The Collected Works of Kenneth White

Volume 1

The Collected Works of Kenneth White
Volume 1

Underground to Otherground

Incandescent Limbo
Letters from Gourgounel
Travels in the Drifting Dawn

Edited by Cairns Craig

EDINBURGH
University Press

Edinburgh University Press is one of the leading university presses in the UK. We publish academic books and journals in our selected subject areas across the humanities and social sciences, combining cutting-edge scholarship with high editorial and production values to produce academic works of lasting importance. For more information visit our website: edinburghuniversitypress.com

© editorial matter and organisation Cairns Craig, 2021, 2023
© the text Kenneth White, 2021, 2023

First published in 2016 by Aberdeen University Press

Edinburgh University Press Ltd
The Tun – Holyrood Road, 12(2f) Jackson's Entry, Edinburgh EH8 8PJ

First published in hardback by Edinburgh University Press 2021

Typeset in 10.5/12 Adobe Sabon by
Servis Filmsetting Ltd, Stockport, Cheshire,
and printed and bound by CPI Group (UK) Ltd,
Croydon, CR0 4YY

A CIP record for this book is available from the British Library

ISBN 978 1 4744 8129 8 (hardback)
ISBN 978 1 3995 1112 4 (paperback)
ISBN 978 1 4744 8130 4 (webready PDF)
ISBN 978 1 4744 8131 1 (epub)

The right of Kenneth White to be identified as the author of this work has been asserted in accordance with the Copyright, Designs and Patents Act 1988, and the Copyright and Related Rights Regulations 2003 (SI No. 2498).

Contents

Acknowledgements vii
A Note on the Texts viii

INCANDESCENT LIMBO: THE BOOK OF THE SEVEN ROOMS

Preface 3

1 Notes of a Nothing Man 7
2 On the Hyperborean Fringe 24
3 A Short Introduction to Eskimo Studies 38
4 The Hermit of the Rue Gay-Lussac 49
5 It's Raining Tea in Darjeeling 64
6 A Little Place in Nowhere 78
7 The Cabinet of White Meditation 92

LETTERS FROM GOURGOUNEL

Preface 101

The Approach 105
Gourgounel 111
Settling in 113
The Roof over my Head 116
Former Inhabitants 119
Madame Teston's Testimony 125
Letter to Those who Live in Cities 128
Old Fireside Tales Retold 130
Underworld Acquaintances 134
Neighbours 136
The Mysteries of the Mushroom 141
Mathieu's Pears 143
The House of the Sun 145

The Baker at La Boule	147
Visitation	149
Dog Days	152
The Lightning	154
Tathagata	156
Seeing the Dragon	159
Reading Chōmei	160
The White Clouds of Wang Wei	162
A Bowl of Tea	164
A Handful of Haiku	166
The Shining Earth	168
The Story of Karma Dordji	171
Epilogue: The Path Through the Forest	173

TRAVELS IN THE DRIFTING DAWN

Preface	177
Part I: The Wake	
Underground London	183
Time on a Dark River	191
The Rocky Road to Carraroe	200
In a Drifting Dawn	212
The Inhabitant of Edinburgh	220
The Big Rain at Tigh Geal	228
Part II: The Gates	
The Blue Gates of Brittany	241
Letter from Amsterdam	250
Winter on the Plains	256
Flemish Weekend	261
Grass on the Streets of Antwerp	269
As a Breaking Wave	276
Night in Barcelona	281
Insular Delirium	286
The Tunisian Journal	290

Acknowledgements

Incandescent Limbo was first published in 1976 as *Les limbes incandescents ou Le livre des sept chambres* in a translation by Patrick Mayoux (Paris: Editions Denoël). It appears in English for the first time in this edition.

Letters from Gourgounel was first published in English in 1966 (London: Jonathan Cape) and appeared in French in 1986 (Paris: Editions Grasset) in a translation by Gil and Marie Jouanard.

Travels in the Drifting Dawn was first published in French in 1978 as *Dérives* (Paris: Editions Les Lettres Nouvelles) in a translation by several hands, and appeared in English in 1989 (Edinburgh: Mainstream).

A Note on the Texts

In 1983, Kenneth White was appointed to a chair in Twentieth-Century Poetics at the Sorbonne in Paris and awarded the Prix Médicis Étranger for his book *La Route Bleue*. Fifteen years after having been sacked from his university post for his participation in the uprising of May 1968, and little more than half a decade since beginning to publish regularly in France, he had become a prominent figure in French intellectual life, sufficiently so to attract criticism from the likes of Deleuze and Guattari.[1] Deleuze, indeed, had been one of the jury members when White presented his doctoral thesis on 'intellectual nomadism' in 1979, a thesis whose success allowed him to escape from his university position as a 'foreign assistant'. It was, however, by no means a standard doctoral thesis: for a start, half of it was written in French – on theoretical implications of 'intellectual nomadism' – and half of it was written in English. This latter part was a study of various American poets who were 'nomads' both in the physical sense that they went exploring the American landscape but also because they set out to gain enlightenment from other cultures, often oriental (Zen Buddhism) or, closer to home, the cultures of Native American peoples. Such intellectual nomads were in search of a 'New World' – 'a newfound world' (G, 174) – which they did not identify with the actually existing United States of America. The thesis, in other words, was a hybrid composition, with each of its linguistic components having a very different focus. Even if the section on American poets treated them as instances of 'nomads' who 'had no history' because they 'only had a geography' ['*Les nomades n'ont pas d'histoire, ils n'ont qu'une géographie*'[2]], and even if the French section traced intellectual nomadism's origins to Ralph

---

[1] For an account of the interactions of White and Deleuze, see Kenneth White, *Dialogue Avec Deleuze: politique, philosophie, géopoétique* (Paris: Isolato, 2007), 9ff.

[2] Kenneth White, *L'Esprit nomade* (Paris: Livre de Poche, 2008; 1987), 64.

Waldo Emerson,³ they had very different trajectories and were later published as separate books. Thus the French section appeared as *L'Esprit Nomade* in 1987 and, although it concluded with a section on American writing from Whitman to Kerouac, the full book on American writers was not published till 2015 in a French translation as *Le Gang du Kosmos*.⁴

The complexities of White's thesis submission and its later publication history, are part of the interweaving of French and English publications in White's career throughout the 1960s, 70s and 80s. The three books contained in this first volume of Kenneth White's *Collected Works* were all begun when White was living in France in the early 1960s. Funded by a bursary he had been awarded by gaining a double first in French and German at Glasgow University, his academic project was a study of the relationship between poetry and politics in the twentieth century. While working on his doctorate, however, he was also continuing to develop a body of poetry that would be published in France by the 'Club des étudiants Anglais' in 1964 under the title of *Wild Coal*, and then, later in the same year, in an extended dual-language edition under the title *En toute candeur*, with translations of the poems into French by Pierre Leyris, the distinguished translator of poetry in English from Milton to T. S. Eliot. A further book of White's poetry, *The Cold Wind of Dawn*, was published in 1966 by Jonathan Cape in London, followed by *The Most Difficult Area* in 1968. In 1966, however, Cape also published *Letters from Gourgounel*, consisting of a series of brief chapters recounting White's experiences in 1961–2 when he had bought and renovated a farmhouse in the Ardèche, a famously fierce part of France in both landscape and climate. By the time *Letters from Gourgounel* was published in London, White was already making a name for himself in France with prose pieces about his experiences in Paris, which appeared in the Parisian literary journals *Les Lettres Nouvelles* (1965) and *La Brèche* (1965), in translations by Michel Gresset, who would supervise White's thesis and go on to be one of the leading scholars of American Literature in France. Further chapters of what would become *Les limbes incandescents* appeared in *la Nouvelle Revue Française* in 1971 and 1975, in translations by Dominique

---

³ Ibid., 50: '*il est probable que la notion de "nomadisme intellectuelle" a surgi le première fois dans le journal de l'Américaine Ralph Waldo Emerson*' ['it is probable that the idea of "intellectual nomadism" first arose in the journal of the American Ralph Waldo Emerson'].

⁴ Kenneth White, *Le Gang du Kosmos: poétique et politique en terre américaine* (Paris: Wildproject, 2015); the phrase 'le gang du kosmos' is quoted in *L'Esprit nomade* and attributed to Walt Whitman, 385.

Aury and Michelle Tran Van Khai, but the book itself was not published until 1976 and appears in English here for the first time.

That *Incandescent Limbo* comes first in this volume is not only because it contains some of the earliest of White's publications in prose but also because it presents the earliest experiences of the character who appears in many of White's later writings and who is called 'Kenneth White'. Kenneth White-the-author and Kenneth-White-the-character share many of the same experiences – growing up in Ayrshire on the West coast of Scotland, followed by student years in Glasgow and Munich and then an escape from Britain to France in 1967 – but they are by no means identical. They have a shared interest in Oswald Spengler's analysis of *The Decline of the West* (1918–22), with its prediction of the end of Western civilization as we have known it, and in Arnold Toynbee's *A Study of History* (1934–61); they also share a belief that the earliest cultural pathbreakers out of Western civilization were French poet Arthur Rimbaud and German poet-philosopher Friedrich Nietzsche. But the Kenneth White of these early texts is a reconstruction of the Kenneth White who originally began to write them, just as the texts themselves are reinventions by a later Kenneth White of what he had previously published.

'Make it new', Ezra Pound had declared during the modernist revolution in literature in the 1920s: many have misunderstood this as a demand for novelty but the 'it' was the literary past, which had to be continually remade for a new historical context. Indeed, the phrase itself is a remaking of the past since it is Pound's translation of a French translation of the ancient Chinese Confucian text, the *Da Xue* (*Ta Hio*).[5] White-the-author takes the same view of his own writings: they are always to be made 'new' with each re-publication, which also means that the character 'Kenneth White' is also being remade in the context of the later understanding of Kenneth-White-the-author. Thus we are told in this edition of *Letters from Gourgounel* (but not in the original) that White-the-character arrived in Gourgounel with a copy of the *Ta Hio* (viii) as part of his library of Chinese and Japanese books and that this library inspires his experiments at recreating Japanese poems. The poems are there in the chapter titled 'A Handful of Haiku' (*G*, 166)[6] but the chapter was not in the original 1966 edition, so when White presents his reader with 'some of this

---

[5] See, Michael North, 'The Making of "Make It New"', *Guernica Magazine*, August 15, 2013; https://www.guernicamag.com/the-making-of-making-it-new/, accessed 6 June 2020.

[6] The following abbreviations are used in the text: '*G*', *Letters from Gourgounel*, this edition; '*G*, 1966', *Letters from Gourgounel*, original London publication 1966; '*IL*', *Incandescent Limbo*, this edition, '*LI*', *Les Limbes Incandescent*, Paris, 1990; '*T*', *Travels in the Drifting Dawn*, this edition, '*T*, 1989', *Travels*

morning's collection' (*G*, 167), to which morning is he referring? It is not some biographical morning in the life of White-the-author but the morning of the text itself, one that belongs to White-the-character.

This reconstructive process is underlined by some large and many small changes in all three texts. For instance, four of the seven chapters in *Incandescent Limbo* have changed position in the sequence: chapters 2 and 3, 'Brief Introduction to Eskimo Studies' and 'Hyperborean Wanderings', have been reversed, making the Nietzschean 'hyperborean' more prominently the gateway to an alternative set of values. Similarly, chapters 5 and 6 have been reversed, with 'A Little Place in Nowhere' following, rather than preceding 'It's Raining Tea in Darjeeling', and the importance of 'nowhere' being reinforced by the addition to the final chapter, 'The Cabinet of White Meditations', of passages such as this,

> A certain amount (even a lot) of knowledge, is necessary in order to penetrate deeply into no-knowledge, and know where you're going (which in no way diminishes the surprise or delight, but prevents panic or mystification). Hence my erratic studies. Hence, too, in order to arrive on the no-way, my physical errances. *Shake the letters until you become unlettered*, says Kanha. (*IL*, 93)

By such insertions, White-the author is able to amplify the significance of the thinking and the doings of White-the-character: the 'erratic studies' of the earlier chapters, which might have seemed random accumulations of accidental happenings, are recast as preparations for a deeper understanding. Similarly, in *Letters from Gourgounel*, the final chapters, from 'Seeing the Dragon' (*G*, 159) to 'The story of Karma Dordji' (*G*, 171) have been recast or added to foreground White-the-character as a student of eastern religion. And in *Travels in the Drifting Dawn* what was the penultimate chapter in the original edition, 'The Big Rain at Tigh Gael', is not only moved to earlier in the book, alongside other Scottish and Irish chapters, but the sections of the book are renamed, Part 1, '*The Solitudes*' (originally '*Les Limbes*' in French) becoming '*The Wake*'.

The complexities of these textual histories – both in terms of when and in which language the books were originally written and published, and when and how often they have been revised – mean that they have several times been 'made new'. Thus *Incandescent Limbo* may originally have been written in English and then translated into French, but the English text as it appears here is actually a much later

---

in the Drifting Dawn (London, 1989); '*D*', *Dérives* (Paris, 1978); '*D, 2017*', *Dérives* (Paris, 2017).

and substantially amended version not only of the original French publications, but of the most recent French edition of 1990. *Letters from Gourgounel*, on the other hand, although originally written and published in English, is very different in this edition than in its original English-language version, with the excision of several chapters and the addition of at least six new ones. Similarly, the version of *Travels in the Drifting Dawn* in this edition involves not only changes to chapter titles – 'The Blue Gates of January', for instance, becoming 'The Blue Gates of Britanny' (*T*, 241) – but a series of substantial excisions: from that chapter, for instance, a paragraph devoted to a detailed description of a harbour scene – 'Welter, clamour, smell and sea and oil and the fat gleaming sliminess, the glut, blood and fleshiness of the fish' (*T*, 1989, 70) – disappears, as does its affirmative conclusion: 'Here I am at home!' Such changes to *Travels in the Drifting Dawn* were mostly adopted in the revised French version, *Dérives*, published in 2017, but that edition did away with the division into two parts while retaining some of the elements of the earlier French and English editions, such as in the conclusion of section 3 of 'The Blue Gates', which was originally described as a 'Letter to an Acquaintance of Paris and London' (*T*, 1979, 70), an atttribution now dropped. In their revisions and rewritings, these texts are, in effect, palimpsests, in which a later White overwrites his own earlier writings and, in consequence, reconstructs his own earlier selves.

In form, *Incandescent Limbo*, develops the aesthetics of fragmentation and juxtaposition pioneered by T. S. Eliot's *The Waste Land* and by Ezra Pound's *Cantos*. Some of the changes in the text, therefore, simply reposition the fragments among other fragments, as when White notes that he still carries with him a piece of paper given to him by his father, which he takes to be an instruction about his own aims as a writer:

> I keep with me (as a talisman?) the sheet of paper on which my father, railway signalman, jotted for me the times of trains when I was leaving Scotland. It's a "Snowstorm Duties" chit, and in the column "Work Carried Out", there's a phrase in brackets which comes across to me as a kind of programme for my own peculiar "snowstorm duties": *Specific details of nature of work must be given. A general description such as Snowstorm Duties will not suffice.* (*IL*, 10, *LI*, 46)

This has been moved from its original location in 'Brief Introduction to Eskimo Studies' (*LI*, 46) to be an introductory element of the first chapter, 'Notes of a Nowhere Man', and also offers a preliminary invocation of the snow imagery which runs through the book, 'turning Paris into St Petersburg' (*IL*, 42). On the other hand, some of the repositionings are also rewritings, as when White recalls an incident in Glasgow:

> That night over in the Gorbals (Glasgow): Wee Harry from Florence Street telling me that if I wanted to write a bestseller (my father had told him I was "writing", was using up enough ink to float the Queen Elizabeth), all I had to do was come over to his place with a tape-recorder and he'd tell me about his exploits as a con-man on the South Side. "Put y'right on top, boy, put y'right on top." "Right on top of what?", I said. (*IL*, 11)

In the French edition this is on page 144, in the chapter 'It's Raining Tea in Darjeeling', whereas in the English version it is in the first chapter, and the final response – 'Right on top of what?' – is not in the French. There are many points like this where White has added, almost as a commentary, an extra sentence to what was in the French edition. So, when he thinks of it always being winter –

> With me it's always winter: winter ending, winter beginning, middle of winter, but always winter.
> They're all trying to tell me it's spring. (*IL*, 34; *LI*, 74)

– the English version adds,

> But they won't fool me. I wasn't born in Glasgow for nothing. (*IL*, 34)

Similarly, a long quote about Bergson and the nature of laughter (*IL*, 72; *LI*, 142–3) has appended to it in English a comment entirely missing from the French: 'This makes Bergson sound like the *Sunday Post*'. At the same time, some more personal statements in the French edition have been removed in the English. Thus there is a section in French (*LI*, 47) in which White claims often to think (*'Je repense toujours'*) about an Eskimo whose kayak was washed up in Aberdeen some centuries ago. In the English version this is attributed to White's researches in the Bibliothèque Nationale, where,

> reading through a number of the *Journal de la Société des Américanistes* (tome 13, n° 2, 1921), I come across this mention of a kayak 7 yards long and 2 feet wide that turned up, end of the seventeenth or beginning of the eighteenth century (the records differ), at the mouth of the Don. In it a man "covered with hair who spoke a language nobody could understand". Every attempt was made at Aberdeen to keep the Inuit alive, but he died within three days, totally exhausted after God knows how long a trip – from where, Greenland? Wild winds, rogue waves and crazy currents must have driven him from his home shore far out to sea, when all he could do

was hang on, following the movement. As for the kayak, it was deposited at Marischal College in the said town of Aberdeen. (*IL*, 39)

However, White's response in the French version is much more personal: it mentions nothing about the source of the story and claims the Eskimo as one of 'his spiritual ancestors. An idiot. A madman' ['*Un de mes ancêtres. Un idiot. Un fou*' (*LI*, 47), who should have remained on the old 'hyperborean continent' ['*vieux continent hyperboréen*'], which is the source of 'ancient illumination' ['*au pays de la très ancienne illumination*' (*LI*, 47)]. In the present version, however, White has added:

If ever I make back to Scotland, it will be in something like that kayak. Adrift here in the asphalt ocean, amid a myriad of shooting stars and the flashing lights of the *aurora borealis*, Kenneth of Whiteland writeth his kayak-book. (*IL*, 39)

'Kenneth of Whiteland' suggests that he may have an autobiographical relationship to Scotland but he has 'become an Eskimo, by naturalization. In fact, even that's just for my passport – I'm really a Hyperborean (*IL*, 42). He is, in effect, 'nation-less' (*T*, 292), because his true homeland is the 'Whiteland' of his writing.

There are, in contrast, other passages that have been added to this English-language edition which reflect White's changing relationship with Scotland and its intellectual traditions. Early in the text we are presented with the following:

A rainy day on the banks of the Seine. In a musty *bouquiniste* booth, I come across this old book: *Mystics of the North-East*. The "North-East" in question is northeastern Scotland, and the author, I see, was Regius Professor of Theology at Aberdeen University. At this, I hesitate. But the price of the book is cheap, so I purchase it. Who knows, maybe in some of these characters I'll recognize distant cousins. (*IL*, 14)

This may or may not be true about the Kenneth White who was in Paris in the 1960s, but it does not appear in French edition, though it fits with a pattern of revisions across *Incandescent Limbo* that foreground White's intellectual rather than just his personal connections with Scotland. Thus a quote from Thomas Carlyle's *Sartor Resartus* – '*My breakfast of tea has been cooked by a Tartar woman, with water of the Amur, who wiped her earthen kettle with a horse tail*' (45) – in the original French edition is extended by the comment, 'Carlyle – another member, slightly bourgeoisified, of my radical Scoto-shamanistic ancestors' (*IL*, 45). In the same section, there is a substantial addition about the influence of the eighteenth-century Scot, Andrew Ramsay, on French culture:

> Another couple of hours rummaging among the *bouquinistes* of the Seine. This time I come away with a biography of Andrew Ramsay, born in Ayr, known in France as the Chevalier Ramsay. Was for a while secretary to Fénelon. Wrote (in French) *The Travels of Cyrus*. Was involved in freemasonry, developing in France the Scottish concepts and practises known as *Écossisme*. It was in a speech of 1737 that he suggested the creation in France of an encyclopedia that would lay out the state of knowledge and thought, an idea taken up by Diderot and D'Alembert. The great *Encyclopédie* (*Dictionnaire raisonné des sciences, des arts et des métiers*) came out in 1751, printed in Paris by one Le Breton. Encyclopedia: *enkyklios*, "in a circle" and *paideia* "education". There's going to be something "encyclopedic" (cyclotronic?) about these eccentric studies of mine: I follow psychomental circuits with a sense of concentric, expanding circles. (*IL*, 17)

This Scottish origin of a major turning-point in French culture was not in the original text but is now prophetic of White's own participation in French culture in the late twentieth century. Equally, White's recovery of the 'wandering Scot' as the tradition in which he can situate himself (re-)writes itself into the text of *Incandescent Limbo*. A café scene in the original, listing the names of tobacco products, including 'Celtique Balto', is juxtaposed with,

> An Irish scholar, twelfth century: "In those first days when youth in me was quick and life was fast, there I was wandering from city to city in fair France for the desire that I had of learning and letters."
> *Monumenta Germaniae Historica*, picked up in the Sorbonne library. (*IL*, 11)

This discovery in the Sorbonne is entirely in keeping with what White-the-author was doing in Paris and of the 'celtic' identity that he projected in works such as *En toute candeur* in the 1960s, but it was not in the original text.

The palimpsestic nature of the texts presented here only underlines, however, the palimpsestic nature of all of White's writings, which intertwine notes taken immediately about his daily experiences, quotations from his eclectic reading and thoughts drawn from his philosophical, anthropological and scientific enquiries. In a passage in *Incandescent Limbo* added to this edition, White quotes Nietzsche – 'We have found the way' – and adds:

In fact, I have several ways in mind and at my disposal: the wild Atlantic western way; the quiet eastern way; the burning southern way; the transcendental northern way. All employing the formula K+L+M (knowledge, literature, meditation) and the more advanced formula K+W (kenning, wayfaring) (*IL*, 25)

In *Incandescent Limbo*, though, not all of these are yet available to the character Kenneth White, who is travelling intellectually and aesthetically northwards, to the lands of the hyperboreans (as indicated by the epigraph from Nietzsche on the title page of 'Room 2') and in the references to Dostoievski's 'underground man':

The snow is still falling today. Takes me back to Glasgow when, around 1955, I was reading among other Russian books, Dostoevsky's *Letters from the Underworld*. In the little red-battered Everyman's Library edition I still have with me, I see underlined this: "Today, half-melted, dirty, yellow snow was falling. It was falling yesterday, and it will be falling again tomorrow." (*IL*, 23)

To this image out of Dostoevsky White adds:

That was the atmosphere of those Glasgow days. A lot of modern literature came out of Dostoevsky's *Letters*: Kafka, Camus . . . Maybe in some sense I came out of them too. But with the accent on the *out*. (*IL*, 23)

White's escape from Glasgow to Paris is necessary but insufficient: what is necessary is to travel further, imaginatively, towards 'some old lost China of the mind' (*IL*, 48) and 'to read the poetry of Li Po, out there on the Szechwan Road' (*IL*, 38). Similarly, White's journey to the south of France in *Letters from Gourgounel* also turns into a journey east, especially in the added chapters which focus on the poetry of Wang Wei ('The White Clouds of Wang Wei', *G*, 162–3), tea culture in Japan ('A Bowl of Tea', *G*, 164–5) and 'Asatori Miyamori's *Anthology of Haiku* ('A Handful of Haiku, *G*, 166–7). None of these was in the original version of the book. White-the-character is thus made more clearly a spiritual time-traveller to cultures that lie beyond the boundaries of western civilization.

The focus on the journey east is made more prominent by a major revision to the opening sections of *Incandescent Limbo*: the first chapter of the French edition invokes its subtitle – *The Book of the Seven Rooms* – to envisage a 'vast penitentiary' in each of whose rooms is an American author. In those rooms, Edgar Allan Poe, Robert Frost, Ralph Waldo Emerson, Henry Miller, e.e.cummings, T. S. Eliot, Wallace Stevens, Thomas Wolfe, Ernest Hemingway and

Henry Adams rub shoulders with figures from American popular culture such as Rip Van Winckle and Jerry Lewis, and somewhere in there, too, is Kenneth White: *'dans une autre, tout au bout, me voici en train d'écrire cela ...'* [in another room, right at the back, here is me in the midst of writing this] (*LI*, 20). In the English-language version, however, this American context has disappeared: the character-narrator is no longer the co-inhabitant of an American tradition. Thus a scene in which the narrator encounters Whitman in Paris is transformed from a surreal dream in the French edition into an ordinary event in the English version:

> 'Hello comrade', said Whitman, met in the Rue Racine, just in front of the anarchist bookshop. Whitman (old ancient mariner) I like him well. The Paris I know wouldn't be the same without him. "Bye, Comrade." This is George Whitman, by the way – but he says he's related to Walt somewhere down the line. Who knows? (*IL*, 53)

The genealogical explanation is not in the French edition, which leaves its Whitman character as a ghostly apparition in the streets of modern Paris, as though an escapee from the penitentiary in which all the American writers – and White himself – were apparently trapped in the book's opening scene. When the poet Whitman does appear in the English version, it is in a much less explicitly American context:

> It's the dawn-chorus in my brain. I hear the yawp of Whitman, the cock-crow of Thoreau, the yark-yark of that bird-thing Nietzsche, Burns – the Scotch cock on the dung-hill, Diderot's athletic owl, Rousseau's persecuted sparrow. (*IL*, 22)

Whitman is now only one of a variety of European and North American writers who belong to a tradition that has come to a dead end, as represented by the writings of Samuel Beckett. White taught a course on 'The Limits of Literature: Beckett and after' (*T*, 178) and saw himself as not only getting *out* but as getting *beyond*:

> *Life in the ditches* – a title à la Samuel Beckett. I can go a long way with Samuel B., as long as he likes to go, right to the end. But that's it, Sam's at the end of something (and there's good reason: it's end city and final history) – he's at the end of something, and he keeps shoving the end a bit further forward, the infinite calculus of despair worked up into perfect no-art. But he never makes the break, never gets beyond the end, he just marks time there, and he does that marking time better than anybody. I'm beyond the end, or trying to get beyond the end, feeling at least the early

will-o-the-wispy beginnings (nothing to do with history, the time and civilization process) of something else. (*IL*, 68; *LI*, 137)

In this version of *Incandescent Limbo*, the journey east is the prologue to a journey beyond the history that has exhausted itself in the West, as underlined in passages added to its conclusion:

> Kakushin, on returning to Japan in 1255 after studies and training under Fu-yen, founded the school of homeless mendicancy known as "the community of nothingness." (*IL*, 98)

Like Kakushin, White has to escape civilization in order to recover the 'centre' that is himself:

> The centre (we can forget "culture"), is where I am, anywhere. I don't need a "literary world", or a "swinging scene". I can swing things plenty myself, and in my own way. As for a "literary world", God save me from that menagerie, whatever the language it talks. (*IL*, 52; *LI*, 88)

White-the-character journeys eastward away from the 'literary world' in order, with Kakushin, to join the 'community of nothingness'. 'A Little Place in Nowhere' ends,

> *The art I practice doesn't need social relations*
> *the way of knowledge is difficult, and you have to walk it alone*
> *I like the pure streams that wind among the rocks*
> *I like my old quiet hut among the pines*
> – that was Wang Wei, long time ago China. (*IL*, 91; *LI*, 130)

The fact that we are not told we are reading a quotation till after it is complete emphasises how Wang Wei may be a 'long time ago in China' but is also intimately present in the moment of our reading.

The journey east does not mean that those American writers who were erased from the begining of *Incandescent Limbo* entirely disappear – Pound, for instance, gets quoted: '*To study with the white wings of time passing*', Canto 74 (*IL*, 88) – but American culture is mostly represented by jazz and blues lyrics. And though Whitman gets a mention in *Letters from Gourgounel*, it too is committed to the journey east:

> One of Wang's key-words is *hsien*, meaning something like "being at peace". It's a state of mind free of anxiety, but beyond that, a mental landscape in harmony with the physical landscape around. Of all the Chinese poets, Wang is probably the one who penetrates most deeply into

the landscape, or lets the landscape penetrate most deeply into his mind. (G, 163)

It is that fusion of landscape and mind – a 'mindscape' – that becomes a key element in the poetics of Kenneth White and which White-the-character has apparently already discovered in Gourgounel.

The reason behind many of these changes, I suggest, is that although White-the-character is finding illumination by travelling east, White the author-critic was travelling, at least some of the time, in the opposite direction, towards increasing engagement with what he called 'the Whitman line' in American poetry, and which formed the English-language half of his doctoral thesis.[7] It is a line – both a poetic line and a line of thought – that White describes achronologically in *Le Gang du Kosmos* as the gradual escape from what America, post-industrialisation, had become, to the recovery of a 'New World': *'d'un éveil en dehors du cauchemar de l'histoire, d'un retour aux sources, une réintégration mythico-écologique'* ['an awakening from the nightmare of history, a return to the sources, a mythic-ecological reintegration'].[8] The 'Whitman line' includes William Carlos Williams and Robinson Jeffers from the earlier twentieth century, as well as the 'beat' poets of the 1950s and 60s, particularly Allen Ginsberg and Gary Snyder. The latter two had, of course, also been travelling east, into Zen Buddhism and other eastern belief systems, but it was the resistance of this line of poets to the corruption of modern society, to the degradation of the 'New World' that White wanted to celebrate.

In 1975 White published two short books on individual poets in this line: *The Coast Opposite Humanity: An Essay on the Poetry of Robinson Jeffers* and *The Tribal Dharma: An Essay on the Work of Gary Snyder*, and, in 1978, a related book on *The Life Technique of John Cowper Powys*. White summarises Powys's views as follows:

> The self, in its deepest ground, is aware of 'a craving ... that neither the passion for communal improvement nor the passion for communal applause can distract from its organic unrest', an 'intellectual restlessness, a stirring of the imagination, a trembling of the waters, a terrible and dangerous questioning, that cannot be allayed by any national or even by any international pre-occupation. In short, 'the soul within us is a microcosm, not a micropolis; and is born for the happiness that flows from a cosmic, not a political or economic life.'[9]

---

[7] This was the title of a lecture course he was giving in 1968 before he lost his job; see 'Preface', *Travels in the Drifting Dawn*, 178.
[8] White, *Le Gang du Kosmos*, 48.
[9] Kenneth White, *The Life Technique of John Cowper Powys* (Swansea:

The 'micropolis' in which Western tradition has invested ever since Aristotle's insistence on the individual as being defined by his membership of a '*polis*', by participation in a political community, has to be torn aside in order to reveal humanity's fundamental relationship to a wider context – indeed, to the widest context, the cosmos. The 'radical question for the naked *self*', White insists, is how it can make 'full use of its body-mind, make its way through the world, work out some satisfying relationship with nature and enjoy the chaos-cosmos'.[10] It is such a turning away from social humanity to the 'inhuman'[11] that White finds in Robinson Jeffers, and takes the house the poet built himself at Carmel on the Californian coast as emblematic of this shift:

> From Carmel, standing at the junction of State Highway 1 and Ocean Avenue, looking south, you can see the Santa Lucia Range rise, green and gold, above the cypresses of Point Lobos. Say the Pacific mist, which has obliterated temporarily the clutter of civilization, has just lifted – what is it you have before you? Is it part of the United States, or the edge of the world?
>
> If you feel it as part of the United States, you have the soul of a patriotic real estate agent. If you feel it as the edge of the world, you're ready for poetry.[12]

Poetry happens at and from the edge where the human confronts that which is beyond humanity: in the words of Powys, where humanity is discovered to be an amphibian with 'one foot on the sandy shore of the traditions of humanity, the other in the salt sea of our non-human cosmos'.[13] The 'Whitman line' is characterised precisely by its desire to reach this 'poetic-cosmo-social consciousness', which means it is also characterised by a 'poetry' very different from the traditions which governed British or French poetry in the 1950s and 60s. Thus White dismisses criticism of Jeffers's poetry by envisaging it in geomorphological terms:

> ... I simply see Jeffers as being concerned with what I take to be the essential – in his own way, working from his own bedrock, with his own

---

Galloping Dog Press, 1978), 9; the quotations are from Powys's *The Art of Happiness* (London: Village Press, 1974; New York, 1935).

[10] White, *Life Technique*, 11–12.

[11] White, *The Coast Opposite Humanity* (Llanfynydd, Wales: Unicorn Bookshop, 1975), 22.

[12] Kenneth White, *The Coast Opposite Humanity*, 17.

[13] White, *Life Technique*, 12. The quotation is from John Cowper Powis, *In Defence of Sensuality* (London: Village Press, 1974).

luminous peaks, and with his own (in a quasi-geological sense) faults. I won't be insisting on the faults, they're obvious enough (over-writing, over-strain, incongruous pile-ups of adjective and metaphor, they're part of the mountain). I'll just be trying to make my way along that mountain, with my eye always on the summit, where it all leads up to.[14]

We can trace this shift of the 'ground' of poetry in a passage in *Incandescent Limbo* in which White mocks the idea of 'The Poetry of the Month':

> Little ribbons of poetry; little shit-pellets of poetry. Poetry of the month. Where's the poetry of no-time, no place? A poetry that breathes in space, and is alive with mental lightning. (*IL*, 72)[15]

This shift of focus on what counts as poetry can also be traced in some of the changes made to *Travels in the Drifting Dawn*: thus in section 4 of 'Winter on the Plains' the original version suggested that,

The cry now is for wide-open poem
a poem plain but curving with power
set bare on reality, a January poem
for whiteness and the winter of ecstasy (*T*, 1989; 89)

In this edition, however, the focus is much broader than on 'poem',

The cry is for a wide-open writing
a language plain but curving with power
set bare on reality, a January script
for whiteness and the winter of ecstasy (*T*, 257)

The 'poem' itself as a linguistic object is no longer the focus but the 'poetry' behind the poem – 'the whiteness' of a cosmic consciousness which the poem makes visible. White finds in William Carlos Williams the precursor who had already travelled into the 'white world', uncovering *'la blancheur d'une clarté au-delà des faits'* ['the whiteness of a clarity beyond the facts'].[16]

In *Le Gang du Kosmos* White uses Jack Kerouac and his *romans à clef* – *On the Road* (1957), *Dharma Bums* (1958) and *Desolation Angels* (1965) – as guides to the context in which Allen Ginsberg and

---

[14] White, *The Coast Opposite Humanity*, 7–8.
[15] In the original French this ends, 'Une poésie qui respire dans l'espace vivant de l'éclair mental' (*IL*, 143), i.e. 'mental clarity' rather than 'mental lightning'.
[16] Kenneth White, *Le Gang du Kosmos*, 208.

Gary Snyder became the key figures of the 'beat generation'.[17] White identifies Kerouac not as a North American writer but as 'being closer to a holy Celt travelling savage roads alone' [*'Kerouac se rapproche avantage du saint celte en voyage sur des routes solitaires sauvages'*].[18] In *En toute Candeur* White describes what he considers essential to his own writing as follows:

> *tout ce que je présente ici est un petit carnet de notes, quelque chose qui n'a ni commencement, ni milieu, ni fin (c'est ainsi que j'aime à voir la vie) et qui, ne partant d'aucunes prémisses, n'atteindra aucune conclusion. Tout ce que j'offre est un peu de spontanéité, un peu de présence.*
> [all I present here is a little book of notes, something which has neither a beginning, a middle or an end (it's this way that I like to see life) and which, setting out from no premises, does not reach any conclusion. All that I offer is a little spontaneity, a little bit of presence.][19]

The method of the 'little book of notes' is one that White shared with Alan Ginsberg and Gary Snyder, many of whose poems are developed from their immediate jottings in notebooks, but the emphasis on 'spontaneity' also links White's writing method with the 'spontaneous prose' that Kerouac proclaimed as the technique behind his own novels from the mid-1950s. Thus *Letters from Gourgounel* starts with a series of notebook jottings ('The following are extracts from the notebook I kept', G, 105) and often slips into present tense:

> I am sitting on the terrace. The thunder is rolling. The south-eastern corner of the valley is shrouded in blue. A great wind has risen. Mulberries are scattering all around me. The grasses and flowers are jerking and tossing. There is panic in the air. The stream is flowing faster, and now the whole valley is filled with the blueness. The lightning flashes. (G, 152; G, 1966, 54)[20]

In the original version of *Letters from Gourgounel*, White seems also to have adopted one of the fundamentals of Kerouac's account of how to make prose 'spontaneous': 'No periods separating sentence-structures already arbitrarily riddled by false colons and timid usually needless commas – but the vigorous space dash separating rhetorical breathing

---

[17] See, for instance, *Le Gang du Kosmos*, 52 fn 117, 217ff.
[18] White, *Le Gang du Kosmos*, 218; Kerouac believed his family was originally from Brittany; see Michael S. Begnal '"To be an Irishman Too": Jack Kerouac's Irish Connection', *Studies: An Irish Quarterly* Review, Vol. 92, No. 368 (Winter, 2003), pp. 371–7.
[19] White, *En toute candeur*, 20.
[20] This chapter is now titled 'Dog Days', in the original it was 'Canicule'.

(as jazz musician drawing breath between outblown phrases)'.[21] Thus in the chapter entitled in the original version 'Mother Catastrophe' we have the following:

> But fruit, ha, that depends on the weather. And you can't trust it. Look at this summer, all storms – all those thunder-claps aren't normal – and last year, no water [...] In the old days – 'in the time of my poor father – the men used to go harvesting on the mountains [...] (G, 1966, 129)

The dashes reflect the 'rhetorical breathing' of Madame Teston's speech patterns, but as well as radically changing the position of this chapter in the new edition and giving it a new title ('Madame Teston's Territory'), White has changed the many dashes back into more conventional grammatical markers (G, 126). Nonetheless, White's aim is to produce 'the abrupt kind of little book I like, with nothing heavy in it' (G, 128) and in this edition he has removed many passages that were in the original and which made it 'heavier'. For instance, in the chapter entitled 'Gourgounel', after the paragraph that ends 'then the naricissi are all around us, glistening in the rain, gently swaying in the wind' (G, 111), there was, in the original, a nearly page-length paragraph about Demeter, Zeus and Kore, and the sentencing of Kore to 'descend into hell in the winter' (G, 1966, 21–2). White introduced this classical narrative with the statement 'I cannot help my mythology, I was brought up on it' (G, 1966, 21), but it over freights the immediacy and the spontaneity of the rest of the description and has been removed.

White's prose – as its continual revision and rewriting underlines – is not attempting to replicate Kerouac's kind of 'spontaneity', which required the almost total avoidance of revision, but it does always aim to avoid anything 'heavy': 'My world isn't a God-world. Before, the world was full of God, now it's full of Man, and I'm at home in neither. Both of them are noisy, heavy, and burdensome' (T, 279). The White world is a light world, and in its presentation of White-the-character as a lone hitch-hiker – 'someone who is first and foremost a pedestrian' (T, 178) – echoes the vision that Kerouac attributes to Japhy Ryder (Gary Snyder) in *Dharma Bums*

> 'I've been reading Whitman, know what he says, *Cheer up slaves, and horrify foreign despots*, he means that's the attitude for the Bard, the Zen Lunacy bards of old desert paths, see the whole thing is a world full of rucksack wanderers, Dharma Bums refusing to subscribe to the general

---

[21] Jack Kerouac, 'Essentials of Spontaneous Prose', https://www.writing.upenn.edu/~afilreis/88/kerouac-spontaneous.html, accessed 6 June 2020.

demand that they consume production and therefore have to work for the privilege of consuming, all that crap they didn't really want anyway such as refrigerators, TV sets, cars [. . .] all of them imprisoned in a system of work, produce, consume, work, produce, consume, I see a vision of a great rucksack revolution thousands or even millions of young Americans wandering around with rucksacks, going up to mountains to pray [. . .]'[22]

White-the-character, as he emerges in *Travels in the Drifting Dawn*, is an outrider of the 'rucksack revolution' – 'I'm up at five, pack my rucksack with a loaf, some apples, a change of socks, a towel' (*T*, 212). He is a 'Dharma Bum', who, in the original version of *Letters from Gourgounel*, quotes at length in the 'Tathagata' chapter, the poem 'The Tathagata as a Raincloud', containing the line 'I Preach Dharma to all beings'.[23] And in a new chapter in this edition, White (the character) declares 'I'll be "turning the wheel" [of the Dharma] in my own way' (*G*, 128). Like Kerouac's central character he is 'on the road' – 'we got on the road again' (*T*, 296) – recording characters encountered in his travels and presenting lightly disguised versions of real people – as, for instance, in the meeting with Joe Torelli (Scottish-Italian writer Alexander Trocchi) in the opening chapter of *Travels in the Drifting Dawn*. White's title for the French editions of *Travels in the Drifting Dawn* is *Dérives*, a word he uses to describe Kerouac's *Clochards célestes* ('heavenly tramps', the French title of *Dharma Bums*), as they set out, like Snyder, *'à "dériver"'* ('to drift') across the wild landscapes of Northern California.[24] White's search is 'for a place of concentration, that's what my travelling is all about, the travelling-writing as one indivisible process' (*T*, 288).

White-the-author would go far beyond the simple commitments of the 'Beat' poets of the 1950s, or the counter-cultures of the 1960s (as, indeed, would Ginsberg and Snyder), but White-the-character, as he comes into focus in *Travels in the Drifting Dawn*, is someone who has been through those times and gone beyond them. In 'Letter from Amsterdam' he comes across

> Hippie Square, with its horde of vague-eyed wanderers sitting on the steps of the national monument, waiting for the end, or the beginning, sitting mostly in stolid silence, though the odd guitar strumming – like a tribal group when its shaman dies, showing signs of unrest, distracted, unable

---

[22] Kerouac, *Dharma Bums*, 83.
[23] *Letters from Gourgounel* (London: Jonathan Cape, 1966), 73. In the current version, the translation has been amended to *I teach the great Law to all beings* (53).
[24] White, *Gang du Kosmos*, 222.

to work, sleeping a lot, talking in their dreams, fleeing individually into the tundra. Well, I'd been like that too, and maybe still was like that a bit, but I was no longer of the tribe, and wasn't waiting for another shaman. I'd maybe just gone a bit further out into the tundra than my companions, and was concerned with my own dance there. The 'underground', as they called it, was so full of phoney shamans (and every shaman is at least part-phoney), that it was better to be entirely out on your own – better, and harder. (*T*, 250–1; *T*, 1989, 80)

White-the-character and White-the-author have this much in common that each accepts that 'it was better to be entirely out on your own'. White-the-Character is a solitary traveller, out 'on the road', in search of the moment when you find 'an ecstasy running through all your being' (*G*, 141). White-the-Author is an intellectual nomad, continually crossing boundaries between different kinds of writing, between the recording of an immediate reality and its inscription in a variety of literary traditions, but focused on fulfilling 'that urge, always present, not to be embedded in history, but to work a way out of it' (*T*, 230). White's writings not only resist conformity with any pre-existing literary genres, but by their palimpsestic accumulations and radical excisions, resist ever becoming 'embedded in history', even in their own history.

Cairns Craig

INCANDESCENT LIMBO

THE BOOK OF THE SEVEN ROOMS

Preface

Paris then was still the liveliest intellectual and literary precinct on the planet.

I'd just completed four years of study (French, German, Classics, Philosophy) at the University of Glasgow, Scotland, from which I came away, after a pretty erratic and rocky course, with a double First, a nomination as the most illuminated alumnus of the Faculty of Arts, and a bursary ostensibly intended for my composing a doctoral thesis to which I gave several provisional titles, one of which was: "Poetics and Politics in the Twentieth Century".

I had a tricky job getting the parish minister of my Ayrshire village to sign the papers of that bursary, testifying to my good character as the Protestant scion of a truly Protestant family. He knew my father was a socialist, if not a communist, and he was well aware of my own tendencies he no doubt thought of as pantheistic, atheistic, or worse. But we finally worked things out and I was ready to go.

That autumn of 1959, I got my things together, with no idea at all for how long I was to be "away".

I can still smell the post-Victorian stench of the Royal Scot as we rolled down to London, recall the sea-salty atmosphere of the coastal train from Victoria to Newhaven, then there was the wild moonlit crossing over the Channel to Dieppe, and the little green French train rattling through the dawn to Paris, Gare du Nord.

A new life beginning, an undefined work-field opening.

Over the years there in Paris I moved from lodgings to lodgings, mostly little cold-water rooms in the top floor of various buildings in different districts of the city. In every one of these rooms, be it in the Rue d'Écosse, the Boulevard Montparnasse, Rue Gay-Lussac, Boulevard Richard-Lenoir, Rue des Fossés-Saint-Jacques, Rue de L'Orient, I had a large map of Paris pinned on the wall. Every now and then I'd close my eyes, point a finger at the map, note the quarter, and go there, mostly by foot, sometimes by subway. The result was a random wandering all over the city. That's one of the aspects of this book, but there are others, a lot harder to define.

If the scene was mainly inner Paris, the actual writing of the book began in Meudon, a quarter hour train journey south-west out from Montparnasse. Meudon had long been a refuge for unorthodox politicals and artists: Hans Arp was still there, and the author of *Journey to the End of Night*, Louis-Ferdinand Céline, whose book I read once every year when I was a student in Glasgow, after living, like a Trappist, in an old house on the Route des Gardes up by the Observatory, had just died there, leaving manuscripts dedicated, ironically, to "the clowns of history" and, sympathetically, to "the animals". In the streets of that quietly bohemian suburb, and in its cafés, I'd hear Russian spoken by exiles from Moscow, Kiev and Odessa. The street I lived in was called the Rue des Basses-Pointes, just up from the Impasse du Progrès.

As to writing, I wrote sections of the thesis, doing a lot of research for it, rummaging in second-hand bookshops and copying out by hand in the Bibliothèque Nationale and in an underground section of the Bibliothèque Sainte-Geneviève, long out-of-print anarchist, communist, dadaist, surrealist, existentialist texts. But it was the manuscript entitled "Incandescent Limbo" that took on more and more the precedence. I wrote maybe half of the book between 1961 and 1963, then, having temporarily left the city, set it aside, and only returned to it in 1970, when I was back in Paris for a while in the aftermath of the 1968 revolt. At first sight, on a first reading, it may seem a haphazard crazypaving patchwork. But closer acquaintance will reveal a latent sequence, maybe even a logic. I was bored with the sociological novel, which had been done and re-done, hashed and re-hashed. I wanted more from my mind than personal phantasma, mental cinema. So, I thought, I'll write this syncopated journal, this kind of flash-by-flash biography, the bits turning up out of my living, thinking, reading, and a live pattern emerging: telegrams from the underground, and sporadic movements on to other ground. Process and project, transitions and transactions. In one of the rare, really interesting novels of the twentieth century, Musil's *The Man Without Qualities*, which ended up in a scattering of notes and sketches mainly because Musil got tired of plodding away at a novel (plot, character, straight, fragmented or complicated narrative), the protagonist is reported as thinking that every time he felt he had the germ of a real idea, *a drop of inexpressible incandescence fell on the world*, changing the whole aspect of things and beings. To put this in the terms of more recent literary theory, I was "deconstructing" long before systematic Deconstruction became the literary shibboleth, and was already going beyond it. Deconstructing with a capital D means, fundamentally, picking holes in mental constructs (Hegelianism, for example), like some repetitive woodpecker that would never actually fly itself in open space. This hyper-anarchistic, super-nihilistic book moves towards such open space, with breakthroughs into it. It's a kind of radical auto-analysis: a graph of catastrophic evolution.

If the book is published only now in English, it's not because, according to the timeworn tradition of "outsiders", it was initially rejected by umpteen publishers. My attitude was even more radical than that of the insider-outsider. I didn't even submit to the system this fundamental re-beginning. I wasn't out to "contribute" to literature or philosophy as understood and practised. I knew it would take time, maybe a long time, for me to work things out, and and open up a general field. I felt I was bringing in a whole new continent. When it amused me to put names to that continent, I called it Euramerasia (because of its main field of exploration), White World (because it had neither map nor formula) or Atopia (because, while being "another world", it wasn't utopian, it was this world without the furniture).

When the first parts of the book appeared in a Paris magazine, *Lettres Nouvelles*, I received a beautiful letter from the man who had founded the Surrealist movement back in the twenties, André Breton, a letter from which I quote this bit: "On Thursday evening, seated with friends as is our habit in the back room of the café called La Promenade de Vénus, I was commenting on the high tone of innovation evident in your text. The editor showed great discernment and even clairvoyance in putting this piece at the head of that issue of his review."

With those few notes by way of background and to focus the context, we can now go into the actual works and days.

K.W.

"The remnant of some unfortunate tribe, he walks the boulevards of the West."
    E. M. Cioran, *A Short Treatise on Decomposition*

"This journey is experienced as going further 'in', as going back through one's personal life, in and back and through and beyond . . ."
    Ronald Laing, *The Politics of Experience*

"The mind of an artist, in order to achieve the prodigious effort of freeing whole and entire the work that is in him, must be incandescent."
    Virginia Woolf, *To the Lighthouse*

ROOM 1
Notes of a Nothing Man

"So reality dumps your dreams on the shit-heap? OK, no problem, all you've got to do is jump over the shit-heap."
FRANCIS PICABIA, *The Testament of a Rapscallion*

I no longer simply exist here, I am a recognized citizen, if only temporary and an alien. My presence is official. There is a photograph of me up at the Commissariat – taken two weeks ago, when I needed a haircut and my face was covered with mosquito bites after a long walk in the Camargue country: I look like a bad case of psycho-something with liver complications. Beside it is written a summary biography: "*White, Kenneth, Anglais, Glasgow, étudiant.*" It's a caricature, but it'll do the trick.

A couple of days ago I was in the Paris Prefectory for my "residence permit". I wasn't alone. I was part of a long, straggling queue. And I had two others like it that morning.

In one or other of those queues, I met a Vietnamese whose name had been spelled wrong and who had been trotting for hours from counter to counter desperately trying to establish his identity. I met the American who'd been supplied with priority tickets for three days – he would stand in the queue, and when he got up to the door, they'd tell him he was too late and give him another red card. He said he was beginning to think there was something fishy about all this. Sure, there's something fishy, pal, we're all fishy characters trying to survive in the murky ocean of a turbid reality.

"He who does not know the Left Bank of the Seine between the Rue Saint-Jacques and the Rue des Saints-Pères doesn't know life", says Balzac in *Old Goriot*, that I read the other night. Tonight I'm reading the same Balzac's *Lost Illusions*. This book of mine begins where *Lost Illusions* ends.

My papers in order, I can get down to work – at all levels.

At surface level, I talk by the hour and get paid for it. I talk all over Paris, about anything: politics, cosmetics, neurotics, diuretics, art, literature, culture, economy. I get it all out of my system. When I'm on my own, I've got only bare life in front of me. I talk with the woman in the art gallery, and fifty million francs worth of the most variegated artistic shit imaginable hung around us. I talk with the man who makes speeches all over Europe – my job is to renew his stock. I talk with the pale-faced miss who's going to Mexico to make a film and hopefully a fortune out of Malcolm Lowry's *Under the Volcano*. I talk with the professor of Arab studies. I talk, I talk, I talk – in order to be able to buy a little silence for myself.

When he was in Paris, Van Gogh would often leave, on foot, for a long excursion – out to Asnières maybe, or l'Île de la Grande Jatte – with one big canvas strapped to his back. He would stop whenever a motif attracted him, paint it, move again, stop, paint, dividing his canvas into so many little sections, so that when he came home, he was carrying a whole museum on his back, a painted notebook. Maybe that's the kind of thing I want to do. While I'm at it, let me indicate a deep affinity with the Chinese painter Huang Kung-wang who carried round about with him for years on end the roll of paper on which he painted his handscroll "Living in the Fu-ch'un Mountains", working at it only when the spirit moved him.

I give lessons. Superficially merely English lessons, but their latent content is what matters. I make people ask themselves questions. I am a missionary, but without a purpose, without a gospel to sell. I am a missionary who just asks questions. They think I'm only teaching them grammar, while all the time I'm destroying their props, burning their costumes, laying deliberate doubt on the sense of their scripts.

The lift at 15, rue St. Dominique, rises with a slow, oh so slow solemnity. I am sitting on the little bench covered with red plush, beside the caretaker, an old man complete with broom and apron, who is going up to sweep the floors. You have the time to meditate on such an ascent. The atmosphere is soaked with a dream-like mythology, a transcendental tranquillity. The old man holds keys in his shiny hands. The notebook in your hands takes on portentous significance, like some holy Book of Hours. You are approaching finality, slowly penetrating the infinite. The lift makes no sound, not one hum, not one creak, it is raised by supernatural, supertechnical power. You forget what you came for, where you are going, you have only the sensation of ascending, the rest is infinite. All images fade. The old man's face is expressionless. A slight jolt, then immobility. Things crowd in again. The old man's broom begins to sweep. You go to teach grammar. The glass case goes slowly back down into the depths.

Paris, queen among cities, moon among stars, so gracious a valley, an island of fine living, and on that island hath Philosophy her ancient seat, who alone, with Study her sole comrade, holding the eternal citadel of light and immortality, hath set her foot on the wildered pasture of the ancient world.
      GUIDO DE BAZOCHES, Archives of the University of Paris

Coming down the Rue de Richelieu, empty and lost, I see a shop-window full of cheeses, yellow, red, brown and white cheeses, and I stop and I smile, and suddenly feel good again. I read the names: Gaperon d'Auvergne, Chabichou, Banon, Bigottes, Poivre d'Âne, Puant du Nord – it must be this stink of the North that makes me feel good, gives me the sensation of a reality. It's peasant reality I recognize here, the last reality we know. For the state of things in which we now live is not a reality. It has not the feel of a reality, it has not the intimate tatchiness of a reality, it is a sequence of boredom and catastrophe. I'm out for reality. All my writing is a tendency towards radical reality.

John of Salisbury's recommendation for a happy life in his *Policraticus*, companion volume to his *Metalogicon* on which I also spent a few hours today in the Sorbonne library: "A searching mind, poverty, quietness, sojourn in a foreign land". I should make out all right.

Dream:
It's my last day in Glasgow. I'm walking away at the edge of the city, along dingy streets. Then suddenly I come smack up against this huge hotel, The Empress of India. It's a bit rundown, but still shining with gold and rubies, and the rooms full of exotic furniture. I think: if ever I come back to Glasgow, maybe this is where I'll live. I continue walking, now along the river, darkness coming down. Here I come across an old mine, that can still be visited. You have to put on a mask because down in the depths the gases are mephitic. The

stone mined is basaltic black with traces of dark red. I pick up a piece. Further along the river, a cold air rising from it and the beginnings of a mist, I see another place. It's a gin-mill, Grannie Bell's. They sell old postcards in there: the misshapen figures with patibular faces of Glasgow criminals. I drink a contemplative gin, then go for a piss. Gazing down at the bowl of the toilet, I see, engraved in dark blue, the letters: Shank's Vitreous China.

I keep with me (as a talisman?) the sheet of paper on which my father, railway signalman, jotted for me the times of trains when I was leaving Scotland. It's a "Snowstorm Duties" chit, and in the column "Work Carried Out", there's a phrase in brackets which comes across to me as a kind of programme for my own peculiar "snowstorm duties": *Specific details of nature of work must be given. A general description such as Snowstorm Duties will not suffice.*

In this café at seven in the morning the juke box is rocking and rolling. Today's warm cigarette smoke mingles with last night's cold remains. Life is great for everybody – so says the Commercial.
Man beside me remarks to the proprietor: "I'm fed up working" – he's got it out, now he's embarrassed, as if he's hazarded some dangerous joke and is apprehensive of its effect. He blushes, tries to smile. "What d'you mean", says the jovial barman, "work's a fine thing, work is freedom". A hunchback to my left says softly: "You don't work, you just rake in the cash." The hesitant revolutionary slinks off, the hunchback continues, louder: "You don't work, you just pile up the dough." "Yes, yes, that's right", says the barman in a superior conciliatory tone as though the man were a halfwit. The hunchback insists: "You just rake it in." The barman's jaw muscles tighten, then he repeats himself: "Yes, yes, that's right", but this time his voice grates. The hunchback now raises his voice, stands up from his stool: "Well, I work, and I don't rake it in." Then his thoughts veer, and he begins to defend his position: "I do something for society. I work. I work by the hour. I earn the same thing every hour. I know exactly where I am. I'll get an old age pension." "That's right", says the barman, unsmiling. The hunchback evidently thinks he has gone too far: "It's very dark, this morning", he says, in the neutral voice of a man commenting on the weather.

Capstan Chesterfield Players Anfa Turmac Smart Memphis Austria La Favorite Disque Bleu Philip Morris Craven A Gitanes Celtic Hello

Weekend Gauloises Vertes Hit Parade State Express ... Smoke. But not my kind of smoke. The weed I use for smoking grows in the desertic backgrounds of my mind.

A girl's face, a face on a poster, a girl's face on a poster, half ripped away.

An Irish scholar, twelfth century: "In those first days when youth in me was quick and life was fast, there I was wandering from city to city in fair France for the desire that I had of learning and letters."
Monumenta Germaniae Historica, picked up in the Sorbonne library.

That night over in the Gorbals (Glasgow): Wee Harry from Florence Street telling me that if I wanted to write a bestseller (my father had told him I was "writing", was using up enough ink to float the Queen Elizabeth), all I had to do was come over to his place with a tape-recorder and he'd tell me about his exploits as a con-man on the South Side. "Put y'right on top, boy, put y'right on top." "Right on top of what?", I said.

Picked up on the quays an old copy of Eugène Sue's *The Mysteries of Paris* that came out in serial form between 1842 and 1843, and read through it this rainy afternoon. Pretty corny stuff about the hero Rudolph of mysterious origin and his Scottish mistress, Sarah MacGregor. But the book did go down into the Parisian underworld that had spread out over the years from the medieval Cours des Miracles, and had not only Paris but the whole of Europe all agog. Anyway it's neither its plot nor its more significant sociological content that really interests me, it's the very movement of the book. It's a *roman-fleuve*, a river-novel, with a myriad of eddies, sworls and swirlings. And Sue himself was not an uninteresting character. After early years as an autocratic dandy, he turned republican and was elected Socialist deputy for the Seine on April 28, 1850. Because of these tendencies and his positioning, after Louis Napoleon's coming into power, he had to go into exile. Went in 1851 to the Savoie which was still then an Italian principality. Died there six years later. Buried in the dissident, free-thinking, non-Catholic section of Annecy cemetery. As a student I had gathered enough Glasgoviana together from the book barrows of Renfield Street and Buchanan Street (about crime rings, gangs, model lodging houses . . .) to write *The Mysteries of Glasgow*. But it would have been like Job on his shit-pile. It's now 8 p.m., November 17, 1961, in Meudon, suburbs of Paris, at the end of another history-cycle. What I'm doing here? Making intellectual leaps over the shit-piles of culture. A transhistorical hurdle race, a metaphysical metropolitan marathon.

To do what goes beyond all merit and even all understanding.
NIETZSCHE

An ontophanic notebook, a supernihilist's book of hours.

Never since Plotinus had metaphysics rebecome to this extent and degree a maieutics of incandescence, writes Manuel de Diéguez on Nietzsche in his book *A History of Intelligence*.

After some rummaging around the Russian bookshop I came across the "Scythian Manifesto" of 1917, published in the review of the "free association of philosophy", *Volfila*. This Scythian association brought together poets and philosophers, revolutionary socialists and libertarian apoliticals (Blok was among them, so was Biely) on a "platform of creation" out to inaugurate a new form of culture: new literary forms, new aesthetic forms, new social forms. The intellectual atmosphere was a blend of subjectivism, elementarism and symbolism. The secretary of the association, one Steinberg, described its members as solitaries "living like islands in the sea of bolshevik Russia".

Dream:
Talk English, he said.
I am talking English.
No, you're not.
Call it Scottish then.
Say your name.
Kenneth White
That's not English.

Went to the Père Lachaise graveyard in order to say hello to Maurice MacNab. An ancestor of his came from Scotland to France in the eighteenth century as part of Louis XV's special guard. Maurice, born in 1856, was never a special guard of anything, except maybe a bottle. He was anarchist, socialist, and songwriter. By day he earned his living as a postman, at night he performed his songs, first in the Café de l'Avenir in the Latin Quarter, then in the cabaret Le Chat noir, up on Montmartre, making it a point of honour to get paid only in alcohol (he was later to write a medical thesis on hangovers for the "Faculty of Montmartre"). A newspaper article of the time said his voice was the roughest and the falsest imaginable, something like a seal with tonsilitis. But he was a great success with the aficionados of the night, always dressed in black like an undertaker, singing his songs full of revolt and black humour, songs such as *Le Bal de l'Hôtel de ville* (The Dance at the Town Hall) or *Le grand métingue du métropolitain* (The Grand Meeting of the Metropolitan). He died, on Xmas day 1889, of tuberculosis and no doubt some other ailments, at the Lariboisière hospital in Paris, having reached, almost, the ripe old age of thirty-four.

As I go through the graveyard I'm singing to myself one of his songs:

C'était tout d'même un bien chouette métingue
Que le métingue du métropolitain!

At this restaurant, down by the dark, slow-flowing Seine. Old hunchback Algerian with satchel and black coat comes in, selling bright-coloured leather wallets. I buy one. I'll put my testament in it.

1 a.m., Boulevard Garibaldi. The streets are black as boiling tar and the light of the lamps is embedded in them. The metro station, which is high up there, the line between Sèvres-Lecourbe and Pasteur being above ground, glows murky yellow, and beside it lies a Bumper Car lot, part of the big fair stretching all along the boulevard. The cars slide round, enamelled in screaming red and yellow and green, and their masts scraping along the netted iron roof strike off sharp little blue sparks. At this time in the morning, only young men are present, lounging in the cars, trying now and then to bump each other, very seriously. I see one fellow being bumped, but he neglects the jolt disdainfully and carries on puffing at his cigarette. Minutes later, I see him throw the butt on to the street with a magnificent gesture and knuckle down to the earnest business of sport. Dull collisions follow each other relentlessly.

A rainy day on the banks of the Seine. In a musty *bouquiniste* booth, I come across this old book: *Mystics of the North-East*. The "North-East" in question is northeastern Scotland, and the author, I see, was Regius Professor of Theology at Aberdeen University. At this, I hesitate. But the price of the book is cheap, so I purchase it. Who knows, maybe in some of these characters I'll recognize distant cousins.

The city is cold tonight.
I am standing in the Rue du Maine, by the little triangular square.
The lights of the Rue de la Gaîté reveal the smoke rising from the tenement buildings, and colour it red, green, blue. A child cries from a yellow window.
A red sign above says: *Gaîté*, and now below at the station I see another: *Départ*.
I walk around the triangular park, then go down towards the Boulevard du Montparnasse.
The moon is suspended just above the brassière advert on the Place de Rennes. Something in me is saying good-bye, over and over, and over again. But goodbye to what, and where am I going?

Where am I going? I'm going madwards, heh-heh, and me chin is running with black, black blood. Me name is Rumplestiltskin, Profess-or Rumpelstiltskin, of Waldorf University. Thank you very much, Madame, and bob's your uncle, your heredosyphilitic uncle, and say hullo to the vagotonic twins. This stone hides boney kingdoms. I am the prisoner of Chillon, my name is Iacobus, I was educated in the Collège des Écossais and I say to all of you: *chlanna nan con thigibh a so's gheibh sibh feoil*. Where are you going now? I'm going outside, where the secrets are.

I've never thought in terms of roots, but for those who do I suppose I'm "uprooted" and this manuscript is a prime example of uprootedness. This was the big theme of Shestov, pseudonym ("traveller-wanderer") of Yehuda Leyb Schwarzmann, who worked in Moscow before moving to Paris. It's there in the title of his key-book, *Apofeoz bespočvennosti (The Apotheosis of Uprootedness)*, 1905. In his book of 1944, *Existential Monday and the Seventh Day of History*, the Rumanian poet and philosopher Benjamin Fondane says he turned the historical museum of philosophy into a hallucinatory experience. Experience is the word. And experimentation. Moving out over a new field. It's not just a question of emigration, but of the extirpation of rooted ideas.

There's only one really necessary and interesting -ism: nihilism. All the rest is just improvisation and combination. Socratic dialogues reduced to this: "What's that up there on the horizon?" – "Nix."

The times are not "a-changing", as the guitar guy puts it. And they won't in any real sense for a while, if ever. The first step towards something else is a paradoxical existence made up of abstract negativism and erratic movement.

The National Library: the biggest collection of ticks, crocks and gargoyles you've ever seen. A man wrapped in a cloth that looks as if it's already gone around ten corpses – pale, chipped nose supporting bifocals – is studying the ways of God. An albino with pimples and a body that's gone through the wringer trottles around, lost to the world. A woman with a face of chewed gristle registers obscene delight when big tomes are thumped on her desk like babies. A youngster who looks healthy enough, suddenly starts biting his pinky and patting his cranium. An English professor with a bald rugby-football head and a nose like the mushroom called the Trumpet of Death studies history. A red, greasy man with blubbery lips – my suspicion is that he also is English (bacon and eggs type) – makes agonizing expressions every now and then as though he were undergoing birth. Prim powdery sixty over there keeps up stiff-lipped concentration. Cow's-lick and podgy fizzog beside her is having digestion trouble.
Vamos.

Waiting in the damp-dark station of the Champ de Mars, under the Quai Branly, looking past the black pillars at the Port de Suffren, and Passy on the other side. A dismal, dripping cave of a station, a whale's mouth of a station, Paris above and behind you, gaping into the Seine.
The train comes clanking in, full of blue smoke and vinegary light. You and a hundred other souls climb in.
Along the river, through the suburbs: ox-blood bricks; honest, poignant allotments; coal-bings; waste lots; factory sheds, marshalling yards; a fruit-ripening plant; an abandoned factory; the lights on up there in Rodin's museum; the viaduct; rain on the hills; the dark line of trees.

Meudon is wet and windy tonight. The butcher clears up his benches, wipes his knives and mincing machine, hides away a basin of fat, slobby meat. The cobbler tap-tap-taps away. In the murky wineshop, a radio is playing noise. Two emigrants from way back pass, talking Russki. Up the Basses-Pointes, then along the ash-strewn pathway that crisses under my steps. Home again. Home again. "God bless all here" says an Irish voice deep in my guts. I reply, valiantly, with "Up de Valera!".

On the platform at Montparnase. Dark skies pouring northwards. On the roof terrace of a building close to the station, there is a plant, a small tree, which is seized, tugged, hauled, jerked, dragged by the wind. You want to see it fly away over the roofs of the city.
Montparnasse, evening. Platform lamps swinging, scattering bushels of light into the wind and the rain.
The city smoulders. To the fore is the great red sign on the boulevard, letters of fire, hot, seething, swelling as you stare at them: *Terminus*.

Meudon is full of exiled Russians, more or less White, more or less Red, some on the verge of anarchistic Black. I got into talk with one of those exiles tonight. Spoke French with a strong moscovite accent. Told me he was writing a history of the Khazars. I'd never heard of the Khazars, but I was interested. Nomad Turks who occupied a large territory comprising the Black Sea steppe, the Caspian and the Caucasus. The name meaning "the wanderers". My man told me it was the Khazars who made possible Russia, because they held back Muslim conquest. Without the space they kept open, the Rus ("the rowers") wouldn't have been able to make their moves from the Baltic. Khazar culture was apparently a mix of turco-mongol Tengriism and a kind of Judaism. It was in close touch with Byzantium. Next time I'm in the Bibliothèque Nationale, I'll look into it closer. I have a fascination for those peoples and politics that got lost from the established map of Europe. Ghost states. Forgotten configurations. White worlds.

The Rue Leblanc – that's right, White Street, goes down from Place Balard to the Seine. On one side of it rises a high wall; on the other, loom factories. Behind the wall, railway sidings. Behind the factories, more factories. Great dusty windows, shadows in yellow light, a beam turning. Grinds, screeches, chugs. Buildings cut out against the reddish sky. It's a cold, wet, raw night. I walk down the street towards the river. Nine o'clock. No one here but myself, a slight rain-mist rising off the cobbles and the lamps naked and sore. Pinned to a dark door in the wall, a notice: "House for sale, in the country – in the Ille-et-Vilaine." I keep on walking down the street, come down to the André Citroen Quay. The Seine is yellow and black. Up near the Boulevard Victor station, work in progress, two bulldozers red in a sea of mud and the rain drifting across the hot light of the work-lamps. There's a fire lit too, an open fire of wood, and an Algerian in yellow oilskins is on his hunkers before it, poking at it and raising sparks – finally he stands up and pisses into it. A goods-train goes by, loaded with cars. On the other side of the tracks, in a big black hangar, a crane is clawing scrap metal from one spot to another, where it gets crushed into cubes. The screech of the metal cuts the night, and behind the screech is the soft throb of an engine turning over on the work-site. I go down to the river and its cold, faraway emptiness. Beyond its shadows and reflections, the cold, faraway emptiness.

Another couple of hours rummaging among the *bouquinistes* of the Seine. This time I come away with a biography of Andrew Ramsay, born in Ayr, known in France as the Chevalier Ramsay. Was for a while secretary to Fénelon. Wrote (in French) *The Travels of Cyrus*. Was involved in freemasonry, developing in France the Scottish concepts and practises known as *Écossisme*. It was in a speech of 1737 that he suggested the creation in France of an encyclopedia that would lay out the state of knowledge and thought, an idea taken up by Diderot and D'Alembert. The great *Encyclopédie* (*Dictionnaire raisonné des sciences, des arts et des métiers*) came out in 1751, printed in Paris by one Le Breton. Encyclopedia: *enkyklios,* "in a circle" and *paideia* "education". There's going to be something "encyclopedic" (cyclotronic?) about these eccentric studies of mine: I follow psycho-mental circuits with a sense of concentric, expanding circles.

This morning, grey, wet, clammy, there was a sparrow on the concourse of Montparnasse station, fluttering about, worriedly cocking its head, skimming here, there, looking for a way out. At length it perched on a signboard. On the signboard was written: *Consult our Tourist Office.*

Nulla dies sine linea – no day without a line, said the Benedictine. I go with that. But also go one further: *nulla dies sine idea* – no day without an idea. Ideas? That intellectual adrenaline. And a poetics that isn't (only) aesthetic, but *semantic*.

To sum up both my psychological disposition and the "metaphysical" atmosphere in which I evolve: white exaltation and black humour.

Rue Henri Barbusse, prophet of Peace (in this street stands the apartment-house Nirvana); Rue Fleury Pankouke, only two red geraniums. I end up in the Rue de la République. Nothing.

I'm in this café – the Café des Sports – and I'm drinking coffee from a cup which has a crack in it as long as the Mississippi-Missouri. In the games-room beyond the partition, meeting-room of the Club des Supporters *"Allez Meudon"*, four muslims are playing table-football, handling the shafts with skill and earnestness, bent low down over the pitch. At a table behind me (I'm holding up the bar), three old sodgers with scarves and caps drink red wine. Beside them is a pin-table – *Serenade* – a pin-table for two ("it's more fun to compete"), illuminated: curvaceous girl guiding gondola bearing cosy couple down Venetian canal.

We are very cold, and we are very quiet, comrades. It is 3 o'clock in the afternoon and the morale is down to the dregs. Even when you think you have some way down in the pit of your belly, it gets lost on the way up. No use looking for poetry or anything. Consult the Bottin.

The clubroom is painted maroon and yellow, with a billiard-table plumb in the centre. Cups and trophies litter the ledges. There is a pennant on the mirror. There is. There is. There is no end to the Bottin.

Suddenly there's a rush of uniformed men into the room.

It's the Meudon brass-band coming in for a drink, a blether and some banter after their weekly rehearsal. They line out along the bar :

"Six coffees, and five glasses of Calvados!"

"Is this on you the Auvergnat?"

"Don't make fun of the Auvergnats."

"Well, I'm a Breton, that's even worse."

"Did you see that dog?!"

"Sure, it's a hunting dog to go fishing with."

Night of insomnia, the window full of moon and wind. I hear a bird. Hark! Must have insomnia, too, it's only 3 o'clock.

I feel like a negative in a cold fluid in a dark room.

A train. First one of the morning.

Why not get up and take the next one into Paris? I remember the last time. Me and the stiff drunk in the Montparnasse café. They finally put him out on a bench. I stayed for a while, then what, I got a train back to here and went to bed. And couldn't sleep because of the coffee.

Stay where you are, that's the only way to get places. Proverb.

There goes the second train.

You haven't a chance with that wallpaper, so don't keep staring at it. Just try to move gravitionly into oblomovian oblivion.

There goes the third train.

There's a cat keeps wailing and coughing. I go to the kitchen door, stand there behind its iron and pane of glass, and look out at the cold afternoon. The cat itself I don't see at first – then there he is, his scream of a face and cold eyes glimmering, grey-and-black in the darkness, hairy hump of sick flesh, coughing and wailing. It's late afternoon, there's bird-song in the glabrous greyness, and I'm hoping the cat will get well soon. It should go away to a wood somewhere, instead of snuffling round the doors for scraps of human refuse that only make it sicker than it is. It should go away alone, and give better powers than the humans it has come to rely on, the chance to cure it. It should make a decision, and get out, even backwards apparently, into solitude and uncivilized animality, not keep skulking round those charitable doorways. That cat and I have a lot in common.

This limbo with its incandescences is situated between Being and Nothingness. I don't cling to Being. And I don't plunge into Nothingness. I do a jig in the intervening space.

These mornings and this weather winter hales me out of bed at about two in the morning. I am told by a friend I do not sleep enough, that I shall be old before my time, that I am burning up my precious quota of youth. Not in riotous living, no, but in a deeper kind of fire, a fire that burns whitely within me, the spirit of whiteness, a holy ghost. Whatever I consume is consumed by this whiteness, it burns me, hollows me out. In winter there is a vigilance demanded of me, and this is the winter of the world. I am a child of winter, and winter claims me entirely, lets me sleep no more than is necessary, and even then my sleep is a winter sleep, a drifting of snow in which I bury myself. I wake in the mornings, in the cold white silence, I rise from my bed and dress, I drink a glass of cold water, and I begin to write. So each day begins. I have come to look forward to my glass of water the way a drunkard regards his drink. I am drunk with my vigil and my icy water. I am drunk with my winter thoughts, the incredible joyance of this apparent misery, I am drunk with a clear-minded clear-bodied drunkenness. My brain is a laboratory of thought, and I use the purest of the waters of winter. Shivers of cold and shovers of enthusiasm, shivers of cold enthusiasm chase over my body. I distill a new brand of transcendental spirits.

Strange things from the sea, spiny craiturs pierced by the point of scissors and slit round and opened – my landlady is regaling herself with sea urchins. "Everything that comes from the sea", she says, "does me good". She stands there at the stove waiting for her soup to cook and spoons out the red-brown, yellow lobes of porous flesh from the shells: "iodine", she says. Iodine, salt, the smell of the sea. In addition to the eatable lobes, the urchins are full of violets, blacks, maroons of globular and tissuey substance. I am looking at the heart of a sea-life, inside its grey-green shell, while my landlady tells how she was introduced to them by a Breton oyster-merchant up at the Place Clichy, and how tonight she paid them four francs the five. I am looking at the heart of a sea-life, a dark, cold passion, I am looking at life, abysmal, generic, feeling its cold radiations, a kind of planktonic mist that is to me what the world of Ideas was to Plato. As I think of Plato, my landlady tells how she sometimes asks for a plate of sea-fruit in a restaurant for, it's curious, everything from the sea does her good. I get the hell out of Plato, and into the restaurant. I see that plate of sea-fruit: the ancient oyster, the black dome of the whelk, the spiky back of the urchin, the ribbed curved cockle, the moon-eclipse of the mussel. I'm walking around with them in their abyssal world – myself eating plankton, like the biggest whales.

I am sitting here tonight in the light of the lamp sooking at a bottle of port given me by a friend a few days back, and which I've reserved for a suitable occasion, a time of *pougra*, as the Siberian ice-storm is called, where the only resource is to bury yourself in the snow and hope. I am sitting here, sipping at the bottle of port, and thinking of the little Portuguese girl who was my first love and with whom I lived for fifteen whole days. To say I lived with her is perhaps to give a wrong impression, since we were living in a school in Paris with twenty of our fellows from all over Europe who had, like us, written an essay on the fair country of France and won a prize for it. I was in love with Francisca Maria Rodriguez Ortega Perez, and it was something, believe me, to be the rival of Jesus H. Christ himself. I was seventeen years old, Tristan White, and I loved her. But Jesus Christ and the Opus Dei won in the end. Maybe, by this time she's doing missionary work in some heathen corner of the globe. Easy enough to say, now that I'm an old dialectical humorist who's been around, but at that time it meant a lot to me, and once back in Scotland, I wrote to her and wrote poems about Francisca and the Red Land, and her necklet of sea-shells (yes, she wore a necklet of sea-shells, and I could not get them out of my head ...). I was working that summer as purser on a Clyde paddle-steamer plying between Wemyss Bay and Rothesay, a continuous shuttle-traffic, half-an-hour each way, checking on passengers and luggage, entering them in the books: Wemyss Bay-Innellan-Rothesay; Rothesay-Innellan-Wemyss Bay, the thud and splash of the paddles, the spray on my face. The old sailor-man (Royal) who engaged me in conversation and told me of the fun and games they had when he was in the service, tapping me on the balls as he did so. The Gaelic man with the round, brown face and the smile, and with the poems, the yards of recitation he'd spin out as we lay berthed at Rothesay. Those nights in Rothesay, counting the tickets collected during the day, and tying them up in piles, little concertinas of snippets of tickets you held in your hand, your left hand, and tried to slip a noose of string round them with your right, and then draw the string close – and the set would break, the tickets would spill back on to the board and you'd have to begin again, cursing blue murder in the hot little counting house, and outside the cool night darkening, the throb-throb of the dynamo, and the lights along the prom. At last you'd get the damn things tied up and packed in newspaper ready to be handed over to the van in the morning, and then you'd go for a walk in the streets of Rothesay before coming back on board for a glass of milk and a dried-up muffin and settle down in your cabin, a little hole near the paddles and where the dynamo throbbed at its loudest and it was hot, hot, and you'd hear the engineer come in drunk, and think of Francisca and never get to sleep. And then suddenly it would be morning again, and you'd be up at the gangway checking on the passengers, before getting down below for your breakfast. And there'd be Saturday nights at Rothesay, near riots on the pier, drunks cursing you upside down and threatening to throw you in the drink and you clicking away conscientiously with your wee counting machine, and thinking of Francisca, port in a storm, whiteness in a red land, sea-shells, a pretty little face with tears on it, because she didn't want to leave you, Christ or no, and in one month's time your heart seemed to have swollen, and the night before your day-off, you'd jump the boat on the last trip to Wemyss and take the bus into Largs and then another bus to Fairlie, and you'd spend the day walking through the woods and over the moors with a letter from Francisca you'd read over and over again, and they kidded you at the Post-Office about the love letters from Portugal . . . Yes, Tristan White, long out of sight, now drinking the last of the port in the darkblue Paris night.

Undifferentiated living – that is the rain and the white mist, the seeping, vagrant substance I like to feel around me, as well as the determination of the sun. Today Meudon is muffled in the stuff.

I lie in my shell, all wrapped up in my albumen-richness, and read of great birds. It's the dawn-chorus in my brain. I hear the yawp of Whitman, the cock-crow of Thoreau, the yark-yark of that bird-thing Nietzsche, Burns – the Scotch cock on the dung-hill, Diderot's athletic owl, Rousseau's persecuted sparrow. And I dream of a bird with white wings, as the ugly duckling dreamed of the swan.

Swan, gannet, petrel, or albatross. In the islands at the back of nowhere, lost in the cold mist, I have seen petrels nesting on the bare crags of the most exposed cliffs, facing the wind and the ocean. A million penguins lived in those same islands.

The rain is falling over the Seine and the Oise, and I, *homo candidus*, wait calmly for birth.

On the night of the Saturday to the Sunday, it snowed. On the Sunday afternoon, I walked along towards the lake of Trivaux and when I came near it saw crowds of people. I didn't know the lake was frozen, solid, and I didn't know it was used as an amusement-ground in such conditions. Every time I'd passed by, it was bare and solitary, except for a few diehard anglers. It was like bursting suddenly into the sixteenth century, catching Brueghel in the act. All the farce, colour and aliveness of the Fleming was there: toddlers unable to keep their balance, skaters, tobogganists. I was surprised and delighted to see the owner of one of the local wineshops, a tired sad quiet man of about fifty I had always seen moping behind his bar, sailing away merrily, lost in a blessed waltz, his beret set firmly on his head, his muffler flying, sure as a bird on his skates, circling, sweeping, gliding, with his poodle in his arms. Fathers show their children how to slide, watch the kids for a long time, wondering if they dare risk it, success will be hero-worship, failure will mean ridicule, the challenge is there – down they go, cigarette in mouth to show they're not really in earnest, arms out to balance, and they've done it, so they do it again and again, with confidence, and their wives laugh with delight. Oh, there are rivalries too – the two couples over there, the women watching the men, one of whom is tubby, small and jaunty and balances well, the other tall, thin, scraggy, makes a mess of it and is scared and would like to stop, but the little show-off eggs him on, taunts him in front of the women and the scraggy one makes another attempt and hurts his elbow and puts his hands into his pockets and looks miserable and cold, while the other, full of glee, bubbling over with mirth and false good-will, continues his triumph. A group of boys, aces on skates, clear a pitch for hockey practice, sweeping off the surface snow with their sticks. A girl, learning to move on the blades, places one foot after the other gingerly, unsteadily, and falls with a rueful grin. It's one chapter of a winter fantasia, and I take it all in, moving round the pond, getting it from every angle, half-closing my eyes to see only the movement and disposition, closing them altogether to hear only the sound . . .

I stand there in the cold, watching, but I get tired of it pretty soon, and go away into the ice-gripped wood on my own.

The snow is still falling today. Takes me back to Glasgow when, around 1955, I was reading among other Russian books, Dostoevsky's *Letters from the Underworld*. In the little red-battered Everyman's Library edition I still have with me, I see underlined this: "Today, half-melted, dirty, yellow snow was falling. It was falling yesterday, and it will be falling again tomorrow." That was the atmosphere of those Glasgow days. A lot of modern literature came out of Dostoevsky's *Letters*: Kafka, Camus . . . Maybe in some sense I came out of them too. But with the accent on the the *out*. It's always snowing in the *Letters*, that yellow, dirty snow. But towards the end there's a little clearing, when the snow falls cleaner, and when, coming back home, exhausted, desperate, after a long nocturanl walk through the city streets, the underworld man feels dawning in his mind a "consciousness of the truth". What truth? That is the question, and the quest.

ROOM 2
On the Hyperborean Fringe

"Let's face it. We are Hyperboreans. We are very well aware in what remoteness we live. Beyond the North, the ice, and death – *our* life, *our* happiness. We know the way. We've found the way out of millennia of labyrinth."
NIETZSCHE, *The Antichrist*

Lonely in the freezing cold, oh lonely. Winter still savage in Saint-Michel. Having skimmed through in a library a book called *The Metaphysics of Happiness*, without results, promenading my unmetaphysical body through the chilled latinity of the quarter. I exist far way in an in-world out-world of being, lonely at times, oh lonely, but in movement, always in movement. I give a New Year greeting to all Hyperboreans.

It's in the fourth book of his "Enquiries" (*Historia*), that Herodotus concentrates on the Black Sea, the lands of the Scythians, the Cimmerians, the Hyperboreans, and the Eurasian steppes: "Towards the North, in the region of the Boreas wind, beyond the last civilised lands . . ." He also tells the story of one Aristeas, born on an island in the Sea of Marmora, who left home for the Hyperborean country, that "immense territory", and was away for six years. When he came back to his homeland, "possessed by Apollonian fury", he wrote a long poem about his travels, before disappearing again. But he or his ghost turned up a couple of centuries later (that would be about 450 B.C.) at Metaponte, in southern Italy, declaring to the folk there that for years, in the shape of a crow, he had been travelling with Apollo in the Scythian Caucasus and that they should raise a statue to this episode. Which was done. Imagine that statue of Apollo and all the crows of the region flocking around it, croaking over it. It's as if, up in the North, Aristeas had got wind of some shamanic Wotan with those two crows, Hugin (thought) and Munin (memory) perched on his shoulders.

"We have found the way", says Nietzsche. In fact, I have several ways in mind and at my disposal: the wild Atlantic western way; the quiet eastern way; the burning southern way; the transcendental northern way. All employing the formula K+L+M (knowledge, literature, meditation) and the more advanced formula K+W (kenning, wayfaring) and implying existential exitiation, fundamental earth-experience and the makings of a world.

Up behind Montparnasse there is the big Inno store. I was in there last night, down in the basement, among the food counters, where a profuse display of nourishment is laid out from all over the world. Need I insist again upon the fact that I have quit Parnassus, its religions, art, and philosophy, for good, and am writing in the basement of the world, looking for real nourishment? *Nach Inno geht der geheimnisvolle Weg*, as Novalis might have said. I stood at the bread-corner and watched the fair-haired bread-girl delivering lengths and rounds and whorls of white, yellow, brown and black panification. And then I went through the cheese section, a cosmos of colour and smell, a worldly stink, terrestrial effluvia: from Norway to Italy in two easy whiffs, through Switzerland and its yellow snows to France, with its lactic delights and nose alarmers. Balls and pears and rolls and pyramids and squares of cheese, bare-fleshed cheese and cheese hid in leaves, in grape-stones, in cinders, cheese like a sun in fog, cheese like an autumn moon, cheese flowing with milk and honey and cheese crumbling in blue putrefaction, cheese, cheese and cheese. And sausages the same: pale, fiery, stolid, dainty, morose, glutinous, lascivious, benign, bad-tempered, dreamy. And ham fat and soft, or burnt clean in the open air of a mountain, thin red gleaming slices of essential pork. And salads: Chinese salads, salads of palm-tree heart, all kinds of delicatessenry chopped up and laid on platters, with green celery and the red glare of pimentos. Mangoes big and soft and heavy as a woman's breast, avocados like jungle-green pears, oranges faithful as ever, Brazil nuts like shrivelled moons, walnuts coralled in secrecy, hazelnuts simple as good-day, dates ancient and sweet on their branches, apples from a ruddy old garden, monkey-faced coconuts, smooth red cola nuts, wrinkled cashews, dry porous almonds – fruits of the earth, the first and last inspiration, the living, nourished Adam. And the sea of our searching: the fat turbot with the slimy white slit in its neck, the gleam of the silvery fishlets in a spray of crushed ice, the sunset redness of salmon, the opalescent reflections, the blind, archaic gropings of crayfish, the pink flimsiness of shrimps, the jocularity of whelks, the contorted secrecy of oysters, the fleshiness of scallops, the ribbed sea-smoothness of cockles, the blue glint of mussels and the orange force of their meat, cod stolid and no nonsense, the smoky brilliance of haddock. My life and my death, this is my element, this is the ground of the world, my meataphysics, the first chapter in the book of a new covenant.

Wandering about in the smoky-black precincts of Saint-Sulpice. It was in a café here that Rimbaud recited for the first time his poem "The Drunken Boat", his first crazy outburst before he set out on his quest for "the place and the formula".

Since Rimbaud, the attempt has been to get at a global formula. Like the integral calculus in mathematical science. Hence on the one hand, in the higher reaches of literature, either absolute essentialism or logorrheic association. I'm trying to get at something else. Archaeo-logical and archi-pelagic. One of these days I'll reach out to a new abstraction. But for the moment I'm in the plenitude of the immediate, in a fragmentary, precipitative kind of way. There's a lot of thought going on too, but it's rushing along fringes and frontiers. In meteorology, they talk about frontology – the study of weather fronts. This book is a chart of high energy mental meteorology.

The tidal energies of conscience.
Waves of thought.
Poiesis.

Displacements, paradoxes, incandescences.

Around this room, as around any focal point of incandescent activity, in concentric circles: a traffic zone of stolid indifference; a clinical zone of tepid intellectualism; an empty space with a whooming wind and bird cries.

Dream:
The place is Germany.
I'm in a station.
"A ticket for Memlik, please."

"There's no train for Memlik."
"Oh, well, I'll go back to Scotland."
When I arrive in Scotland, having taken the long way round, I'm dressed like a Persian. I give a long talk in some institution which nobody understands. Maybe, I think, it's because I'm talking Persian.
After the talk, I walk in the streets.
I walk, walk, walk . . .
Getting nowhere.
Finally I go into a station.
"A ticket for Germany, please."
And I'm back on the Luneburger Heide, feeling quite at home.

Took the underground to Notre-Dame-de-Lorette. Walking in the Faubourg Montmartre with the ghost of Isidore Ducasse at my side. Born in Montevideo, looking across the Plata at Buenos-Aires, schooling in French lyceums at Tarbes and Pau. It was in a hotel in this quarter he wrote the *Songs of Maldoror*, black humour with a vengeance. Rain falling on the Rue Richer, the Rue de la Chaussée-d'Antin and the Square Montholon. Went into one of those old Paris restaurants, a *bouillon*, where the waiters do a quick black-and-white ballet among the tables, for a bite to eat: a dish of vinegared leeks and a fish roasted in fennel. Outside, the rain still falling. Walked north up to the Butte. All Paris laid out before me, beautiful as the meeting of Schopenhauer and Eugène Sue on the top of a piano all of whose keys are black.

In a café on the Rue des Trois-Frères up in Montmartre. A guy leaning on the zinc counter to the waitress:
"What did Paul die of?"
"What you'll die of."
"What would that be?"
"Antiteetotalism."

I met Manuel, the mad Maoist from Madrid, this afternoon in the Sorbonne library. We had a coffee together and then went for a walk. A very picaresque and profitable promenade. Manuel has taken it into his head to get a little revenge on the "big capitalists" by snaffling in the shops a little of anything that takes his fancy. "Recuperating", he calls it. He also finds it thrilling, which gives the action psychological as well as political significance. He makes it a point of honour to rip off four caramels every morning from a big sweet-shop he passes by on his way to the library. On this walk with me, he was out to surpass himself. I lost him in the crowd at one point and got a couple of steps ahead of him, and when I turned round he was offering me a caramel, newly acquired. But that was only the beginning. The net result of our stroll consisted of:

 23 caramels
 1 large cowrie shell from a South Sea Marvels stand
 1 bottle of after-shave lotion
 2 cakes of soap (1 bath-size)
 1 copy of the Surrealist Manifestos
 1 copy of Lenin's *Que Faire*.

 This afternoon I went to see a Japanese exhibition in a small gallery in the Marais district, where I had a good long look at a couple of portraits of Daruma (i.e. Bodhidharma, i.e. P'ou-ti Ta-mo), and looked long also at Hokusai's old monk with a *sutra* beside him. Outside, when I left the gallery, rain was falling through the blue-green air. I came down through the Marais, and across the metal Pont Saint-Louis (rain and wind, a barge passing turgidly up the Seine, people crossing in a crowd) and went down past Notre-Dame to the flower-market where I wandered round the flowers for a while (the rich, dark-coloured, heavy-scented flowers) in the murky light, and then hit the big Paris night. Then later, much later, after walking in the night of Paris, after long walking in the black streets of the fifteenth district, I come back into Montparnasse, to the Rue Bréa, which is full of lights, red signs and green signs, and at the corner of the Rue Jules-Chaplin the prostitutes stand like blond-flamed candles slowly burning down (the devadasis of a sordid temple) while the night-club ten yards up the street has lit-coloured photos of bodies, of breasts, of buttocks, of bellies from dark-brown to tawny gold. Venus wasn't born here but there is semen-foam in the gutters, the quarter reeks with it, and there is blue milk, yes, in the breasts of the prostitutes.

 Dream:
 I had lost everything, and suddenly I was free. On the pier, I told the girl sitting behind the desk piled up with magazines she should leave, there was freedom enough for everybody. She did not believe me. Walking along the shore, I heard young boys discussing me, saying I could have won the race if I hadn't broken my ankle. I was warmed to them, but I no longer cared about the race. I walk along the shore: waves and seeweed and sand. I come to Rory's house, I go in. We talk

of brotherhood. I stay the night. In the morning Rory is dead. There is a crowd of people round the house. I show a chart, written in Scots, but one part was written in German by my grandfather when he was in Poland. I continue walking along the shore.

"Ah, that horrible Pantin . . ." So spoke to me a man, evoking his grimy, murky, gloomy life in Pantin, north-east of Paris. "Ah, that horrible Pantin!"

It is just after 6 o'clock in the morning. The underground train is deadly yellow, cold, smarting with light, packed with people crammed together, some trying to read their newspaper, the woman in front of you reading in a brochure about blood: "Blood is a thick, red, viscous substance, the cells of which are immersed in an albuminous salty solution . . ."

Porte de Pantin. You can hardly call it dawn, but a grey coldness has taken over from the night, growing over the rail-yards, over the slaughter-houses of La Villette.

You come along the Rue de Paris, you go down the Rue Auger, dipping into closes now and then, exploring backyards, reading the chalk marks of children: *Josseline est jantille.* From there you fork off into the Rue du Congo. A man in a torn black coat stumbles over the threshold of a café growling: *M'sieurs-Dames,* and wheezes away up the street before you. Down the Rue Hoche, then, and you're at the Ourcq Canal.

It's dark green in colour, cold, still, the Ourcq canal. The morning hovers in a chill milky vapour. The sun heaves up out of the grey fuzz of the sky, pale orange, then disappears, then returns slightly redder now, then paler.

You walk along the canal, quiet, quiet. Lorries, mainly meat lorries, and in the canal, a couple of barges. One, an open battered hulk, filled with sand. The other, all black and brass, spick and span. North Africans shuffle by, muffled in balaclavas. You come to the Pont Delisy, and the café *Au Bord de l'Eau – Articles de Pêche,* the big cane fishing rods in the window, and pass on till you are stopped by an iron rail. You turn right down a path used as a rubbish dump to the Église Saint-Germain de Pantin, and look away down the road to Châlons-sur-Marne.

Yesterday evening I spent with Alphonse, a Parisian from Burgundy, and his wife Lucienne. Alphonse is a burly fellow with a big, but weak heart and enormous moustaches. The older he gets, he tells me – he's only thirty-nine now – the more anarchistic he gets; at the moment he's just waiting for a chance to beat up any cop that tries to hassle him. His wife collects books, fine costly editions which she'll read maybe when she's retired. Alphonse's main preoccupation, apart from the *boulot* (he's a carpenter) is food and wine. Weak heart or no, he's already had an attack, he still eats like four and drinks the same, talking of his wine the way his wife talks of her books, telling me how he checks the corks every fortnight and displaces the bottles only with very great care. He gives me a tip how to clear troubled wine: you just slip the white of an egg into it and as the albumen sinks it picks up all the floating sediment and leaves the wine crystal clear.

I meet the small man with the leather jacket and the grey stub of moustache at the Odéon metro station. We begin to talk. He tells me he works in the hospitals, does a tour of them nearly every day, collecting instruments for sharpening and adjustment. Sometimes too he goes to the Saint-Antoine hospital to collect blood. They have the open heart operation there on Fridays, from two till nine. It's marvellous. He's often up in the cupola having a look-see. There are always foreign doctors there looking on, for Paris is a great place for the open heart. One day a doctoress fainted – "Some are oversensitive, like" – and he had to cart her away. He can carry 95 kilos – "it's a knack". Sometimes there's a brain operation too. That's really something. They saw round the skull and open it "like a tin of polish". We travel from Odéon to Convention, via Montparnasse and all the hospitals of Paris. When he leaves me at Convention, he says: "Take care of yourself". I pat myself to make sure I'm all there.

I'm in the Grande-Chaumière art academy in Montparnasse with my pal the painter Lauvin. He's over there in the corner, swishing away with his bit of charcoal: the shaved bullet head, the big nose with the wire-rimmed glasses bent over the paper. It's a forty-five minute pose, and the model's already been at it for half-an-hour. She's a tired hulk of a woman, reddish, running to fat, with long streaks of varicose veins on her legs. Lauvin looks up and gives me a wink. The place is hot and dusty and quiet, except for the swishing of charcoal on paper. At last the pose is over. The model stands up, bends her knees – her arse is puffed and creased and red – scratches her muff, yawns. Lauvin gives her a wave, then moves around the big yellow room sketching the lamps, the stove with the twenty-feet pipe, anything at all. Coming over to me, he says it's no use drawing that model, as well draw a violin. She's a fly one, takes it easy, no muscles working: "nothing doing". Not that he minds, why should they bust a gut just so a lot of bums can make sketches? The young ones always start eagerly; they go to the Louvre and study poses, they read up porno books and give you things that would curl your hair. He had a girl-friend who did just that, and he had to tell her after a fortnight to take it easy or she'd have everybody writhing on the floor. When the next pose is taken, he gives me a nudge, gives another wave to the model, and suggests we scram. Which we do. Lauvin has taken it upon himself to show me the whole subterranean art-scene of Paris.

Now that March and Spring have come to the city, the sky is palest blue as though still diluted with snow and the air is rocking with warmth and expectancy. But I still travel sometimes in the underground, and in the underground I am always meeting madmen who speak to me as though they wished to be understood. This one had come straight out of an Irish tale by the looks of him. An old man, beggary, with three coats on his back, a rucksack at his feet, straggly coarse grey beard round his face, a felt hat, round and black, on his head, his mouth full of brown twisted teeth on the left side and empty on the right. It was only after I'd got on the train that I noticed people had made a space around him. I stood alone with him in that space, and he began to sing. It was a gentle, high-pitched singing, pleasant and strange to hear – but he suddenly interrupted it and began convulsively to bite his wrist, and then screamed out: Why! The singing was then resumed (in French it was, but I couldn't make out the words), interrupted every now and then by those convulsive bitings of his wrist. Then he began to talk to me, saying: "There are no old fellows like me around any more." Followed another incomprehensible rigmarole, then the gesture of stuffing his mouth with food. "Isn't that true?", he said, laughing, and began again to sing. When I left him at the Odéon Station, he was still singing.

Charlet? Charlet? Who the hell is Charlet? There's a statue to him in this little square, up by Denfert-Rochereau, where the rain has come to sleep. In the cold quiet wetness under the trees there's only me and an old woman dressed in a skirt with pyjamas showing beneath it, wrapped in a shawl, a towel round her head, smoking a cigarette. It's the middle of the afternoon, the dark side of four. I'd intended to visit the catacombs (just the thing for Spring) but this isn't the first or third Saturday in the month. Anyway I found something better, much better than the catacombs. It's that little structure there of iron and glass, attached to the square. The finest piss-house I've ever seen, a palace of a piss-house and only twenty-two centimes the cabin. I walk up and down the pavement first to get a good look from the outside, and also, to try and work up a piss, just to make the pleasure complete. No piss, finally, but I go in. It's cosy in there, Madame Pipi in the background solid on her throne, dressed like a nurse, and the six cabins, three on each side, flanking a black and white marble alley. Madame Pipi even has a petrol stove to keep herself warm. I make for a *cabine*. I'm just about to turn the handle when Madame says: "The paper's to the left, monsieur." So I take a couple of sheets just to please her and enter. What a place! I've got friends who would willingly rent a place like this for twenty-two centimes a day, I might do it myself yet. There's the shugs, a wash-hand basin and a mirror, and the whole caboodle deodorised into the bargain. All you need now is a shelf for books – even then the cistern would do – and you're all set. It might not even cost you twenty-two centimes. If you could prove you were a "notorious indigent", as the forms put it, you could get it for nothing, from 9:30 a.m. to 7 p.m., and maybe you could even wangle it for the night with Madame Pipi if she took a liking to you. After having a good look round and pulling the plug just for realism, I come out, amazed and delighted. I go to Madame Pipi to pay what I owe:

"Fine place you have here", I say.

"Not bad", she says, with republican modesty.

I'm coming up the Boulevard Saint-Germain, late on a Saturday night. Just in front of Lipp's, an old woman wrapped in a dirty coat and with a basket in her hand suddenly spreads her arms wide and shouts: "I've got the fever, I'm as hot as hell!", and hirples away down the street. In the Rue de Rennes, a tramp is asleep in a doorway, a bottle overturned beside him, and the wine spilled darkred over the pavement. Up at Montparnasse, a man is making bird-sounds, raucous chirp-chirps, with a device he holds in his mouth, and which he is selling one franc apiece. Whenever girls pass, he chirps louder than ever and trips after them in a big, heavy coat, flapping his arms, shouting: "Look out, girlies, here comes the man." There is a lone prostitute in the Rue d'Odessa. And the rain is falling.

Dream:
The planets must have stopped. The moon's up there huge and glabrous, ice streaming from its nose, snow falling like dandruff from its greenish hair. The sun must be buried away deep down in the abyss of night, like a naked dream. What I'm really writing for is to get things in movement again.

There's a blockage somewhere, a spoke in the solar system.

It's slow going, boys, I'm ice-bound, icicles are dripping from the masts. The air feels like sandpaper. I drink this piddling black coffee and it freezes in my stomach, it'll never get the length of my head, I've poisoned myself for nothing.

Got to persevere. Standing on the prow looking into the grey distance. Not even a seal.

I climb up the mast. Nothing.

I climb up the mast again, tie a brush to the top of the mast, and climb up the brush. I see just a faint redness way down there behind the horizon.

I abandon ship. I begin to trek, I trek for years. I make snowshoes from my bones and my hair, I suck my own marrow for nourishment. On Chrismas, as a special treat, I eat an eye and an ear.

Once I found a mouse. But I didn't eat it. I kept it as a companion, I talked to it all the time. I taught it everything I know. That mouse can now speak Irish, Welsh, English, Scotch, Spanish, French, German, Italian, Portuguese, Russian, Finnish, Hungarian and a smattering of Japanese. He later taught linguistics for a while at America's new Mickey Mouse University, before resigning in disgust at the low intellectual level and going back to the fields. I don't know what I would have done without that there mouse.

I went on and on. I kept a diary. When my paper ran out, I tattooed myself, using a specially invented system of runes. The most interesting part of this diary is set out on my left buttock, but it has not yet been published (for moral reasons). Besides, since about that time I invented an even more abbreviated system of writing, which I have now forgotten, the semioticians are having some trouble with the interpretation of the signs.

All I can say is that the truth will come out some day. As it is, my bum is at the centre of modern linguistic controversy. The biggest thing since the Dead Sea Scrolls, and promising to be infinitely more important.

I will not depict for you the anguish and the terror of that journey. You will read it once my bum is published. Let me just say that I was really glad to stand there finally with one foot on the horizon and the other on the sun – before giving the latter such a dunt with my heel as sent it spinning round so fast my back was blistered before I had retained my balance, and mangoes were beginning to grow all around me.

Yes, mangoes.

I now have a mango-growing ranch in what was once an icy desert. And I am reckoned by those who ought to know the most original writer to have appeared in the universe since God drew up his notes for it.

My life is that big spumy river, naked as hell, and ten times as cold. I think in barges. The barges of the White Inspiration Co., that churn up the river here from Rouen and further. I stand on the bridges like Resolution and Independence looking down on my life.

And so I move into another winter. With me it's always winter: winter ending, winter beginning, middle of winter, but always winter.

They're all trying to tell me it's spring. But they won't fool me. I wasn't born in Glasgow for nothing.

To think that I who know nothingness inside out, who wear it as pyjamas every night, and as underclothes during the day-time, to think I should go on living, go on living to think. To think about nothingness and going on living. I'm just about as naked as you can be without being a public nuisance.

I should go to a solitude where there is sun. But with me up to now it's always been crowded winter.

There's a big hill of rain growing out of the silence, wispy trees now, black pines, a lake dripping with slow waves, a boat, a chain, a rock, a stalk of bamboo, a hut and a sage. The sage is writing. Rain falls in big blue moons on his paper. Two sparrows chirp.

It's all coming out of the silence. The sage looks up and I recognize myself a thousand years ago. It is the year 900, and there are two sparrows on a bamboo stalk.

I go out into the rain. I strip myself naked. All the hairs of my body try to grow roots in the earth. I go down to the hissing sighing lake, and walk into the waters.

Rain, and a new level of silence.

   Ah, girl in black

where are you going
with your red kerchief
your soft red lips
and your crazy eyes

what doors are going to close on you

you whose notch at this moment
is an open door to paradise

Under her sky-blue slip was the fattest mount of Venus I've ever seen, a beautiful little bombolation of a thing with a mass of silky black hair flattened like grass under wind from the tightness of the nylon that had covered it, I ran my fingers slowly over and through the muff, then slipped them suddenly down below into the thick-lipped juicy lovely notch, at which she gasped and began to move and moan so that the desire that had been tightening in me leapt in me all the way from my belly to my throat and I put her in the bed, put out the lamp, and went quietly into her, like a boat on a slipway.

At various times different places have a pull on me. There was a week when I couldn't keep away from the Boulevard Magenta, another when all the gardens of Paris seemed to be holding out plants to me, another when all I could think of doing was walking up and down on the concourse of the Gare du Nord. And so on. I get it into my head that I must go somewhere, and no sooner is it in my head than it's in my feet and I've got to go. It's a superstition. I'm a survival from some great catastrophe and I'm tying to re-establish connexions. I walk and write for the same reasons. To make the right movements and renew the lost relations.

At the moment it's dark sleepless night, and I'm going over again what I can hardly call the *events*, let's say the *characters* of this afternoon, especially at its initial point: midday.

It all began with a great silence. I felt it as I came up the Rue de la Montagne-Sainte-Geneviève, felt it more dense and intense with every step I took upwards. I was looking for signs.

At midday the city is quiet. Only those who don't eat are about. Midday is a kind of night. At night only those who don't sleep are about. The world spends its time digesting and sleeping. It's because I need to do little of either that I have so much time on my hands.

Midday, quiet, climbing. The sun was white and there was a slight wind blowing. Blowing sunlight like veils. As though the sun were trying to hide something from me more than anything else. Or was that the only way it had to attract my attention and key me up to the highest pitch of expectancy? I climbed, and the veils fluttered before me. There was no tenseness, or weight, but a hovering, a presence, hovering, perhaps one of those presences, or that presence, I'm looking for.

In the Rue Laplace I saw children playing peever, and I stood still to watch them, and asked a little Chinese girl what the game was called, and she told me, quickly, turning away, *La marelle escargot*, and began to hop on the chalked spiral, and when she'd finished she darted a look up at me and smiled, but was puzzled. I stood for a long time watching them, standing still, in the shade, opposite the Chinese restaurant. And then suddenly I moved on.

Came into the Rue Valette, and from that street, having seen a courtyard, went into it, along a narrow corridor. It was a cobbled yard, the dirty white walls rising high all around it, and the sun held in it.

I stood in the courtyard, full in the sun, and a black cat came out of the shadows. It was a cat with the greenest eyes I have ever seen, pure emerald, flowing, endless, with only the savage black stab of the pupil to personify them. The cat came up to me, and I was fascinated by its eyes. I stared into those cat eyes. We were the only two live things in the courtyard, and I wanted to stare myself into the eyes of the cat, but it wouldn't stare for long, turned its head away, even stretched out on the cobbles and pretended to go to sleep. But it rose again, and came circling round me, meeting my eyes, and the greenness widened and became more luminous and I *fell into the ocean.*

When I came to, the cat was gone, and the face of a woman was glued to one of the windows gazing at me. When I looked up, she turned away quickly. I left the courtyard by the way I had come.

Wandering around the halls of the Louvre this afternoon, I stopped for a while before the copy of the Venus of Cnidos, the loveliest Greek statue I know. I was thinking also of that Hindu statue of Lakshmi up in the museum in Edinburgh: a black statue, a little jaded with dust, but so many fingers, whether in India or in Scotland, had, in passing, touched the humpy little love-hole that, contrasted with the rest of the body, it shone out brilliantly. I stood there in contemplation of the breasts of Venus and the love-hole of Lakshmi, till one of the guardians told me it was closing-time. Then I went out into the evening of Paris, looking for the breasts of Venus and the love-hole of Lakshmi in the one living body, with the sensation of eternal life flooding my expanding brain.

Dream:
At one time I'm on my back and ice is growing over me. I've got about ten seconds to find a comfortable position. If I don't find it, I'm liable to spend a million years in agony. But I'll only know after about the first thousand years. I try to relax. I settle down. The ice grows over me. I'm too nervous for sleep. I just keep staring at the thickening ice. I never knew silence could be like this. There's a shoal of fish due west of me, glinting green and red, fanned out, in perfect profile, moving northwards. Further on there's what looks like a door, a big

keyhole. If the ice shifts, I say to myself, I may be able to get through there. Northwards there's a horse, no, a woman, a woman wearing a cloak of poppy leaves. Caught in some act or other, I'm curious to know what. Around her fly a few blue seagulls with orange beaks and an icy white foam streaking from them. There's a steeple with a golden yacht at its summit. I say to myself: that's the old village. At these words, everything changes colour, and I know that the first millennium has passed. The poppy leaves have turned mauve. The seagulls are yellow. I begin to feel pain, at first I don't know where it's coming from, but then I realize the pinky of my right hand is crooked. I try to straighten it out. The whole icy landscape becomes a stormy sea, I'm dragged along the sea bed, tossed in currents, and am finally thrown up by the tide on an island. It is night. I lie on the white sand. In the morning, I find a grove of mangoes, and eat, after my thousand years fast. I decide I will stay here for ever. But the mango trees begin to move away, and soon the fruit has changed into an infinite constellation, and I'm in the middle of a desert. I see a goat. It skips off, a bell tinkling around its neck. I follow it. The desert changes colour many times, but I'm still following the goat, its silky whiteness blazes like fire.

The last I saw of my self, I was still wandering in the desert.

ROOM 3
A Short Introduction to Eskimo Studies

"I tell you, either we discover a new common language, or we turn into Eskimos."

BRICE PARAIN, *A Little Treatise on Language*

First night in the new quarters. Realising I don't have a pillow and that it would be pleasant to have one, I use Dasgupta's *Obscure Religious Cults* wrapped up in my pullover.

Al Hack has gone back to the United States with his esoteric rucksack, to start up a desperado post-Comanche community in the ten square miles of Arkansas desert that have come to him in a will. Kenzen has returned to Japan, to perfect his studies in a Hokkaido monastery. I'm the only one of our kind left in Europe, and it's getting harder every day, every way.

Nil desperandum. Even the Great Manitoo himself (according to that Ojibwa initiation scroll I have pinned above my bed) made three attempts before he managed to create the perfect world.

Went to the Chinese restaurant, Long Phong's down the road. Not a soul in there – except, if we stretch a point, the three old Chinamen laughing their heads off at the bottom of my soup-bowl. I was through with the soup, and half-way through my chicken and bamboo, when a tubby little Chinaman came in with an umbrella, did a lightning-job on a bowl of rice, rifted twice, and was gone. I sat alone sipping tea for a while, then came back up to my room, to read the poetry of Li Po, out there on the Szechwan Road.

*When ice fills the skies
and the girls close their thighs*

– that ain't exactly true, thank God, but it's a nice little couplet nonetheless. Came to me this morning when I was waiting for the bus. I am always thankful for small mercies.

Dream:
Scene: a Greyhound bus-station in Cleveland, Ohio.
This girl shows me the photo of a baby she's just given birth to in San Francisco.
"I sure hope I ain't the *fader*", I say, laughing (I was learning Swedish at the time).
"Oh, but you are", she says.
"*Kenavo*", I say (I was also learning Breton).
And suddenly I had an urgent rendez-vous with a band of Sami in Lappland.

At the Bibliothèque Nationale, reading through a number of the *Journal de la Société des Américanistes* (tome 13, n° 2, 1921), I come across this mention of a kayak 7 yards long and 2 feet wide that turned up, end of the seventeenth or beginning of the eigthteenth century (the records differ), at the mouth of the Don. In it a man "covered with hair who spoke a language nobody could understand". Every attempt was made at Aberdeen to keep the Inuit alive, but he died within three days, totally exhausted after God knows how long a trip – from where, Greenland? Wild winds, rogue waves and crazy currents must have driven him from his home shore far out to sea, when all he could do was hang on, following the movement. As for the kayak, it was deposited at Marischal College in the said town of Aberdeen. If ever I make back to Scotland, it will be in something like that kayak. Adrift here in the asphalt ocean, amid a myriad of shooting stars and the flashing lights of the *aurora borealis,* Kenneth of Whiteland writeth his kayak-book.

*I'm walking on ice
on thin ice
I've become poor
like this poor earth –
the new country*
            Magic formula, Greenland

Sometimes, if I let myself go, and I do, I'd just prowl round and round this room like a mad wolf, with sheer despair gnawing at my belly – and then at other times, I'm quiet in myself, serenely happy to sit here in the empty room, with the bare walls and the skylight.

The shamans are born in the Far North, at the source of the terrible sicknesses.
An Eskimo informant to Rasmussen

Sinking back, sinking back – through storms, through blindnesses, in long opaque crawlings and sometimes sudden shifts, sinking back. Losing identity to achieve at last (perhaps?) an anonymous density.

> *Downwards and deep down*
> *one had to let the journey go*
> Travel song, Netsilik Eskimo

It all goes on behind a great wall of China, in a silence in which words like writer, poet, artist, philosopher, scientist, psychologist, fade into insignificance.

> *The sky's full of cloud and the day is dark*
> *wild duck in the north wind and snow's going to fall*
> KAO CHE

"All alone?" is how the little old red-haired waitress in the Russian restaurant just off Saint-Michel always greets me. "All alone again, mister Ken?"

I am the lone white wolf, little mother, the lone white wolf from the transcendental steppes . . .

When she sees me reading a book, she says: "Ah, study, study". When I don't eat much, she says: "That a man's meal?". When I eat more, she says: "Now, you really eating Mr Ken."

> Midnight:
> *Excoriated*
> *playing cold music*
> *on my skeleton*
> *getting to know*
> *the empty room*

Scotland in the room with me tonight (the Scotland of Michael Scot and Dr Long Ghost) in the shape and fumes of a bottle of old malt whisky straight from one of the islands. I'm in a seventh-floor room in Paris, hardly room to move in, drinking whisky, thinking of Glasgow nights (the big prostituted river), Edinburgh days (the east wind cutting everything away to a desperate bleakness), and the study at Culross where I holed up in the sixteenth century studying alchemy. In other words, transcendentally drunk, like all bedevilled Scots from here to eternity. It's time the Tibetans came to evangelize us, the last crowd left us in one hell of a mess.

In winter the white house seems more poverty-stricken than ever
A dog barks behind the straw door
In the night of wind and snow, somebody's going back home
                                                        LIU CH'ANG CH'ING

Dream:
Wandering with Lena in the streets of Munich.
We go into a bookshop she knows, an antiquariat place, where we look at a collection of old antiquarian prints: villages, towns, hills and seascapes with boats. I tell her how much I like them.
Then suddenly I'm up on an island, somewhere near Heligoland.
I'm walking round and round the island, writing about it in ten different languages.
At the end, I'm standing at the edge of a cliff looking out into a grey nothingness.

The wee Eskimo girl (igloo breasts and ice-greeny eyes) just about clawed the back off me. "Did I do that?", she asked this morning, all surprised at her nocturnal ferocity.

Atungai was a great shaman who was seized with a desire to travel round the world. But he wanted a woman with him, a strong woman, childless. So he began to look up all the childless women till he found one that suited him.
Then he set off. And at length he came to a high, steep cliff. When he'd come to the top of the high, steep cliff, he started travelling around the world. He was a great shaman, he kept to the outer edges.
When he had met all the different people of the earth, he came home. But he came home by a different road from the one had taken on the way out. He was a really great shaman, that one.
                                                        Netsilik Eskimo legend

They still take me for a Scot. But I've become an Eskimo, by naturalization. In fact, even that's just for my passport – I'm really a Hyperborean. Nobody knows much about the Hyperboreans. The Hyperborean is engaged on an erratic path to a far-out something. What people see are the erratics (the stones he leaves on his path), what he sees are flashes of the far-out thing. Nobody can define anything in that area. It's nine hundred miles beyond literature, nine thousand miles beyond civilisation.

> *I awake from sleep*
> *with the morning cry of the grey gull*
> *I arise from bed*
> *with the morning cry of the grey gull*
> *I take care not to look*
> *towards the darkness*
> *I turn my eyes to the light*
>
> Eskimo formula for warding off sickness

Writing about the old yellow ancestor, Charles Baudelaire, of "modern poetry" (bah – a numb expression, but let it pass), a critic said that he was away out on a Kamchatka. It was still just a literary image, but the critic smelled something through his cultural catarrh: a high, clear air his snitch wasn't used to.

The paleo-siberian element in the actual workings of our mind in these dark days.

The K-territory.

Paleo-siberian, and the way east.

Kamchatka is linked to the North-Japanese island of Hokkaïdo by the Kouril archipelago.

Archipelago – a word I've always loved. Image of a world.

The white archipelago.

> *I do not like the man who talks a lot. The actual practice is far more important. Until the full realization of truth is obtained, a man should keep his mouth shut and get on with the work.*
>
> MILAREPA

"Einstein can take to his bed."

He's a long Russian, about sixty years old, here with me, 2 o'clock, in the little restaurant, and the snow falling outside, turning Paris into St. Petersburg.

"Yay, he can go off to bed . . ."

Sergei is a mathematician, out of work – lives over in Montparnasse, in a couple of rooms with a wife and five kids. Wants some peace and quiet to get on with his work on differential analysis. All he needs, he says, is a rocking-chair – with a villa around it, somewhere in Switzerland.

The man who sits
in the dark rain domain
watching the blue moon

I also study mathematics:
A profound change has taken place during the present century in the opinions physicists have held as to the mathematical foundations of their subject. Quantum mechanics provides a good example of the new ideas. It requires the states of a dynamical system and the dynamical variables to be interconnected in quite strange ways that are unintelligible from the classical standpoint.
DIRAC, Quantum Mechanics

In the café, young English journalist, here to write an article on underground Paris:
"I'm from the Black Country."
Hell, we're all from the Black Country, boy. Some of us are trying to get into the White Country.

The passionate desire which induces men to flee the irksome tasks of daily life and permit the soul to live its own inner life has made them discover by instinct the strangest substances. They have discovered them even in areas where nature is parsimonious and where what she does offer seems far from possessing the properties that allow men to satisfy this desire. In N.E. Asia, in the region of Siberia, crossed by the rivers Obi, Ienissei and Lena, and limited to the north by a sea of ice and to the east by the Sea of Behring, the Samoyed, the Ostyak, the Tunguz, the Yakut, the Yugakir, the Chukchee, the Koryak, the inhabitants of Kamchatka, discovered at some remote period, in the Agaricus muscarius, the properties which allow them also to enjoy hours of a state which to them is happiness.
L. LEWIN, Phantastica

Woman last night, about thirty-five years old. Dark teat-circles, dark belly, darker where the skin puckered.

A long voyage of discovery.
Finally, earthquakes in Manchuria.

Ile: gniak: a
kangerse: wimak: i
qoula: nemak: i
ile: gniak: a
kangerse: wimak: i
qoula: nemak: i
ayange: leca: k: a
a: kit: ean: ikit: e
toqoume: wara
erce: rwaman: a
toqoume: wara

In an old number of the Annals of the French Academy of Sciences I picked up on the quays I come across mention of one Archibald Scott Couper, who, in June 1858, published, in French, a paper on *A New Chemical Theory*, concerning the structuring of atoms in a molecule, in particular the linking together of carbon atoms to form larger molecules, eventually a new element. The son of a mill owner at Kirkintilloch, north-east of Glasgow, Couper studied at the universities of Glasgow, Edinburgh and Berlin, before moving to Paris, where he worked at the private laboratory of Charles Wurtz. It was there in Paris he wrote his paper *Sur une nouvelle théorie chimique*, which he asked Wurtz to present to the French Academy. Either because Wurtz was slow in moving, or because the Academy set it momentarily aside since Wurtz wasn't a member of the said Academy, publication of the paper was delayed. With the result that a paper on a similar theory by August Kekulé appeared before it in Germany, so that it was Kekulé who got all the credit and reputation. The result for Couper was a bout of depression and total disappearance from the field of science. His theory was in fact more complex than Kekulé's, involving more subtle connexions and structurations. He also invented new means for writing out his formulas, using, in addition to the elemental symbols of the periodic table, a system of dashes and dotted lines. But it was all lost. Couper's bout of depression was to last thirty years, which, till his death in 1892, he spent in silence at the family house in Kirkintilloch, watching the Kelvin flowing by.

Atoms of sensation, experience, knowledge, cognition coming together at a high energy level to create a new element of living and thought.

My breakfast of tea has been cooked by a Tartar woman, with water of the Amur, who wiped her earthen-kettle with a horse-tail.
CARLYLE, *Sartor Resartus*

Carlyle – another member, slightly bourgeoisified, of my radical Scoto-shamanistic ancestors.

In the Russian restaurant, snow again, falling darkly. "Like Russia", says the little old red-haired waitress. A drunk from Minsk or Pinsk goes out to the pavement and slowly rubs snow over his pow to cool his brain. I stand out there beside him and we talk about the heroes of our time. The ontological heroes. From Ishmael to Lermontov.

It is difficult to descry white bears in the desert of ice. So before setting out on his expedition, the hunter covers his face with his hood, and holding a knife in his hand, sings the magic formula:

Eya! Eya!
from the eyes of what animal
shall I receive sight?
from the keen eyes of the grey gull
I shall receive sight.

A rawcold morning, and I go for a walk in the Marais district. Hardly started when I come up against the Irish Hotel (next door to it a café, Le Celtique), which puts me on the chill and windy shores of Outer Celtica, where I stay till they turn into the islands of Japan, for there is a Japanese exhibition running in a little gallery in the Place des Vosges – *real space, metaphysical space*, with a quotation on the catalogue from Kandinsky: *The white rings out like a silence that might be understood.* Thereafter walking aimlessly, down any street: Rue du Roi-Doré, Rue Payenne, till eventually I come smack up against the Cirque d'Hiver, where I go down into the underground, looking for the eye, the breast, the door.

In the empty room:
At such times the atmosphere is so dense that it is difficult to breathe. The earth, the ice, the branches of the trees, crack with a dull noise. One can hear the ringing stroke of an axe on a tree at a great distance.

CZAPLICKA, *Aboriginal Siberia*

There's the hound of dawn yelping in the sky.

Well, I bought this novel, five hundred pages of it, American, the ravings of old angel midnight, and I bought also a half-bottle of whisky and thus fortified (it was like old times in Glasgow), I sank into the night. Now it's after ten the next morning. The novel's read and dead, the bottle's empty, and there's nothing to be said, nothing at all, at all, at all.

Old Red Bone beating his drum.

> *Earth root*
> *great earth root*
> *I give you*
> *this song text:*
> *the dark pillars of the world*
> *are growing white*
>   Magic words, Netsilik Eskimo

To the lost tribes of the Yougakir, Chukchee, Koryak, Ainu, Gilyak, Toungouz, Samoyed, Ostyak, Vogul – greetings and salutations. The night is dark, brothers. The moon is shut up in a madhouse, raving about the long-gone sun. The stars no longer talk the bright logic. The sea crawls sluggishly, rank with the carcases of poisoned whales. Men of the tundra and the taiga, our spirits travel in mist and in fog, and there are no songs. We travel farther and farther into our silence. Waldemar knew of us, but who knows Waldemar? Soon even the rocks will have forgotten us.

With that girl this afternoon, impression of a sap-filled, firm-rooted birch tree gleaming in cool, clear air.

"Paris", Al Hack used to say, "ain't exactly Paradise." True enough, friend, but it'll do for the time being. It's an incandescent limbo.

In this dawn, I walk alone.

When Milarepa came back into his cave, he found five demons with eyes as big as saucers. One was crouched on his bed, preaching a devilish sermon, two were listening and laughing, another was making a weird meal, and the fifth was flipping impatiently through the pages of a book.

> *The gull*
> *the one who*
> *cuts the air with its wings*
> *the one that is usually*
> *above our heads*
> *gull you up there*
> *come down towards me*
> *your wings are red*
> *up there*
> *in the coolness*
> *ayaya!*
> *ayaya!*
>
> Magic words, Netsilik Eskimo

Snow falling thickly over Paris. The Bois de Vincennes is a collection of perfect Sung paintings.

Ah, while I was ill, snow fell, wet and melting, and I got up during the night to look at the landscape. Never has nature seemed to me more touching and sensitive.
VAN GOGH

At 2 o'clock in the morning, the bridges of Paris have blue eyes.

When Milarepa received Gambopa, who was to be his foremost disciple, tea was brewed, and Milarepa pissed into it, "which made it very delicious".

Two barges coming up the Seine side by side like a couple of amorous whales, with gulls screaming around their bows.

While they're all making plans for the future, or gesticulating noisily on the scene, I'm away out and up here on my own, beating the old shaman drum.
The signs on my drum are: a fish, a gull, three bones, a dancing figure and an arrow.

Maybe after all I should make tracks for China, some old lost China of the mind. Maybe that's what I'm doing (the long way round) – no use arriving in China just another foreign devil. Yes, going to China the long way round. Whose China? My China. No China.

When you can live in a quiet hermitage
Why think about straying in other lands?
Since you meditate on your Buddha Guru
Why need you circle Lhasa?
While you watch your mind at play
Why need you see Samye Temple?
If you have annihilated doubts within
Why need you visit Marngo?
Since you practise the whispered lineage teaching
Why need you sightsee at Loro and Nyal?
If you can penetrate to your self-mind
Why walk in circles round the Kradrag?
                                        MILAREPA

The Seine booksellers – a gull perches on a copy of the *Kamasutra* and lets out an atlantic yell that amounts to a *sutra* in itself:
Ka! kaya gaya! ka!

ROOM 4
The Hermit of the Rue Gay-Lussac

> "The tendency of the mind towards the universal is what makes for original works in philosophy and poetry."
> SCHOPENHAUER, *Parerga & Paralipomena*

Underground in the morning, crowded underground in the morning, whine of the train, hot silence, bodies packed and lurching, and suddenly out of the mass a woman's voice:

"If you don't want a clout on the face, you'd better stop your damn fumbling."

The gentle voice of Paris. Not speaking to me, but to a furtive fellow who leaves us abruptly at the next station.

One of the first things I do is get five months of hair cut off my head. No use putting up signs for the long-hair-hating police; there's work to be done here in the pen and I don't want any interfering. Ready to start in again. Come and go, come and go, where will all this end?

Telegram to whomsoever it concerns: "Gone to the heart of darkness."

At that time, my one thought was to disappear entirely from the circle of my normal relations. So I searched around for some discreet lodgings and finally found exactly what I wanted in the temple of the Shingon sect, in the vicinity of Matsuba Street, in the Asakusa quarter.
TANIZAKI JUNICHIRO, *The Secret*

Yes, the secret. The only way some of us can survive and get on with the real work is by being as secretive as hell.

The engineer to whom I'm giving English lessons says the Third World War (which he speaks of as if it were next summer's holiday) will not be so disastrous as alarmists make out. It will, he says, be fought with *small* atom bombs. Oh, that's fine, I say, I really was worried for a while.

> *When you're strange*
> *Faces come out of the rain*
> *When you're strange*
> *No one remembers your name*
> *When you're strange*
> THE DOORS

Unbelievably happy here.
In this wretched room, bare as a monk's cell, in the heart of Paris.
The rain beats on my window, traffic hisses and roars on the Rue Gay-Lussac.
My manuscripts and books lie to hand, on those rough wooden shelves. Sheaves of notes pinned to the wall.
Just so, just right.

Impasse du Cheval-Blanc (White Horse Passage), Place de la Bastille. Can't pass by this place without thinking of the old Chinese poem:

> *In the tenth year, they arrived in India*
> *that is, Tsa-in and those who travelled with him*
> *there they met Ksyamatanga and Cho-fa-lan*
> *and obtained many books in Sanskrit*
> *these they brought home on a white horse*
> *which is the reason why*
> *when the emperor came to build a monastery*
> *west of Lo-yang*
> *where they could get down to the work of translation*
> *he had it called the White Horse Monastery*

At nine, I go down to the Chinese restaurant to have a meal: a crab salad, a curried beef and rice, with, as a treat, a half-bottle of Côtes de Provence.
Been working all day.

Rosy reflection of the wine on the white table-cloth.
Red dawn in Siberia.

He crossed the river and went into the Wei country.
Pi Yen Lu

Just a few yards down the street, Paul Valéry worked with a blackboard and a skeleton. Midwinter exercises. But my way, and the probable outcome, different, very.

Came across another interesting old text in the Sorbonne library, from the *Bibliotheca Philosophorum Medii Aevi,* entitled *De Contemptu Mundi.* By one Bernard Sylvestris, a Breton, twelfth century. Panic philosophy. A vision of the elements: "Out of the turgid confusion came the power of fire and broke the primitive darkness with a quickening flame that flickered over the waters along with flying shadows." Evocations of Rome and Venice, the Tiber and the Po, the woods and coasts of Brittany. "Through Nature to knowledge". Plenitude fashioned in full: *integrescit ex integro, pulchrestit ex pulchro.*

That mongol face. Lost in the crowd. Perfectly beautiful, an antediluvian quiet. I say "mongol" – maybe tartar. Because it wasn't typically Chinese, Japanese, or Indochinese. Seemed further back, further out. Almost wished I'd never seen it. Obsessing me, and will obsess me. Will probably never see it again.

With the passage of the centuries both Buddhism and Hinduism accentuated the psychological introspection we meet with at the very dawn of Indian religious life. On to the mandala was projected the drama of cosmic disintegration and reintegration as relived by the individual, sole contriver of his own salvation, that is to say of his return to the logos spermatikos.
TUCCI, *Theory and Practice of the Mandala*

In the queue for underground tickets, someone touches my shoulder and says as I turn round: "*Entschuldigen Sie, sprechen Sie deutsch?* ('Excuse-me, do you speak German?')" Tall young fellow, scraggy. I say: "Yes." "*Wunderbar*", he says. From Frankfurt, in Paris for two or three days. Wants to know if I can recommend him a cheap hotel. Then asks me about "trips" – "*Wo kann man Trips kaufen?*

('Where can you buy trips?')" I don't catch on at first, then I realise he's looking for acid. I tell him where he'll find a hotel, also where he may be able to drop some LSD. But to come to Paris from Frankfurt (where he says everything is *müde*, tired, because of too much money, *zuviel Geld*) with the idea of tripping out of it as soon as you arrive seems a bit queer. But then I don't come from Frankfurt.

Little Tunisian couscous-place down Saint-Severin way. Girl comes in, quiet, blond, good-looking. From Vancouver. Searching for work. Just another girl lost in the city, carrying promises.

Dream:
Guy's house is burning all around him.
He doesn't phone up the fire brigade, he phones up a jazz-band and asks them to play *Tin Roof Blues*.
"This place isn't held together by carpentry", he says, "it's held together by psychiatry."

The Englishman in the café:
"Paris is finished. New York is the culture-centre now."
To hell with that, you Sassenach nitwit. The centre (we can forget "culture"), is where I am, anywhere. I don't need a "literary world", or a "swinging scene". I can swing things plenty myself, and in my own way. As for a "literary world", God save me from that menagerie, whatever the language it talks.

He should regard all things around him as constituting the mandala of himself as Vajrasattva.
                                                            Shrichakrasambhara Tantra

Suburban station, around ten in the morning. Spent the night with the Pakistani girl. We got to her place at 11 o'clock. While I went to shave and shower, she put new sheets on the bed, with a towel on the sheets, because it's the third day of her period.
"Bite me, bite me."
If she likes to be bitten, she's a biter herself, the girl from Karachi. In fact I've never met up with such a biting girl. Almost bit my finger off, and the tip of my tongue, and sank her teeth more than once into my shoulder. Like going to bed with a shark.

Towards the early morning, she wanted to suck my zob, and I knew what I was risking. But all went well.

"Hello, comrade", said Whitman, met in the Rue Racine, just in front of the anarchist bookshop. Whitman (old ancient mariner), I like him well. The Paris I know wouldn't be the same without him. "Bye, comrade." This is George Whitman, by the way – but he says he's related to Walt somewhere down the line. Who knows?

The psychoanalyst to whom I have offered my linguistic services wants to learn English via Edgar Allan Poe. Okay. About sixty years old, white-haired, still good-looking, Russian extraction. Beautiful apartment on the Boulevard Saint-Germain: vase with golden leaves (*The Golden Bough*), and easel with half-completed painting of a blue flower (*blaue Blume*). Says she's losing her memory, everybody is – with the bad air in towns the brain is not sufficiently oxygenated. A few weeks ago, a man tried to kill her, throw her out of the window. A homosexual. The following week, he'd met a young fellow, and he sent the young fellow to the psychoanalyst. She phoned the first man, interpreting: "You think you're my phallus, and since you want to leave, you're sending another one in its place." "Damned thoughtful of the fellow", I said.

The tattva is something that cannot be known through others, but only by one's-self. It is calm, undeveloped by words, exempt of all concepts.
NAGARJUNA, *Madyamikaçastra*

We're lying quietly side by side, me and the Karachi Kid, after a bout of erotic yoga, when suddenly she starts reciting the list of the forty-nine imams:

Mowlana Ali
Mowlana Houssein
Mowlana Abideen
Mowlana Mohammadinil Bakir
Mowlana Dzafar Sadik
Mowlana Ismaël
Mowlana Mohammad ben Ismaël
. . .
Mowlana Shah Karim

Either sheer exuberance, or it's to counteract the effects of foutering with an infidel.

Later on, she tells me, nice touch, that when she was a little girl, her mother used to wash her eyes with tea, to make them bright.

The psychoanalyst. Tells me of a former patient of hers. An American girl. Could talk only when she'd lain out on the floor with her shoes off. In the second year of her analysis, she met a man, and they were living together – but not making love. On going to bed, the girl would put on two pairs of pyjamas, a pullover, and a nightgown. Said she felt the cold. That lasted two years. The girl now lives in Boston, is married, has six kids, and is a psychoanalyst. That's what they call a cure.

Dream:
"One day", he said (old grey-bearded man in a red robe), "after a lot of vedanta and zen and tao, you'll be sitting on the banks of the Ganges (which, by the way, is the secret continuation of the Clyde) and you'll be wondering how it was before you were free, and then you'll see me coming along the bank in my red robe, and when I smile at you in passing you'll remember, but we won't say anything, not a word."

In this yellow café, evening coming down cabbage-blue over Les Halles – bats flying across the moon – the guy with the black, metal-studded, hell's angel jerkin and the ivory monkey on a string round his neck yawns and says: "Shit".

Up in Montrouge:

> *White satin kimono*
> *with bird-design on back*
> *when I open it I see her well-spaced breasts*
> *the wide curve of her hips*
> *the smooth flat belly*
> *and the dark curling hair of her cunt*
> *ah!*

Over in the National Library to read about Osaka. If they ever asked me to write down exactly what my studies are . . . That girl, Japanee, and Osaka as *mandala*.

The psychoanalyst with her sixteen patients a day. She wonders why she does it. Would like to live in the country. But what could she do? All she knows is psychoanalysis, and the peasants aren't up to that yet. No, there is one thing she could do – cartomancy. She learned it as a child, from her Russian mother. She could be the witch of the district. She would like that a lot, she says.

Dive, smoke, moozik. Guy (American) reading *Ulysses*. When the record starts up, his stumpy cigarette holder (not holding) starts beating time in his mouth. Thighs also move, kind of frog-like, but keeps reading *Ulysses*. English-talking old long-haired Indian over from London says with LSD you fuck like hell: "You haven't had sex till you take LSD", this to English student who's maybe looking for a groovy guru. I like that little Chinese girl with the cute breasts, but it's the French kid who's making eyes.

Night in a hotel off Pigalle. Original idea was to go out to Créteil, but when we got out there, her parents were away all right, but her sister was waiting for her fiancé, so we decided to go elsewhere. Not back to my place, where I've been holed up for three days writing, and which I've had enough of for the moment. The hotel then, dark and quiet, up the carpeted stair after signing the cards (whispered to her to put age 21, vague ideas of laws concerning minors), musty room with mirrors behind a yellow door. She slips off her dress without more ado, and gets into bed, breasts bare, hair spread over pillow, but pants still on, snatch still secret, waiting for me to uncover it, and come into it, and move in its wet red darkness that trembles with lightning the long dark night. Next morning, Place Blanche, quiet rain falling, I see a great white flower blossoming, a white-glistening rain-petalled flower, its roots in all this multicoloured shit.

In Buddhism Tantra of vajra love, it has been taught by gurus that each Dakini has her secret nerve in her vagina but their situations are different from one another . . . In Dakini A vagina, her secret nerve may be situated on east side but in Dakini B it may be situated on west side.
   C. M. CHEN, *Discriminations between Buddhist and Hindu Tantras*

Two American girls in the underground from Châtelet to Louvre: "The unconscious ... subliminal awareness ... minimal sense perception". Beside them, mirroring herself in the window, a French girl wets the sleek curl on her cheek.

In my room:

>   As I gaze at this rough rock
>   with a clutch of grey crystals
>   niched in its hollow
>   bittercold archaic waters
>   trickle through my brain

Chinese class at Censier.
On the walls of the room, slogans:
     INDOCHINA WILL CONQUER!
     WE LIVE BY HOPE – UNFORTUNATELY
The Russian instructor in pidgin French:
"Next time, I give third part the method, yes? To work in the house, yes? Very good. Now translate, very quick."
The passage to be translated runs:
"The new China Agency announces that the plenipotentiary ambassador of Norway on mission to Pekin left today Nov. 21st to resume his duties . . ."
I sit at the back wondering where the hell's Li Po? Maybe I got into the wrong class? It's true it was the smile of that little Chinese girl I was following rather than the notices.

In a café with the Cormorant (the Cormorant is head-man at an international institute for literary research, and fellow of the so-and-so society, but he's really a cormorant, a black sea-bird on a lonely rock). He tells me about being up in the Orkneys during the War where he taught a Scottish poet how to write and how in the house where he was billeted there was a reproduction of Mona Lisa on the wall. The Mona Lisa finally got on his nerves, so he wrote this little rhyme, for relief and release:

>   She stares at me from off the wall
>   from breakfast until supper
>   it might have been better after all
>   if Leonardo had just gone up her.

French girl, very young, very Catholic, aristocratic family, met her a couple of years ago – suddenly turns up out of the blue, had heard

I was in town again. Is engaged, about to be married to a fellow at the École Polytechnique, in a couple of months, and wants me to deflower her. Why the hell, I asked, since she was going to be married in eight weeks? She says that's just it, she wants it to be me, had had this idea since she first met me. Has been sleeping around for a year or more, but never allowed anyone into her. Well, okay. In no time at all, she's flipped off jacket, pullover, pants, brassière and panties, and is lying out on the bed. There's a kind of naïve speed to it, and she lies there with a "come and get it" look that gives me an erection and a laugh at the same time. Beautiful breasts, very hairy cunt – real little equatorial forest.

A letter out of Brussels, from a woman with a Slav name, telling me she is preparing an anthology of poems on the theme of The Future, and sending me some texts in English which I might be kind enough to translate into French (tariff attached). Once I'd done the translations, I was to phone her at an address she gave me in Paris where she'd be within ten days. Well, I did the job, which was one hell of a chore, but I needed a little cash, and this afternoon I phoned her. "Please come to my mansarrrde", she says, with an accent you could split with a hatchet, "you must enterrr the courrrtyarrrd and take the thirrrd stairrrcase on the left, and on the fourrrth floorrr, there is a little doorrr which you must pliss go thrrrough, and go up a crrrowd more of little steps, and you will then see a doorrr with a white paperrr and my name is on it." I did as instructed, feeling like a gink in a spy story, with vague expectations of meeting up with a lively piece of green-eyed slavonic Lou Salomesque energy in the flesh. I meet this woman on the staircase (she was going out to buy a pack of fags). "I am surrre you did not eggspect to see me so old?" she says, and leads me – tousled grey-haired smokey-eyed old harridan speaking about ten languages and telling me the why and wherefore, which I don't care to know, of this anthology of poems on The Future – up to her two-roomed attic, where she has all her portfolios of Hungarian poems and Spanish poems and Finnish poems about the Future over the floor, and can't find what she wants in them. For ten minutes, she makes the papers fly like a Siberian snowstorm, then suddenly (puffing furiously all the while) gives up: it is impossible. She must have left them in Brussels. I'm thankful for that, get paid and make a hasty getaway.

Coming up the Boulevard Saint-Michel in the rain – sounds from a music shop. A saxophone. Johnny Hodges! And suddenly I'm back up in old Glasgow again, the tenement building on Park Avenue, the flat with the eight rooms, six for students (Scots, French, Indian, African) and two for prostitutes. Studying like hell, in that room infested with mice, rain coming in the window (despite the renewed wads of pink evening newspaper), ragas and kitsch from the room next door, the landing reeking with joss-stick perfume. Downstairs, the Nigerian engineering student, Ezra, at his sax – rank bad at first, really rank, then gradually smoothing up and mellowing out, Johnny Hodges his god:

Whoa Babe
Empty Ballroom Blues
Echoes of the Jungle
Night Wind
Good Gal Blues
Rockabye River . . .

Glasgow long gone, but still there on the edge.

At Vandamm the sinologist's place, over in the 12th district: a darkbrown apartment on the sixth floor. Vandamm at his desk, a nude bronze statuette to hand under the lamp in case he feels lonely, Buddhist texts lining the wall behind him, and Chinese, Japanese, Sanskrit dictionaries. He's working on the translation of a *sutra*. We drink Belgian beer and he tells me how he's getting on with the text: *The sutra of the samadhi in which you get the Buddha to appear before you.* "What do you think of that?", he says. I tell him there's no room for that kind of stunt in my place.

In the sauna:
I'd come out of the heat-chamber and after taking a shower was lying out at rest, thinking of the text in hand, when suddenly the noise of a car's horn put a stop to all that, and I found myself in a most pleasant area, with nothing on my mind except maybe the sensation of a tree, a tree growing in me – or no, maybe even that's too imaged. No tree, only the sensation of a big growing inner silence. Expanding consciousness, or unconsciousness, I don't know.

Invited by this woman (about thirty years old) for lunch. So I go, 12.30. Fine-looking legs coming out very naked from a very short skirt. Lunch takes its time: steak and potatoes and wine and salad and cheese. Every time she gets up to bring over a dish or a bottle, I get another eyeful of her thighs, but there is time, there is time, so I keep my hands on the cutlery. After the coffee, she brings out some darkgreen stuff in a little round packet. Says she'd like to turn on with me, she knows it would be "a superb experience". A half-hour or so later, having taken our time also with the smoke (eye-to-eye through the smoke, and quiet, though she kept crossing and uncrossing her legs), we're on her big, low bed in the little room, surrounded by wailing hi-fi equipment, and I'm caressing her wet thighs, belly and buttocks, like God (to borrow a myth once isn't habit-forming) when he made the first creature out of the good red clay, and she's become momentarily a field of pure sensation.

Back then to my hermeneutic hermitage.

In the macrobiotic restaurant, rue Pascal:
> MASTICATE MORE, TALK LESS
> TALK LESS, BREATHE MORE

A fellow who works there tells me the macro people are lugubrious, though the place is supposed to have good vibrations. Adds that big cities make people nervous wrecks anyway. He's going to get out soon, to Brittany, with his old lady, reckons they can make it on a macrobiotic diet with two hundred francs a month. Yes, I said, and they've probably got that edible seaweed over there too. He noted that. But it's not only for economic reasons he's going to Brittany, oh no. He's going to Brittany because a druid (he's into druidism) said recently that Paris was going to disappear pretty soon, in a tremendous cataclysm. Not only Paris, but the whole of France – except Brittany. This summer he's going down to Montségur for the Cathar convention, asks me if I'd like to go with him, he likes my vibrations. I thank him, tell him sorry I can't make it, I'm all booked up.

The Chinese girl (longest, most slender fingers I've ever seen), has a mole on the lobe of her left ear, which she says is a sign of latent madness. A fortune-teller in Singapore told her she would be a successful scientist, that she should avoid violent sports, and that, having married a man pale-faced and on the fat side, she would be subject to miscarriages. It don't sound promising. But we'll see.

Moses Lakeman over from the States, on a flying visit to Paris. I meet him in a café. Tells me he's "stoned out of his mind" with cool

dope from Mexico; is wearing a sweater with the slogan in big letters over the breast:
                    SUPPORT YOUR LOCAL POET
Really gone State-side, Moses. Last time I saw him, he was very English and very worried, hunting for his umbrella in a London pub that contained thirty other umbrellas, all identical, all belonging to wet English poets. Moses has a paperback Dante under his arm. I say I've never read Dante, except for some bits of the *Inferno* which went well with Glasgow. He says he thinks I should and makes me a present of the book, which I accept – but I doubt if I'll read it. Not now. Too full of symbols. What I'm looking for is a space. Have had enough of total discourse. For the moment I'm gathering elements for something else.

Talking with the Chinese cat in her room – she's drinking her favourite cinzano blanc, I'm drinking whisky. Strange girl. Lives on the moon. Spends her time reading novels (very well read in the lesser known porno classics), dining in the best restaurants, and going to the cinema. Subsidised by her father, a business man in Singapore, whose only condition is that she write a thesis. For periods at a time, she does reading for this thesis – on an eighteenth century French writer – in the National Library (that's where I met her). There, she's "courted" by all kinds of characters. One in particular, a psychologist, also working on a thesis, has been hovering round her for three years. They take tea together, and he tells her about his family life, and his work, and his problems, and she listens. If he hasn't managed to see her, to spill his psychic beans over a pot of tea, he phones her. He hangs on the phone for hours at a stretch, telling her he's been dreaming about her (e.g. she's walking down this street and suddenly she takes down her panties – black panties, of course – and crouches to piss on the pavement), asking her if she's in bed, if she wears a nightdress or pyjamas. She keeps him going. For three years this creep's been creeping round her, talking his head off, because he can't get round to sleeping with her. It amuses her, or did up to recently, she's thinking now of telling him to drop dead. She says a hundred years ago in China she'd have been a courtesan. Here now, the moon life: novels, fancy restaurants, movies. So far as the mind's concerned, we live on different planets, and while she's drinking her cinzano blanc and I'm drinking my whisky, I have a sense of interplanetary communication, interstellar talk. But whatever regions her mind may have chosen to dwell in, her body is still real genuine antique Chinese, that is, at the centre of the earth, and that's where I finally meet her, in the ancient taoist darkness.

I'm continuing my Chinese studies in an autodidactic kind of way. General terms for love-making: *chiao-kou, chiao-chieh, chiao-hui, chiao-ho* ; also *chiao, chieh* and *ho* used alone. Sex in present day Chinese: *hsing* (literally, nature). Vulgar terms: *jin, k'an, shang-ma*. Dignified expressions: *fang-chang* (the affair of the bedroom); *yin-yang-chih-tao* (the way of yin and yang). Literary expressions (mostly derived from the legend of the lady of Wu Mountain): *yün yü* (clouds and rain); *wu-shan* (Wu Mountain); *yang-t'ai* (the Yang Terrace).

In bed since eleven last night, we get to sleep around six. At eight-thirty, the alarm goes off, a vicious red alarm clock on the dresser beside the photos of her family. Five minutes later the clock on her radio goes off. Got to get up. I tell her to stay in bed, but she gets up and starts to make coffee while I go into the tiny bathroom under her hanging little silky things to freshen up. Out then to the table, coffee pot and cups ready on it among ballpoints, pads, and Chinese brushes, her dressing-gown half-open showing one snuggling breast, the dream of the red chamber, rain falling outside. I gulp down the coffee, kiss her goodbye on tit and lip, run up the street, go underground, come up again at Odéon, and by nine o'clock I'm conducting a class in translation at the university. It's an east-west, overground-underground life.

Need to go further up north. Maybe fed up with Chinese sophistication, or sino-european sophistication. Further up north. That Mongol girl. From the Chinese courtesan to the Mongol girl. Further up and out to the Mongol girl. But where the hell *is* that Mongol girl?

> *As the sun sets*
> *over Singapore*
> *the foreign devil*
> *goes out the door*
>   (exit foreign devil)

I'd been working in the American Library, Place de l'Odéon, and then around midday I was walking in the Rue de Médicis when I suddenly felt pure joy. For two days I'd been in limbo, but here suddenly, for no reason at all apparently, I was full of joyance, shivers of pure joyance running up and down my back and I felt too the sensation of blueness (from the sky), and the fresh smell of running water (from the gutter). And it was with blue waters running through my brain and those shivers running up and down my spine that I made for the little pink-fronted cheap Chinese restaurant where the Cormorant has invited me to lunch. "How come you always look so mysteriously happy?", he says.

A sudden outburst of Shiva's own consciousness of his potential possibilities, carrying along with it a joyous feeling of self-realisedness.
SUDHENDU KUMAR DAS, *Shakti*

I suppose I'm too much of a barbarian to care for or appreciate sophistication. It's not that I have beliefs or values or a seriousness that are rubbed the wrong way by sophisticated play. It's just that the play itself bores me. I prefer a dance that happens further back.

Om, A, Hum, Ha, Ho, Hri!

Up the yellow stair to my unholy hermitage. The face of an old hermit on my door, cut out from an illustrated magazine. *Kensho jobutsu.* Inside, six months of manuscript pinned to the walls, the book of tomorrow, tomorrow's dawn. Rain falling on the Rue Gay-Lussac.

Absolute mongol quiet
the steppes of the mind

The Lao girl has been coming everyday for the past week. Each day she wears a new dress. Her notch-hair is shaven – at the moment, a slender black fern – and when I asked her why the first day, she said: "to be smooth all over". She tells me – her pronunciation in French is very liquid, full of l's, as though she had a well in her throat – about the Mekong, and Vientiane, Luang Prabang, and about the moist green loveliness of the rice-fields with the monk's bell sounding over them. Vientiane, long river, ricefields ... Saying "Vientiane", and seeing (probably little of it left in the modern town), that curving Siamese-Laotian architecture, the "long river", the Mekong, and I imagine myself taking my time coming up it, all time at my disposal, a whole life; and the ricefields, the green music in the wind, the rich substance, a simple economy. The eternal dream. All that in her. In her nakedness.

The long black coarse hair
the compact body
full delight

Now I know the body of the Lao girl, my plans to study a language (Chinese) fade. Could a language go further than the sensation of my hands on her breasts, my lips on her lips, my belly on her belly, my being in her being? Why learn the letter of a language when you can live with the spirit in the flesh?

Now it's dark blue night
over the city
with the great space all around me
and you golden flower within me
the eastern art I made my study
is your flesh your bones
the curve of your eye
your tongue and its tones
in the presence
of your naked breasts
religion has no reality
and the smooth beauty
of your loving belly
realizes philosophy.

ROOM 5
It's Raining Tea in Darjeeling

"His vajra revelled in the profoundest of tantras."
Life of Marpa

Looking for lodgings once again:

Well, when I was first in New York
I moved from room to room
When I was first in New York
I moved from room to room
Didn't move because I had to
Kept on movin' 'cause I had the blues.
     LARRY JOHNSON, *Take these blues off my mind*

Jean-Luc, the actor, trilby hat and swagger, derby coat and holes in his shoes, has a room in the Rue des Fossés-Saint-Bernard: walls hung with jute, and two armchairs from Dahomey, sculpted massively out of tree trunks, legacy of some colonial uncle. He's got a couple of beds there, and invites me to share the room and its expenses with him.
OK.

There's that traffic, which is the symbol of non-sense, and my thought, which is trying to get hold of elements of sensitive space and do a new dance. Birds dance, animals dance, fish dance, leaves and flowers dance, even a rock dances an immobile dance, but that traffic doesn't dance, it just whines and snorts and tries to get somewhere, a whole lot of somewheres, fast, destroying thought and all that resembles thought, as it goes. It's that kind of circulation and circuit I want to get out of, but not just into some kind of nirvana.

Meet a fellow in the café, Italian, came to Paris six years ago, and says he should have come a damn sight sooner, he's making money hand over first. He's in the carpet business, which he extends into general interior decorating. Ready to buy anything: old furniture, old guns and pistols, old picture-frames, houses, the lot. Cash galore. Mind you, he says, it makes for worry, because you've got to be always at it, always on the lookout for a deal. But you can enjoy yourself too. He has a Jaguar, he tells me, to move about in at weekends, and he's just bought a house on the outskirts of Paris for ten million. Yes, Paris is great, he says, he never realised you could make so much dough. A few months ago, he made a little tour of the Nièvre, buying up old rusty guns in antique shops and farmhouses, brought 'em back to Paris, cleaned 'em up a bit, and within a couple of months he'd them all hanging, at ten times the price he'd paid for them, in bourgeois apartments in the city. You've just got to have the eye, he says, put your finger on the new thing, and, bingo, you've made it.

Rue des Fossés, eleven in the morning, looking around me: the big half-circle window filled with sun; the jute-lined walls; the heavy wooden armchairs; Jean-Luc's sleeping-bag-covered bed in one corner, mine in another; the long table in the centre of the room; the rough plank-and-brick bookshelves climbing up one wall; the array of foodstuffs on the wide shelf running along the window. On the table at the moment, the tea-pot, one of my manuscripts and an oval box of *beurre salé du Pays Nantais*.

Let Dawn, house of Dawn, rejoice with the Frigate Bird which is found upon the coasts of India.
KIT SMART

Late October, cleaning the windows: first with plain water and a sponge; then with raw alcohol and a rag; and finally a brisk rub with a fistful of newspaper. Stripped to the waist, hanging out over the Rue des Fossés, getting it all clean and clear. "Hey", shouts a taxi-driver up at me, "Hey, you look warm!" Warm? I'm radiating. Now down into the streets. When you get high, go down.

An iranian eye
In the blue night

"*Bonjour Maurice, tu viens boire un petit verre, vite fait?*" – Rue des Martyrs, seven in the morning, Pigalle awakening, smoky blue light, the sounds, the lights, the smells of Paris.

Ensconced in his apartment above the Rue de Bretagne, Meister Lucien enjoys his "contemplative solitude" (which, he says, has a necessary basis of physical and emotional satisfaction: "prick not happy, mind not clear and quick"), smoking blue tobacco, drinking white wine and black coffee, handling books among the ten thousand volumes collected in his rooms. Epicurean, sophist, sceptic, he regales his friends and practises what he calls "conceptual" or "useless" conversation. The concepts range from the quality of green peas through all the images of human aberration to the particular dialectic practised at Nalanda.

A gathering of elements around the distant hills (half-sleep phrase this morning). Brainstorm weather.

Thus have I heard – at one time the Lord dwelt in bliss with the Vajrayogini who is the Body, Speech and Mind of all the Buddhas.
                    Opening of *Hevajra-tantra*, tr. Snellgrove.

Blue Waters, old friend
so now you've become
a regular Buddhist
duly initiated
in a Nepal monastery
with a specially appointed goddess
meant to grow in your brain
while I keep walking
these common streets
in an undefined ecstasy

Ecstasy ... What I mean is that I'm in some sense *outside myself*, engaged in an undefined field. And it's as though I'm waiting for a root-action to take place within this field, giving it density if not definition. If you have density, you don't need definition.

Jazz sequence N° 12:

Misty mornin'
Sing it low
Really the blues
Rain is such a lonesome sound

Gone away blues
Five long years
Boo's tune
Angel eyes
Howlin Wolf
Trouble in mind
Walkin' down a lonesome road
I'll just keep on singin'
West coast blues
I have my moments
Crazy rhythm
Hobo flats
Walk right in
Dallas rag
Uptown
Wild side
Rattlesnake boogie
Big Joe talkin'
Highway 49
Down in the bottoms
Walk on little girl

The breakfast sessions with Lucien. Around 7.30, I phone from a café in the Rue des Écoles, just to make sure it's all right to come over (he prefers it that way). I phone: "OK?" "OK", he says, "I'll get the coffee on." By the time I get to his place in the 15th district by metro, the coffee is ready, a rich black smell in the morning air. A small man, Meister Lucien, seventy-two years old, full of beans, up at six, has his morning shit ("If you don't shit right, you become a shit yourself"), and is ready for talk. "Well, how are your studies getting on?", he asks me, just to set the ball rolling, and I tell him about the week's readings and cogitations, and that sets him off on a monologue taking in, for example, Sextus Empiricus, David Hume, the impact of Kant on Russia, the dialectics of Nagarjuna, and all the while he's jumping up to get hold of books, piling them up on the table: the Loeb Classical Library's four-volume Sextus, René Pintard's *Le Libertinage érudit*, Schayer's translations from the *Prasanapada* . . . So it goes on for three or four hours. The weekly session.

Hare Krishna Hare Krishna Krishna Krishna Hare Hare Rama Hare Rama Rama Rama Hare Hare . . .
Put the last dregs of Christianity, transcendentalistic twaddle, puppy love, spiritualist acne, and general swamification together, and

you get that shaven-pated, glaikit-looking Bhakti-boy wailing and clashing his *karatala* up the Boulevard Saint-Michel.
Hare Krishna Hare Krishna Krishna Krishna Hare Hare ...

The casualty ambulance goes howling round the city. Every street corner has its potential suicide.

Life in the ditches – a title à la Samuel Beckett. I can go a long way with Samuel B., as long as he likes to go, right to the end. But that's it, Sam's at the end of something (and there's good reason: it's end city and final history) – he's at the end of something, and he keeps shoving the end a bit further forward, the infinite calculus of despair worked up into perfect no-art. But he never makes the break, never gets beyond the end, he just marks time there, and he does that marking time better than anybody. I'm beyond the end, or trying to get beyond the end, feeling at least the early will-o-the-wispy beginnings (nothing to do with history, the time and civilisation process) of something else. In limbo too, sure, but my limbo is *incandescent*.

R.T. the novelist, met on the Boulevard Saint-Michel, tells me about the island he's just spent four months on, off the coast of Brittany. Rented a room in the island's hotel. Says how he was sitting in his room one day with a glass of red wine before him when suddenly the wine *lit up*. It was a burst of light from a cloud-break over the sea reflected in the glass.

Let's get out of the time-process, into a more abrupt territory, with different levels coinciding, a fresher geography, a more lively weather of the mind.

Presenting the ritual biscuits and coffee this morning, around the usual hour of eight, Lucien cries: "You've got to feed the brahman!". After the coffee, he clears the table and brings down a volume of the *Kokka* and we look at some Japanese paintings. Lucien's pronunciation of English has to be heard to be believed: "Wilt dooks", he says, referring to one painting. He's miles better at Sanskrit. We talk about some Sanskrit books. Compared to what went on in Sanskrit literature, English still has a long way to go.

In a café in the rue du Temple with Phileon the Jew. He tells me a dream he had just recently. There was a step-ladder with twenty rungs. Then a long, winding staircase. Then another ladder with twenty rungs. He probably climbed to the top, but he doesn't remember. What he does remember is the notice at the bottom: NO LORRIES ALLOWED.

"We're leaving for the Indian Ocean. For good. Have house and land and material on the island of Reunion. The wherewithal to create an agricultural community. If you are interested, contact us." – notice stuck on a tree, Boulevard Saint-Michel. My workfield is here, at least for the time being.

Lucien: "I don't air my opinions in public."

Late october. Traffic humming, chugging, whining by. Red lights, yellow lights, white lights. All those people. Sitting here after eating a meal (potatoes with oil and pepper and salt with some cheese on the side and a beer) looking out of the half-moon window. All those people, all that traffic. Night in the city.

I'm gonna pick up ma baby
we're gonna swing tonite
I'm gonna pick up ma baby
we're gonna swing tonite
til the sun is shinin brite
       JAY STUTES and SHORTY LEBLANC

Mad dog in the wilderness kingdom.

Meet a student in the café. She tells me she's writing a thesis on the sacred in modern literature. The sacred – seems a hopelessly heavy word. I quote her Bodhidharma's phrase to old Wu: *no sacredness, emptiness*.

Pont de Sully:
Sun red-sparkling through the mist.

Lunch with Linkfuss (teacher at the University). Extreme leftist, excluded from the Communist Party. In the circles he frequents, the struggle is no longer between left and extreme-left (old chestnut), but, within the extreme-left, between politicals and culturalists. Linkfuss is a culturalist.

He tells me a story. Up visiting a friend and colleague of his (Wailing Wall Waldenburg) in Pigalle with two woman colleagues, he leaves with the two women around midnight.

Midnight, Pigalle. A striptease hustler catches on to them: "Come and see the show!" Putting his arms round the two women, Linkfuss answers: "We put on our own shows." "Leftist!" shouts the hustler, which shows maybe that even striptease hustlers in Paris have a political conscience.

Left of left, you're in your own territory.

Midnighters. Aware there may be no tomorrow, but knowing their own dawn. The body-mind can blaze within its own energy even when the world goes to ashes. Shiva dances in the cremation grounds.

Lucien: "This is the school of scepticism, the aporetic school, a school for intellectual liberteens. I say 'school', but there's nobody less attached to the concept of school than I am."

The dakini, *dancing and making the mudra of fascination, will gleam forth.*
Bardo Thodol

The secret signs by which the yogi and yogini recognize each other are laid out in the Hevajra-tantra. Sign seven:
If he indicates the sole of the foot, she should dance with joy.
Vajragarbha's commentary:
This asks the question: 'How shall we go to these places?' To which this is the reply: 'First the dance, and then by entering complete tranquillity, in this way we shall go to those places.'

The girl from Venezuela, six months in Paris, living at the Contrescarpe, tells me she is, *cómo se dice,* reflecting on her political ideas – the social and economic situation of Venezuela as compared with, as she pronounces it, *Cuva*. Hem, hem. Dark skin, mass of black hair, smoking like a volcano. I noticed she used the word "magic" a couple of times, in different contexts, and remarked on it. Yes, she was, *cómo se dice*, interested in magic, in particular the cult of Maria Leonza, from the province of Yara-something (I didn't catch the name), which is the magic area of Venezuela. A magical revolution??? While I'm thinking that one out, she tells me I should go to Latin America. The people are all anarchists, she says, whereas behind every idea in France there is a hunk of cheese and a bottle of wine, the French wear slippers on their brains. In Venezuela, it is all crazy, crazy. "You would love it", she tells me. "Venezuela is the place for you. Come to Venezuela."

What is here is everywhere; what is not here is nowhere.
                                                            Vishvasara Tantra

As a radical sceptic, Lucien enjoys all dogmatisms. He looks to dogmatic forms and structures, in order to take them apart. I enjoy his scepticism because dogmas, heavy and hindering, there are, and plenty, but I have less interest in dogmatics, I tend rather to disregard them and go all out for the life-wave.

Night. Smothered moon above the Rue des Écoles. Police vans gathering in the street, rolling up grey along the pavement. In the quarters, I take a shower, eat some bread and cheese, and get down to work.

Erratic movements and studies – the necessary preliminary to a whole *unedited* domain of being.

Those personal poets with their little pink clouds floating across the sky. Better by far the big dark storm clouds of the chaos-writers. But best of all, the lightning-stroke in clear sky of those who have broken through.

Sometimes I just want to go away into a corner and laugh. Everything going on seems so egregiously corny.

Zeising's definition of laughter:

Comedy is a nothing in the form of a something. It is not only a contradiction in itself, it contradicts the idea of perfection that is part of our build-up. In other words, it negates the spirit of the absolute. When God approaches the Nihil, a world is produced, and when his image, man, encounters the Nihil, laughter is produced. The universe is the laughter of God, and laughter is the universe of the man who laughs. The laugher raises himself to the level of God. He becomes, within his limits, the creator of a hilarious creation. He is the destroyer of the Nihil, the contradictor of contradictions.

This makes Bergson sound like the *Sunday Post*.

Sunday morning. I'm at the long table with a pot of tea. The sky a quiet, smoky effulgence, the window rattling every time a car passes. Ten o'clock. I've been up since nine (worked late into the night), now doing a piece of translation for *Le Monde* to earn myself a few pennies: *The Poetry of the Month*. Little ribbons of poetry; little shit-pellets of poetry. Poetry of the month. Where's the poetry of no-time, no place? A poetry that breathes in space, and is alive with mental lightning!

What it's all about. Putting yourself into the changes. Seeds arising from the play-of-chance (the welter), you develop them. From this comes your reality. When one thing's complete, another grows. Each growth is delight in itself. And the final outcome of the growth, the delights, is a beautiful clear calm light which is the whiteness of the "white world".

Conversation with American in café. Lives In New York. Gets home after work in the late afternoon, bolts his door behind him – he makes the gesture of methodically closing five separate locks – and turns on the television. "Even what I have left of freedom has to have a taste of pollution", he says wryly.

Afternoon. I'm lying on my bed just letting my mind drift. Jean-Luc's on his in the corner, reading a book on poker to perfect his game (he makes good pocket money off it). Tells me about the difference between the American method, where it's fifty-two cards no matter what the number of players, and the French or modern method, where the number of cards is according to the number of participants. He prefers this method, says the American game can become one awful mess.

Have trust in the deep blue light of dazzling splendour.
I've just come across this phrase from the *Bardo Thodol*. Reminds me of that dream I had in Glasgow, years ago, towards the end of a very dark period. A rock, and the rock opened up, and inside there was that dazzling blue gleam. Also that rainy morning in the Botanic Gardens, Glasgow. I was walking in there as I often did, that grey morning under the rain, in a kind of limbo-state, neither here nor there, when suddenly I was confronted with this blue flower, the rain pearling its pale blue petals. It was the Tibetan Poppy. Blue floods of coolness. Glasgow, which is mostly considered as the home of kitchen realism, was for me a kind of transcendental laboratory. Clinically considered, I suppose that's psycho-pathological territory. I was "mad" in Glasgow. A cyclothymic phenomenon. And what am I now? An open system. Wanderings in an open field.

The dancer from Madras (met her after her show last night). Beautiful. She had to turn up soon. The time is now. The field was waiting for a root-action.

The story goes. that the brahman Saraha, who is supposed to have been master to the tantric Nagarjuna, met in the person of an arrowmaker's daughter "the yogini of his field of work, who could free the essence of his being", that he led with her the wandering life of an arrowmaker, and that finally they both rose into the sky by magic.
                                                GLASENAPP, *Buddhist Mysteries*

A rainy morning, over at Lucien's place. After we've talked for a couple of hours, he warms up some *sake* left him recently by a Japanese visitor. We sit sipping the *sake*, and finish off the bottle. Lucien, who is from Nantes, says he prefers a good white wine. Me too, as to taste. But that *sake* has an *atmosphere* to it.

A dancing girl (patra) must be slim, beautiful and young. She must have small round breasts, be sure of herself, witty, and pleasant. She must know when to begin a dance, and when to end it. She must have long eyes, be able to express herself with or without instruments. She

must know how to keep the beat, and how to bear herself. A young girl possessing all these qualities can be called a real dancer.
                                  NANDIKESVARA, *Abhinaya Darpanam*

Blue waves of the Indian Ocean. Whitefoaming, sunglistening, longcurving. An adjective a mile long is what I need.

Mahamudra
Mahamudra
Mahamudra

R.T. the novelist, whom I think of as "the old Vosgian", in his attic room at the Porte d'Orléans. Dust-layered cases in a corner, books higgledy-piggledy on shelves and on the floor. He reads me from his little book of remarks and quotations, a notebook to which he consigns the kind of realities that take his fancy: the definition of a strange word in Johnson's dictionary; a fragment of a letter from Chateaubriand in which he says he's going to send a folding bed to the Pope, who is ill. He tells me he hesitates a long time before making an entry, it has to be just right. Leaving the little book aside, he goes into his kitchen to ready the meal and I go with him. As he fries a couple of sputtering steaks, he tells me how earlier in the evening he'd had a visit from an insurance agent. The agent had told him all he should be insured against and had run up quite a list of eventualities. When he'd finished, R.T.'s cat went and pissed on his shoes, and R.T. asked him if *he* was insured against *that*.

She is neither too tall, nor too short, neither quite black nor quite white, but dark like a lotus leaf. Her breath is sweet, and her sweat has a pleasant smell like that of musk. Her vagina gives forth a perfume from moment to moment like different kinds of lotuses, or like sweet aloe wood. She is calm and resolute, pleasant in speech and altogether delightful, with beauteous hair and three wrinkles in her midriff. Having gained her, one gains that siddhi *which is Joy Innate.*
                                                      Hevajra-tantra

Jean-Paul (long hair much receded at the temples, stubble of beard) in his room, rue de la Victoire, scraping a little trintle of *afghani* on to a paper and mixing it in with tobacco (supplies are pitifully low), tells me he doesn't know where he is at the moment, feels outside definitions, just back from Amsterdam where he says he had "a mystical experience", wondering if he isn't going to go down and join the del Vasto community in the Larzac. "Don't do that", I say. But that's what they all do, once they've had the slightest inkling. They join a kindergarten or a penitentiary.

Champion Jack Dupree – *Rattlesnake Boogie!* Doing my crazy dance, making faces at myself in the mirror. The dance of the cosmic clown. Police-ridden, traffic-tortured, head-aching Paris humming all around, but I'm here at the centre, in the eye of the storm, doing my dance, happy-mad.

> *When the soul rests*
> *at the centre of the lotus*
> *it acquires knowledge*
> *knowing all there is to know*
> *it sings, dances*
> *teaches, and creates joy*
>
> Dhyanabindu Upanishad

The philosopher from Berkeley. Black beard almost hiding his face, bites his nails. Tried a Californian Zen monastery for a while, and "got the crap beaten out of him". Never again, he says. Now wondering what he thinks, what he should think, what there is to be thought. For the moment, Hegel and Marx are doing a wrestling bout in his mind. He's discovering Europe. Yesterday's Europe. But maybe he'll catch up.

I didn't go to India. I put myself into the changes. And India came to me.

> O dombi, *your hut is outside the town limits.*
> *As you walk, you seduce both Brahman and Buddhist.*
> O dombi, *I shall unite with you. Kanha is a bearer of skulls, naked*
>   *and without hate.*
> *There is a lotus of sixty-four petals. The* dombi *climbs on to it, and*
>   *dances.*
> Dombi! *For you I throw away my luggage.*
> *You are a* dombi *and I am a bearer of skulls.*
>
> KANHA, *Dohakosa*

They're all doing something. This one's getting himself zazenated by a Japanese; this one's getting gurufied by an Indian; this one's brooding in transcendental meditation – and I'm just sitting in my cave (visited by the *dombi*), writing notes on the wall, watching the rain fall over the world.

International telegram:
>   IT'S RAINING TEA IN DARJEELING

Letter from C.P., artist, England: "What's wrong with my life? Where am I going? Why am I in such a mess? How can I unclutter my mind? How can I achieve a life that goes like an arrow, straight and clean to its target?"
Stop sitting on your own shit, mate.

According to the *Hevajra*, there are four kinds of joy in the process of realization. The first comes from the desire for varied contact; the second from desire for deepening bliss; the third from the communication of passion; and the fourth, arising from these, is the blankness of perfect truth.

India
What is India?

A dark cave
A dancing girl

The hidden yoga

The vajra entered rapidly into the vajra-lotus where it remained planted, and Vajrapani entered into meditation.
>   Mahabala-nama-mahayanasutra

Just read a learned article, sci-en-ti-fic, by Dr B.K. Anand, Dr G.S. China and Dr Baldev Singh in the *Indian Journal of Medical Research*: "Studies on Shri Ramanand Yogi during his stay in an air-tight box."
That's not exactly my kind of yoga.

Six o'clock, met the Cormorant in the Rue des Écoles. Said he was very glad to see me, and invited me to go with him for a beer to a café where they sold coal and where there was a white rabbit. So we went to the café, saw and stroked the rabbit, which was real, right enough, and the idea of it obviously tickled the Cormorant. He told me he was now living in a hotel with Lafontaine, Apollinaire, Machiavelli and Dante. After a couple of beers, he extended his invitation to have dinner with him in his favorite little Chinese restaurant. So we went there, quiet little place. Now and then, the Cormorant touches his heart and says it isn't working so well any more – "must have pumped too much poetry out of it". He tells me that when he retires he's going to buy a pair of boots, no, two pairs of boots, and just walk – to Rome first (for a long time the Cormorant thought he was a Catholic), then Yugoslavia, Romania . . . till he gets to China. Then he'll turn back, and keep walking till he feels it's time to drop, when he'll look for a wood with a nice bed of leaves.

All this must be done with circumspection, that no disclosure come about. Through lack of secrecy misfortune will befall you.
Hevajra-tantra

– I learned long ago to keep my mind wide-open and my mouth shut.

ROOM 6
A Little Place in Nowhere

> "While his thought remained unknown, he was nameless. But he broke the circle of ignorance, and penetrated emptiness."
>
> BIANJI, *Sanzang's Journey to the West*

Positively the littlest room I've ever let myself in for. It's up on the sixth floor. You come climbing up the usual steep and narrow, dark and murky service stair, jouk under the lines of manycoloured, manyshaped, drip-drip watch-your-neck washing, and there you are. Another temporary abode.

Took over these lodgings this morning, Saturday. Rain falling. At Passy, as I came along in the underground, where it comes up for air, I saw a red-and-orange barge ploughing laboriously up the Seine.

Now sitting here in the 11 o'clock quietness at my table, writing this. Flap and whirr of a pigeon's wings outside the skylight.

It's a clean compact little place. There's a good heater, and a two-plate gas stove for cooking. Shelves for books, and shelves for my rice, tea, etc.

It'll do.

> *I got a mind to travel*
> *Where I'm goin nobody knows*
> *I got a mind to travel*
> *Where I'm goin nobody knows*
> *Whatever highway I travel*
> *Will be one more lonesome road.*
>
> JUKE BOY BONNER

Went down to the shop on the corner to buy a pan. Got it, then said I needed six nails (to fix my sheaves of manuscript on the walls of my room), but the lady of the shop tells me she can't sell me six nails retail. In fact she has me understand that all the old ironmonger shops failed because they sold nails six a time. She makes me feel I'm not up to date about ironmongery at all, in fact I'm positively from the backwoods. Anyway, I've got my nails – enough nails to build an ark.

My manuscripts? A process of getting to know myself, or rather, travelling through myself. On the hundred and one uncertain paths.

Big Portuguese talk-fests up here on the sixth floor on Sunday nights. Three or four households (or rather, roomholds), all with doors wide open on the corridor, making one big noisy family. At first I think hell, I'll never be able to live and work in this din, then I remember that passage I read years ago, I think it was in Seneca (Latin studies in the attic room, Fairlie, Scotland), where he tells how he did his philosophizing in a room above the bawling public baths. So I take down one of the manuscripts and start working.

No idea what time it is. Got into my sleeping-bag on the bed, and tried to sleep, but couldn't. I'd opened the skylight for air, but that let in the noise of traffic and the air was no pleasure to breathe in anyway. So I closed the skylight again. Less noise, but still couldn't sleep. More on my mind than noise, or bad air. I lay there in the darkness, then I got up, put on the light, and came to the table here to try and write it all out. But it's no good. My mind won't work, and I'm left with this vague, but heavy, feeling of anxiety. Suddenly, noise from the corridor. A jabbering quarrel between two Iberian banshees. They must be scratching each other's eyes out. Wonder what time it is. Probably only a horrible 3 o'clock in the morning.

Always been too much concerned with a feeling of space to bother about my place in the world, and never any thought of time, that is, the future. Sometimes get the impression now that the world and time are coming in at me, getting their revenge as it were, coming in to ruin not only what space and presence I've won, but my very self, for having dared to claim that space and presence. Sometimes, panicking, I even envy those who have a niche (profession, family, home) and a future (even if it just means more of the same). I get afraid of my own particular activity. It takes a hell of a lot of (even an infernal kind of) self-confidence, what the Greeks called *hubris*, and the devil-thing in Christianity. No support from society, nothing to fall back on there. Society has its norms, whereas this is definitely ab-normal. It isn't socially justifiable (and this is an age when society is all-encroaching), not being concerned with world mechanics. It's a pure self-thing. Some get roped-in as artists. They *want* to get roped in. So they can suck at "success", which is infantile. Dependent on appreciation for their existence. At best, art is a half-way house. Whereas here there's no house at all. At most, a room in nowhere.

May the rhythmic and difficult dance protect us! – part of the stanza of benediction pronounced at the beginning of Sanskrit plays, referring to the dance of Shiva between two worlds.

> *Woke up this morning,*
> *felt around for my shoes*
> *yes, I woke up this morning,*
> *felt around for my shoes,*
> *you know how it is*
> *I got those old walkin' blues.*
> ROBERT JOHNSON

To work and live at *all* levels, know what it feels like in *all* areas, enjoy your "polymorphous (per)versity" to the full. Few people being aware of the multiple possibility (society being based on a refusal of multiplicity, and on a drastic curtailment of possibility), some will know you at one level, and define you accordingly, some in one area, some in another. But you'll be defined by none of these partial views. Your dance takes place beyond them all – in a "nowhere" so far as fixed locality is concerned. Your centre is that "empty room", in which *anything* can happen. Most of those who become aware of this "empty room" make haste to fill it with furniture, and the furniture slowly stifles them. You're trying to live without furniture. What you're after, what you're in, will come across to people (and you like people well enough, if you loathe their furniture), as a draught, a stroke of lightning, a faint perfume, something like a memory, a strange gesture, a foreign word, an absurdity, an irrelevance, a madness.

Remember, if at moments in your dance you stumble a bit, and almost break a leg, or even your neck, and lose the rhythm, and really find yourself abandoned in a blank emptiness, just keep cool, take it easy, have a look round, try a few more steps – and away it'll go again.

The *pançakrama* (five stages), according to Nagarjuna:
(1) *kayavisuddhi*, solitude of the body.
(2) *yagvisuddhi*, solitude of speech.
(3) *cittavisuddhi*, solitude of thought.
(4) *sukhabhisambhodi*, total awakening in joy.
(5) *yoganaddha*, integration of the body-mind.

To get out of "normal" relations, out of talk, out of time – meeting life otherwise. Always meeting life. Your "monastery" is right in the middle of things.

Egocentric? Yes, what else can you be *centred* on? It's when you centre on the ego, concentrate on it, and *go through it*, that you enter the open field. Before that, you're wrapped up in all kinds of *camouflaged* egoism.

> *From Cold Mountain monastery*
> *beyond the walls of Ku-su*
> *the sound of a bell at midnight*
> *reaches the traveller*
>   CHANG KI

Morning. Massive throat-howkings and spittings. Sound of water running into plastic pails from the tap in the WC on the landing. Rattle of cups and spoons. A baby's howling.
Up. Dark-grey novemberishness.

> *This joyance is wild and savage like a deserted place.*
>   RUYSBROEK

Remembering the village tonight:
The cluster of birch trees I used to make love to, high overlooking the firth.
My father's signal cabin: the smells of paraffin, creosote and tar; the green and red flags; the wall clock with the initials of signalmen carved inside; the big ledger with train times and events within the section duly marked in.
The empty space of moor – gulls wailing; leaping hares; the wind.

G. F., painter, had written me from England to get him the catalogue of the widely-publicized Polokhanov show at the Musée d'Art

Moderne. So I went over there to do this little chore, and while I was at it had a look at the show, but there was nothing for me, nothing at all. Fortunately there was a young girl wandering round in there it was a pleasure to set eyes on (unfortunately, she was accompanied). When I came out, it was dark and I went into a café to sip an espresso before walking up to the Étoile and then down the Avenue de Wagram. All these "artistic" problems – I want the real white flow of being, nothing else.

As I climb up the service stair, my nostrils are filled with the gutsy stench of cooking. It's even in my room. I'll have to buy some perfume-sticks. For the moment, I want to wash. Quite a complicated affair. Means filling up my basin down at the tap in the WC, then kneeling down in front of it here. It becomes like a rite, and I treat it as such. This place is well-heated at least, which means I can work in it naked.

> *Sri Rama Benzoin Perfumery Works*
> *Kolar, Mysore State:*
> *50 assorted sticks*
> *rose jasmin and musk*
> *and among them*
> *a long black hair*
> *from the head of the Mysore woman*
> *who packed them*

– I'll offer it to Kali.

O goddess Kali, he who on the midnight having uttered your mantra makes an offering to you in the cremation ground of a pubic hair from his female partner wet with semen poured from his penis into her vagina, becomes a great poet, a lord of the world and always rides an elephant.
From the Karpuradistotram

As yet, only the little girl back from school, wandering up and down the corridor singing to herself. She has a nice voice. But what a life for a little kid like that, wandering up and down the murky corridor. She ought to be playing with shells on a beach in the Red Land.

And me?

The room is redolent with smoke perfume, and I dream of Mi Fu's junk on the Blue River, and the colours and smells of India. I open a book, and the mention of Shiva, or the photo of some corner of a temple, is enough to set me off. I go from North to South. I'm up in the Himalaya, among the rhododendron, the giant rhododendron of the Himalaya, then I'm away down South at Mahabalipuram, and there's a lotus growing in my brain, a thousand-petalled lotus, and my feet are beating the darkred earth. Therafter I leave India for great China, and I'm over again on the Blue River, evening coming down, dragons running along the banks, herons silent at the water's edge, the water lapping up against their legs. My heart's a drumbeat, calling for space, for space. Back to India, on the dusty roads, alone, alone as the sun, moving from village to village. Or in a market place, and crazy flute playing going on all around me. That drumbeat, that drumbeat. It's filling the whole earth, that space-beating drum. When did my heart turn into a drum? When did my whole being start beating on this drum – for space, for space. If I don't get real space for my heart, it'll burst. But where the hell is that real space? It's that still-ghostly world, you fool. The white world (to name it is too much) – that unseizable, quicksilverish amalgam of multiple existence and non-existence. Becoming more and more evident. The evidence coming out of the incandescence.

Around the drumbeat
the bones cry

around the drumbeat
the symbols fly

around the drumbeat
all things go by

Over this afternoon in Montparnasse, talking with Blue Waters (old Vietnamese acquaintance), about monks travelling up and down the Mekong, about *mahayana, hinayana, tantrayana*, about Bhutan, Sikkim, Little Tibet. Blue Waters is an electronics engineer, fed up with electronics. Has a photograph of Lhasa on the wall above his head, and is about to take off any day.

Rue du Petit Musc. Compact, dark-skinned body, with the exaggerated breasts of an *apsara* on an Indian temple.

The karmamudra *has breasts and hair, and is the basis of pleasure in the realm of desire* (kamadhatu). *The* jnanamudra *arises in the mind and is the basis of pleasure in the realm of form* (rupadhatu).
Naropa: Sekoddesatika

Karmamudra, plus *jnanamudra*, towards *mahamudra*, the great seal, the great gesture.

Dream:
I'm in the train from Paris to Marseilles. Why Marseilles? No reason apparent. Anyway I know I'm just going there to come back. And in Paris, I have a few addresses, but none of them my own. An unsettled feeling. Yet there in the train I'm at home.

All the Portuguese doors are open on the corridor, and a great racket is going on, somebody banging away on a shaky guitar, but I don't mind a bit, not a bit, let it rip!
I'm in Kailasa.
Up on Shiva's mountain, drinking Highland hooch.

The seven factors of enlightenment:

mindfulness
investigation
energy
joy
serenity
concentration
equanimity

Expansion and multiplication of the self. The polymorphous chaos. Then the burst into not-self. The lightning-stroke. And the high, clear air. The process.

"*What's that*", *asked Kyō-sei.*
"*It's the rain*", *answered the monk.*
"*All living things live upside-down lives, deceived about themselves, pursuing objects*", *said Kyō-sei.*
"*And you yourself?*"
"*Near to not being deceived.*"

"*What do you mean, 'near to not being deceived?'*"
"*To speak about it in abstract terms is relatively easy, but to say the Reality itself is difficult.*"

From the *Pi Yen Lu*

No, it can't be ... Sitting in this room at midnight, in the middle of Paris, I hear a ship's horn on a river, and see a drifting fog. But that was Glasgow, years ago. All time at my door.

I'm a long line of ghosts, and none of them holy, but in me the ghostness is to become a light, all these souls in the murky lanes of history moving towards light, "concentrated in its own place like the sun", as Fa-hien says of the *sambhogakaya*.

Afternoon, after working all morning in my room, I went over to the British Institute to give a talk on "the state of modern poetry". Found the place closed, dammit. And had a meeting with a man wanting English lessons at 6 o'clock, which meant a lot of time to kill. Thought of going to a cinema, but they were closed too. National mourning, b'jees, some politician or other kicked the bucket (I wasn't aware), and the nation was supposed to be in mourning. I went down Boulevard Saint-Michel to the Seine – fortunately it was still flowing. So I sat there on the stone parapet, watching it flowing and grey cloud scudding over the city. There everything got cool and spaced out again. Came back to my room, made myself a pot of rice, ready for a long night's work. Rain battering all hell on the skylight.

Eating my rice here alone
thinking of Hi K'ang:
Hi K'ang
called "lone pine"
whose first concern was
to "nourish his life"
and who perched his heart
on a precipice
of mysterious obscurity
saying
"without bells or drums
joy can be perfect"

And Chong Huei, bureaucrat
wrote to the Generalissimo

> *condemning Hi K'ang as a loner*
> *enemy of the State*
> *"no servant of the Empire*
> *despises the State and the Age*
>
> *corrupts morality*
> *must be executed"*
>
> *executed 262 A.D.*
> *thirty-nine years old*

At two in the morning, this place is silent, full of quiet substance. I look at my little sack of "whole rice", and laugh to myself.

> *Dream:*

The first time I came into the land of Bod was from Hsi-nang-fu past the Koko Nor, over the Salt Plain of Tsaidam, a dreary expanse of territory, 150 miles of it, and the North Plain of Chang Tang. This time I come in to the South Side, from Darjeeling through Kalimpong in Sikkim up the Chumbi valley to Gyangtse. Here in the bazaar at Gyangtse, eleven thousand feet above sea-level, I walk through the dirty, laughing, milling crowds and read one of those long, narrow books with four lines to the page: on this occasion the poetry of Milarepa, who spreads the doctrines of the White Order founded by Marpa. Next day, as I'm setting out on the way to the big monastery of Tashilhunpo, I fall in with a Red Cap monk who is drunk on beer and tells me he's just been to the holy lake of Manasarowar in the West, and shows me a poem he's written on the rich, lush blossoms of the rhododendron. On the heights, we see blue sheep, snow lynxes, and many wild yak.

> *Rain falling*
> *bus passing*
> *lovely dark face*
> *Alma-Trocadéro*
> *gone*

I suddenly see myself lying on my bed, ill, in the little attic room, Fairlie, maybe ten years old, with my father's railway coat (rough black cloth with big silver buttons) flung over me for extra heat. That room, full of the sounds of the sea, and gull cries at the window. And then – skylight to skylight – I'm at a table littered with books and papers, sheaves of notes pinned to the wall, and that was student days in Glasgow. When I die, as I probably will one day, and there will be a little ceremony at some crematorium, I'd want there to be no music, just a few minutes' recording of gull cries.

Hans van Buren, Dutch poet, in Paris for a few days. We go to a restaurant in the Rue Monsieur-le-Prince, eat and talk, and when we come out at midnight, he's telling me about the Noh plays he's just been reading, and he quotes me these lines from the Nishikigi:

There is nothing here
but this cave in the field's midst
a dark place
unlit and unfilled

I ask him to say it again, and I say that's it, yes, that's it, and I don't know if he understands that my excitement is based on more than the appreciation of some "good poetry".

I've read much hindu literature
over the past years
more than a hundred well-studied books
but when I stood there with the girl
in the pale blue sari
and might have been expected
in that intellectual gathering
to make some appropriate conversation
all I could think of
was the pale blue sari
and her nakedness under it

There are about half-a-million Portuguese emigrants in Paris and on Sundays they're all congregated up here on this sixth floor.

December afternoon, cold and raw. I went over to the Musée de l'Homme where there was a Japanese exhibition. Listened for a while to shamisen and koto music in a dark room.

Then came back up here.

Another one of those literary texts to translate for the newspaper. Those fellows get carried away by their syntax. It goes on and on. You hope and pray at some point or other it's going to enter more abrupt territory. But no, never. On and on, smooth as butter, full of flattened-out meaningless meaning.

Those two little German cubes at midday made a pot of vegetable broth which was very delicious (especially as, on an afterthought, I'd dropped two eggs in it), spooned up direct from the pan on the table, with a hunk of bread on the side. It's a great thing to be able to do some cooking in a little place like this; good to hear the gurgly music of boiling water. Going to make myself some hot milk now, which I'll drink with bread and dates while going on with my work. It's about 9 o'clock, and I've got a long night ahead of me. I'm liking it OK here, yes, happy, happy as hell.

Another whiff from the village: Yoni Macleod's famous Loch Fyne kippers. And another glimpse: Red Anderson trying to teach me the fiddle. Whiffs and glimpses . . .

To study with the white wings of time passing.
POUND, *Canto 74.*

Description from a history of China of the T'ang capital, Ch'ang-an:
"The population was a motley crowd of a pronounced cosmopolitan character. Buddhist priests from India rubbed shoulders with Nestorian monks and Taoist magicians, merchants from Samarkand with silk-dealers from Soochow."
That's my kind of city!
But I won't always live in cities.

Friday morning – after two days work and running about here and there, suddenly this morning, empty space, and no quiet lotus.
To get some peace, some fullness, I went over to the Musée Cernuschi, and there I looked at pages from *The Cabinet of the Ten Bamboo*, and at a painting of lotus in the wind on Lake Shinobazu, and another of the Kia-ling river, and read about Li K'an, bamboo painter of the thirteenth century, who wrote a treatise on the bamboo, the hollow bamboo that is the symbol of the wise man who has emptied his heart of passion.
I came back to my room about 11.30.
I'll make myself some tea.

Proverb: *When in the shit make tea.*

Yes, it's Shit Creek, citizens. We're all up Shit Creek, paddling like hell, getting nowhere fast. Some have bigger boats than others, some prettier than others, some more expensive than others, but all the boating's going on up Shit Creek.

Artaud, taking a taxi in Paris, banging on it with his stick and shouting: "To the madhouse at Ivry! To the madhouse at Ivry!"

Raindripping morning, dull and grey. Coming back up the stairs after wandering about the city for a while and buying, in a jumble of an oriental bookshop, three or four Chinese texts, I feel happy again. Is it because the Chinese seems to go with the rain, or because the printed mass of the books gives me the sense of substance I need? I don't know. Anyway, whatever its source, the feeling's there, and it's thinking of scholars, hermits, monks, sages in bamboo groves, taoist wanderers and recluses that I open the door of my room. Inside, above my table, the travels of the Chinese Buddhist Hiuan-tsang in search of manuscripts – from China, across the desert of Gobi to Samarkand and Nagarahara, in the seventh century. Up one wall in a corner, the plates from Avalon's *The Serpent Power*, showing the tantric lotuses. Further on, a photograph of migratory birds in flight and, on another wall, this quotation from the *Candrapradipasutra*:

> *If someone asks you*
> *to make a gift of the Dharma*
> *at first you must say*
> *I have not studied it deeply*

Over again at Montparnasse with Blue Waters. He tells me the Buddhist group he belongs to is going to be inviting a Tibetan *rimpoche* from Darjeeling to give a series of lectures on the Brgyud-pa sect, along with a four week preliminary initiation. He and his group ("dedicated people", he says) are looking for premises to open a Meditation Centre. He wants me to join the group – and come to meet the *rimpoche* – but I refuse (again), gently, quoting to him from the Tibetan yogi and wander-poet, Kunlegs, also of the Brgyud-pa sect, but a "crazy man" (*smyo*):

> *For guru, my own thought*
> *for practise, pure appearance*
> *letting everything happen as it comes.*

Sunday, morning of rain. *Walking in the soft-falling rain.* Saying this phrase to myself over and over as I looked for a café. Most of them shut. Finally found one in the Rue de Tocqueville, where there's a Sunday market.

I'd been looking for a quiet place, to do some work on a translation for the newspaper. But here there was only noise – raucous talk, pin-tables bashing and clanging. I left after five minutes. Out again into the rain. Feeling miserable.

Then in the Rue Jouffroy I saw a grocery, a tea specialist, with varieties in bowls on display, and I read the names:

Black Dragon
Tarry Souchong
Great Lord
Forbidden City
Rosy China

– and feeling better (any bit of grotesquerie, rising out of the numbness is enough to set me up again), walked on.

Good in here this afternoon. Dark rain pouring over Paris, making music on my skylight. I've been working all morning – now just sitting in the 3 o'clock afternoon light, listening to the rain.

Last night, I worked things out in my mind, right to the end, and there was no anguish, no bitterness, all serene.

That could be a Glasgow sky out there, they're all mingled. It could be years ago, in Scotstoun, Martinmas, leaves falling, the gulls, eyes and breasts of a girl.

The rain falls harder, the images come faster.

Eating my soup, rain still battering on the skylight, this phrase, from nowhere apparently:

"What are you looking for? It's here."

Went over this morning to *Le Monde* to deliver the latest translation.

Then walked about the streets for a while. Into a café to read a little. The ten thousand voices of the world.

Back to my room, 2 o'clock. Put some order in the books and papers lying about. Lie down on my bed. Rain pin-pointed on the skylight:

*The art I practice doesn't need social relations
the way of knowledge is difficult, and you have to walk it alone
I like the pure streams that wind among the rocks
I like my old quiet hut among the pines*

– that was Wang Wei, long time ago China.

ROOM 7
The Cabinet of White Meditation

"This domain free of emptiness and non-emptiness, that is the Shiva-reality"
ABHINAVAGUPTA: *Anubhava-nivedana*

In the outskirts again. Not Meudon this time, Brunoy. My entry-gate to Paris now not Montparnasse, but the Gare de Lyon. A quiet villa, with a bit of garden before my window.

Isolation – and the density of the psychic atmosphere that goes with it.

Waiting for my rice to cool
watching the yellow-leaved sapling
dancing in the wind

Sitting quietly, writing materials and a few books here on my table. Looking over at the bed covered with my old blue sleeping-bag, where the juice of the girl who was here yesterday has left stains.
"What are the commandments concerning meditation and wisdom?" asked Kô.
"I've none of that useless furniture in my room", answered Yakusan.

To know the diamond of the mind, and have it radiate, without the shit of the "literary life" – that is the project.

The phoney religion trade is a flourishing business. All those swamified fellows with their auras, their vibrations, their telepathies, their mystagogeries. A technicolour mush in place of the West's lost God. A population ill at ease in their skins, carrying the whole decline of the West under their T-shirts, tongues hanging out for spirituality, blind eyes looking for the Light, hands grasping for symbols. I'm away out elsewhere.

Not the underground, otherground.

Religions: men standing on the bank of a river and shouting at the other bank to come and get them.

A strange Paris under snow and I'm reading, in the *Council of Lhasa*, a controversy on quietism by Buddhists of India and China in the eighth century. The text of a *sutra* is brought up in which it is recommended to "produce a thought that is attached nowhere". I say the phrase over and over to myself, looking out the window at the snow.

> *I have often had occasion to allude to the apparent connection of brilliancy of colour with vigour of life or purity of substance. This is pre-eminently the case in the mineral kingdom. The perfection with which the particles of any substance unite in crystallization, corresponds in that kingdom to the vital power in organic nature; and it is a universal law, that according to the purity of any substance, and according to the energy of its crystallization, is its beauty or brightness. Pure earths are white when in powder; and the same earths, which are the constituents of clay and sand, form, when crystallized, the emerald, ruby, sapphire, amethyst, and opal.*
>
> RUSKIN

A certain amount (even a lot) of knowledge, is necessary in order to penetrate deeply into no-knowledge, and know where you're going (which in no way diminishes the surprise or delight, but prevents panic or mystification). Hence my erratic studies. Hence too, in order to arrive on the no-way, my physical errances. *Shake the letters until you become unlettered*, says Kanha.

The work of bringing in another element. Nothing to do with the mechanics of literature.

Morning meditation: "Life like a dome of many-coloured glass stains the white radiance of eternity."

> *Look into the mirror of your mind, the radiant light*
> *The mysterious home of the Dakini*
>
> *Life of Naropa*

Living alone like this (and I mean alone – i.e. the *mind* also alone, without radios, newspapers, etc.), you gradually come into a kind of waking dream state, a beautiful cool calm atmosphere. If for some reason or other I lose this state, I can work myself back into it by really concentrating on some image for a while: the birchwood poster, or the photo of the little Cham dancing-girl, or the heron at the edge of the pond ... I remember I had something of the same during my walks through Glasgow, but then it was more pathological, shivers running up and down my spine, endless associations. In Glasgow, I was almost clinically "mad". Now I've made it to the other side. Well, almost (ssshh).

> Japa, mandala, mudra *and* dyana *are the substance of the yogin's technique for the gaining of that intuitive and indefinable realization which is his goal. As methods they have only a conventional value, and their real existence is submerged in the final undifferentiated unity. For the perfected yogin, for whom all things are in all, all speech is* mantra, *even a footprint is a* mandala, *any gesture is a* mudra, *and all thought is* dyana.
>
> SNELLGROVE, note to the *Hevajra-Tantra*

The way of the hermit:

> *Bamboo studio*
> *rain*
> *the necessary books*
>
> *enter girl*
> *smooth body*
> *perfect*

The *bodhi*-mind is not transcendental. To say it is "transcendental" is to imply that it is in the same series as what it transcends, only further on, or higher up, whereas in reality it is on its own, outside all series, and moves about freely in the "non-transcendental" world.

During the English lesson I gave to the psychoanalyst this afternoon, we were translating from a book written by a French intellectual just back from Japan. In the preface, the man has a complicated screed in which he indicates his very contorted and very sterile-sounding thought-process, saying it is a method for him to attain to "what the Japanese call *satori*". I couldn't help saying to the psychoanalyst that if that fellow had been anywhere near *satori* he wouldn't be talking about it in such a constipated way. "Have you had *satori*?" asked the psychoanalyst. "If I had, I wouldn't say so", was my answer, and I left her to figure it out.

Half-awake this morning. A man staggering about in the snow, then disappearing into it. Thereafter a series of perfect little Japanese landscapes.

> *Reading*
> *fourteenth century Japanese:*
> *"the nature of man*
> *is no different from that of the universe"*
> *looking out the window*
> *at the blue sky*
> *of this cool December morning*
> *and the young birch tree*
> *always out there*
> *dancing at the slightest breeze*

Saw a film in a little cinema up by Place Blanche. About a band of legionaries who've fought in Algeria and Indochina, and now settled and domesticated – except for one, the leader, who decides to carry on the same risky existence alone. The film wasn't up to much. But bits of dialogue struck me, between the leader and his closest mate. To this man, he says: "There's only three professions for a man: king, poet or captain. Unfortunately I'm not a poet." The other says to him, as a warning: "Remember the Chinese story about the seven circles. The man who stops at circle 1 is a coward. The man who crosses 2, 3, 4 and 5 is courageous. The man who crosses circle 6 is foolhardy. The man who crosses circle 7 is a madman." They've got it almost right, but not quite.

Malevitch's *White square on a white background* (1978), described as "a pure experience of an objectless world, the last space of cosmic rest, man re-established in original unity, in communion with the all." For me, too static, monolithic. This absolute whiteness is a moment, which should not be fixed. After it, there is a dance. A way of moving, way of doing, way of thinking. With Malevitch, there is not a way at all, there is "God".

She looks at the necklace round my neck, and the bracelet on my left wrist. No name-disc, no amulet, nothing.
"Godless and nationless", I say.
She smiles: "Your religion is sex and your country is women."
She's wrong, but that's how she sees it for the moment.

Ah, Hiroshige, what a cool, flowing state you were in when you made *Mountains and River along the Kisokaidō*, I've been looking at it all afternoon, drinking tea, rain falling outside on the remains of snow. I've let a lot of things (memories and bits of ideas, but mainly memories) float down the waters of the river, and I've walked on many paths over those hills. It's not nothingness up there, only the scared would call it that, it's that cool, flowing state you must have known when you made the print. Where a man is absolutely disencumbered, and is "out of his mind".

> *The two causes*
> *by which the mind works*
> *or does not work*
> *are on the one hand the store*
> *of inherited memories*
> *and on the other the air*
> *inhaled and exhaled*
> *unconsciously*
>   Yogakundali Upanishad

The six great elements – earth, water, fire, air, space and consciousness.
What an elemental poetry means.

"He who sings far-out songs has few accompanists"
            (Liu I-min's letter to Chao).

Reborn in my own space.

From the matricial hills to the white world. That's the first part of the way. After that, wide-ranging navigation.

Home again, said Chang-yin
and all he meant was a tree
growing at the edge of a precipice

– lines I wrote about a while back when I started all this.

I used to know them almost by heart, the first seven books of the Old Testament: Genesis, Exodus, Leviticus, Numbers, Deuteronomy, Joshua, Judges. Known to the biblical backroom boys as the Heptateuch (Greek *hepta*, seven, and *teuchos*, book). Beginnings, wordings and namings, cryings in the desert, inspired prophesying. There's something of that in this seven-roomed book of mine, this heptarchy of heptalogical residencies. Situated somewhere between the Dead Sea Scrolls and the diary of Gogol's madman: "Everybody thinks that ideas are born in the brain. Not so. They are blown in by the winds around the Caspian Sea." Ah well, my heptaglotic heptad is coming to an end. Is that the sound of a Black Maria I hear, or some strange heptachordic music?

Reading *haiku* and there's a ring at the door:
"We offer you a free journal. And we would like you to read it. It contains a very important message."
Jehovah's Witnesses.
Time is short. God is about to destroy the present utterly corrupted world. We must throw ourselves into His arms, for afterwards will come the Kingdom. For further information, phone 32 25 42.

All those people crucified with Christianity, and the others beshitten with sentimental Buddhism. Burn Buddhism, the way to get to the white thing. As for Christianity, it is bad fuel, all blood and tears, too wet.

Peace in my own bones.

A transpersonal being and activity, outwith the person-public nexus. A writing which isn't addressed to the world, but is a breathing space, a cool area. Ninety percent of literature is wrapped up in that person-public nexus, nine percent is concerned about the breakthrough into "something else", in about one percent you see the breakthrough actually taking place.

"It isn't a book, it isn't a book . . . If only you'd make it more continuous". It's a touch here and a touch there that really enlightens the mind, and leaves it free. Writing for walking along a mountain path.

When they ask me if I belong to the northern school or to the southern school, writes Tao-tsi – and I might add, or the western, or the eastern school – *I reply with a laugh that I don't know if I belong to a school or if a school belongs to me.*

Kakushin, on returning to Japan in 1255 after studies and training under Fu-yen, founded the school of homeless mendicancy known as "the community of nothingness."

Final scene: over Paris, a resplendently setting sun. Tomorrow, above the quays of my cosmopoetic city, will rise, in part due to what I've done, another, stranger dawn. I may still be living here, or maybe I'll be gone.

LETTERS FROM GOURGOUNEL

Preface

In his late manuscripts, Nietzsche speaks of the most crying need of our civilization: "temporary isolation ... a kind of deepest concentration on oneself and self-recovery – not to avoid temptations, but obligations". It is the desire to "get away from the tyranny of stimuli and influences which sentences us to spend our strength in reaction, and does not permit us any more to let it *accumulate* to the point of *spontaneous activity*".

After four years at Glasgow University (with a break of isolation in between at Munich) I left Britain, where I felt I was bound to live more and more by reaction only, and went to Paris. But after two years in that city, I found reactivity again setting in, and removed a few miles out of it to the relative quietude of Meudon, where I lived in a house surrounded by a garden, and began to feel and live and express the kind of life I wanted.

It was there in Meudon that I heard of the Ardèche, part of what was then called "the French desert", where houses were being abandoned by locals, the last remnants of the French peasantry, making for the big city. With the intention of acquiring such a house, before they all went to rack and ruin, I did some more translating, gave some more lessons in English, performed one or two other jobs in order to gather in some extra cash, and began to study the territory.

"In the month of May 1844, travelling from Nîmes to Le Puy", wrote Michelet in his book *The People of France,* "I crossed the Ardèche, that harsh country, one of the hardest Nature has ever made." It sounded like one of those "places" the old travellers and hermits were always looking for, a kind of Thebaid. That was exactly what I wanted.

One of the foremost nineteenth-century French poets, Stéphane Mallarmé, taught English at a college in the Ardèche. He said that the very name, "Ardèche", summed up his life: *l'art* (art) and *la dèche* (slang for "poverty"). A more serious etymology might see in the name: *ardesco* (I burn). But it's maybe better to think in terms of the Celtic *ard*, meaning "height" (as in Ardrossan, where I'd gone to school). I liked to put the two notions together, arriving at "the burning heights".

As to the name of the house I finally found, *Gourgounel*, that word gurgled, it spoke the language of deep sources.

In a poem written later I talked of the "twelve books" gathered at Gourgounel. It was a symbolic number, but roughly true. In addition to studies on the language, literature, culture and politics of Occitania (a principal reference, by the way, for renaissance policy in Scotland), I had Nietzsche's *Ecce Homo*, several volumes of Chinese and Japanese poetry, including the four haiku books composed by Blythe, a few sutras such as the *Lankavatara*, and the *Ta Hio*, which advises the meditant to "read the signs in the sky and follow the lines of the earth".

Along with these oriental affinities, I had very much in mind Schopenhauer's "natural monk", the man who, feeling that his faculties reach beyond what is required for normal social life, prefers to relinquish family, profession, career, live apart, and concentrate on something more unique and universal.

If there was a great deal of contemplation at Gourgounel, there was also a lot of sheer physical existence, both in and around the house, in the chestnut wood, and on the paths of Mt Tanargue ("thunder mountain") that rose on the horizon.

I went to Gourgounel for the first time in 1961, and the book's first version was written in the summer of 1962 within the space of three weeks' total exhilaration. When it was published at London in 1966, it was haled in the press as "a fascinating curiosity of literature", standing outside "the mainstream (or muddy eddy) of contemporary classifications." In France, where it came out in 1979, the book was seen both as an unusual literary gesture and as a socio-political stance.

It is certainly a book not easy to define in the terms of normal literary discourse. But there are at least analogies to it in world literature.

An eleventh century Chinese text by the scholar Lieu Tsong-yuan has this:

"South of the river Kuan there's a stream flowing East. I decided to settle there for a while. I never learned its accepted name, so I had to give it one. Since I felt a bit crazy myself, I called it Crazy River. Society can make no profit out of Crazy River, but it reflects all the movements of nature. I tried to live with it and follow its way. That's how I came to write this Crazy River Collection."

Another old Chinese writer (sixteenth century), Yuan Hong-dao, of his book *Clouds and Stones*, has this to say: "This isn't for minds that are low, limited, mean. It's for those who want some space and freedom, something vast and luminous. The literature I love comes from the minds and hands of hermit monks and fervent travellers, not from those of literary vulgarians."

And there are examples in the West as in the East. Speaking of Thoreau, the hermit of Walden Pond, who was out for an extravagant literature, "as wild as lichens", Emerson said that he could have taken part in the construction of the United States, but that he'd preferred to "go and gather blueberries". Thoreau wasn't there at Walden just to gather blueberries. He was trying to get in touch with basics, to work out other developments from there. Witness his later essays on economics and civil liberty.

It was with a similar set of complex motivations I went to Gourgounel.

K.W.

"When the rivers are poisoned, go to the mountain well."
W. B. Yeats, Letter to Ethel Mannin

"For what I have in mind, I want to write at my own place, out in the wild."
Montaigne, *The Essays, Book I*

"Poet, thinker – these are names for the nameless one that finally comes to dwell in the finest of worlds."
The Kena Upanishad

The Approach

On a morning of April, 1961, I boarded a train at the Gare de Lyon in Paris, making for the South. At Montélimar, I hired a bicycle for one franc fifty a day (a new tyre thrown in) and got out on the road. I cycled round the territory for ten days. The following are extracts from the notebook I kept:

Joyeuse
I met her in the church at Joyeuse, an old, quiet woman in black, the caretaker. She was waiting patiently, the big church key in her hand, for a corpse to arrive from Grenoble.

She lit the lamps of the church for me, and led me around the chapel, showing me a painting – "a copy of Raphael, signed" – and the confessional "all hand-carved, yes, all hand-carved."

She was a peasant's daughter, she tells me, in the Lozère. Twenty cows they had, and twenty-five pigs, a fine place. Her sister is still there, but will soon have to leave, for she is very ill. It is a pity to see the old place die. But, then, if you are ill, what can you do? She herself was very ill from the age of twenty to thirty, with rheumatism, in the back, everywhere. But, ah, life is short, and we are not of this world.

She says that Joyeuse is poor, that the people abandon the villages because there is no industry. And yet, she goes on, you can live on the land, the earth is good, everything comes from the earth. I ask her if you can really get a living. "*Mon pauvre monsieur*", she replies, "there are chestnuts galore – *en pagaille* – and you need no more than that to fatten a pig. You can keep hens, and when you get a new brood, you eat off the old ones. And then there are mushrooms. Why, the priest of St André bought himself a car with mushroom money, and it's mushrooms that keep it running too. And then again there's the fruit – apples, peaches, cherries." At Rosières once she saw stalls selling peaches stretching for two kilometres, she never thought you could sell so many peaches. "Oh, you won't be a millionaire, but you can live, the earth is good. And then, anyway, we are not of this world."

Sablières
The priest of Sablières is a burly fellow, in his early thirties, his wide cassock bound by a thick leather belt in which he sticks his thumbs.

He tells me the people are sluggish and backward. They won't even prune their trees, as a result the fruit is small or the trees fall barren. They can never reach agreement among themselves: if a house is to be sold, there may be ten owners, they can never decide how, where, when to sell, so the house just falls to ruin. The same with the hills: the forestry commissioners stress the need to reforest them, but when they write to see who owns the property in order to set the work in motion, they get no reply. If anyone shows the slightest initiative, say in levelling out some of his terraces so as to work them with a machine, they say he is *fada*, an *imaginaire*, crazy. If by any chance he succeeds and makes money, they say "look at that rich devil". They live stagnant lives, in filth and ruins, scrabbling away stupidly at a patch of ground. What produce they can bring to market is paid very small prices.

Up in Thines, he says, a young woman is trying to interest the people in handicrafts. But they're so embedded in their rut that they're slow to follow the suggestion. He says industry would save the district, and has hopes that the lead-mining at Largentière may give employment to a few men.

In 1900, the *chef-lieu*, chief town (whenever I say "village", the priest corrects me), had 1,800 inhabitants. Now it has 230, and there are more than fifty bachelors over thirty.

In summer, those who are fit go down to the Midi and work a season at the vine-harvest. They come back with a thousand francs, maybe, and that sees them through the year.

"They are poor people", says the priest.

I next have a talk with the village carpenter, who is a joker. He urges me to buy the house next to his, because if someone doesn't buy it quickly it will fall to bits, and he's not anxious to have a wreck next to his own neat little place. "You buy it", he says. "I'll tidy it up for you for next to nothing, and don't worry about electricity, we'll rig up a little meter on my wires and you can tap them." "Is that allowed?" asks the priest. The carpenter gives him a big wink. "You buy it", he says to me, "it'll cost you next to nothing."

As for work in the village, he can't make out: *"Je ne m'y tiens pas."* At one minute he's planting vine-roots, then it's potatoes, now and then he does some carpentry.

But yet, he concludes, he won't leave Sablières. Or, if he did leave, he wouldn't sell his house. It would always be useful to have a place up in these mountains in troubled times, a man needs a place he can come to for refuge. The priest laughs at him heartily: "So you'll be the last to leave, carpenter, it'll be you will make the last coffin." "Ay", says the carpenter, "and the devil will help me into it."

I meet an old woman in the street and walk with her part of the way. She is suspicious and reserved at first, but soon opens up.

We pass the house where she was born, no longer inhabited, used by a family of peasants as a store-house. Peering through one of the small windows – "Our ancestors", she says, "I don't know, they seemed to be against light" – we see a smoke-blackened room, strewn with chaff, and a fox-skin hanging from a rafter (the peasants get three francs each for them, "hardly worth the shot" she tells me). The outhouses are crumbling and overgrown with weeds. The old woman potters around them, telling me about the past, when there were two thousand people here. She stoops down and picks some sprigs of parsley from between the stones: "Look, I didn't know that was growing here. It is very good. My daughter who is a nurse in Grenoble told me that if I needed vitamin C I could get it just as well from this as from the pills."

The peasant who uses the place comes strolling up from working among his vines to see what's going on. "He'll think I'm trying to sell the house", the old woman whispers to me, "and he's a dullard, he'll never make anything of himself."

The peasant can't be more than thirty years old, but his skin is ghostlike, and his teeth black, irrevocably rotten. He leans on his hoe and stares dully around him, answering the woman, who rates him for allowing the house to fall into such disrepair, with a shrug of the shoulders. "Why didn't you flit to here anyway?", says the old woman, "I would have liked to see the old house lived in, and your own place is much too small for your family." "If I came here, what would happen to my place? The same." "But that's not the kind of attitude to have!" cries the old woman. The peasant shrugs.

We leave the house and the peasant and move down to the present abode of the old woman. No, she is no longer a peasant herself, her son is in the meat-trade, she lives with him and his family. The meat-trade does not satisfy him, he says he would like to go back to the land, but, she says, "I tell him: my poor man, you don't know anything about the soil, things won't just grow well because you ask them." She says she knows one man in the district who has levelled out all his *faïsses*, his terraces, and who works them with a machine. That is the kind of man they need, he has made a success. He came up to Sablières once and he said: "I see everything grows wild here, your peasants haven't had an agricultural education." "Ah", concludes the old woman, "that is what is needed, an agricultural education."

Just in front of the house, she shows me a cherry tree which brought her sixty francs last year. She invites me in to meet her daughter-in-law. They regale me with a bowl of hot milk, sugar and bread.

After leaving the old woman's house, I go to the grocer's, that is to say the post office, to buy a bottle of local wine, some bread and a cake or two of *tomme*, fresh goat's cheese.

I tell the grocer about the carpenter's suggestion that I buy a house in the village. He looks up at me, startled and speechless, then says: "No, no, this isn't a country for you, it's hard here, *c'est pénible*." It is a phrase I hear very often.

Granzial
Moth-eaten, shabby hills. The sun long set in this valley, the atmosphere is rust-red. An oppressive silence all around. I pass a small letter-box set in the wall of a ruined house: *La levée de MARDI est faite.*

I call on a family mentioned by the carpenter of Sablières during our conversation, and say simply I am a stranger, travelling around.

I'm invited into the house by a shy, sunburnt girl of about twenty-five. She talks very fast, then is suddenly silent, then bows her head, then starts again, in savage spurts: "Where do you come from?", "Ah, do you like it here?", "*C'est pénible, c'est pénible.*", "Have you heard the news?" During the silences, I ask her questions about the country and drink the wine she has placed before me in a cup. She tells me how the grocer's van calls once a week, and about the low price they get for their chestnuts and their wine, and how dear it is to repair a house, the mason has to have sixty francs a day, plus his food. "It's dear to feed a man. Drink the wine", she continues, "the men drink a lot here."

Her mother comes in from the fields, all excited at the idea of a visitor. Will I have something to eat? Some coffee then? "Well, drink up the wine, drink up the wine." She talks even faster than her daughter, and I find it hard to understand her because of her very bad teeth. Her eyes are staring, as though fixed in perpetual surprise. When she is not speaking, her mouth is open, and she nods her head vigorously at what is being said.

She too has a lot to say about the hardness of their life, how all loads must be borne on the back across the steep hills, how the population is dying away, only one old man living over there, and an old woman up there behind. There's a house for sale, she tells me, in the valley, but it's dear, the fellow who owns it likes money: "*Il aime les sous, oh oui, il aime les sous.*" He's played tricks all over the neighbourhood, that's why he had to leave. He used to sell beeswax – it's good for the furniture – he would just mix a little earth in it to help on the weight, till he was found out. And then he sold that cousin of his, the carpenter at Sablières, a goat that gave no kid, sold it for seventy francs too, what use is a goat with no kid, it just dies sooner or later. But that's the way it is in the valley, everything just dies, sooner or later.

Nouzareth
Monsieur Jouve is the last man in Nouzareth. His house is surrounded by ruins, a crumbling chaos of stone. Beyond this slump of stone, the mountains rise white and blue, covered with chestnut, oak and pine. The sky is moving fast. There is a storm brewing.

When I call on Monsieur Jouve, he is busy working at his house in the company of a mason. He is covered in plaster, and says he doesn't dare shake my hand, but I've to come away in and drink a *canon*. He says his wife will be up later, she's out guarding the goats.

He calls in the mason who's working in the next room, and we settle down at the table. He pours from a bottle of wine, his own. "You can drink it freely", says the mason, "it makes you talkative if you want to talk, but it won't give you a headache" (he draws the edge of his hand across his forehead). "Now that other stuff, wine X – I say X because there are thousands of them – they'll praise it, put it up for prizes, whatever you like, but it'll give you a headache, you never know what's in it, it gets you. Is that not right?" he asks Monsieur Jouve. "Yes, that's right", says Monsieur Jouve, "we like good stuff here, we don't go in for prizes."

We talk of fruit. Jouve maintains he'll eat a peach at his peach tree, and it tastes wonderful, but he'd never think of bringing a peach into the house. As soon as it's under a roof, he says, it changes taste, once it's on the table, it's uneatable. And as for markets, shops, they're abominations, he'd never eat a fruit that came from there. You never know what poison you're swallowing, and the taste is lousy compared with a fruit fresh-pulled, with the dew still on it (he moves his hands in the air, and his eyes express delight).

He says he's tried to sell fruit to the merchants. But they won't have it, his fruit isn't pretty enough for them. Maybe it's got a dark spot on it where a fly sat, so they say it's got no commercial value. Commercial value! Cut out the black spot, and you've got a fine fruit for eating! Whereas their fruit, the commercial fruit, oh, it may be nice-looking, but it's full of that damned chemical poison. But they don't understand, people don't understand.

The mason says maybe they're not very rich up there, but they've got some good little things up their sleeve. Maybe they don't live any longer than other folk, but while they're alive they can enjoy themselves better. "You can get pork that you know is pure meat. You can get trout, and mushrooms, but, oh, you've got to get up early for that, for Jouve there's up at the crack of dawn and he knows all the spots. And there are chestnuts, and wood for burning, you don't need to worry when your wood-pile is running low, the woods are there, men will never burn them all, the woods will be there when men themselves are burning." He laughs abruptly and sips his wine.

"But it's a hard life too", he continues. "I'm a mason now, but I've done a lot of jobs: it's hard to earn money, once you've got a wife and kids you need clothes and, oh, there's never an end to the ands. I work well below the trade union rate, have to, otherwise I wouldn't get any work at all, the people are poor." And then the wine, he knows folk who get ten centimes (a penny) a litre for it. And the chestnuts, "why, you could pick a whole day, eat your evening meal with spikes in your fingers (all right, that's just a detail, but it matters), you'll get thirty centimes the kilo for them, and what do they sell them for in Paris? I'll tell you: two whole francs the kilo . . ."

Well, I'd travelled around quite a bit, I'd met and talked with a lot of people, but I still hadn't found the place I was looking for, that essential place I imagined, full of solitude, silence, wind and sun.

On the tenth day, however, I came upon Gourgounel, an abandoned farm in the valley of the Beaume.

Gourgounel

That morning I had arrived in Largentière, sought out the house-agent, told him what I was looking for, and he had said: "*D'accord, d'accord, d'accord*", and then: "I think I've got it." He phoned up the owner who was a retired post-office clerk, and an hour later we were on our way, through the fir and chestnut woods, climbing, past the villages of Luth, Joannas, Rocles, along the Tanargue road. The Tanargue, that is the mountain range facing Gourgounel: the mountain of Tanarus, which is Thor, the Indo-European weather-god. Tanargue: the field of thunder. In this area the people say: *lou troun toumbo oqui vounté sen dévé*, the lightning strikes where it must. Sounded exactly like the place for me to make my home. The car turned and climbed, along the boulder-strewn torrent of the Beaume, and then we stopped: "*Nous y voilà.*"

The meadows along the river are packed with narcissi. We cross the stream by the plank with the handrail, and then the narcissi are all around us, glistening in the rain, gently swaying in the wind.

We climb up the narrow path to the house. In many places the path is completely overgrown with whin and fern, and the seller of the house has to cut a way through with the big knife he has brought with him in anticipation. We are soaked through, and the two older men have made heavy weather of the climb, but at last we arrive at the little meadows around Gourgounel, and I see the house before me: a very plain structure, built on rock, flanked on one side by a little tower, its base hidden in brambles, and on the other by a stone *magnanerie*, a silkworm-house. We go into the yard. The yard is sunken and you descend into it from the field above (a field now chock-full of whins) by a short flight of crude stone steps. From the yard you go up two steps into the house.

What a sight met us there that morning! The former inhabitant, a refugee from Marseilles, had died there three years before, and the place was exactly as he'd left it, which is to say: piled high with tins and bottles, the table still littered with crockery and food, even to the bottle of green milk and the plate with the last meal's fork lying negligently on its rim. Over all this chaos and from the smoke-caked rafters hung cobwebs, and there were spiders everywhere (I later found a couple of frogs in the fireplace). We went into the centre room, where there were more bottles, with evil-looking contents, and some queer electrical apparatus, and a bed with a filthy, torn mattress, and a pile of books and papers. We then moved into the third room, which our friend had filled with hay, it being handier to have it in the bedroom than in the hayloft.

We then went down into the cellar, the foundation of which was bare rock, and then went back to the living level, and climbed up the ladder through the trap-door to the loft. The whole layout pleased me. I liked all the different heights and depths of the place. I went out into the yard, and had a look out over the terraces and the great green chestnut wood ... "Well, what do you think?" said the house-agent. "I want it", I replied.

Three days later (I extended my stay in order to get the business over, and be able to go back to Paris knowing Gourgounel was mine) we were in the notary's office at Joyeuse and the papers were signed and the money paid.

Let me quote from the title deeds, in the original and ancient legalistic French:

Pardevant Me André Archimbaud, notaire à Joyeuse ... les immeubles ci-après désignés, situés sur le territoire de la commune de Beaumont, canton de Valgorge (Ardèche) savoir:
1) Une maison à usage d'habitation sise au lieudit "Gourgounel" avec terrain attenant en nature de châtaigniers, pâture de lande, figurant au plan cadastral de ladite commune de Beaumont, sous les numéros 287, 288, 289, 290 et 291, de la section A, pour une contenance de un hectare un are and trente-huit centiares.
2) Une parcelle de terre, en nature de châtaigniers et pré, sise au lieudit "Côte Longue", cadastrée sous les numéros 245, 247, 251, 252, 254, section A, pour une contenance de un hectare quarante-six ares quatorze centiares.
3) Une parcelle de terre sise au lieudit "Gourgounel" en nature de pré et châtaigniers, cadastrée sous les numéros 255, 262, 292, section A, pour une contenance de quatre-vingt-sept ares quarante centiares ...

And so I returned to Paris as the new owner of Gourgounel. It was in the city that I received my copy of the deeds, together with a cadastral survey on tracing paper of all my "parcels of land", which I pinned to the wall of my seventh-floor attic and waited for the summer.

Settling in

I came to Gourgounel that July, and for the fist three days I was panic-stricken, in a landscape and a climate utterly strange to me. I had lost my habitual self completely, felt exposed, abandoned, confronted by colours I had never seen, forms I did not know, above me a sun such as I had never experienced. I lay under the mulberry trees, out of the blaze of the sun and the sky, with the perpetual hum and *kree-kree-kree* of insects all around, and now and then a hawk gliding over the massive chestnut wood. I lay there during the day, and at night I rolled out my sleeping-bag, and slept under the stars. At night I felt better, but dawn came like a knife.

Several times I went up to the village of Valgorge, to see gardens and sit on the terrace of the one hotel, patronized mainly by *Marseillais*. On the road to Valgorge, about three miles up the valley, I had to pass two or three houses, grey stone houses with closed shutters and black portals. There was the house of one old woman in particular. Hearing footsteps on the road, she came out the first day and asked me in a high-pitched voice who I was. The rag covering the entrance had been dragged aside, I caught a glimpse of blackness, blue smoke and fire, and then this old woman was there on the edge of the road, with grey dishevelled hair, brown-creased face, a grey shapeless frock. She'd already heard of me, and when I had arrived: "Ah, you are the new one at Gourgounel?" Had Camossetto left any books? Once he had repaired her radio. Was I liking it up there? "*Vous ne languissez pas trop là-haut?*" (Are you not wearying all alone up there?). The weather was very hot. "But you have the fresh air up there, *vous avez le bon air là-haut, heh, heh!*" I got away from her as fast as I could, promising myself I would make conversation with her once I was able, she was obviously half-crazy with loneliness. I was half-crazy myself but I didn't want to talk. So I left her that day, and did not stop the other times, merely waving to her as she came out of her house repeating: "*Vous ne languissez pas trop là-haut?*" The phrase got on my nerves. The sun kept blazing.

On the afternoon of the fourth day arrived the postman, Martin

Martinesche. I was lying under the mulberry trees when this head with the képi appeared above the stone wall, and then the ... but I shall tell you exactly how Martin's body appears to the casual observer. His post-office regulation issue pants are about ten sizes too big for him. The fly reaches down to his knees, and the seat drapes over his hurdies in folds. His body also has a curious way of moving about the landscape. His feet are splayed and encased in heavy rubber boots, which already hardly makes for agility. But Martin is also a walking wine-bag. So that his movement at times can take on a kind of lumbering, stumbling, mumbling lurch. Martin drinks wine all day and every day. Every house at which he delivers a letter pours him one, two, three glasses of wine, and he doses himself liberally mornings before beginning his rounds, evenings after completing them. Yet he is never offensively or stupidly drunk. Apparently he has never yet made a mistake in his deliveries, and has one of the most prodigious memories the postmaster has ever met up with. It must be said that a great deal of what Martin imbibes comes out almost immediately in sweat, which explains the great purple patches on his post-office summer issue. He has a round which entails a great deal of climbing up paths no more than goat-tracks, a round which takes him five to six hours right in the middle of the day.

That day he saw me under the trees, and came towards me with a stuttered: *"Bonjour la maison"*. We shook hands. Then, with the sweat pouring down his face, and his head nodding continually, he delved into his big leather bag to get my letter. There and then I arranged with him that he need not deliver my mail right up to the house, but could leave it somewhere down by the river, and I would collect it myself. This idea suited him very well and he suggested, subject to Madame Ribeyre's approval, the window-ledge of the grange at Ribeyre's farm on the river-bank.

When Martin left, I read the letter. It was from friends in Paris, people who thought I was just a leetle bit mad to go away into the back of the beyond and commune with nature and a poetic goat – a waste of brains and energy. Though they conceded, ironically and kindly, that from such a premature retirement and such an oriental quietude, something might come. They were waiting to see the something.

It was probably this which made me get down to work.

I plunged into the dust and filth of the house, piled up rubbish, swept the windows and corners and rafters of cobwebs, made gentle eviction moves on spiders, axed old bits of furniture, broke down the makeshift "improvements" Camossetto had made – for example round the fireplace, where he had built up a great heap of earth to prevent draughts from the door – rummaged through books and papers and set aside what might be of interest.

Then, finding tools in the cellar, an old mattock and a shovel, I went to the edge of the terraces where the woods begin, and there dug a huge hole. A neighbour, Marc Abeillon, appeared on the second day of my digging, and thought I was off my head. I was up to the eyes in earth by then, and I did not stop digging that hole till I had to cut steps in the earth to climb out. In the hole I shoved all the rubbish of the house, lock, stock and barrel. And then covered it all over with earth, and knew that in a year's time the spot would be overgrown with ferns and brambles.

After five days of furious working and on the fifth evening, I sat in the cleaned house on the two chairs I had salvaged along with the beautiful old *maie* (a long wooden trough with a lid, used for laying the dough for bread) I had disengaged from the filth on it and around it. This, together with a shaky cupboard and an old chest, was all my furniture. It was all I needed – except for a bed.

That night I laid a couch of whin on the floor, and intended to sleep on that. But I had got to like sleeping out of doors, so I went back under the mulberry trees.

The Roof over my Head

The house needed re-roofing, the roof had hardly been touched in forty years and had slipped badly. It leaked prodigiously. In the crannies and spaces I found most of the last occupant's old wardrobe, the worst hole sporting a complete pair of grey serge pants all to itself. The whole thing would have to be laid bare, and the tiles set back firmly in place. I had obtained promise of help from my neighbours, Virgilou Escudier and Marc Abeillon for the laying of the tiles. But I had to find the new material: planks, nails, and tiles also, for many of those already on the roof were cracked.

For the tiles I went to Pouzache at Largentière. It was his wife I saw first, and she had bad news for me. The kind of tile I wanted – the round *tuile du pays* – was hardly made now. All that could be had was the flat one, the "mechanical tile", the *tuile mécanique*. Most of the little artisans who made the old Roman tile had been run out of business. Certainly the big tile-works at Marseilles still made a few for special orders, but it had been a hard winter with a lot of frost, and there's no use trying to make tiles in frost. Did I really want to insist on the round Roman sort? Yes, I said, if it was at all possible to have them. Well, they *were* expecting a lorry-load soon, but were not sure how many would be on it. How many did I need? Five hundred. That's a lot of tile. I had a lot of roof to cover and if the tiles were to be going out of manufacture, I wanted to have a few in stock. A roof is supposed to last fifty years but there's always a tile slipping or cracking, and I didn't want to have to stick in those flat square things if I could help it. Well, they would see what they could do. At that moment, Pouzache himself came. I stated my case again. "*D'accord . . . ça ira. . .* you'll get your tiles . . . I'll have them up there in a week . . . I like the round tiles too." Four days later there were five hundred tiles waiting for me at the side of the road. I carried them up to the house seven at a time. They weighed over six pounds each.

The nails I also bought in Largentière, at mother Breysse's *quincaillerie*.

I get to the door of the shop at about four in the afternoon. Closed.

Funny. I retreat a few steps and see mother Breysse sitting quietly at her window, knitting.

"Hello", I shout, "is the shop closed?"

"Why, no", she says, in great surprise.

"Well, the door's locked, and there's no handle on it."

"Oh, she cries, "I must have forgotten. I'm always forgetting that handle", and down she comes, all apologies, a little old woman with silver hair and puckered face. "That handle will be the ruin of me. It's always getting forgotten about..."

When she hears I want nails, she asks me to follow her to the annex across the road. It's a dark poky little hole of a place, and she mumbles something about the electricity being cut. I tell her I need three kilos of 8-cm nails, and twenty single ones of 17. There are packets of nails in niches all along the wall. She gets down on her knees, peering into the darkness, murmuring: "Eighty, eighty, where the devil are those eighty nails... ah... no... ah, maybe... no..." She gets hold of them in the end, and lugs the packet to the counter, on which stands a magnificent pair of antique scales about a yard high, with copper pans. Three kilos? she says. She lays the weights on one scale, and the packet on the other, and begins pulling out nails from the packet. By the time three kilos are left on the scale, there are nails covering all one corner of the table, nails rolling on the floor, all clinking and shining. Then we come to the 17-cm fellows. It takes a long time for her to find these too, but find them she does in the end, like the others, triumphantly, and laying the bag of 8-cm nails back on the scales, sticks the 17-cm ones into a packet, one by one, on the other side, and calculates her price. It comes to about seven francs. I pay, and we come back into the sun again. Mother Breysse tells me if I come back to the shop again and the handle's not on the door, just to give her a shout.

I have nails and tiles. Now for the planks. For these I go to Luth, just outside Largentière, and to the carpenter there. He tells me he has not been in his shop for two months, but has been working on his land. I am a stranger here? Up at Gourgounel? Ah, any mushrooms this year? Seen any game? During the winter he was up there and saw a wild boar and two flights of partridges but had no gun with him, "It's always like that". He notes the measurements for the roof-planks, and I tell him I'd like two or three other planks for a bed. Ah, for a bed? You have a mattress at least? I tell him I'll make a paillasse or get one made. Well, the roof-planks will be ready in about ten days and he'll deliver them by lorry. But maybe I'd like the planks for the bed a bit sooner? He could send them up by the bus, though the busman's a bit *"lunatif"* ("moony" – that's only one of the carpenter's linguistic inventions) and never twice the same, so you never know if he'll do a job or not. I say he can bring the whole lot up at one go, whenever it suits him. Fine. He tells me, as we come out of the shop, that he's growing old, and it's only now he's getting to know the Ardèche. He and a pal of his often go for a trip on Sundays. Last Sunday they were at a little place up behind Loubaresse, which he recommends to me: you can get bread, butter and ham, and as much cheese as you want, and the price is five francs for two! He says he'll be going back. I say I may well take a turn up there myself some time. "It's a real treat", he says, as we shake hands.

A fortnight later, with all the material gathered together, Escudier and Abeillon came up to Gourgounel and we spent three days there putting the roof back into shape.

It is a fine roof, I think it is a very fine roof. Storms can come now, rain can pour in deluges if it likes. I'm ready for it. Ready for anything.

Former Inhabitants

"*C'était un silence affeux: l'image de la mort s'y présentait partout*" (there was a terrible silence, and the image of death was everywhere). This is from *La Belle au bois dormant*, The Sleeping Beauty. Thorns and trees were so thick around the house where the Sleeping Beauty lay, such a great and menacing obscurity encompassed it, before the awakening, that it came to have the reputation of a witches' rendezvous where evil spirits held sabbath, or the home of an ogre. Well, Gourgounel had its witch, who was not an evil spirit certainly, but a peasant-woman who had read the *Petit Albert*. And the place had also its ogre, if a lonely and poor man who, when he was thirsty, just lay down under the duds of his goat and sucked, can be called an ogre.

There are many stories of wizards and witches in these parts. I've heard of a man in La Boule, just on the other side of the valley, who, twenty years ago, could conjure up rats and send them to infest the house of anyone he didn't like. And up behind Gourgounel in the hills is a hollowed-out stone said to have been the eating-bowl of a witch whose chief amusement was to roll down slopes with her long yellow hair flying wildly and emitting sparks. The witch of Gourgounel was well known in the region, and it is said people used to come from as far as Marseilles and even Paris to consult her, and receive her simples. She was, in the patois of this country, a *fachinaïre,* in common parlance, a *guérisseuse,* or healer. I have suggested that the *Petit Albert* was probably her vade-mecum. Now since modern readers may know little or nothing of this famous book, it will be as well here to say something about it.

The *Petit Albert* (there are in fact two books: the *Grand Albert* and the *Petit Albert*, but in the countryside the latter name usually covers both) is a *grimoire*, or gramarye, that is, a book of natural magic or necromancy, *Admirables secrets de magie naturelle*, written down by one Albert Groot, a German of Dutch extraction, in the thirteenth century. He was a monk, and a pioneer in natural science, and rapidly won in those supernatural times the reputation of a sorcerer possessing occult powers. He came to Paris where he was illustrious and where he did a great deal of teaching – indeed the Place Maubert, where he taught, is named after him: the square of Master Albert. His books of secrets may have been in a kind of code, incomprehensible except to a few, which could explain the apparent absurdity of most of their recommendations. Or perhaps, representing, as they do, translations from ancient Arabic, Greek, and Egyptian texts, so many errors have slipped in that they are now more or less senseless. Be that as it may, they were published first in a complete and collected edition in Lyons in the year 1621, and from then on, and up to very recent times, absurd or not, they exercised a very strong influence, perhaps especially in the country districts. As aforesaid, I'm pretty sure it was her possession of the *Petit Albert*, together with what knowledge of herbs she may have acquired, which made the reputation, and, so they say, the little fortune, of the *fachinaïre*. Armed with the *Petit Albert*, she could give advice on practically anything.

If, for example, a man was about to leave his home on a long journey and wished to ensure the fidelity of his wife, he could do so easily by the following method. First, he had to take some hairs off the head of the said wife and chop them up into dust. Then, he had to smear his penis with good honey and sprinkle the hair-dust over it. Thus prepared, he was to make love to his wife, and could rest assured that in his absence sexual activity would disgust her. In order to bring her round again on his return, he was to use his own hair, add a little civet to the honey mentioned above, and proceed in the same manner.

If a man wished a woman to become pregnant and give birth to a boy, he must take the womb and the entrails of a hare, dry them, and reduce them to powder and then mix them with wine. The resultant mixture he must give the woman to drink. The only other condition is that they turn love-making into a more or less full-time business. If by any chance a girl is born, there was something wrong with the hare.

It may be news to some people that Dioscorides in his Tenth Book, Galien in the Tenth Book and Egenetus in the Seventh Book of their treatises, are full of admiration for the medicinal qualities of human excrement. Thus, they affirm that with no other remedy than ordure they can cure sore throats. The method is as follows. You give a young man of good humour and perfect health rabbits and well-baked bread to eat for three days, letting him drink only claret wine. The excrement he produces on the first day can be thrown away as useless, but those of the second and third days must be gathered up and carefully preserved. Mixed with an equal quantity of honey, they can be swallowed down, or else applied externally. As mentioned above, this is a sure-fire cure for quinsy.

While on the subject of excrement, Albert assures us that one of the finest cosmetics for a woman to use is the dung of lizards. There are, however, several other ingredients in the truly finished product. First of all, you take the lizard droppings, then cuttle-bones, then tartar of white wine, then scrapings from the antlers of a stag, then white coral, then rice flour. You pound all these together in equal quantities. Next, you prepare a pot of water distilled from almonds, vineyard slugs and the flowers of the great mullein, and drop your first mixture into it, leaving the whole to steep overnight. After which you pound it again in a mortar. It is now ready for use on face, hands and breasts, and should be preserved in a container of silver or glass.

Improvident people may not know the medicinal value of old shoes. So Albert tells them. Reduced to ash, they are excellent for all bruises and chilblains on the feet. An oil can also be extracted from old shoes which is excellent for tumours.

Talking of old shoes, in my cleaning of the house, I came across an ancient pair of wooden clogs which may well have belonged to the *fachinaïre*. There was a rose and a cross cut out on each toe as decoration. At first I laid them outside the door of the house, then, after a couple of days, I bunged them in the big hole with the rest of the stuff. I hope the *fachinaïre* went with them. She is reported to have said that she would never leave the house until she had transmitted her gift to another person.

The next man I want to speak about, my predecessor, was certainly smitten with something.

Camossetto was from Marseilles. His parents had owned a dry-saltery there, and were quite well off. When they died, they left him no money, but a big house. He himself was a draper to his trade, but when the war broke out in '39, he was sent to work as a mechanic on an aerodrome. The war and the work, however, got on his nerves, and he fell ill. Exempted from service, he was advised by a doctor to go and live in the country. This advice he decided to put into effect, and set about selling the big house he owned. But Camossetto was naïve, perhaps a little simple, perhaps just a little absent-minded. Anyway, the house was swindled out of his possession without his having got a penny for it. With what little money he still had, he moved up country through Provence, and arrived one day in 1941 or so in Largentière. There he heard of a house for sale – it was Gourgounel – and for a nominal rent, because his case excited pity, he was allowed to occupy it until a real sale was effected. He occupied the house for seventeen years, his main concern being how to get hold of enough cash to buy it.

One of his most brilliant ideas for acquiring wealth was to marry a rich wife. So he advertised in the papers, saying he was a big strong handsome man with a prosperous farm in the Ardèche, and wished to marry a serious woman who would be willing to share his life ... and the expenses of the farm. His advertisement provoked a response from as far away as the Belgian Congo, where, as my informant, old Calixte Habauzit, told me, "all the women have jewels and cars". Camossetto and the Congo woman exchanged letters and photographs, and increased in intimacy, until one day the woman actually arrived at Valgorge, not in a car, but off the bus. There, she inquired after Camossetto, and was met with raucous laughter. Camossetto, the people said, he's a big fool who lives at Gourgounel, and they told her stories of the man, for he was already well known in the district for his appearance and his ways. The result was, the woman stayed overnight at the hotel in Valgorge and left again the following morning, presumably for the Belgian Congo, without ever having seen Camossetto, and without ever writing to him again. He never understood: no one ever told him the woman had been there. The people at Valgorge chuckled in secret.

Swindled out of his rich Congo woman, Camossetto – *"moi, Alexandre Camossetto"* – remained poor. For bread, he collected whins and split wood for the baker at La Boule. And if at any time there was an old decrepit goat for sale (usually to the slaughterhouse for melting down), Camossetto would buy it for food. He also had a little garden, and managed to eke out a living. Indeed, with time, he did fairly well. First, he was not averse to begging around the doors, and thereby amassed a great deal of stuff: old coats, old shoes, old furniture, which he would sell *sub rosa* for a few francs to people who didn't want to beg, but who had a use for the coats, the shoes, and the sticks of furniture. This went on for only so long, till the donors got wise to him. But meanwhile he had found something else. In Marseilles he had been connected with an Adventist religious group and, having written to the headquarters of this sect in the United States of America, he found himself showered with supplies of canned foods, which explains the great quantity of containers I had to clear out of the house. He probably ended up the best-fed man in the whole canton of Valgorge. But it was money he wanted. He had visions of wealth and power. He finally took to magic to get it. Perhaps he had become a little nutty. One of my neighbours had this to say of him: *"L'araignée dans sa tête a dû avoir une patte détraquée"* (the spider in his head must have had a gammy leg). It was when I sorted out his books and papers (careful copies and first drafts of letters he had sent) that I was able to augment these scraps of information concerning him which I had gathered from people here and there.

The books ran from cheap booklets on *Le Secret de la réussite*, to pseudo-scientific texts on occultism (*Cours oriental*, by Professor Rimpotché Tawagompa), to more or less serious books on hypnotism and magnetism: *Les Forces supérieures, Les Guérisons miraculeuses, Les Puissances surnaturelles, Transmission de la pensée, Les Secours spirituels, Voici la lumière, Au seuil de l'initiation.* The original impulse, as became clearer still from the letters, was the desire for money. But this, allied to his obviously extreme credulity, led him up all the paths of spiritualism, and made him easy meat for any self-styled sage or spiritual adviser.

We find him, for example, writing to the Fakir Birman, asking for his three-monthly Astrological Calendar, so he will know his lucky days. The Fakir – "*Dans l'ennui, venez à lui*" (when in trouble, come to him) is the motto – writes him back. In a letter dated "*Heure sidérale 8*", he gives Camossetto "the astrological position that presides over your existence" (Mercury, in conjunction with the Virgin), ending up by declaring that he, Birman the Fakir, knows all the secrets of the rites of the sages of Ancient India, "whose representative I am in Europe", and suggesting that he, Camossetto, procure a special "fluidic talisman" devised by the Fakir, which will guide him through life, and which will cost him ten francs.

Another letter to the Fakir Birman, who this time appears as the founder of the Indopsychic Foundation and "the guide of the elite of Parisian society", asks whether he should take up commerce or bee-keeping and whether he should get married. Yet another asks for tips concerning the National Lottery.

From the Fakir Birman we move to Professor Balydson of *Les Cendres sacrées de l'Orient* (The Sacred Ashes of the Orient), with whom Camossetto is negotiating about a Chinese talisman with radioactive power. For this talisman to become Camossetto's own most prized and sacred possession, Balydson needs a lock of his hair and twenty-five francs. Later, in a letter from the Professor delivering the goods, Camossetto is warned that "the results may not be immediate", and advised never to become discouraged.

We next find our friend trying the "Institut Tahra Bey". Specialized in the Occult and Psychic Sciences of the East, this institution offered graphological and psychometric studies to its adepts. Tahra Bey finally sends a talisman with the following recommendations: "Wrap it in a white cloth about ten o'clock on the evening of October 15th, and stitch the cloth with black thread. The medium will then be in contact with you." It is easy to imagine Camossetto up there at Gourgounel, in that room piled up with tin cans, under the smoking oil-lamp, waiting for the medium . . . and then going to bed on that lousy mattress, another twenty francs down the drain.

In a series of letters to Tahra Bey, Camossetto tells his life story: how he had worked as draper in the Paris-Mode shop at Marseilles and had fallen in love with the girl in the glove department but hadn't been able to score. She left the shop, but liked to walk in the Jardin Zoologique, so every Wednesday, Camossetto went to the Zoo to read the newspapers, hoping to meet her. But he was too shy, or maybe the occult forces were not in his favour. He found his morale getting lower than ever. He then approached marriage bureaux to try and find a wife, incurred "enormous expenses", but no wife ever turned up. Then he got a job in films as a stand-in, but his big feet got in the way of one of the star actresses, so they gave him the heave-ho. Next the war broke out. He worked for a while on the aerodrome, and then came up to into the hills, where he lived with "my goat and one hen, the only livestock I possess – with a cat."

In February 1950 he terminated with this pathetic paragraph: "I am sorry to have written you so much but I am all alone in this abandoned farm and life is sometimes very sad especially at this season, and yet there are days when I am glad to be alone, isolated, in a way like the Initiate . . ."

They say he died of pneumonia because he claimed he could live without fires in winter.

Madame Teston's Testimony

"Ah, in our regions life is very hard." And Madame Teston unrolls her rigmarole of woe.

I had heard of her before: how she set up Private Property notices all over her fields; how she prevented road-builders taking "her" stones and "her" sand from the river; how she flew into rages of passion – she is a small, stringy woman – whenever it was suggested that a roadway pass through her meadows to allow access to and exit from the homesteads on the hills.

Hers is the biggest farm in the district. It has remained the same size for generations, but she and her husband, along with her son, can no longer work it. To hire labour is too expensive, and her son is often ill. She says he is *chétif*. He is tall and looks powerfully built, but his shoulders are hunched and there is a twist to his lips. He gets bad headaches and suffers from colic. This is what prevented him going away like the young men of the other farms, who now have a "place" in the post office, or the *gendarmerie*, or a factory, and get a monthly wage and just wait for a pension. Ah, the happiest today is the worker, who has nothing. He is supported by the State. While the owners are being throttled out of existence.

It was different before. Now you have to spend precious hours guarding the animals when they're out to graze, because of the roads, whereas, in the days of her "poor father-in-law", he could let the goats and pigs fend for themselves. The land stretched intact all round the house. The animals stayed out as long as they wanted, and returned on their own. But now, while the men are in the fields, she's out with the beasts. The result is, she gets behind in her repairing and washing: the work piles up. It's only in the winter, when it's the men who go out to guard, that she gets her darning done, and the other countless chores. She would pay someone to do the housework, but it's dear, and then where would you find anybody? These regions are deserted now, the young people go away, and they're right.

It's finished here, finished. She'd never advise anyone to come there to farm. You work your guts out and what is there after it? There are no neighbours. Go up to Valgorge, four kilometres away, for a game of cards? You'd rather go to bed. Their only amusement is the radio. The two men there work like slaves, but they can't do everything. All the hay can't be brought in, and chestnuts rot every year. And there's the weather. They had looked forward to about eight hundred francs off their cherry trees, but all the rain this year had caused the fruit to split, "my poor son was in a rage when he saw that." You lose all that, but there are still the taxes to pay, and the insurance.

There's only one resource, to make things easier, the seasonal work in the Vaucluse: the strawberries and the tomatoes, and then later on the grapes. But her husband is too old for that now, and her poor son is ill. That's all there is to get out of the bit, that, and a good herd of animals. Maybe fruit. Her poor son is going to try raspberries next year. Raspberries are beginning to take on here.

But fruit, ha, that depends on the weather. And you can't trust it. Look at this summer, all storms. All those thunder-claps aren't normal. And last year, no water. And even the seasonal work, there was more opportunity for it in the past. The good days are over here. In the old days, "in the time of my poor father", the men used to go harvesting up in the mountains, on the plateau. But now they have machines for that. Or else they would trek down by Montpellier and Sète, to the salt-flats, where they'd work and earn a penny. Her poor uncle lost a leg there. But there too the machines have taken over. You can rest in your hole and rot, that's all.

You must have a steady job with a wage somewhere. That's the only hope. Her poor son is ill, he has headaches, but he may go away yet, and she hopes he will, he has no life here. Her younger daughter worked for a while at the nylon factory down in Largentière. It wasn't well paid, but she lived at the hostel there during the winter and would come home at the week-ends for provisions, "a pot of soup, a hen, some potatoes", so that she was able to put something by. She had a bed there and a stove to cook on. And the wages would have got better. But the silly bitch, the pumpkin, "*la courge*", has gone and got engaged to a peasant up at La Boule, where she'll be with him and his parents on a bit of farm, and a pretty mess it may turn out. She's going to marry her on Saturday. She supposes everybody should be happy at a wedding, but she's looking to the future and she doesn't see much happiness.

It's true that the factory doesn't please everybody. Some girls work only a week, or two or three months. And whenever the seasonal work begins they abandon the factory for the fields, because they prefer the open air. The factory gives them insurance during the winter. But from May on it runs with only half its hands. They say the mines in Largentière are not paying much. The best is the worker in the city. He has nothing to worry about. He gets his wage every month, and insurance, and allowances for his children, and will get the pension. It's better to have nothing and be nothing. That's the way to be happy. It's the State nowadays. There's no use owning anything, it only strangles you, you never get out of the bit. It's finished here. The country is too hard, you can't work it with machines. How do you expect to work a machine on these slopes? Her eldest daughter is down on a farm in the Rhône valley, and is pretty well off. But here it's no use. You kill yourself to have enough to eat. And that just allows you to go on killing yourself. It's not like that in the town. Independence is finished anyway, it's better to be easy and have a safe wage. What use is independence if it only lets you kill yourself with work and die of boredom?

Letter to Those who Live in Cities

"They ask me why I live in the blue mountains. I smile without answering", says Li Po. Well, let me try to give some kind of answer.

I've come to this place to undertake a certain type of work. The idea is to set a whole mass of matter – knowledge, imaginings, feelings, all the accumulations of the past ten years or so – to the process of fire, and see what comes out of it. Maybe nothing more than one of those little "sparks" Meister Eckhart speaks of, but that will at least be *something*.

The sixteenth century German alchemist, Kunrath, puts it this way: "Study, meditate, sweat and work, and a healthful flood will come to you from the great world, waters that for us are the true and natural water-of-life".

Another approach would be from the East.

I've just come across this in an old Chinese text: "This chapter will take readers right into the heart of Ts'ao Ch'i, a district through which the Ts'ao stream still winds its course and where in the year 502 an Indian master built Pao Lin (Precious Wood) Monastery, foretelling that some one hundred and seventy years later a flesh-and-blood bodhisattva would come there to turn the wheel of the Dharma."

I'll be "turning the wheel" in my own way. Don't ask me for a definition of the Dharma. Stcherbatsky wrote a whole book on the subject and he was no farther forward at the end than at the beginning. Besides, there's a sutra that says:

> *If someone asks you*
> *to tell them about the Dharma*
> *start off by saying*
> *oh, I haven't gone into it very deeply.*

As like as not, I'll wind up by writing a book about all this myself. But it'll be a very little book, the abrupt kind of little book I like, with nothing heavy in it, the topogaphy full of accident, strewn with rocks and erratic growths, occasional pools and running streams.

I'd like it to be said of this book what Chen says of his book of Vajrayana meditations: "People have described it as a very fragrant work since at the time of reading it they noticed a sweet smell in the room."

Old Fireside Tales Retold

The land around the house has been left alone for about two decades, except for the patches where neighbours have won hay. Same with the wood, except where the neighbours again have cleared a space around the chestnut trees which give the best fruit. On the meadows, whins and thorns have taken over, sweeping across the terraces, curling round the mulberry trees, shooting lithe roots into the walls. I have nothing against whins and thorns, but there was an overpopulation problem which had to be seen to. For the past few mornings I've been out there with mattock, shears and rake to clear the place.

Thinking about old local tales . . .

There were great juicy-green eglantines with glistening red thorns. They say the devil tried to use the eglantine as a ladder to climb back into heaven, whence St Michael had booted him. It shoots up with a demonic force, bearing its bobs of fire, turning from juice-green to jade-green, making straight for heaven, and the devil is dancing about its root, his old bat-wings fluttering fit to rip. The angels see the eglantine moving up, and up, and up, and up, and they know the devil's in it, for a thorn never got so near heaven before. They run to Michael who runs to God, who shoves a cloud away from his window, and looks out. Uh, huh, mmm, ah . . . He breathes gently at the mounting thorns, and the tops wilt, incline, as though in salute or submission, and start growing downwards again. Satan sees this, and starts blowing with all his might from below, but it's no use, all he achieves is to put a vicious twist on the thorns. That's why eglantines are the way they are.

Take the whins, now. The whole region is overrun with them. So much so they are a family name here. The Latin name for whin is *genista*. Travel a while round the Ardèche and tell me how many Ginestes you meet up with. I'm not saying that all the people called Gineste have the character of whins, at least I don't think this is the case. But what is the character of the whin anyway?

Here is the story:

Mary was fleeing from Herod with Jesus in her arms. No man

comes to her aid, but the plants are ready to help. They hide her from the eyes of the soldiers and muffle the sound of her steps. But not the whin. It refuses to be silent. "If I want to crackle, I'll damn well crackle", says the whin. Well, Mary got away as was to be expected, and there was joy in the kingdom of the grass, but the old whin kept crackling away all by himself. That's why the whins were used as horses by the witches.

Whins and eglantines, all in all it was a hellish business rooting them out. Now I'm taking a rest in the clearing, thinking up more stories. I've got a headful of them. There's that clump of heather over there, dark purple, the hills here are covered with it. What about the heather? There's a story I have in my repertoire culled from various recondite sources about heather beer.

There was this Irish elf once who hurt his wing on a coarse winter night and was taken in by peasants. He stayed with them, all through the winter, and the peasants were none the worse for it, good luck being in the house. The elf even ate at their table, and that's where his tongue tasted beer for the first time. He became so human and corrupted, the poor little fellow, that he forgot the taste of dew and developed a craving for this other potion, though human food didn't go down with him very well. When he finally took his leave of the peasants, he was glad to get back to eating berries and nuts, but he still had a hankering for beer. He raved about beer among the other elves, until they were almost as bad as himself: "Give us the recipe for this stuff", they said, "we can make elixir, we'll manage this too." But the beery elf didn't know the recipe. He remembered, however, hearing the word "Denmark" in connection with it. Denmark! So off went the horde of Irish elves to Hamlet's kingdom, to consult their Danish counterparts. For a week they did nothing but visit breweries. They saw the grain fermenting and the addition of the hops, and they saw the brown liquid and the froth. Then they went back to Ireland, and they began to search for the ingredients. They were pretty silly elves after all, for, as far as the story goes, one of them, landing in a clump of heather in bloom, thought the globes of heather were like the hops he had seen in Denmark, even finer, for pink seemed to him much better than common red or yellow. Eureka! he shouted, which in elf language means: "Come on guys, this is it!" And they all came rushing to harvest the heather. This they brought to a marsh to be soaked. "And the green things", cried a wee elf with a squint in the eye, "the green things to give the bitter taste?" "Here they are", cried the rest, pulling out the green shoots of heather. They tossed the lot into the marsh, and sat around it on their hunkers waiting for the beer to froth. When the evening mists began to stream off the marsh, they could wait no longer and ladled into the water. The elf king tasted it.

Very fine. Everybody tasted it. Very, very, very fine. Only the little old elf who had been with the peasants sat dolefully sipping in a corner, murmuring to himself: "That is not it, no, that is not it at all." But nobody listened to him. And ever since the elves of Ireland have been drinking heather beer. Many a night, if you listen intently, you'll hear them singing away in chorus. No need to tell the words they sing, the curious can find that out for themselves.

The sun's high up the sky now, and I'm grateful for the shade of this apple tree to rest in. I won't tell the story of the apple tree, anyone can do that, I'll tell about ... ouch! ... that thistle I've just put my hand on.

There's no use telling the story of the thistle, without first telling the story of oats. Everybody knows that when Eve and Adam took the apple, men were condemned to earn their bread by the sweat of their brow. That meant the creation of cereals by God Almighty, for in Eden, cereals there were none, not even cornflakes – Adam and Eve lived on figs and pomegranates and almonds. Well, God invented cereals, that is to say: wheat, rye, barley, and gave them to man. "Sweat", he said, "and make bread to eat." Sweat they did, but at least they had something to eat: bread, good whole bread.

The upshot was that the devil grew jealous. He also wanted bread, he wanted a cereal. Men, the damned sinners, had it. Why not him? After all, as a devil, he was only doing his job. God thought it over. "Maybe work will do you good", he said, "I'll give you a cereal to sow and harvest." And he gave the devil oats to be his own, but on one condition, that he never forget the name. O.A.T.S., oats, he must never forget the name. The devil was delighted, and hirpled away over the fields, crying: "Oats, oats, oats", in case he should forget the word ...

A long time passed. Then came the moment for one of God's periodical visits to earth, just to see how things were going. So down he came from heaven on a horse of cloud which, naturally, became a real horse when he landed, and set off with St Peter. They rode for hours and hours, till the horses became tired and hungry. "Our nags could do with a peck of oats", said Peter. "You're right there, Pete", said God, "but, dang my hide, I done give oats to the devil, remember?" "Wasn't there a condition to the lease?" said Peter, very business-like. "Sure was", said God, "but that old devil will never fail to meet it. Why, he keeps on singing 'oats-oats-oats', all day long. He won't ever forget that name." "We'll see about that", said St Peter, who was a pretty smart cookie for a saint.

At that moment, as was to be expected, the devil came along at a jog and hollering at the top of his voice: "Oats! Oats! Oats!" St Peter hid behind a rock, and when the devil passed, jumped out and shouted: "Woo! ... Grrr!" The devil nearly jumped out of his skin. When he saw who it was, old Pete from heaven, he was furious: "That's a hell of a trick to play on a poor devil", he cried. "Who do you think you are? Me?" And he continued to call St Peter for all the names in Christendom, until ... When he was out of breath, Peter sidled up with a grin on his face and whispered: "What's its name, eh, the name of your cereal?" The devil went white as a sheet. He stammered, and scratched his head, and mumbled, and stamped his foot, and looked up at the sky, and then grunted:

"I've forgot."

"I know it", said Peter.

"What is it? Please tell me."

"No fear."

"Go on."

"Nope."

"I dare you."

"Well ..."

"I dare you!"

"It's ... thistle."

I told you Peter was a wily bird. "Thistle!" shouted the devil: "Thistle, thistle, thistle! I've got the name again: thistle!" And he rushed away dancing over the fields, his tail doing sixty to the dozen.

Peter tipped God a wink, and quietly led the two horses to the side of the road where oats were bending in the breeze. The horses ate their fill, and God and Peter went majestically on their way.

Meanwhile the devil was planting thistles. And he's been planting thistles ever since.

That's my story.

But it's midday now, and the grasshoppers are going crazy. It's too hot here. I'm going into the house. Marc gave me a little goat's cheese yesterday, called a *picadou,* and I'm going to eat it with some bread. I'll come back out here in the evening.

Underworld Acquaintances

Today, second August and, on a third day of rain, I met the queerest lizard I have ever seen. I had gone out for a stroll between two thunderplumps, and there it was on the grass, beside a clump of fern. It was about four inches long, black, jet black, with yellow blotches from head to tail and on its toes. It was fat and slow and sluggish, not like the other lizards I know: the little fellers, brown, silver and green that skim over the walls of the house on the hot days, and their bigger cousins like that big blue-and-green devil I've seen once or twice. Maybe its slowness was due to the weather, I do not know, but when I touched it to see its movement, expecting to see it travel like lightning, it just waggled its trunk and then began plodding. It plodded its way into the clump of fern.

I discovered later that "lizard" was a salamander.

That was a big black beetle on a yellow stalk of grass: Mr Scarabee, at home. His legs were metal-blue, with the little crotchets of the feet light-brown. In the interstices of the head and neck and body, you could see the varnish red of the flesh. He had two pairs of antennae, the upper two, the long ones, like twisted and waxed thread, waving slowly, the short secondary ones trembling all the time.

I had been hacking and howking away at a big thorn bush, and there on the remains of a bright red stalk glinting with thorns was a snail, slimy pale flesh in a pink-and-canary yellow shell. I watched it ooze its way up the stalk, negotiating the thorns. When it came to the top, from the other side of the stalk, it loomed up, its long peelie-wallie neck with two horns slowly prodding the air. I had been examining tiny creatures like ants and ladybirds for so long this body seemed huge to me. I watched it swing from one stalk to another, a tricky business. It stretches out its neck, farther ... then ... farther ... till it touches the stalk in view. The body ripples and the hump of the shell moves along it. You can see all the strength of the body concentrated under the shell, a muscular yellow mass, while the tail now is no more than the palest of glistening mucus. Then, the shell settled, the tail lets go, always in slow motion, and our snail is ready to take the new road.

The frog hides the winter away in mud and comes out in the spring. As such it is a symbol of continued life, and I believe that in the Coptic Church the paschal lamps are in the form of frogs. I seem to remember also seeing in some museum terracotta figures of pregnant women that looked like frogs. I met this one at six this morning, when I was out cutting whins. She was brown and white, thrush-coloured, with eyes maroon-red and black-pupilled, and her throat pulsing, pulsing all the time. She was like a living stone.

There are no vipers here, I am glad to say, but there are grass-snakes in the stone rubble around the house, and down in the river. I was going down the path this morning about eleven o'clock when I heard a hissing and there was a fellow about a yard long scuttling away into a thicket of thorn. The other day at the hay-making, Escudier got one wrapped round his leg. It was more scared than he was, though he found it hard to keep calm. He had only his hayfork with him, which, made of light wood, he might break in trying to strike. He stood still for a while and the beast slithered off, hissing furiously. There are vipers farther up the mountain. They say the magician at La Boule, a few years back, had a formula for enticing them down if he wanted to annoy somebody.

Neighbours

The inhabitants of Valgorge, which locality figures on my postal address (*Gourgounel – par Valgorge*), are nicknamed in patois *courto-fusto*, which is to say: short-beam. And the reason for this appellation is, so I've heard, that some years ago the people up there cut a beam, a *fusto* in dialect, for a construction, but, when they measured it from one end, they found it was too short. Being methodical people, however, they proceeded immediately to measure it from the other end, but it was still too short. There is a saying in the district: *"C'est comme la fuste de Valgorge, elle est trop courte des deux bouts"* (it's like the Valgorge beam, too short from both ends).

So far as administration goes, however, Gourgounel, and the hamlet Les Praduches (little meadows) of which it is a part, comes under the *commune de Beaumont,* Beaumont itself being a little stony village up in the hills, where the mayor is a carpenter. Now the people of the commune of Beaumont, to which I now belong, have also a nickname: *pendjo-chabro,* strangled goats. Apparently, for several years at the beginning of this century, up there in Beaumont, there was an epidemic of suicides by hanging, exactly in the fashion of goats, who often succeed in strangling themselves on their tether. I am then a *pendjo-chabro*, and I have *pendjo-chabros* all around me.

Madame Tauleigne is a Gibraltar of flesh, and has not moved from her house in twenty years. Immensely fat and rheumatic, she uses an old brush for a crutch, and lumbers from bed to bench making wry remarks while her husband, a rake of a man, works away at his fields, his sheep and his cooking. *"To, bon Dieu"* is Madame Tauleigne's favourite phrase, followed by an expression of sudden pain which twists her round, brown face and a *"Mon Dieu, je vous l'offre"* (My God, you can have it), the "it" referring, I presume, to her life. It was Madame Tauleigne who told me that the spider in Camossetto's head must have had a gammy leg. She also comes away with phrases like this to describe a village on the abrupt slope of a mountain: *"Quand un chien aboie il faut qu'il se cale entre deux pierres"* (when a dog barks, he has to wedge himself between two stones). Or again, of an old disused and overgrown path up behind Gourgounel: "*Il faut qu'un lézard s'aplatisse pour y passer*" (a lizard has to flatten himself to get by). She was very glad to see me, for she hoped I would be able to photograph her. She had heard of a healer in Lyons who just needed to look at your photo to tell what was wrong with you and send you a cure. When I told her I had no camera, she said it was just as well, the man would have thought she was a pig. The word she used for pig was *habillé de soie*, a silk-wearer.

Speaking of old Paudevigne, Madame Tauleigne told me: "He thinks he's eternal." Paudevigne is about ninety years old, and came back to his farm only five years ago, tired of living in an old folks' home in Carpentras. I had come across him one Sunday morning, quite suddenly, a thin and ancient white-powed man lying under the chestnut trees reading the newspaper. He had told me to come and pick cherries at his place if I wanted, and I had gone with him. That night I shared his supper of cherries and bread broken into a plate of salty water. And the following day I was working with him in his garden, turning over earth with mattocks. He wants to grow a lot of fruit and vegetables in that garden; poultry also he intends to raise, and has already set up a big pen, from which the fox stole twenty chicks in the first week, but which he has now reinforced. All his produce he plans to take to market, but for that he needs a road, and from the Valgorge road to all these farms, there's nothing but little paths. When he lived here thirty years ago, he had negotiated for a road with the authorities, but it had never come. Now he's back, he's renewed his agitation, but everybody thinks he's just a mad old man, and still the road does not come. Old Paudevigne took down a rusty tin from one of his shelves and showed me all the *papiers timbrés* (papers with official stamps, awesome to the peasants) which he had sent and had sent to him concerning the road. He is determined to see it realized. But he's getting old, he says, and tells me any time I'm passing by his place to come in and make sure he's not dead. Not that he's intending to die soon, not he. Of course, he feels tired and sick now and then, but he doesn't let it worry him: "You just try to get a hold of yourself, and that helps a lot. Some people get worked up. I just go to my garden and let it pass."

About the time when I was working in Paudevigne's garden, Marc Abeillon came to take in the hay from the little *faïsses* of Gourgounel, and with him came Virgilou Escudier to help him in the scything. It had not rained much in May. "It's the month of May that makes the grass grow here", said Marc, so the cutting was poor. When the hay is poor in these regions, they say that the winter will not be hard, but if it is plentiful, you must make sure you lose none, for the winter will be long. Hence the proverb which Virgilou quoted to me:

"*Quand il y a peu de foin, ramassez avec la fourche; quand il y en a plein, ramassez avec le rateau*" (When there's little hay, take it with the fork; when there's a lot, gather it with the rake). The two cut the grass, and left it to dry in the sun. But the difficulty was there, for long and heavy storms were soon to break out, and the hay was soaked time and time again till in places it was rotten and useless. Up at Gourgounel, during one of the few moments of sun, Abeillon came with his wife and daughter and Escudier's little daughter, and a big sheet made by sewing six sacks together, called the *linçao*, in which they carried the grass, and laid it away in the grange with red salt sprinkled through it to preserve it. If only we could have more north wind (*lou soulédré*), said Marc. "*Le vent du nord, ah pétard, c'est ce qu'il nous faut ici. Quand ça souffle du nord, vaï, il ne pleut pas*" (The north wind, godammit, I tell you, that's what we need here. When the wind comes out of the north, you can be sure you won't get rain). But even when it did blow in those days, as it did along with all the other winds of the Tanargue: *l'aouro* (the north-west), *lou ven* (the south-east), *lou ven blon* (the south), *lo troverso* (the south-west), *lo biso* (the west), *l'onguiola* (the east), it was never for long: "*Le vent du nord, que ça soufflait, il n'a pas duré longtemps, ah pétard!*" (The north wind was blowing there, godammit, but it didn't near last long enough).

It was agreed between Marc and me that in return for the hay and the right to harvest chestnuts from the Gourgounel woods, he would supply me with fruits and vegetables. So about once every week in the next few months, I'd be round at his farm, and we'd dig out something or pick something off a tree, and I'd go back to Gourgounel with a sack over my shoulder and in my hand maybe one of Madame Abeillon's cheeses on a plate, covered with vine leaves.

I got cheeses from Madame Ribeyre too, for which I paid forty centimes, and once when I was down at her place there was a big earthenware jar on the table, filled up with the dark slabs of honey her son had just drawn from the hives. She pulled out a couple of slabs and set them on a plate with a goat's cheese for me to eat, which I did, with relish.

Virgilou also had hives, and his honey was every bit as good as Madame Ribeyre's, rich with heather and whin. When I went to visit his home for the first time, approaching it, I heard a little girl, his daughter, singing this local refrain about the expressive capacities of a certain Madame Lacrasso's arse:

> *Uno, medouno, metreno, m'éclaù*
> *tolo, bardolo, gengivo, fournaù*
> *taïro,*

rouveïro,
francasso, petasso,
lou quioul de Madame Lacrasso

The dogs had already announced my arrival to Virgilou's wife and she was out on the porch to welcome me, and bring me into the kitchen, where Virgilou had been having a snooze at the table. The shutters were closed, and now they were opened a little. The fire was blazing with a fine perfume of wood and whin and the evening meal was simmering upon it. Virgilou, a small well-built man with a twisted smile and beautiful eyes, got up to shake my hand, and asked his wife to go fill a bottle of wine from the cellar and bring some glasses. When the wine was brought, he said: "*Faï bé faré vivara lou moulis*" (you've got to keep the millwheel turning), and poured me a full, dark glass. While we drank, the little daughter was sent to bring in the goats, three goats, whose milk provides five cheeses a day, the majority of which are preserved as winter supplies, the soft, white *tommes* having dried and hardened and tightened into sharp-tasting little *picodons*. I could hear the little girl calling: '*Volé, volé!* – come, come!" to the goats. She has a brother who at the moment is down in Carpentras, working at the tomato and melon harvest. This brings the family in a little money. Virgilou himself makes a little from the chestnuts, being able to get twenty centimes a kilo for them now, which is good compared with five centimes a few years back. No one wants his wine, he's even been told to pull up his vines, but he says he'll wait till "they" come. Sometimes he does a stint on the road-gang, but he hates having someone supervising his work. Sometimes he works as a wood-cutter, and he is the regular butcher of the district, though this is work he abhors. When the time of the *tuailles*, the "killing", comes, it is he who slits the throats of the pigs and bleeds them, before handing the carcasses over to the wives who make the ham, the sausages and all the great variety of *charcuterie* they know. These hams and sausages are stored away in the cellar or hung on the rafters of the house.

I like sitting there with Virgilou, and when Raymonde comes back with the goats and they have been milked and Madame Escudier pours the milk into a jug so it looks like a big snowy mushroom, and Raymonde says: "*Eï fouan* – I'm hungry", and she is given a cup of milk and a hunk of bread and honey, that also I like. And when later at night I climb back up the hill to Gourgounel with soup and bread in my stomach and a moon riding in the sky, I am so full of liking I talk to the moon and wink to it before lying down under the mulberry tree to sleep.

In the morning I'm usually wakened by Habauzit and his goats, their bells ringing as they scatter up through the wood, the dog (*lou tchi*) keeping an eye on them. Habauzit, well over seventy now, plods up after them, a stick in his hand, a bag slung over his back containing bread and wine and maybe a bit of sausage or cheese, and which on his return will be full of mushrooms. The goats must be taken out to feed before it is too hot, and old Habauzit spends about nine hours a day with them. While in the woods, he maybe whittles away at prongs for his hay-forks, using chestnut-wood because it's handiest, though it is not so hardwearing as ash or acacia. He has a lot of time for thinking and the results of his reflections are such as this: "*Les années se suivent et ne se ressemblent pas*" (the years follow each other and are never alike). It seems to me he must have borrowed that one. More like himself is this thought: "*Les années poussent trop vite*" (The years grow too fast). He could not understand at first how I, who "might have gone anywhere in the world", should have come to Gourgounel and be happy there, but finally he reached this psychological conclusion, accompanied by a shrug of the shoulders: "*Si on est heureux et qu'on se croie malheureux, on est malheureux; si on est malheureux et qu'on se croie heureux, on est heureux*" (If you're happy and think yourself unhappy, you're unhappy; if you're unhappy and think yourself happy, you're happy).

That may not be the last word on happiness (defined in Gourgounelian as "complete existential time-space"), but it'll do for the moment.

The Mysteries of the Mushroom

I was out in the wood at six, and had just started stalking, when I heard the snap of a twig. I crouched down behind a whin-bush, and saw ... Escudier with his sack on his back, slow-stepping, his eyes glued to the ground.

My first impulse is one of rage: damn the man! and I pick up a stone to give him a little fright, the bloody poacher, picking the sweet fruit off my land. But this proprietorial reaction goes out like a light, I let the stone slip from my fingers, and settle down to watch Escudier at work. He's like a cat on its hind legs, with a squashed blue cap on its head and a bit of a fag between its lips. There he pounces! In the bag, and it's a good bagful already. I watch him reach his tenth, then I make my way quietly back to the house. If I want to beat Virgilou, I'll have to be up earlier.

There are fellows here in the season who do not sleep at all. In the daylight they wander about with fingers twitching and nostrils sniffing. At nightfall, you'll see them slink into the woods, and in the mornings emerge with a sly smile on their face and a bulge on their back. If you ask them, they have never heard of mushrooms, wouldn't recognize one. They say it's just that the air of the woods is good for their ... eh ... bronchitis.

The next morning I was up at half past four. It's a strange delight to be prowling about in the twilight of the wood at that hour, knowing there are mushrooms that have just sprouted up through the soil all around you, their moulded, velvety tops and their fat, solid stems. At that hour in the morning, the wood is full of rich, earthy, musky smells, perfumes, spices, and when the first ray of sunlight appears rippling over the chestnut leaves, lighting the dew, you feel an ecstasy running through all your being.

There is something really *tremendum et fascinosum* about mushrooms. When you come across one, in the great rustling silence of the wood, brown and secret, it seems to have a halo, seems to vibrate with a mysterious life.

The prize of my hunts was a mushroom which no creature on earth would ever think of eating, except his lordship the slug. It was a *cèpe*, no doubt about that, its origin was recognizable. But what a *cèpe*! It must have been a thousand hours old.

It was huge. The fingers of my right hand could not reach round its stem: it was fourteen inches in circumference. The height of the stem was ten inches, and the diameter of the crown also ten. But what was truly amazing was the colour. If I say that the stem was of red ink, vinegar and blood, that the under part of the crown was of the darkest orange, that the upper crown was pale yellow, pale green with streaks of red, does that convey an idea of the thing?

You have a great brainish, livery mass before you, with two or three brown slugs slowy wending their way through their paradise. You have the massive carbuncular stem, with dead chestnut husks stuck in it. This stem tapers towards the crown which is rutted and weevilled and pitted. It looks like a moon of flesh. A putrid planet.

If I'd had some formaldehyde and a big enough bottle, I would have preserved this marvel.

Walt Whitman once said that with a red tomato in his hand he could walk through the world and confound all the philosophers. How much more so with that monster mushroom!

Here I am speaking of the *cèpe*, but I wish to record that when, later on, one morning in August, the twenty-fourth to be exact, I found my first *oronge*, I was beside myself. There it was at the foot of a chestnut tree, opened out from its vulva, impeccable, with a delicate luminous orange reflection: total earth grace.

Mathieu's Pears

The village of Sarrabasche consists of three hamlets: Le Mas, Sourirou and Paytou, all of which cling to the face of the hill like limpets and look out on hills upon hills.

I was bound for Paytou, which is as much as to say: the little place. More particularly I was making for the house of Mathieu, who, as I had been told by Madame Abeillon, had a meadow full of pear trees that were choc-a-bloc with yellow fruit. Monsieur Mathieu is Madame Abeillon's cousin, and Madame Abeillon had told Monsieur Mathieu about the stranger at Gourgounel who ate so much fruit, and Monsieur Mathieu had said: let him come, then, and welcome, my trees have about four hundred pounds on them, and the fruits are falling like raindrops.

So I went. And I was expected.

When I came upon the hamlet of four houses at about nine in the morning and stood on a wall to shout down to a woman I saw and ask for the *Maison Mathieu*, she looked up smiling and said: "*C'est ici, Monsieur*", and waited while I clambered down the wall and up the lane.

The terrace of the house had piles of pink potatoes in the corners, a vine growing over it and tin cans full of flowers on the ledge. The woman asked me in. There were jars of preserved vegetables on the mantelpiece of the living-room and three big framed certificates on the walls. One, decorated with views of the Lac d'Issarlès and other curiosities of the Ardèche, was the Certificate of Primary Studies won by her daughter, now married with two children in Montélimar. The other two were of a military nature. One certified that Jean Mathieu had been at Verdun and had three ribbons with medals pinned on it. The other was a *Souvenir de la Grande Guerre* and had a photograph of Monsieur Mathieu plumb in the middle of it, needing a shave. Madame Mathieu and I talked away together till Monsieur, still needing a shave, came in from his potato-field. We were introduced, and the talking continued. Here, said Jean Mathieu, we have a little of everything and a lot of nothing.

We went out to the pear trees. They were dancing in the wind, and all round the boles there was fruit lying in the grass. "It's a treat for the pigs", says Madame Mathieu. "For me too", I say, and I begin to gather.

When I had a big basketful, Monsieur Mathieu invited me up to the house to have a drink, but I said I got all the drink I needed from the pears. He laughed at this: "You're not a spendthrift", he cried. I said I supposed not, for I got all my food from them too. He became serious. Ah, he saw no inconvenience in that: "*Pour celui qui aime, c'est bon*" (it's good for him who likes it). As for himself, when he liked something, "*j'ai pas besoin de deux plats*" (no need at all of two dishes).

The House of the Sun

Mid-afternoon. Rain, cold and the monotonous threep of a bird.

I lit a fire and let blue smoke fill the room. When the smoke was thick and acrid – the rain outside still pelting – I sat down at the *maie* and began to write.

And suddenly I was alive again.

Was it the blue smoke? I had eaten nothing, I swear it, and the wine-bottle in the corner, a present from Habauzit the philosopher, was untouched.

It must have been the smoke of the fire.

It was chestnut wood and cherry wood I used. I give this knowledge gratis to all future seekers-of-inspiration.

It is no longer 3 o'clock. It is eternity. Even if it is raining, I am now in the house of the sun. And there, at the centre of reality, I remember:

I remember the lake of Pannecière, which I saw on the way down here. It was blue, so blue, and green paps of hills around it. There were small fields too, blue with wheat. I came down little roads bordered with hedges. In the fields lazed herds of white cattle. At Château-Chinon I walked round the crown of the world, and then I came into a beech wood – grey, green, brown and gold – to eat the bread baked by the baker in Tannay.

I remember, I remember:

The bakehouse in Fairlie, the Baker's Lane, where I lived as a child. The ground-level room lit with yellow light, musty with flying flour. Dan the baker making rolls, turning a lump of dough in each fist. The fiery depth of the oven. Hot rolls, hot rolls, on a winter's morning.

I remember:

Bread and margarine in Munich. A January diet of bread and bad margarine. Food for gods! The loaf and the margarine there on my table, beside the books. And the room reeking with smoke from the stove. Ah, the hellish cold that was there! The icy tangle of grass outside my window. I was desperate then for light, waiting for the fiery magnificat, for sunrise in hell. I painted on the cardboard that lined the walls of my room. I painted for colour. And for heat. By the end of the month I was living in a circus. A circus of dragons. I painted nothing but dragons.

The thunder is striking now. The rain is coming down in torrents. Strike on, pour on, erratic sky! I am lord of the smoky house of the sun. Intact, immune.

Hosanna! My life is a hosanna!

Now, but was not always.

That dim dookit in Glasgow. The pale flowers on the wall-paper, the narrow skylight, the gas-ring, the table with the stains, the mice ... The long evenings of fog ... And in the room next door to me the high-pitched laughter and jangling music of some India. The oatcakes, the tins of red beans. The rotten carpet. The walks in the streets, the perpetual walking. The stations, the cathedral, the Barrows, the lodging houses.

Gather round me, memories, so I can burn you, turn you into a new kind of energy.

The Baker at La Boule

La Boule is a little village on the other side of the valley, and in it there is a bakery. Now, I have loved bakeries ever since I was a child living in the Baker's Lane in Fairlie, so that when I first met Chabanel delivering bread to Les Praduches – laying down loaves on a plank fixed to a tree – we soon got into conversation, and he said I must come up to work with him one morning.

So it was that one morning around six, I left Gourgounel, and set out on the three-four-mile up to La Boule. The early sun glinted on the granite and gneiss of the terrain, the streams flashed, the air was icy cold, and all round blazed the blue immensity of the hills. It was well before seven when I arrived up at the bakehouse. Chabanel had already been working since half past four. There was a new batch of loaves all wrapped in cloth waiting for the oven, and a new load of dough was ready to be shaped.

In general there are two shapes only now: the *flute* and the *navette*, weighing either seven hundred grams or two kilos. The old crown-shape, called the *ardéchoise*, is no longer favoured. "People are too refined now", says Chabanel. So he makes long loaves, only long loaves. Sometimes in summer there are visitors, and they like their bread soft, hardly baked at all. But the peasants like it baked hard, so it will last longer. He starts shaping up *navettes*, and, for fun, calling me his *mitron*, his apprentice, tells me to make a *bonhomme*, a breadman, which he sometimes supplies for parties and anniversaries.

I struggle to make a man out of the wad of dough he has given me. But the body is a miserable shape, the head lolls on a non-existent neck, the arms and legs hang on for grim death. I bash it all together and start again. The second attempt is not much better, nor the third. The fourth finished, I have something I think slightly more presentable, so I present it. Chabanel inspects it with a bleary glint in his eye, then he points at the navel: "*Il manque la pipe, il manque ce qui sert le mieux*" (the pipe's missing, the most useful thing isn't there), he says. So he cuts out a big penis of dough and plasters it on. "That's fine", he says, and I roll *navettes* with him for the next hour. When he decides he has enough, all those long dough-lengths lying under cloth on the trays, we leave the bench and look to the oven.

Chabanel rakes out the cinders, then cleans up the inside of the oven with a wet mop on the end of a long pole. Pine faggots, bought for fifty centimes each from the sawmill, have been burning in there, and the temperature now is high enough. He brings the trays close to the oven, gets a tin of bran down from a shelf, along with a razor-blade, and takes hold of his long wooden spade. He spreads bran on the spade, flips a loaf from its cloth on to the spade, cuts three slits in it with the razor-blade, transfers the razor-blade to his teeth, opens the oven-door, shoves in the loaf, gives the spade a flick, and the dough reposes at the far corner of the oven, there to bake for about half an hour. Soon there are a hundred loaves in there.

After this work, we go and have a breakfast of bread and cheese and wine. While we're sitting there at the table, Madame Chabanel comes in with a live hen in one fist and a butcher's knife in the other. This knife she sharpens on the edge of the oven, the poor hen looking on, then retires to the backyard to do the dirty work. Chabanel now tells me I should start a nudist camp up at Gourgounel and make a lot of money. Or else I might be thinking of taking up the trade of sorcerer. Did I have any snails I'd care to sell?

Breakfast over, we pull out the loaves. Chabanel lifts them burning hot off the spade, wipes them on his pants to clear them of the pine cinders, and piles them on the floor. Since he insists, I take my bread-man. But I pitch the doll, the idol, into a ditch at the first opportunity.

And make my way back up into the dense reality, the existential intensity, of Gourgounel.

Visitation

It was a hot afternoon in August, and I was sitting up among the whins, reading, when I saw an old man step out of the wood, a net bag full of mushrooms in one hand, and a twisted bit of stick in the other.

When he saw me, he shouted: "*Bonjour la maison!*" and came up to shake my hand. He told me he lived in Largentière and had come up here today with one of his sons who was fishing at the river. He had made use of the time to take a stroll through the wood, and had come to have a look at the house where he had been raised. He was ninety-five years old.

"My great-grandfather", he said, "lived in Chastanet, and was a very rich man, the wealthiest in the whole, canton. But he ate it all up, *il a tout bouffé.*"

"How was that?"

"He was very intelligent, and he liked to talk. He was councillor for the district. And when he had to attend a meeting somewhere, he would spend ten days over it. He would take his cart and off he would go on the road, stopping wherever he liked, at the inns and all, and give dinners to everybody. He was a grand man, and he ended up a poor one."

"What happened to him?"

"He took this farm here and began to work. But he died very soon, and my grandfather took over."

"What was it like in those days?"

"Ah, there were no roads, then, not a single one. My grandfather helped to make that road up to Valgorge. Before that, there were only mule-paths. The *pajols*, the men of the mountain, would come down with their wheat, and they would leave here again with wine. They had many vines here, but in 1870 the phylloxera came and it was finished. My grandfather tore up his vines and planted those chestnuts yonder."

"And your father?"

"He carried on where my grandfather left off. He had eight children, and I was the eighth. When his fifth child was born in the fifth year of his marriage, he bought another farm, La Parot, there down the road, and worked the both of them in order to feed his family. He worked hard, everybody had to work hard. I have always been working, and I am still working yet. I remember when I was that high" (he stooped and held his hand about a foot from the ground), "my father gave me a sickle and told me to go and cut the ferns from round the chestnuts. I've never been afraid of work. Nobody has worked more than me. We lived on what we grew. We didn't buy biscuits at the grocery."

"You didn't stay on the farm though?"

"When my father died and the share-out was made, there was not enough for any one of us. So the house was sold, and we each went our separate way. We had to find jobs – *il fallait avoir une situation*. I went to Marseilles and became a tailor. But I soon left there to go to Lyons, which is more famous for clothing. Then I came to Largentière, sixty-nine years ago, and have been there ever since. There were five tailors in Largentière and I was the sixth. I worked well, I had a good shop. I sent my sons to school till they were seventeen. That was unknown in my day. My sons have a better situation than I ever had, and they got it easier. One of them could have been a commandant in the army if it had not been for the capitulation. He wished to go and join de Gaulle in Morocco, but they told him he could not be accepted in his former rank, so he refused. His colonel had been pleased with him, and wanted to send him to the officers' school. He could have been a colonel, no, not a colonel, a commandant."

"What about his other brothers?"

"They became miners, in the coal-mines, near Alès."

"And the new mines in Largentière?"

"The engineer told me the other day that the Ardèche has the richest mineral deposits in the world. There are layers three metres thick. It is deep down, at three hundred metres, farther than any of the old mines. Some of these old ones are being re-opened and pushed farther. There's a whole world underground waiting to be discovered. It is great work. There are four sorts of minerals, lead and silver and ... I forget. Six hundred miners have come to swell the town."

"Where do they come from, the miners?"

"From everywhere."

"The Ardèche?"

"Some are from the Ardèche."

"Where do the others come from?"

"Oh, everywhere. Some are to come from Poland. There is one Pole there already."

"It's important, then?"

"Yes, yes, Largentière is growing. They are building new houses up on the plateau. It is like a pot boiling over. My sons have wanted me to move and go and live with them. But I am happy where I am. I haven't done much tailoring since my wife died, but I have my garden, and I pass my time there."

I invited him into the house, but he said he'd prefer just to stroll a while round the meadows and the wood. I let him go off on his own.

About twenty minutes later, I saw him coming out of the wood again. He was quite a distance from me. He raised his stick in salute and shouted: "*Bonsoir la maison!*" and made his slow way back down the hill.

Dog Days

These are the dog-days. At night Sirius burns bright in the sky, and in the afternoons the thunder growls. Calixte Habauzit has heard a mysterious howling in the woods. The verbena plant is flowering.

As the dogs madden, the fox becomes more cunning. Paudevigne lost four chicks last night.

I am sitting on the terrace. The thunder is rolling. The south-eastern corner of the valley is shrouded in blue. A great wind has risen. Mulberries are scattering all around me. The grasses and flowers are jerking and tossing. There is panic in the air. The stream is flowing faster, and now the whole valley is filled with the blueness. The lightning flashes.

I come into the house, which is full of draughts, and sit down at my table. In the window before me is framed the opposite slope of the valley with its terraced fields and orange roofs, then the chestnut wood, then finally the grey craggy crests of the mountain. The wind howls in the cellar, and there is a chattering of birds in the loft.

I go out again to gather a few stocks of the plant melissa, and I boil myself a drink. Then, still restless, I take out crayons and paper and begin to draw. I draw a white butterfly and a red flower. Ideogram for something?

There are six panes of glass in the window. On the top left pane a wasp has been buzzing. Now it is flying about the room trailing with it the remains of a spider's web.

The thunder is growling directly above the house.

I had lain down on my bed, and had fallen asleep. When I woke, the window was filled with greyness, and the brute stones of the room were black, with here and there a patch of the yellow earth which was used as cement when the walls were raised maybe two hundred years ago. The thunder is still rolling. There has been no open storm, only this perpetual menace and unrest.

I had been dreaming of winter in Glasgow. I was walking down the High Street, making for the Trongate. It had been raining and the air was cold. It was drawing on to night, the windows in the tenements were yellow. I walked down the whole quiet length of the street, seeing not a soul. When I got to the Trongate I was lost in the crowd. There was a man selling poppies. And a choir singing.

Rain has begun to fall. I hear it spattering down the chimney and, looking up, see the lines of it through the window, and hear the murmur and whisper of it.
   A Japanese poem of the thirteenth century says this:

> *Ah, like the clouds we hasten through births and deaths*
> *The path of ignorance and the path of enlightenment*
> *We wander over them dreaming*
> *Only one thing remains in my memory, even when I wake*
> *It is the whispering of the rain*
> *Which once at night in my hut I listened to.*

The Lightning

"*C'est tellement bizarre, vous ne savez pas, le tonnerre comme c'est.*" (It is so strange, the lightning, you cannot know what it's like). It was Madame Abeillon who made this pronouncement.

They speak of the lightning here as if it were a person. A familiar spirit.

When it strikes a herd, they say, it kills one beast, then jumps to a second far off, then hits a third near the first one maybe, and ends up by knocking over a gate just for the hell of it.

When lightning breaks in the sky, they shut doors and windows to prevent draughts, for "it rides on draughts", and put a basin of water before the hearth "*pour qu'elle se noie*" (so it will drown).

Old Habauzit told me to fix up a wire from the house to a tree and from the tree to bury it in a wet patch of ground, say up by the spring. It would take that road and let the house alone. "It's so hot it likes water."

Madame Escudier was standing at the door of her house the other day when the lightning struck. It gave her "a punch in the face".

In all the houses, during a storm, the rooms are full of great flames. The lightning plays with the rudimentary electric installations. It's like the descent of the Holy Ghost.

All through the afternoon, thunder had been rolling in the hills, hesitant, unsettled. Madame Escudier had looked up apprehensively at the sky and made the single comment: "*Ça carcaille*" (it's really rumbling up there). It continued so till the evening, then seemed to die away.

At three in the morning I went outside for a piss. The atmosphere was clammy, and an owl was hooting in the wood. There was silent lightning trembling away down in the southern sky.

By four, when I was seated at my table, the storm was there in earnest. Great masses of doughy cloud rolled in the air. The thunder cracked prodigiously and trundled all over the sky. The window was lit up by pale purple flashes. The rain fell in torrents.

In the lulls, I could hear the dawn chorus, faintly.

I sat at the *maie*, the storm all around me. A little white moth appeared at the window, grey at that moment, and fluttered there for a while before disappearing.

When the window flashed with that pale purple vehemence, the flames of my candles seemed to gulp for air.

The rain came in under the door opening on to the courtyard, slithered in a long black mass to my feet at the table. The wind came up through the floor boards. Suddenly a window blew open. I closed it as well as I could with a stick.

At seven, I went out to the *faïsse* to get a wider view of the landscape. The mist was thick on the valley, and the mulberry trees rose out of it, ghostly. The chestnut wood was swaying and tossing, and I could hear the river roaring down the hillside.

There were snails everywhere. And the meadows were covered with those little white mushrooms called *bouffes* in patois.

I decided to go for a friendly stroll among the *cèpes,* though I was pretty sure that Escudier must have been at them early down the morning, lightning or no lightning. I could imagine him there at the base of a tree, drenched to the skin, sucking at the shreds of a fag, waiting for the mushrooms to sprout up, ready to snaffle them before they had time to know the bitterness of existence.

But no. For in the first few steps I took, I found three beauties. No Escudier could have let that go by him. I continued my prowl with confidence. In the end I collected four or five pounds. I ate a pound or so at midday. The rest I cut up and laid out in slices to dry, intending to sell them at the café-grocery down the road.

Tathagata

It was the eighth day of the storm, a Saturday. I had been informed that a camp-bed I was expecting from Largentière would be on the buggy-bus of Valgorge and that if I was on the roadside at 3 o'clock, I could collect it.

It had been seven wild days and this eighth was wilder.

When I got down the hill, I found that the footbridge over the river had been ripped from its moorings. The river was swollen, brown and white, and turbulent. At a point a little farther down it had spread to take in two hillocks and rushed in a triple track.

I splashed along the meadows and crossed at the stone bridge near Teston's farm.

The thunder was roaring, the lightning flashing, and the rain was pelting down. I ran up to the roadway.

Posted beside Ribeyre's shack, I waited for the bus.

It did not stop for long. The driver came to the back door and handed me out the bed:

"*Pardon*", he grimaced, "*ça continue!*"

"*Incroyable*", and I gave him a quick thanks.

I decided to wait there in the doorway and looked out through the rain. It was driving in great grey scrolls over the hillside. The clouds were low, mingled with the wood, and moving at fantastic speed, changing shape all the while, the wood lurching under the wind like a sea, a heavy, oily sea. There would be a blue slash in the air and a drip of blinding light, then the rolling darkness again, and the thunder, great, trundling peals of it.

I had brought a book down with me for reading in the shack while waiting for the bus: a collection of Buddhist texts from India, China and Japan. I opened it at random. The text I came across was from the Mahayana school and was called "The Tathagata as a Raincloud":

> *I am master of the great basis*
> *I teach it to all beings*
> *making allowances for their several capacities*

I am like a great cloud that rises over the earth
covering all and shadowing heaven
and this great cloud
full of water and wreathed with lightning
lets the thunder bellow and refreshes all creatures
[...]
I teach the great Law to all beings
whether their understanding be deep or shallow
whether their faculties be sharp or blunt
setting aside all tiredness
I rain down the rain of the great teaching
when I rain down the rain of Dharma
the whole world is wondrously refreshed . . .

The rain clouds kept racing over the hills. The rain fell unceasing. It was Nature's great sermon: the storm-sermon. I watched and listened, remaining there in the shack for another hour or more. Then I shouldered the bed, and made back up the road to Teston's.

The river was roaring hardly less than the thunder.

When I came to the farm, I noticed what I hadn't noticed on the way up, being in such a hurry, that the materials for my projected house-repairs (the rough facing of a room) had arrived: the sacks of cement were in the grange and the sand had been dumped on the grass.

But so much rain had fallen that there were streams everywhere now, all hastening to the river, and two of them were taking my sand with them.

I would have spaded the sand to another place, even in that deluge. But Teston's farm was deserted. And the toolshed was locked.

The pile of sand had already crumbled, big slices had broken off, and those greedy burns were spinning it away to perdition.

I began to build a dyke with stones, and deflected the streams as well as I could. No saying how long that dyke would last. Not long if the rain continued as it was. The streams would soon rise above dyke and all.

There was nothing to be done.

I hoisted the bed up again on my shoulder, and crossed the bridge. The meadows were more flooded than ever, and I splashed through them towards Ribeyre's grange, to see if there was any mail.

There was no mail.

With the bed on my back, I climbed up the hill.

Once in the house I unloaded the bed. The book of Buddhist texts had become a mass of pulp.

I lit a fire, and unfolded the bed before it. Then I stripped and rubbed myself dry, cut myself a slice from the loaf on the table and sitting down before the blaze, chewed my bread in peace.

The Buddhist texts I had propped against a stone near the fire, and the pages dried as I turned them in my reading.

I read till night fell, occasionally replenishing the fire.

Then I lay down on the bed. The storm was still raging.

I watched the red ash flicker.

Seeing the Dragon

It was back there in the fourteenth century. A student was travelling in South China in quest of the Tao. One day he came across an old man meditating in a mountain grotto. He greeted the old one who, without saying a word, offered him a bowl of tea and went on with his meditations. The student quietly sat down beside him. In the evening, they ate rice together, still without a word. In the middle of the night, the old man got up and went for a little stroll. The student did exactly the same. The next day passed in a similar way, and the six following.

On the seventh day, the old man broke the silence:
"Where do you come from?"
"The North."
"What made you come here?"
"The desire to see a man of the Tao."
"My face is quite ordinary."
"I've already noticed that."

Then the old man said that in all the thirty years he'd spent in his grotto, he'd never had such a pleasant and intelligent companion, and he accepted the student as disciple.

One night when the young man was out walking in the mountains, he felt a stroke of lightning pass right through him, and he heard thunder in his head. It was as though the mountain and the whole world and himself too had disappeared, and this sensation lasted "the time it takes for a stick of incense to burn down".

After this experience, the young man felt transformed, strangely purified, glowing with an inner light. He went to see the old man about it. "It's nothing at all", said the old man. "Up here, it'll happen to you so often you won't even think about it."

In the old forgotten books that speak of such things, this experience is called "seeing the dragon".

Reading Chōmei

I've cooked and eaten my rice, and now, at my table, with the lamp beside me, I'm reading Chōmei, who completed his Hōjōki ("Notes from the Ten-foot-square Cabin") at the end of the third month of the second year of the Kenryaku era, that is in 1212. He was living then in a hermitage on Hino Mountain, south of Kyōto.

"The same river flows unceasing, but it is never the same water. Here and there appear flecks of foam, then they disappear, never remaining long. So it is with men and their dwellings on the earth . . ."

Chōmei is so pessimistic about life he's almost amusing. Not only does he see in his contemporary world nothing but a series of calamities, fire, famine, earthquake, one after the other, which was pretty close to reality (back there at the start of the thirteenth century was a really tough time) but he comes away with statements like this: "If you live in the centre of town, you're liable to have your house burned down. And if, to avoid the risk of fire, you move to the outskirts, you can be sure you'll be pillaged by robbers."

He was about thirty-four years old when he built his first hermitage. Years later, maybe twenty, he moved to another one, smaller than the first. And then, ten years after, he moved to one still smaller, as fragile as the cocoon of a silk-worm, he says. This was the "ten-foot square cabin" in which he wrote his book. He had a few books in it, and a couple of musical instruments (koto and biwa), and to the north he had a little garden where he grew vegetables and medicinal plants. There was a forest near by where he could forage firewood, and he had a fine view all around. He was happy there, at last:

"When I'm in the mood, I accompany the sound of the wind in the pines with the piece called *Autumn Wind*, and I accompany the flowing waters of the stream with the piece called *Flowing Spring*. I'm not a very skilful musician, but, then, I do not play for an audience, I play for myself."

He'd go out and gather what wild plants and fruits he could find, or go gleaning in the rice-paddies at the foot of the mountain. And when the weather was fine, he'd climb up the mountain and enjoy the view of Fushima, Toba and Hatsukashi. When he felt really fit, he'd cross the mountains on foot and make a pilgrimage to the temples at Iwama or Ishiyama. Or else he'd cross the plain of Awazu and pay a visit to the tomb of Semimaru, the poet and biwa-player. Or else again, he'd cross the river Tanakami and pay his respects to the remains of the poet Sarumaru-Dayū. On the way back, he'd maybe gather edible ferns, or break off a cherry-tree branch, just for its beauty, feeling, though, he should have left it on the tree.

Sometimes, on quiet nights, looking at the moon, he'd think of old friends, and there would be tears in his eyes. Or he'd see glow-worms in the bushes, and they'd remind him of the lamps on the fishing-boats at Makishima. He realizes just how far from the world he is when the deer of the forest come up to him without fear.

What a chance for someone who wants to go the whole way to complete liberation! But he's so contented with what he has, even with a little sadness and some nostalgia, that he doesn't really try too hard to progress on the Buddhist path. He just floats along, enjoying the view of the landscape.

His name was Kamo no Chōmei. He wrote poems, and played the biwa.

The White Clouds of Wang Wei

I was lying with my back to a mulberry tree, watching the clouds pass by, when I heard voices down in the lower part of the wood, where the mushrooms are most plentiful. I couldn't see who the voices belonged to, and was not over-curious to know anyway.

But those voices answering one another across the little valley reminded me of a poem by Wang Wei:

> *King shan pu chien jen*
> *tan wen jen yü hsiang*
> Hills empty can't see people
> only hear voices speaking

I like this Wang Wei. Especially that series of twenty short poems entitled "Poems of the River Wang" that date back to the mid-eighth century.

Wang wrote those poems in a house he'd bought at Lan-t'ien, a few miles south of the capital city of the time, Chang'an. He had to get away now and then from the irks and constraints of his official functions. After his success at the famous *chin-shi* examination, he'd occupied several such posts. But he'd always managed to have on the side a little place to retire to.

It was in the quiet workroom of his Lan-t'ien house that he wrote the River Wang poems, the *Wang-ch'uan chi:*

> *Nine slim supple bamboo stems*
> *are reflected in the blue-grey waters*
> *I'm walking in the Shang on paths*
> *even the woodsmen know nothing of.*
>
> *Wild autumn winds and showers*
> *water rippling fast over stones*

*waves rising now here, now there
white herons flying up and down.*

One of Wang's key-words is *hsien*, meaning something like "being at peace". It's a state of mind free of anxiety, but beyond that, a mental landscape in harmony with the physical landscape around. Of all the Chinese poets, Wang is probably the one who penetrates most deeply into the landscape, or lets the landscape penetrate most deeply into his mind.

Various elements of earth and sky are present in Wang's poems, but none more recurrent than "white clouds". Of his house, he says it is "the home of the white clouds", he speaks often of his desire to be "in the company of the white clouds" and he describes the white clouds as "inexhaustible".

A Western commentator says those white clouds represent "some immaterial, ideal region of the mind".

This is altogether too metaphysical, too platonic.

A Chinese commentator is closer to the mark. He speaks of "world" (*ching-chieh*) and makes a distinction between poets who "have a world" and those who don't, content simply to describe a state of things, portray a condition.

Both idealism and realism, those philosophantine fabrications, are beside the point. What can really take place, at the point, at the limit, is the transfer of deep sensation to the higher spheres of the brain, where they can deploy in an emptiness that is a plenitude.

No easy thing to do, or even to say.

Which is why I decided that day just to let everything go on in silence.

Over in the woods, the sound of talk had gone, and there was only the whispering of the wind:

*High hills, no people to be heard
only the rustling of the grass.*

A Bowl of Tea

No, no, I'm not going to try and condense Okakura's little book and write about the tea-schools of Japan. I'm just going to concentrate a little on the bowl of dark red tea I've got here now and which I'm drinking as I sit at my table overlooking the valley, with at my elbow a jam jar full of wild flowers.

Everything's quiet, my mind included. Only the occasional flutter of a magpie among the mulberry trees. Blue stillness of the valley. And the sky blue above it. Blue on blue. If my friend the painter were here now, the one who painted *Perfume of Spring*, he'd paint it for me, blue on blue. But he's not here, he's in another country. So I'll send him this little poem I've just composed while letting my eyes roam over the valley:

Settled here
among thorns and mulberries
I watch the blue smoke
of a distant village
rising in the air

– he'll know what I mean.

To come back to my bowl. It's a very plain affair, bought cheap in a Chinese shop in Paris a few months back. It's a very ordinary bowl, but it's full of red tea, and out of it comes now a story:

The master (this took place on Mt Kwai, and the master's name, but does it matter? was Ling-yu) was sleeping when his disciple came to greet him. "I've just had a very complicated dream, said Ling, please interpret it for me," and he told the dream. Hiang-yen (that was the name of the disciple, but does it matter?), didn't say a word, but went away, prepared a bowl of tea, and brought it to Ling. "He's understood a thing or two", thought Ling to himself.

There's still some tea in the bowl, so here's another poem:

*I pick flowers in the wood
and quietly look at the southern mountains
the mountain air is pure
and the cry of the magpie
does not break the stillness:
penetration clear as morning light.*

A Handful of Haiku

A morning of quiet rain, and I've been sitting at my table, with a pot of tea at my elbow, working at Asataro Miyamori's *Anthology of Haiku* (Tokyo, 1932). When I say "working at", I mean I've been reworking Miyamori's translations, for while he can hardly be faulted for interpretation, his versions into English leave a lot to be desired. He writes a stilted "poetic" style that deprives the haiku of all their freshness. And a haiku without freshness is like a knife that doesn't cut. Can you still call it a knife?

Freshness. That's what Aso insisted on, in his essay on haiku and Bashō: "In the *Sanzōshi* it is stated that freshness is the flower of haiku art. What the deceased master sought above all is this sense of freshness. We are always looking for freshness, which springs from the very ground with each step we take into nature." And Bashō himself advised: "Let your verses resemble a willow branch struck by a light shower and sometimes waving in the breeze."

So, I've been reworking Miyamori.

When he translates a haiku of Buson's as follows:

Behold! the spring sea undulates
and undulates the whole day long

that's no good. I have to get rid of that grandiloquent, pulpit-sounding "Behold!", and I have to get rid of that numb and dumb word "undulates", while still giving the impression of undulation. I finally work out this:

Ah, the waves of the spring sea
waves of the spring sea
all day long

Likewise, when Miyamori translates one of Bashō's wilder ones:

*The sea is wild! The milky way extends
far over the island of Sado*

it's flat, it's got a dead word "is", it's got a numb word: "extends", in short it's not up to the mark, so I try something else:

*A wild sea
and the Milky Way
bounding over the isle of Sado!*

And so on, haiku after haiku. Here's some of this morning's collection:

*In the evening breeze
the lake water laps
against the heron's legs*

*Winter wind
a shinto priest
walking in the forest*

*Who's keeping watch here
his lamp still burning
cold rain at midnight*

*Passing dew this world
passing dew, yes, no doubt
and yet*

*To awake in this world
ah, what delight
a morning shower*

*Yesterday it struck east
today it strikes west
the lightning*

*First winter rain
from now on my name will be
"traveller".*

The Shining Earth

On a Sunday, at dawn or just before it, when that fore-light shines which I am pleased to call the Lady of Asia, I woke and was aware of the great calmness that was on the face of the world. I went outside, seeing a strange yellow light on the walls of the house, and stood for a while in the yard, in the strange light and the silence.

Away down in the east there were banks of clear, washed cloud in pale colours. There the sky still twitched and trembled with lightning, like a horse ridding itself of flies.

Up by the Tanargue in the west, the cloud was smooring up the hills in fantastic shapes. A great rolled mass of dark-grey cloud hung suspended above the valley, and below it, trying to clutch on to it and heave themselves up to it, wove countless spirals and wisps, ghost-like shapes dancing at great speed. Over the mountain spread a dark illumination, and the cloud phantasmagoria took place against this background.

I stood looking for a while, excited by the sight, then went back to bed, tired as I was with having studied late into the night, and with the idea too that I might sleep my way into that reality, which no effort would allow me.

When I woke later on, there was a west wind blowing wildly, and the sky was clear, so very clear. The whole earth was shining. The forest was gleaming. The river, that had been brown in colour during the storm, though still turbulent, was emerald green. What glory!

The oak tree was dark-green and shining, and I thought of Columba who, in a hymn, said he saw an angel on every oak-leaf in Derry. I know what he meant.

There was a marvellous luminescence everywhere, on tree, stone and sky. And the great wind was blowing.

I went out to finish off the mule-path I had been cutting through the wood. I had been working for about two hours with axe and mattock when I heard someone moving through the undergrowth and waited to see who it was. It turned out to be Jean Teston, with a little cloth bag over his shoulders, on the hunt for mushrooms. He had only one *cèpe*, but was depending on the *chanterelles*. "You're hard at it!" he had shouted on seeing me and when he came up we had begun to talk about the storm, the ruined hay, and my materials that had been stored near his place. It seemed I had lost about half of the sand. He said I'd be able to get some from the river, he'd lend me a sieve.

After a dinner of carrots and cucumber and bread, I decided to go up to Valgorge to buy a new pair of shoes, the blue canvas shoes with the thick rubber soles which are so suitable for the rough paths here. It was the first Sunday of the month and I know there would be a travelling merchant in the village.

I went down to Ribeyre's shack at the side of the road where I kept an old bike I'd bought and had scarcely got it out when up comes Abeillon on his. Short and dumpy is Marc Abeillon, in blue dungarees and vest and a blue cloth cap all-shapes balanced on his ear. I noticed the feet in the sandals were newly washed.

Marc also was going up to Valgorge. He was also going to buy shoes. Maybe the whole valley was going to be buying shoes.

To walk a new world?

There was a shirt-seller in Valgorge the next Sunday, and I needed a shirt. He had his van parked, and his stall laid out beside it. Shirts he had, all sizes, pink, blue and grey. No one was buying a shirt till I stepped up. "What size do you think?" I asked the shirt-man. "Two", said he, the shirts being marked from one to four. I pulled off the shirt I was wearing, and tried the "2", but it was on the tight side. So I took it off, and tried the "3", which was fine. Which colour had been for me a matter of hesitation. Tempted by the red, and then fingering the blue, I finally took the grey. And I went on down Valgorge with my new shirt on my back and the old one in my hand.

At the Café Rieu, a man appeared with an accordion, and shouted to me:

"Want to dance?"

"I don't know how", I said, and went on dancing down the road. I was just a little sorry for the man with the accordion.

I'm not an organized dancer, I don't know any special steps, just the old pedestrian one-two, one-two, but there is a dancing god within me, and I have a dancing soul. Sometimes it feels more like a lurch than a dance, but it's a movement anyway, vigorous and sprightly, whereas souls in general are flaccid and flat, or hard as nails. I'm a dancer, all right, but you'll never get me in a ballroom, I don't like to follow the band. I am wary even of an accordionist.

What do I dance to? Let's say, the music of the earth. Not the spheres, no, just the world, the common-or-garden world.

The Story of Karma Dordji

Karma Dordji came of a very poor family. In the monastery where his parents had placed him, he often had to bear the mockery of monks issued from the higher ranks of society, and he became more and more determined that he would "show them".

After a few years of the normal monastery routine, he asked permission of the abbot to go away into the mountains and meditate on his own. The permission was granted. So Dordji went off into the mountains, built a hut, lived naked and let his hair grow. He was all set. In no time at all he had a big reputation as a hermit and ascetic, but he was still far from feeling he had what he wanted. So he went back down to the monastery and this time asked permission to leave the country and look for a really extraordinary master. Permission granted.

Thereupon began a long wandering search for the perfect master, the one that would give him the powers he desired. He wandered about for a long, long time, but still no luck. Then one day he built a cairn in a lonely mountain gorge and began a series of prayers, begging the gods to give him guidance. On the seventh night of these prayers, there was a roaring of waters in the gorge, the mountain torrent came rushing through it and Dordji was swept away in the flood. Half an hour later he was deposited in a valley, still alive, and convinced that the gods had answered his prayer. And, sure enough, when daybreak came he saw a house, a house with white-washed walls that sparkled in the rising sun, and he felt sure that this was the place and that here he would find the master he'd been looking for.

Stark naked as usual, Dordji stalked up to the hermitage. On the way he met a monk who was coming down the path to fetch water. "Go tell your master", said Dordji, "that the gods have sent him a disciple."

Introduced, stark naked and wild-haired, to the lama, Dordji told his story, rather grandiloquently. The lama, who was of Chinese origin on his father's side, that is, more than a little sceptical by nature, listened, interspersing a few ironic remarks that Dordji didn't notice. When the wild man had finished, the lama smiled and said: "Why don't you wear any clothes?" That started Dordji off again and he went into a long spiel about the ascetic Heruka, and his marvellous feats, and how he wanted to obtain great powers like that. The lama turned to the monk and said: "Take this poor fellow to the kitchen, give him a seat by the fire and some hot tea to drink. Try to find him an old sheepskin coat too. He's been chilled to the bone for years."

Down in the kitchen, where he was given quarters, Dordji couldn't help enjoying the comfort, but his pride was hurt. Especially as the lama seemed to have forgotten all about him. Time passed. Still no sign from the lama, and the comfort became more and more irksome to him. There he was, ready for all kinds of austerities, holed up in a kitchen. But he was still convinced that it was destiny itself that had brought him there, so he stuck it out.

One day the abbot of a neighbouring monastery paid a visit to the hermitage. When he saw the strange figure of Karma Dordji with his old sheepskin coat and his hair hanging to the ground, he asked him what he was doing there, he looked so out of place. Dordji was only too glad to tell his story, and to tell about his ambitions. "So you want to learn magic?", said the abbot, "well, when I leave here just come along with me."

Dordji went with him, and when they arrived at the other monastery, the abbot, true to his word, provided Dordji with a hut near the monastery and a whole library of magic grammaries. Delighted, Dordji got down to work.

He studied magic diligently for two years. Then, gradually, new thoughts began to come to him. Certain phrases in the books took on a new meaning. And instead of poring over them with his head down and memorising magic formulae, he'd spend hours at the open window of his hut, thinking of those new meanings he was beginning to see. And then he began going for long walks over the mountain, looking at the flowers and plants, and the clouds in the sky, and the water flowing in the streams, and the play of light and shadow.

In the evenings, after lighting his lamp, he'd just sit quietly, no longer trying to add to his stock of magic, no longer trying to evoke the deities. He'd just sit quietly, late into the night, sometimes till dawn, and he felt himself at the edge of a shore, watching the rising tide of an ocean of whiteness, and ocean of luminous whiteness, coming towards him, washing over him.

He left the hut some time later and spent his life as a wanderer.

Epilogue:
The Path Through the Forest

It was about four when I left Gourgounel that morning. The moon was riding in the sky and a wind was blowing.

I struck north up the valley, passing through Valgorge and Saint-Martin, and began to climb up to Loubaresse. Of living persons I had seen only the baker of Saint-Martin.

But just beyond Le Couderc, ten kilometres or so from Loubaresse, there was a rowan tree, heavy with berries, lurching in the wind.

It was hellish cold on that road. The morning came blue-green over the hills, and the sun rose in a great chilly flame down in the east, from a nest of dark mountains.

I climbed up to the Tanargue.

Great rocks – the Rock of Abraham, the Coucoulude – rose craggy around me from the whin and heather.

When I got to Loubaresse, I saw men in the fields turning hay to dry. Some of it was almost black with the great quantity of rain that had fallen in the past weeks. It would be useful at most for litters, no animal would eat it.

I went on past Loubaresse to the Col de Meyran. From there to the east you can see the Alps which the peasants here call "The Mountains of the Morning". Here too you see the Cévennes beginning, and they roll away there to the south-west.

It was about seven now.

I looked down the valley of the Beaume, and the hills plaited the one into the other. I saw some of those streams that flow down from the Tanargue: the Valos, the Trivigeyre, the Aulagnet, the Coucouru, the Vernade.

The scene at the pass is one of devastation. The fir trees are silver and scraggy: grotesque skeletons. This is the home of thunder. What growth can you expect on an anvil?

It is still hellish cold. With those stunted and mortified trees around me, I feel I'm in some glacier circle.

But the great green forest stretches before me.

I enter into it.

Pines and birches tower up all around me, muffled in moss, bearded with lichens.

I can no longer hear the wind. There is only the silence.

I come across the trickle of a stream, and follow it upwards. It would be easy to get lost in this forest. But a stream makes the best of guides.

I spend the morning walking through the forest, stopping here and there to lie for a while beneath a tree.

At about midday I eat the bread and raisins I brought with me; and spend the afternoon exactly as I did the morning.

Five or six hours later, I start back on the homeward journey.

I'm walking on the road back to Gourgounel, which I now know for sure to be first base, source base, of an itinerary that will no doubt lead me to other places, other spaces, towards maybe a newfound world.

TRAVELS IN THE
DRIFTING DAWN

Preface

"It was the best of times, it was the worst of times, [...] it was the epoch of belief, it was the epoch of incredulity, it was the season of Light, it was the season of Darkness, [...] we had everything before us, we had nothing before us." So says Dickens in *A Tale of Two Cities* about the period before and during the French Revolution.

The times I want to speak of were those I thought of as "the great drift".

They had their basis in a lack of any confidence in history. For long it had been thought that history was leading humanity to some glorious or at least happy future. That is what has disappeared gradually since the Red Star faded in the East and the Supermarket took its place.

With me, it disappeared totally a lot earlier.

What was taking place in my mind, partly as the result of long readings in History, partly as the result of contemporary observation, but mainly as the result of fundamental cogitation, was a move, to put it first in very general terms, from history to geography.

The earliest texts of this movement, that of "the drifting dawn", were written between the years 1963 and 1967 when, back in Britain after four years of intense study and vagrant experience in France, I was living, just off the Great Western Road in Glasgow, teaching French poetry from Rimbaud on at the university that had seen the first analysis of capitalism (I'm thinking of course of Adam Smith's *The Wealth of Nations*), and engaged, outside the university, in a group I'd started up, the Jargon Group, devoted to cultural, even ontological, revolution. The others were written when, after coming to the conclusion that Britain, Scotland unfortunately included, wasn't ready for anything like revolution, I'd left again for the Continent.

That re-departure for the Continent coincided both in time and in theme with the '68 Revolt in France. I participated in that revolt, without belief or hope (such words have no place in my vocabulary), but simply because it might be the last time that radical questions would be raised on the public scene. My participation in the revolt was manifest and obvious enough (I organized meetings, wrote articles, printed tracts) for me to be expelled from the university where I was teaching a course on "The Whitman Line – democratic vistas and leaves of grass". That left me with a lot of time for moving around, and getting this book together, whose general aim is not too easy to ascertain.

Here's what I wrote in the preface to the original French edition:

"Drifting, drifting ... that's the way it looks on the edges of our civilisation. A drifting, a searching, beyond all the known grounds, for an *other ground*. It's this *other* ground that is the theme of the heregathered texts: a space of being, an area of the mind; and the way(s) to it. So that the book is a book of travelling, the account of a displacement going deeper than geography, by someone who is first and foremost a pedestrian, sometimes a hitch-hiker, always a precarious inhabitant, just passing through. Europe at one time knew a species of wandering monks, quiet but determined – they went by the name of Key, Maklou, Kolomban – whose traces can be found from Galway to Prague and from Cologne to Madrid, and who brought a moving brightness to its sky. The drifter of this book often thought of them, and their like on other continents (Tu Fu: "What am I other than a lone gull drifting between earth and sky"), but there is nothing religious about him, his mind being marked rather by a laughing *gai savoir*. Again, if he may seem to have retained some archaic connections, he is essentially the modern man: facing a void that may contain unedited possibilities."

What I had in mind was a text spanning sense and intellect, written according to an anarchic method, containing, as John Scot Erigena says in the *Periphyseon*, "all that is and all that is not".

In French thought of the time there had begun a gradual drifting away from Marx and Freud, who had for long been the main structural figures. There were parallels between that movement and mine, but my own drifting went on in a space that wasn't just post-Marx or post-Freud, but post-historicist, post-humanist. I was living then down in South-West France, near the Spanish border, which I crossed now and then. But I also crossed many another border. Especially after I'd managed to get myself another teaching post, marginal, but which provided me with a modest salary, while not eating up much of my time. That was at the new leftist University of Paris VII, where I did a course on "The Limits of Literature – Beckett and after."

Around 1966, I'd published some books in London, at the house of Jonathan Cape, *Letters from Gourgounel,* a book of poems entitled *The Cold Wind of Dawn*, translations from the work of André Breton, including his long poem on utopian socialism and harmonics, *Ode to Charles Fourier*. But after that break of mine with Britain in '67, and my participation in the revolt of '68, I felt outside everything. Down there in the South-West, facing the magnificent range of the Pyrenees, I enjoyed for years a kind of splendid isolation. I felt I had an almost limitless time-space at my disposal, and I wanted to keep it that way as long as possible and feasible. That said, I was also piling up a lot of work. Poems emerging from the peaks and valleys of the Pyrenees, and from the Atlantic coast of the Basque country. Essays ranging from politics to metaphysics. And texts arising from a whole series of travels.

The book of the drifting dawn, the first of what I was going to call "waybooks" (as distinguished from so much "travel writing" which I found no more intersting or necessary than the mass of novels) only appeared, in French translation, under the title *Dérives* ("Drifting"), in 1978, at the house of Maurice Nadeau, *Lettres Nouvelles*, one of the French publishers with the most international outlook. The original English manuscript remained in my archives till 1989, when a publishing house in Edinburgh got in touch with me across the wide uncharted waters of intellectual exile. That marked my renewal of contact with the British scene and the English language context in general.

But enough of dates. What counts is the movement. The drifting dawn still goes on. So, let's start off again from Underground London, before moving out into other areas, other territories.

K.W.

"I'm at the heart of the times, and the way isn't clear."
OSSIP MANDELSTAM, *The Voronezh Notebooks*

"Blue soul, obscure journeyings."
GEORG TRAKL, *At the Fall of the Year*

"Out on the roads, feeding on cold well-water and ship's biscuit, eager to find the place and the formula."
ARTHUR RIMBAUD, *Illuminations*

PART I

The Wake

"Sociable, though living in solitude [...]. An enthusiast, without religion [...]. A scholar, without the ostentation of learning."
> DAVID HUME, *Private Notes*

"Scotland would have been our bunk, Mary Stuart, I'd have loved to show you off to the port of Glasgow."
> JOSEPH BRODSKY, *Poems*

Underground London

> ... *it is not the underground that is better, but something different, quite different, for which I am thirsting, but which I cannot find. Damn the underground!*
>
> Dostoyevsky

I

When I phoned that morning from the floozy precincts of Victoria, I was invited to come right over, and soon found myself before the decaying yellow facade of the house in Bayswater where my co-abolitionist and resurrectionist Joe Torelli, late of Glasgow, New York and Chihuahua, had made his temporary abode, open to all vagrants, poets and undefined individuals.

It was friend Joe himself came to the door – long and thin, beak-nosed, with a purple-stoned necklace round his neck and a crimson fez on his head – and ushered me volubly into the kitchen. There sat Luke, one of Joe's followers, wondering aloud what to do with the seven pounds of hot pot which a girl-friend of his had brought over with her from Mexico in the innocent guts of a teddy-bear. Since this had been the subject of conversation before I turned up, and since it was pressing, it was now resumed.

'Now look here, Luke, we just can't have all that stuff-lying around here like it was liquorice allsorts or something. I mean it's crazy, man, *crazy*. You can get fifteen years for that, you understand? You don't want that, do you? More important, *I* don't want it.'

'OK, man, lay off.'

'And don't think you're going to be able to just get out there and sell it on the streets. This is a *civilized* country. Pot is *strictly not allowed*.'

'I know, man.'

'Well, now you *know*, you better start *thinking* some. The sooner that stuff's out of this house, the easier I'll feel. I mean seven whole pounds, it's *crazy*.' He turned to me: 'This cat's dangerous to have around,' he said.

Luke grinned:

'Let's have some cawffee.'

2

In the year of our Lord, 1614, in Cassel, Germany, the world of alchemists, paracelsians, theosophists, etc., was startled by the publication of pamphlets bearing the title: The Fame of the Fraternity of the Meritorious Order of the Rosy Cross. *These were the proclamations of certain anonymous men who claimed to have achieved a synthesis of all the sciences and to possess the true and occult truth concerning the universe. 'Europe is with child,' they cried, and kept on publishing inflammatory pamphlets by the score.*

(Introduction to the Portfolio)

3

'Man, it's happening,' said Joe, 'and when it really gets under way, why nothing's going to stop it, nothing.'

'That's for sure,' said Luke.

'You must give our friend the whole Portfolio with all the plans,' said Joe, 'so he can get boned up on all the various aspects of our activities. These islands have seen nothing like it since Boadicea put on her blue paint and went on the war-path.'

'Damn right,' said Luke.

Joe went over to a table littered with paintings and bits of sculpture, took a syringe from a blue egg-cup and, sticking it into his left arm, pressed the bulb, replaced the syringe in the blue egg-cup, and continued:

'We're negotiating at the moment with a wireless station outside the three-mile limit which we intend to use, and I mean *use*, for propaganda purposes.'

'Radio revolution,' said Luke.

'Then,' said Joe, 'I've just been invited to Cuba by Fidel Castro to give talks on psychedelic sculpture to revolutionary students. Not that I want to get mixed up with the Cuban caper. Communism's strictly for the dodos. But we can use the opportunity.'

'Yeah,' said Luke.

Suddenly there was a commotion in the street outside.

'Ssssh,' said Joe, with upraised, silencing finger, then, with shoulders hunched and on tip-toe, he slipped into the hall-way and stood there listening, like something out of the Arabian Nights. Luke and I came up behind him.

'Are they in?' said a voice.

'Try the door.'

'Knock it bloody well down.'

Squaring his shoulders, Joe went heroically to the door and opened it.

Three workmen, trying to manoeuvre a length of lead piping, grinned cockneyly up at him. Joe grinned back:

'It's this lead pipe,' one said.

'OK,' said Joe, and held the door open while they completed their manoeuvre. Then he closed the door, thoughtful.

'Here,' he said, 'get that damned pot. I don't want to be scared like that again,' pulling a table from the wall and revealing hollow spaces in its frame.

Luke returned with three brown-paper packets. The two of them began stuffing the pot-packets into safety.

Then we went back into the kitchen, and Joe began to expose his shit-hot ideas concerning psychedelic toilet paper.

4

In 1957, or thereabouts, at the Star Observatory, Green Bank, West Virginia, USA, a project (Project Ozma) was set in motion with the aim of seeking out life on other planets. This will entail a systematic survey of all likely stars in the neighbourhood of the sun, the most likely being those of the K group.

(Introduction to the Portfolio)

5

Next morning, we're rolling through the streets of London in a taxi driven by Luke, having collected from their hotel Paul, a jazzman, and Heinrich, a poet who had just published a new series of *Utopian Upanishads* in San Francisco and who, with a trip to Nepal behind him, was to be working with Joe on a book called *High on Hasheesh*.

'If you feel your bottom's hot,' said Joe, 'it's because of what's under the seat.' The pot had changed its hiding place.

'Does Luke always buy taxis?' asked Heinrich.

'Yes, it's handier for our purposes,' said Joe, 'we preserve a certain, mmm, anonymity that way.'

When we arrive back at the house in Bayswater, we meet Joe's loving wife on the stairs.

'Is lunch ready, lover?' says Joe.

'No,' says his wife, like to a jerk.

'Any food in the house?' says Joe.

'No,' says his wife, and moves, indifferently and stolidly, off.

'You bitch,' says Joe, then, 'I think all of us mother-fuckers had better go round to the joint on the corner.'

So we go round to the joint on the corner which is Bill's Cosy Café, one of Britain's best, and when the waitress has come up and is nonchalantly slopping up the stew-juice on our table, she asks what we want, and Joe asks if she has any corned beef.

'Like, not out of tins,' he says.

'All corned beef's out of tins,' she says.

'No,' says Joe, 'all corned beef is *not* out of tins, but if all you have is corned beef out of *tins*, then give me some *eggs*, unless they also come out of tins.'

'You can have eggs out of hens,' said the waitress, who was a pretty smart cookie after all, and took the other orders for stew and cheese and beans.

6

'Tonight at ten. Meeting of the friends of Mt Shasta and other arctic explorers. Bring your stuff.'

7

And His kingdom shall be established in your lifetimes and your days, and the lifetimes of all Israel. Orion, the nebula of Orion, like the proto-ghost of a giant purple bird. The Crab, a great luminous brain in space. Under the ribs. In the veins. Back to root sources. What dada did. Eternal eros. The old calligrapher who loved geese. The original face. Chaos and creation, alienation and creativity. A Mexico of the mind. European euphoria. A no, a yes, a straight line, a goal. Cats and catharsis. Mister Charlie Parker. The big secession. A new anthropology. The hyperborean wild swans. The Amber Road. No Thule the ultimate one. *Brumosa extrema ultima.* Dreamers, mystics, and intellectuals. Explosive incandescences, tormented irradiations. Black, ochrous, sulphurous, purple, copper-yellow. The great waterfalls of the Gullfoss. Curiosities of erotic physiology. Sex and revolution. Work the dumb oracle. Joyce – the sick catholic; Lawrence – the hysterical puritan; Miller – the obscene mystic. Artaud, Daumal, Bataille. Saints and prophets. Ariane and Dionysus. How to connect with the social-political men. The Ishmaelites, cunt-worshippers. Red totem among the trees. Wakinyan! Wakonda! Ketchimanetowa! Buffalo-girl dressed in white leather. Lone Man born from a red flower. The platonic education of desire. Psyche receives wings from eros. The place and the formula. Significant space. Hegel – 'thinking is essentially the negation of what is immediately before us.' The emergence of new modes of existence with new forms of reason and freedom. Psycho-experimental speculation. Hemp used as a de-inhibiting factor in tantric practices. The basic shakti coiled up in the base-centre of the yogic body. Numinogenic. Enstasy and ecstasy. Shiva the lord of herbs. Oneiric delirium. Paranoid use of language. Lingo-lingam. Consciousness overflowing beyond the limit. Take in more of the complexities and possibilities of the real world. Ecstatic materialism. Imaginative energy. An aberration from the point of view of practical utility. Break-away from merely adaptive behaviour. The red and dark-brown arkoses of Applecross. Blue boulder clay crossed by gneiss. Up in the barren red. Hindu girl with a blue muslin sari. Provide the word 'art' with a new content. 'The white of a clarity beyond the facts.' In the Tarahumara mountains. 'Let every body become a dancer and every spirit a bird.' Not either-or, but and . . .

8

'*The strange mad Satyrs are twisted and contorted to make exquisite patterns, they clash their frenzied crotala and wave great vine branches. But in the midst of the revel the god himself stands erect. He holds no kantharos, only a great lyre. His head is thrown back in ecstasy; he is drunken, but with music, not with wine.*'
(Harrison: *Prolegomena to the Study of Greek Religion*)

9

I'm sitting next morning in a Lyons tearoom on Tottenham Court Road, whiling away the time before boarding the Royal Scot, when I meet the tractor. Not a Massey-Harris, or a Fergusson. A human tractor. Who introduced himself as a diabetic. . . .

I'm sitting there quietly and absorbedly, having eaten a spicy London bun gizzered and stuffed with oozy yellow butter, and half regretting it, when a voice speaks unto me, saying:

'Enyseea?'

I look up, uncomprehendingly. Then, suddenly catching on, I say:
'No,'
and the man sits down. It's the tractor. He has a slopping cup of coffee with him and a bag full of –

'Fojemro,' he says.

'What's that?' I say.

'Foiemroevimoin,' he says. I take time to work it out. Fortunately,

I've had some training in linguistics. Bringing the sounds into relation with the situation, I get his message.

'Yes, four jam rolls every morning,' he says. 'Got to. I'm a diabetic.' Then:

'What part of the country do you come from?' he adds.

'North,' I say. 'Scotland.'

'Thought you was a foreigner,' he says.

'It took me a while to catch on to you,' I say.

'God a gumboil,' he says, pointing to his right jaw with a jam roll. 'Gives me gyp. Have a look,' he says, and opens his gub wide. I appreciate.

'Must be a bother eating these doughnuts every morning,' I say.

'No,' he says, 'Enjoy id. God plenty of dime. Oud of work . . .'

'What's the badge?' I say, wanting to he friendly, pointing to a little green-and-gold badge in his lapel.

'Scripture Union,' he says, and then in one long screed and in a flat monotonous voice, gulping air between each section, he reels off:

'Man shall not live by bread alone but by every word that proceedeth out of the mouth of God. Matthew four, verse four – Thy word is a lamp unto my feet and a light unto my path. Psalm 119, verse 105 – Every house is built by some man but he that built all things is God. Hebrews three, verse four . . .'

'Where'd you get all that?' I say.

'I'm a tractor,' he says, and putting his hand in his waistcoat pocket he brings out, between index and thumb, a diminutive red-bound book.

'Littlest Bible in the world,' he says. 'Here, you can have it.'

'Thanks again,' I say.

'Personal Bible. Read a verse of that every day and no harm'll come to you.'

'Thanks,' I say.

'Here, I'll sign it,' says the tractor, and takes out his pen. I slide the book over the table. On the first page of the book of the Little Bible Ministry, the tractor writes: Albert Henry Morris.

'That's very kind of you,' I say.

'I sell them 2d to them I think as can afford it,' he says, 'but you can have that one free.'

'Thanks a lot.'

'Thou shalt love thy neighbour as thyself,' says Albert. 'Good luck to you, Jock.'

'Good luck to you, Albert.'

10

'I've heard that, in England, a fish broke surface and uttered a couple of words in such an outlandish language that scholars have been trying to work out their meaning for three years – so far in vain.'
(Gogol's madman)

11

At three o'clock that afternoon, after five hours watching the landscape I take a seat in the dining car opposite a middle-aged Englishwoman who is studying the tea menu. She doesn't half study that menu, and one thing she's noticed is that you can have Indian tea or China tea. So when the waiter comes up with the pot and starts performing his functions, she says:

'Is that India or China?'

'It's tea, Madam,' he says.

'Oh,' says the lady, and blushingly opens her individual pot of jam.

I've already got down to work. So that pretty soon I'm asking for more bread.

'More bread?' says the waiter.

'More bread,' I say.

'More bread coming up,' he says. We've already established a communication, we two. It's heartening.

I demolish the supplementary bread, pour myself a last cup of tea, and settle back in my seat.

'It's been a lovely day,' says the Englishwoman.

'It has that,' I say.

'The hills look beautiful,' she says.

'Ay, they are beautiful hills,' I say, giving the lady her money's worth.

'Are you going home on holiday?' she says.

'No,' I say. 'I have just been on a long, long holiday, and now I am returning to work.'

'May I ask what your work is?'

'I'm a golf course attendant,' I say.

'Oh, how nice,' she says. She'd have said the same thing if I'd said I was a lavvy attendant.

'A lot of balls,' I say.

'What?' says the Englishwoman.

'I say there's always a wheen balls knocking about, you know, the wee white balls that they knock about, and that they try to put into the ground, you know, the wee hole in the ground.'

'Oh yes,' says the Englishwoman.

'Of course the hole must be as wee as the ball is wee,' I say. 'You understand. There are, as you might say, varying degrees of weeness. A great many people think that wee is always wee. But there is wee, and there is wee-wee,' I say.

'Oh, yes,' says the Englishwoman, faintly.

'Are *you* going on holiday, Madam?' I say.

'Oh yes,' she says. 'I'm going to stay with some friends.'

'Might I enquire whereabouts, Madam?' I say.

'In Largs,' says the Englishwoman.

'Largs,' I say, and then sombrely: 'Largs.'

'Do you know Largs?' she says.

'Madam, I was born there. Just on the north side of Kelburn.'

'Oh, Kelburn estate!'

'No, Madam, Kelburn golfcourse. And the first thing I saw when I opened my eyes was a wee white ball.'

At this, I give her a big, beaming smile, excuse myself, and go back to my mooly compartment.

12

Approaching Glasgow, approaching Glasgow . . . Mile after mile of scabby factory ground. Wishaw – Motherwell – Uddingston – Polmadie . . .

> *Napoleon was a mighty man*
> *a mighty man was he*
> *he sailed right up the Geddes burn*
> *and captured Polmadie*

A crowd of plastered Scots come lurching up the corridor with a bleary-eyed besom at their head, who cries:

'Look, boys – Belsen.'

Time on a Dark River

'Oh' he says, 'I got a map.'
'A map?' I says.
'Sure,' he says, 'I got a map dat tells me about all dese places. I take it wit me every time I come out heah,' he says.
                    Thomas Wolfe, *You Can't Go Home Again*

I

Today the packing-case containing my books arrived from Liverpool. It had come over in the s.s. *Karin* from Bordeaux, and had spent some time under rain in the Liverpool docks. When I opened it, I found the books covered with a dark green fungus. I scraped and rubbed off the fungus and stacked the books in what a few days ago was a coal cellar. The packing-case itself was a hefty thing, and when the haulers helped me to carry it up to the house, we strained under the weight of it. One of them asked me if it contained rifles. He was an Irishman. The other asked me if it wasn't dead bodies. He was a Scotsman. Myself, I was wondering if it didn't contain a chunk of the moon. I'm a Chinaman.

At eight or thereabouts I go down to the Maharajah Stores for something to eat. On the way I pass the Hong Kong Foodhouse – we're a cosmopolitan crowd up here on the hump of the world. Mrs Maharajah is a real Indian with a shawl and a pearl in her nose. When you ask for biscuits, she says: Wat you want, biscot? Mr Maharajah is big and tall, with a sinister squint in his eye, and says: toodle-oo. I come out with biscuits and a pomegranate; but I leave the biscuits alone and make do with the pomegranate. The biscuits were foosty; I shall eat no more.

The pomegranate was rotten.

2

Sunday afternoon.

One of those holy, obknoxious Sundays such as there are fifty-two a year in this ghoul-haunted precinct, and to while away the weary time (big, dutiful clocks all over the cancerous landscape), I go for a walk along the docks, coming down Byres Road, then along Dumbarton Road, then, in Argyll Street, taking the old Kelvinhaugh way down to the river, arriving at Kelvinhaugh Ferry. I cross the river on the ferry, then re-cross, and then re-cross again (the river quiet, the sky a soft grey, the ships berthed in total tranquillity), till the ferryman says to me:

'Are ye enjoyin' yersel?'

Crossing and re-crossing the old Clud on the ferry on that grey afternoon, watching the river-flow and the gulls. After ten or so crossings and re-crossings, I move away along Queen's Dock.

There the smell is strange, and yet vaguely familiar. Whisky – thousands of barrels lined there along the quay filled with sourmash bourbon whisky from Kentucky, USA, with, further on, a load of rye from Indiana. All those barrels, and drunken gulls swooping and yelling over them.

Here and there, too, along the docks, sitting on piles of rope or timber, wee men with bunnets and coloured mufflers reading pink newspapers.

Glasgow. Glasgow.

3

In the early dawn:

She rides a red horse
up Sauchiehall Street
'See you in Tibet'
she says

and disappears
into a smoky shebeen
down by the docks.

4

Night at Charing Cross, standing at the foot of Hill Street there, wondering where to go and what to do, I see a plaque on a railing:
Rudolph Steiner Centre
Inquiries Welcome

So I decide to go and make inquiries. I push open the gate, enter the gas-lit close, climb to the first floor, see no Rudolph Steiner Centre, continue up to the second floor, and there I see two doors, still no Rudolph Steiner Centre, but on the wall next to one of the doors, I see written in thick pencil the word: Otto (German, like Rudolph, I'm getting hot), so I ring the bell, and then, no answer forthcoming, ring the bell again, which brings an old woman to the door:

'Excuse me,' I say, 'I'm looking for the Rudolph Steiner Centre.'

She looks at me as if I'd said I was looking for Rudolph the Red-Nosed Reindeer. Then:

'It's not here,' she says, 'It's down the stair. And it's not open on a Sunday.' She says Sunday with a religious knell in her voice.

'I'm sorry for troubling you then,' I say.

'Oh, it's quite all right,' she says. 'Only it's a *Sunday*, you should have known, and it's late, it's nearly ten o'clock.'

'As late as that,' I say, 'I'm sorry. Good night.'

Ten o'clock. I go back down the stairs. This time I see a small brown plaque on one of the doors. I ring, just in case. No answer.

Ten o'clock. I continue up Hill Street. Quiet up there. Only an occasional television set shining coldly-blue in some of the big windows. As I walk, I look into the basement kitchens: an old man sitting at a table in semi-darkness with a cup of tea before him; in another, there's just a big bushy orange cat sitting on a table among the crockery, all alone in its glory.

Then, on the pavement before me, chalked in large letters, I see this rhyme:

I am a mole
and I live in a hole

Along Hill Street, then down into Woodlands Road, then finally I'm in Otago Lane North, at the edge of the River Kelvin, just under the flashing advert for Red Hackle Whisky. I stand there in the out-and-in flashing light, and watch its reflection on the dirty old Kelvin. I stand there for a long while, then I begin to do a bit of a dance, all on my oney-o, singing to myself.

Let the Midnight Special shine her light on me.
Let the Midnight Special shine her ever-lovin light on me . . .

5

I wasn't born in that house, but all my earliest memories are attached to it. I knew it was in Nielston, but I had only a very vague idea of its exact location. I took a bus for Nielston in Clyde Street, hoping I might find it.

I come off at the bus-terminus in Nielston, and recognize nothing. It's late on in the afternoon. There are few people in the streets, but I hear shouts now and then from the football pitch.

I stand undecided at first. Beyond the area of new houses, the hills stretch bare and cold. I wonder if I shouldn't go straight out to them and forget the house. But at length I go down into the old town.

Coming down the main street I see, down a side-lane, a set of railway signals, and I follow this. My father was a signalman in Nielston at that time, and I know the house was near the tracks. This path brings me to the station; but again I recognise nothing. I look round for a while, but there are no signs at all. Everything non-committal, meaningless. It seems the house is lost for good. Impossible to ask directions. 'Do you know the house where I used to live?' Absurd. 'Who are you?' It's only by following out the signs myself I'll find anything. But there are no signs, not the slightest one. The building opposite the station has blind windows, old and dilapidated, and nailed on its wall is a notice: British Legion.

I've almost given up, when it strikes me that the station here is Nielston High. There must, then, be a Nielston Low. Perhaps the Low one will be my source.

I enquire of two young lads at the corner if there is a Nielston Low, and if so where it is. The station exists. They tell me to go back up the main street, and cut down to the right by Toni's Chipshop.

November, Saturday, four o'clock and the shadows beginning to gather. I cut down Holehouse Brae. 'D'ye know the Mull?' the lads had asked. I had said I knew no mill – 'Ye'll pass it anyway on the road doon'. Once there on Holehouse Brae, I think I recognise it vaguely, but only very vaguely.

It's only when I stand in Lochlibo Road that I feel I'm near the place, yet the house I see before me still has no meaning.

I stand there, and look over to the cold hills and the black branched trees on the sky-line, and then I see a flight of wild geese travelling southwards. It's well and truly winter now. I feel the coldness eating into me, and the geese flying out of sight there down the sky. I stand there with the factory looming up behind me, and then my eyes are caught by the gas-lamps being lit in the station, and then past the station, along behind a wall, I see a grey inconspicuous house, and I know that's it. It's by the side of the line, and I recognise the path leading down to the station, and I recognise the garden, though it's smaller than I had imagined. I think too I recognise the cold hills and copses behind it.

This is the house, isolated from the rest of Nielston, beside the railway-track, with only the hills behind it. I walk round about it, not remembering much, just glad to be there.

The sky is red now in the west, and through the black entanglement of the trees is a wonder to see. Such soft and multiple skies there are here on this seaboard, skies turned inside out, like a fur-lined glove. I stand there quiet, with the grey house, red sky, black trees, then I turn away suddenly and begin to walk back up the brae. I'm thinking of nothing, but a bit of an old Irish poem is in my head:

*Crimson the bracken
it has lost its shape
the wild goose has raised
its accustomed cry.*

I come back to my lodgings in Glasgow.

6

*Wiiiiiiind
nd
staaaaaaars
nd
wiiiiiiind
nd
staaaaaaars*

the day's born deid.

7

I continue flinging crazily about the city.

Today, fog and drizzle. A smoky, leaden indistinguishable mass. The river a wide, misty, empty-looking expanse.

Saturday – I've been through the markets of Shipbank Lane: *The Bonanza, Paddy's, The Popular, The Jolly, The Cosy, The Super* ... In the lane, on the cobbles running with dirt, a big fire is burning.

I go over the bridge into South Portland Street. Dark-grey tenements lining a wide, empty roadway. Thousands of uniform windows bare or with a dismal rag of curtain. Pale faces behind them. Also dark faces. For many Pakistanis live here – witness the *Kashmir Butcher*, the *Pak Store*, the *Ravi Traders*, the *Wali Dairy*.

South Portland Street continues into Abbotsford Place, in the middle of which lurks a pub called *The Rising Sun* and at the end of which, in Turriff Street, stands the *Glasgow Talmud Society*, and the *Glasgow Maccabi Association*.

Other institutions of the area: *The Medical Missionaries, The Muslim Mission, The Church of Baptized Believers.*

The Gorbals. Ancestral grounds. All the ghosts.

I find myself in Portugal Street.

There's a play park there, a monstrosity of a play park. A pond, full of bricks and old plaster. An underground cavern, on the outside of which, painted with whitewash, you can read: 'Paddy, you mancit bastard. Buddha. Itali.' There are five thick poles too, with a conglomeration of dirty, frayed rope festooned around them. The ground is beaten earth, uneven, strewn with bricks and bottles. The whole surrounded by a high wire fence.

The building opposite deserted – all the windows smashed, except three, in which a blurred light is shining.

It's half past two. Time for 'Bright Hour' at the *Medical Missionaries*.

I go into the *Oriental Café* round from Kidston Street. When I was a kid, if I remember rightly, this café was called *Joe's*. The Gorbals have been orientalized.

I drink a coffee, eat a biscuit; and then start walking again – up to the Gushetfaulds, then down into Eglinton Street . . .

I'm still walking when night falls.

8

Queen Street station
fog swirling round the newspapers
a voice booming
arrivals and departures
lonely oh lonely
then the train
the countryside of darkness
the blue rain
and the screeching
of yellow stations on the way
and then at Falkirk
by the gate
that girl
in the fawn tight-belted raincoat
black hair
her eyes
her eyes rain falling countryside
how many times

9

*West Café . . . Southern Café . . . New Bridge Café . . . Bluebird Café
. . .*

If I settle anywhere now, with the least chance of concentration, it's in one or other of the most unfrequented cafés of the city where I sit in the gloom and go through my crazy meditations.

I'm walking down Buchanan Street, with darkness falling. In Renfield Street the starlings in their thousands are squealing frantically.

I go down to the river and cross it, but stop for a while on the bridge watching the reflections of the city lights in the oil-black waters, watching the grey-snow bank where a dog is loping about and howling into the night.

Over on the Gorbals side, I stop – rain is beginning to fall, turning the remaining snow into slush – in the *Southern Café*. I once wrote a short story in there, it was called *South Side Suicide* (a very euphonious title, no?) but that was a long time ago, when I still told myself stories. Now it's more a kind of geography I do.

Out of the *Southern Café* I turn into South Portland Street, intending to maybe spend an hour in the Gorbals library, but the place is closed (I've forgotten it's one of those damned Sundays). So I walk up Portland Street, and come upon a large building with smoky-yellow lighted windows where, on a plaque, with difficulty deciphered in the murky dark, can be read that this institution was founded by Isaac Wolfe. I climb up the stair of the building and push open the door: a vast room, bare but for benches round the walls and a serving counter down the middle. A few men seated round the walls look up as I come in. The other thing that attracts immediate attention is the great star of Israel painted at eye level on a partition just inside the door. *Mishpochah, mazeltov!*

I come back out into the cold, wet darkness.

And go back up to the *Bluebird Café* near Queen's Park, where I drink a coffee and eat a sandwich. The rain is falling thickly now over the city, over my old moon city, and it is Sunday night in the winter of my soul.

From Queen's Park I walk to Pollockshaws, another two miles or so, maybe three, and then retrieve my steps down the same monotonous road, back into the Gorbals where I take my last repose in the *New Bridge Café* and then cross the bridge hearing seagulls over the river screaming in the darkness.

10

About to draw the blinds
I see over the rooftops
and the ten thousand chimneys
with the night-fog
settling down over the city
a dark, red sun.

11

It is almost the end of the winter, the month of March. The grey sky is mottled with blue and, where the sun is curdled in cloud, a distant yellow. In the city the stronghold of a bank has been raided, and a murder trial is about to begin. It is the month of March. We are waiting.

On the suspension bridge over the river, the people wait, loiter and watch, for the old Clud is being dredged – a rust-red dredger by the name of *Sir William H. Raeburn* is anchored in the stream with a hawser attached to a capstan on the quay for extra security, and is dredging, dropping its heavy iron maw into the river with a splash, letting it descend with a rattling chain, raising it again with mud and water dripping from its cracks, and swinging it round in a half-circle, depositing the sludge in the hold. Already the *Sir William H. Raeburn* is lying low in the water, the plimsoll mark eight. The people stand on the bridge, me among them, and watch.

On the bridge there are comings and goings, but always a knot of loiterers who watch the dredger and, perhaps, hear the cold clamour of the seagulls, people with time to spare. And there is one who sits darkly with his right leg under him beside a chalk circle in which is written: *God blessed you*. And the passers-by, reading the phrase, wonder: when? Either that man has made a mistake, meaning to write the more common: *God bless you*, or he is being very, very subtle. Subtle or no, as people pass without giving him a tosser, he curses them, and prolongs his curses so that he has just finished with one customer when another turns up.

There is quietness here on the river – only the cursing voice at the centre of the bridge now, and now and then the screech of a gull, and the dull chain-rattle of the dredger. A pale blue mist wavers in the air, deeper, concentrated under the bridges, while from St Enoch's station come puffs and billows of white smoke that dissipate themselves calmly into the sky. It is the month of March and there is a quietness.

I stand there on the bridge taking it all in, watching the people pass: the Pakistani woman in the orange dress, the drunk Scot in the green suit mumbling to himself, the wee man with the black coat fastened with pins shuffling along in a hen-toed gait, and then I break away and go to St Enoch's station where, on the concourse, there are more people sitting on the benches waiting for their trains. And I wonder if that blue-lit *Enquiry Office* could answer the really big question which is forming somewhere vaguely in the depths of my mind, but which I can't yet formulate (it will remain a lump in my throat, inarticulate as love, and perhaps it is a kind of love).

With all the details gone, what remains in my mind is smoke, or mist: smoke rising spirally and quietly from fantastic chimneys, smoke hanging over the proletarian city, or the first mists of spring rising up from the wet earth as the sun's heat grows in strength and comes closer. The beginning and the end is smoke. Acrid smoke, bringing tears to the eyes.

I go back to the bridge. The *Sir William H. Raeburn* is still dredging, and the people are still watching, and the beggar is still cursing. I stand there, with the bridge gently swaying under me, and look over the city to the sun that, disengaged now from the misty cloud, is gleaming white in a ring of red fire . . .

It is the month of March, and we are waiting.

The Rocky Road to Carraroe

> *Well, now you know or don't you kennet or haven't I told you every telling has a taling.*
>
> James Joyce, *Finnegans Wake*

1

There weren't many passengers that spring night on the Dublin boat. As I stood on the deck when we were already a good way down the river, after having left Anderston Quay, Glasgow, in the purple fogs of evening, as I stood there by the rail listening to the seagulls in the big mauve darkness, the only other people on deck were a bunch of bottle-swinging mashers and herries getting ready to spend a happy vomiting night of it. I waited up there till we were past Gourock, and into the open, then went down to my bunk and settled into my Irish green blankets for sleep. I'd just spent one of the craziest winters of my life in Glasgow, but I felt very good lying there in those blankets, good and warm and at my ease, and began dozing off with a line of Whitman's in my head: '... out of the cradle endlessly rocking...' I'd been away from poetry and everything else alive for months, and the fact that I could feel inside a poem again this way kind of reassured me. I wasn't completely lost. 'We are all lost here in America, but I know we shall find ourselves again.' That was Thomas Wolfe... In the big America-Russia of our age... We are all Americano-Russians or Russo-Americans... But I was going to Ireland – What was Ireland?... It was maybe (it suits me to say so) with this question-no-answer on my mind that I fell asleep.

2

According to an Irish poet, over Dublin and its river 'the sun comes up in the morning like barley-sugar'. Well, that morning as we came up the Liffey, the barley-sugar had kind of melted a bit in the drizzling rain, and what remained by way of light was a diffused dusky yellowness, out of which rose Dublin for all the world like another Glasgow, so that my spirits were slightly dampened and my hopes slightly crushed, not to speak of the soiling of illusions I didn't have, when my foot touched for the first time the stones of Holy Mother Ireland at the end of the gang-plank. And as, in one of the dark dock streets, a Co-op cab was waiting for a passenger, I obliged by getting into it and moved off in the direction of St Stephen's Green, which was the first locality that came into my head. And there it was, after rolling through the drizzly streets, lanes and alleys, and paying 'five bobbies' to the long-coated and incredibly ugly cabman, the Green, where I walked about for a while and the seedy ghost of James Joyce (Ireland is a helluva literary country) singing a song beside me, something like 'Bless this House', but which ended up in a phrase of some hideous and outrageously garboyled jargon that was an offence not only to the King's English but also to the Pope's Irish, and must have been the lingo of Beelzebub himself before the world got all rationalized and sad.

But soon I was feeling hungry, so I quit the ghost stuff, and wandered around for a while in my hungry flesh, till I came across this big *Oriental Café* into which I entered, into its murky light full of the smell of coffee and the spice of buns, and sat down on a red plush bench, with a great contorted headpiece rising at my back, and all around me the oriental wallpaper and the many-coloured plate-glass windows, and ordered coffee, cream, butter and buns. By God, it was a strange place, a real sight for sore eyes, but it pleased me to be there in that dim old nineteenth-century baroque retreat, watching the antics of an old fellow looking like the Taoist god of longevity snuggling up to a young fur-coated woman who edges away from him and finally protests, to which he for his part protests that 'the seat's not reserved', at which she gets up with her coffee and moves to another place, leaving him with his filthy coat and his red rheumy eyes and his desolation. Ah – and over there a Bloom-like character with his mouth full of bun is examining the 'Love Map of Ireland' in *The People*. The Love Map of Ireland – with the northern part of the country striped in black. There's apparently no love in an Orangeman.

Talking of Orangemen, and the rest of the dissenting Five-per-Cent, when I left the doomsday café and resumed my explorations of Dublin's fair city in the morning, I saw a plaque on a doorway and on the plaque was engraved the information that behind this door was quartered the *Incorporated Association for the Relief of Distressed Protestants*, while next to it was another intimating the presence of *Kilroy's College*. So that's where the bugger came from? Dublin, the name of a 'fair city', was beginning to take on a grotesque substantiality. I was beginning to like it.

3

And I continued liking it the next couple of days, during which, having found myself a room at the *Hanrahan Hotel* in Harcourt Street, I went fishing the Dublin streets for images: a peach tree struggling into blossom in the grounds of Trinity College; the pale faces of long and slender girls passing up and down O'Connell Bridge. And sat in the thick warmth of pubs. And hunted for old books in the second-hand bookshops along the river. And sat late at night in my room with the red-tree wallpaper reading Irish poetry. But it was not only, and not even mainly, Dublin I had come for in Ireland, I wanted to go over west, into Connaught, the Gaeltacht, which is why, on the afternoon of the third day after my arrival in Dublin, I was out on the road to Galway, with a bottle of Irish Mist in my rucksack and a foosty-looking box of Black Magic chocolates given me by a fairy, looking for a ride. And it came, the ride, right across Ireland, to Castlebar in the County Mayo.

I enjoyed that journey – the rolling of the car through dark boggy lands under the drizzling and then pouring rain, but most of all I enjoyed the talk of the man who was driving it, good, rich, high talk such as I had not been able to indulge in for a long time. He was full of anecdotes concerning books and writers, this man, and had a deep, richly human appreciation of writers and writing which was a delight to listen to. It was 'character' he liked in a writer and writing – 'he was a great character', he'd say – but deeper even than the appreciation of character was his love, even his reverence, for genius – 'he was a strange genius of a man'. It was real substance he was looking for all the time. No bally baloney – he told me the story of Brendan his friend Behan who, asked if he would describe his writing as futuristic, replied with truculent candour: 'what the fuck is futuristic,' or words to that effect. 'He was probably elephants too,' added my friend Kevin, 'he was nearly always elephants.' And he told me of Patrick Kavanagh lecturing at Trinity College, also elephants. And then there was St John Gogarty, a marvellous talker and a humorous devil, who wrote a beautiful poem of eulogy to Britain and her armies during the '14–'18 war, a poem for which he was highly commended and I'm not sure if he wasn't even awarded a medal, but the lines of which began, so it was later discovered, with carefully chosen letters, which arranged in line spelt this: 'The whores will be busy.' Since, too, we were making for the County Mayo:

> *Towards the Eve of St. Brigit the days will be growing*
> *The cock will be crowing and a home-wind shall blow*
> *And I never shall stop but shall ever be going*
> *Till I find myself roving through the County Mayo*

we talked much of Raftery, the blind minstrel from the County Mayo, whom I knew I'd find more traces of in the County Galway, where most of his later wanderings took place, and I told brother Kevin how I'd first come across the name of Raftery in a book of verse that contained a wonderful translation by Padraic Fallon of Raftery's famous poem 'Mary Hynes', and how from that reference, I came to borrow, through the intermediary of an Irish acquaintance, Douglas Hyde's book on Raftery from the Irish consulate in Paris where I was then living. 'You're an amazing sort of off-beat fellow,' said Kevin, and, for the first time in ten months, I felt a little glow of delight.

And so it went on, from Raftery to Synge, and to Daniel Corkery's book on Synge, and to some of the phrases in it that I liked, such as this: 'Ireland is a passionate country: like the face of a passionate man it is either dull and expressionless or else ablaze with vision,' or this: '... the bleakness and intensity that we always find in Irish literature at its best ...' And then as we were passing Mullingar, scene of the fair in Joyce's *Ulysses*, brother Kevin began to quote from that 'chaffering allincluding most farraginous chronicle,' evoking adventures of the 'lovelorn longlost lugubru Booloohoom,' finishing with his apotheosis, which goes hilariously and preposterously so: 'And they beheld Him even Him, ben Bloom Elijah, amid clouds of angels ascend to the glory of the brightness at an angle of fortyfive degrees over Donohoe's in Little Green Street like a shot off a shovel.' That 'forty-five degrees' kills me.

It was a great talk. And when it came to an end, too soon, at Castlebar, we took leave of each other exchanging addresses and promising to write letters till the next time we met in Ireland.

It was Saturday night, and I slept the night there in Castlebar, in the County Mayo, prepared the next morning to hike or hitch-hike down through the Connemara hills to Lettermullan or Carraroe, and maybe then be able to get a turf-boat to take me out to the Aran Islands.

4

Next morning, then, Sunday, I was out of Castlebar, and on the road to Westport. I had walked halfway along it when a car stopped, with a couple making for the chapel in Westport, and took me into town, where I made for a hotel and a bit of breakfast. I was sitting in the hotel lounge drinking coffee and eating arrowroot biscuits when a dozen or so young men invaded the place from the dining-room, after a communal breakfast discussing politics, and settled themselves on armchairs and couches, evoking past campaigns. 'We went through them like a dose of salts'; 'Did you see her coming down there with her cavalcade of bully-boys like a blidy Boadicea'; 'And Michael bloody well Patmore he says to MacLuskey "up wit yer mits" he says' – and preparing a new one. I left after about a quarter hour, but it was enough to see that Irish local politics can be a pretty colourful and explosive mixture.

It was a fine morning on the road:

> *My thanks, for this fresh April*
> *for the blue crisp waters*
> *and the golden grasses*
> *for the open roads*
> *and her breasts in the wind . . .*

and I was happy walking there, especially round that little loch with the shining blue waters and the long golden grass, and the wind blowing gustily over it. I must have been about five or six miles from Westport on the road to Leenane when a car came by going down the way to Clifden. It was a man and his wife were in the car, and he started talking about Craogh Patrick which we could see from the road, and how there was a stone up there with the mark of St Patrick's knee, and how St Patrick had dumped all the snakes of Ireland into the sea, and how 'one of the loveliest things you'll see' is the torchlight pilgrimage up the holy mountain on the last Sunday in July.

Intending to walk down through the Twelve Ben country by Loch Inagh, I left St Patrick's vehicle at Kylemore and set off across the moorland, where for the next three hours the only living things I saw were wind-ruffled red-marked sheep and a Connemara pony who didn't bray a single patriotic word but just looked at me out of his big brown eyes.

It was coming on evening, and a cold wind blowing when, just before the place called Recess, a car picked me up, going down to Galway by way of Maam Cross, Screebe, and Costelloe. When I told the driver of my intention to try and get a turf boat down at Carraroe, he began talking of the people down there (I remembered what Synge had said of 'the half-savage temperament of Connaught') telling me of the local feuds that often get settled at the dances – 'the country's dance-mad' – where 'they fight dirty and tough', and 'you might see somebody get split'. But, no, I wouldn't see anybody get split, because the time was Lent, and 'by the grace of the bishops of Ireland' there are no dances in Lent.

I left that car at O'Flaherty's Bar, with a couple of miles' walk to get down to the village of Carraroe.

It was going on dark grey night now, and as I walked down through that rocky end-world, with now and then a stocky pale-gleaming cottage and piles of turf all along the rock wall lining the road, and the black sea rushing in the darkness, I was beginning to regret the sun and the wind and the clarity of the afternoon. It's a place of stones, down there, a most fantastic place of stones, and if Renan was right when he said that 'the stone . . . seems the natural symbol of the Keltic races,' I was in the midst of Keltic landscape with a vengeance.

At Carraroe itself, I went to the grocery-post office to ask about the possibilities of lodging. The kind woman there made several phone-calls, but most of the places that receive guests in the season – the area is invaded by students of Gaelic from Berlin – were not yet ready. Finally, however, I was to be fixed up with a Mr Jim McGlone who, at present attending a concert in the village hall, would turn up at the pub in a couple of hours' time. So I went to the pub.

There I spent a warm and pleasant time with three old-timers huddled round the fire, only one of whom, and the most garrulous, had the English; the same asked me if I didn't have the Irish, and when I said no, he said it was just as well, because they spent their time cursing one another. Well, the fire blazed, we exchanged drinks, and talked, my friend with the English sometimes translating a remark from the two Gaelic men, he himself telling me of his experiences in the army, until he said to me, 'D'ye know the sad man's song?' and when I again avowed my ignorance, he said it was 'Time, Gentlemen, Please', and it very soon was.

It was then Jim McGlone turned up, not from any village concert, but from next door where he'd been playing darts, a brutish-looking sort of bloke, and I accompanied him to see in his house the room I was to have. Leaving me seated in his kitchen (his wife I think was still at the concert), at a liberally littered table, with before me a plate of old meat sandwiches, one of which had two mouthfuls missing – 'At my place you get a good feed' – he went, by his way of it, to get the room ready.

It was a mess, the room, when I finally saw it, with facepowder strewn over the dressing-table, shoes scattered on the floor, a pair of wilted pyjamas lying on a chair, and the bedsheets no more attractive than the sandwiches, obviously slept in not only the night before but many a night before that. He waxed indignant and abusive when I declined his hospitality. What did I expect for twenty-five shillings? And I wasn't to think I'd find anywhere else to sleep in Carraroe, begorrah, no, and when I came back to him, the price would be doubled. He was a very accommodating fellow. I left his happy home, and the door banged behind me. Outside, it was pitch dark, and it was raining. I made off in the direction of a guest house I'd seen advertised on the street.

When I arrived there, I saw light in a window, but when I rang there was no reply. So I rang again, and shouted up at the window, but still there was no reply. 'The boogars are deef,' I said to myself, and went to the bungalow next door, where there was also a light (the place no doubt crammed full of deaf Irishmen, I thought), to enquire what was up and why the guest house turned a dull ear to prospective guests. At the bungalow, hallelujah, my bell-ringing got a response. A man came cautiously to the door and told me that the owner of the guest house was up at the concert and would no doubt be down very shortly. So I thanked him and went back to my post. It was damned cold, what with the wind and the rain, and I was also feeling hungry. At length, however, a car drew up, got parked on the other side of the road, and I was just waiting for the woman who now appeared to come up to the door of the guest-house where I was, when I realised she was making for the bungalow. False hope. I hunched down beside the stairs out of the wind. Then somebody else turned up. The police. In the person of one burly specimen who was curious to know who I was and what I was up to. I told him I wanted into the guest house, and that I was waiting for the owner who, I'd been told at the bungalow next door, was up at the concert.

'Oh, but the concert's been out this good half-hour,' he said.

'Well, she must he with friends or something,' I said.

'That's strange,' he said.

I waited. There was after all a chance that he would invite me along to the constabulary.

'Did you not see a car coming down here?' he continued.

'I did,' I said, 'but the woman who got out of it went into the bungalow next door.'

'That's the owner, that's her,' he said.

'But she saw me standing here,' I said, 'and the man in that bungalow knows I'm waiting here.'

'That's strange,' he said.

I waited for him to put his next two and two together. Either invite me to the constabulary, or come with me to the bungalow next door.

'You'll have to do something,' he repeated, and putting his leg over his bicycle and pushing off, left me with the recommendation:

'Action! Action!' and I never saw him again.

I went back to the bungalow, asked to speak with the owner of the guest house who I'd been told was there, and was informed by her from behind the door, which wasn't even ajar, that she wasn't going to open the guest house for me at this time of night. Hospitable bastards. I told them what I thought of them.

But that didn't give me a place to sleep. I began to wonder if I'd better not spend the night walking on into sweet Galway Bay. Going down through the village, however, I decided to try this other house

I saw with a light in it. A man came to the door, and he was listening to my story and request when his wife came up behind him and said curtly, 'we don't take lodgers,' and then disappeared again. The man had just time to tell me there was another house up the road might put me up before his wife bitchily called him in. Knowing this was going to be my last effort, I went to the house he'd mentioned, and after explaining all the circumstances again, got a room and a bed there, for which I was grateful, though they were both damp as hell, and went to sleep half-dressed, with my pullover still on my back, cursing and shivering.

5

At eight or so next morning I was out again in the village waiting for the bus to Galway. The rain was still failing. I knew I wouldn't be going to the Aran Islands after all, Carraroe was enough (there were no turf boats anyway at this time of the year, the old-timers had told me), and as I stood there taking a last good look at Carraroe I was pretty sure that the phrases Synge uses to describe the islands were exactly applicable to these stony grounds also – 'a mass of wet rock, a strip of turf, and then a tumult of waves.' And that morning there at Carraroe was like the fog-weather Synge found on Inishmore – 'the same grey obsession twining and wreathing itself among the narrow fields, and the same wail from the wind that shrieks and whistles in the loose rubble of the walls.'

After a night in a damp bed, I was ready to leave this desolation, and was glad to board that Galway bus. During the journey, to pass the time, and to get the night's experience out of my system, I scribbled down:

The Curse of Carraroe

Carraroe is in Ireland
in the district of Connemara
full of people with names
like Flaherty Murphy O'Hara

But above all there's one McGlone
whose Christian name is Jim
from Galway away to Athlone
there isn't a moron like him

Mick Nolan's the name of the guard
a hopeless excuse for a man

> *if I were an Irish bard*
> *I'd turn him into a hen*
>
> *Then there's that bitch O'Leary*
> *Christian right to the core*
> *turn up at her place late and weary*
> *she won't even open the door*
>
> *That's maybe enough for one day*
> *though I surely could add to the list*
> *(for example O'Neill and O'Shea)*
> *but I think you get the gist*
>
> *On Carraroe and its people*
> *to conclude I say this curse*
> *may they all drop dead in their chapel*
> *and roast in hell or worse.*

6

And so to Galway, that 'grey city of stone and mist and water' as Padraic Fallon calls it. Galway, where I settled into a room in a good hotel, for warmth and comfort and, lying down on the bed – outside the rain had not slackened – reread my notes on Raftery, just to get myself into the mood of the place; and stood later by the Corrib river, soaked to the skin, watching the fishermen; and walked out to the end of the breakwater with Galway behind me drenched in spray; and hunted in a fine bookshop for an old book or two; and went up to Galway University library to get myself looked down upon for not having the Irish (now can I help it if practically the only Gaelic I ever heard spoken was '*Slanjy va*' or something like that slithered on the tongues of rid biddy drinkers in the Q-Irish city of Glasgow?); and then finally, got out on the road again, in the direction of Kiltartan and Ballylee, as writ the said Raftery:

> *That Sunday, on my oath, the rain was a heavy overcoat*
> *On a poor poet, and when the rain began*
> *In fleeces of water to buckleap like a goat*
> *I was only a walking penance reaching Kiltartan*
> *And there, so suddenly that my cold spine*
> *Broke out on the arch of my back in a rainbow*
> *This woman surged out of the day with so much sunlight*
> *I was nailed there like a scarecrow ...*

That woman was, of course, the famous Mary Hynes (an old fiddler, not Raftery this time, another one, said of her: 'Mary Hynes was the finest thing that was ever shaped') whose praises Raftery sings in his song:

> For Mary Hynes, rising, gathers up there
> Her ripening body from all the love stories
> And, rinsing herself at morning, shakes her hair
> And stirs the old gay books in libraries
> And what shall I do with sweet Boccacio?
> And shall I send Ovid back to school again
> With a new heading for his copybook
> And a new pain?

and whose presence in Ballylee, especially after it had been sung by Raftery turned that obscure little hamlet into a place known throughout all the west of Ireland and further. As Raftery writes himself with extravagant humour:

> If I praised Ballylee before it was only for the mountains
> Where I broke horses and ran wild
> And not for its seven crooked smoky houses
> Where seven crones are tied
> All day to the listening top of a half door
> And nothing to be heard or seen
> But the drowsy dropping of water
> And a gander on the green
>
> But, boys! I was blind as a kitten till last Sunday
> This town is earth's very navel!
> Seven palaces are thatched there of a Monday
> And O' the seven queens whose pale
> Proud faces with their seven glistening sisters,
> The Pleiads, light the evening where they stroll
> And one can find the well by their wet footprints
> And make one's soul . . .

7

Ballylee, then, on a cold wet morning, with Raftery and Mary Hynes, coming out along the hedgy and stone-walled roads from Galway (a bit of the way in a lorry, and the rest on foot). Looking, after the rich words of the folk-poet and the famed beauty of the woman, both of them factors which attracted the poet to this area:

> *Some few remembered still when I was young*
> *A peasant girl commended by a song*
> *Who'd lived somewhere upon that rocky place [. . .]*
> *Strange, but the man who made the song was blind . . .*

for Yeats' tower, that ruin of a 'gaunt tower' which he considered as 'a permanent symbol of my work plainly visible to the passer-by. As you know, all my art theories depend on just this – rooting of mythology in the earth':

> *An ancient bridge and a more ancient tower,*
> *A farmhouse that is sheltered by its wall,*
> *An acre of stony ground,*
> *Where the symbolic rose can break in flower,*
> *Old ragged elms, old thorns innumerable,*
> *The sound of the rain or sound*
> *Of every wind that blows;*
> *The stilted water hen*
> *Crossing stream again*
> *Scared by the splashing of a dozen cows;*
> *A winding stair, a chamber arched with stone,*
> *A grey stone fireplace with an open hearth,*
> *A candle and a written page . . .*

When I got to the tower that morning, drenched to the bones, I found a representative of *Bord Failte* wrapped in tweeds and huddled up against an electric heater, reading a book on Yeats, waiting to show an expected party of visitors round the place. By God, it was cold in that there tower – the guardian invited me to share the heater with her, the first, she hoped, of more to come, and we had a talk in which she recounted some anecdotes concerning Yeats, while I listened and enjoyed the heat. Then when the party came I wandered round the rooms myself and ended up, while they were talking literature by the heater, sitting in the fine big room above the stream, and quietly freezing.

From Thoor Ballylee, then, I got on to the Dublin road and was picked up before long by a laconic Irish-American who'd been everywhere, including Honolulu, and who had come to Ireland to settle down, in a cottage he had on the coast, called *The Yankee's Palace*, which had authentic thatch on the roof and genuine green Connemara marble on the floor.

We got in to Dublin at seven o'clock, and that night, after walking round and round the streets again, I took the boat back over to Glasgow, composing, as we came back up the Clyde, this little poem:

Thud. Thud. Thud. Thud.
The boat coming up the river
Dead slow under the rain

That's how it was.

In a Drifting Dawn

Mind travelled in the north, towards the dark waters
Chuang Tzu

1

Morning of December 23rd, I'm up at five, pack my rucksack with a loaf, some apples, a change of socks, a towel, and make for Queen Street station along Great Western Road, quiet, quiet, only from the far end of Bank Street, the noise of milkcrates, the streets frost-sparkling, Kelvinbridge humped in whiteness (smell of warm bread in the air), and board the 5.55 for Tarbet.

2

Dawn's beginning to break. A dark-blue drift in the night sky. I walk down to Arrochar, and continue round the loch. Daylight comes. Ice everywhere – hanging tusks, moulded jellyfish. A satin lustre on the rocks. Dawn wind chill – a newspaper blows by in the still semi-darkness. I go up into a wood, lie down under a fir tree, and eat my breakfast (an apple, a slice of bread).
　When I come back onto the road, there's a lorry parked.
　'Where are ye goin'?' says the driver.
　'Inveraray.'
　'Come on, a'll take ye part of th' way.' I climb up into the cabin with him.
　We chug and rattle up the *Rest and Be Thankful*. I'm sitting on a hot tank that almost burns my backside off. Man starts talking:
　'The black frost's a bugger,' he says, 'only one thing fur it – go slow.' We go slow. It's a long drag. I look at the hills. Massive and blunt, bulging, capped with snow and with ice that dribbles down to the valleys in gobs and streaks. There's a grey smoor clinging round the white-grey tops.

'Ye get tired lookin' at them,' says the driver.
We come to the crossroads. He's going on to Dunoon.
'Thanks.'
A black lochan, ice-gripped. Those black rocks, the ice streaming over them, clinging to them. Yellow grass. Red bracken.
Now at the top of Loch Fyne. Sand banks. Layers of seaweed. Black, black waters. Seagulls keening in the wind.
Along Loch Fyne, the shore. I pick up a lump of quartz, put it in my rucksack. A beauty:

> *I walk on the shingle towards the town*
> *picking up here and there a gnarled stone*
>
> *I see a rock the colour of blood*
> *with dark weed matted on its head*
>
> *walking now faster into the wind*
> *the bitter cold gripping my hand.*

Look! That cormorant skimming away there – black against the greydark – over the waters.

3

Approach to Inveraray:

> *Two fine bridges before you come to Inveraray*
> *at two in the afternoon maybe*
>   *after walking twenty mile*
>   *and the wind blowing like hell*
>
> *At the first fine bridge there are swans*
> *and two old boats like skeletons*
>   *while in the grey sky lost*
>   *the sun drifts like a ghost*
>
> *The town is just a hundred yards away*
> *wind-buffeted and drenched with spray*
>   *since our feet are no longer light*
>   *we'll crawl in here for the night.*

4

The Temperance Hotel.
It's cold, it's freezing. I look down at the backyard. I sit on the bed. Then there's a knock at the door, and a face appears:

'Oh, I thought there was no one in. It was just something I wanted out the cupboard.'

She goes to the cupboard, and takes out one of the biscuit-tins with which the thing is packed. So I'm in the room where they store the biscuits. What else do they store here? It must he their refrigerator. Maybe they're waiting till I freeze before they cut me up. How about a little gallows' ballad to dance some heat into my bones?

They stuck him with a kitchen knife
because he asked for heat
they've taken away that poor man's life
and fifteen shillings neat

Out of the wild and the wind he came
his possessions on his back
he asked at the inn if there was room
they answered: come in, mac

They put him with the brussels sprouts
in a room that was ten below
they gave him a bed that was made for smouts
and left it there to grow

You'll be all right there, they smiling said
and sidled out the door
the man lay dressed upon the bed
in case he should freeze to the floor

The air grew colder, hellish cold
till he could no longer stand it
he cried aloud to the whole household
by God, if you've heat, please send it

The devil heard him is my guess
hence the assassination
they found that poor man in a press
with a knife in his constitution.

I go to the toilet. There's a notice pinned up there: 'Don't sit here, there's work to be done.' Back in my room. I'm trying to keep alive, when another knock comes at the door and a head appears. Somebody else at the biscuits. 'Just help yourself.' I add: 'I'm freezing.'

'Oh,' she says, 'come away down to the fire.'

I ask her if maybe when I come back up to sleep, I could have a heater.

'Oh, yes,' she says, 'and a bottle in your bed as well. All the boys get a bottle. Archie'll see to you.'

I go down to the living room, where there's a roaster burning in the grate. Supper's at six.

Just before six, the residents come in. A work-gang. Pylonmen and tunnelers. 'Rory's on it again,' they say.

'If he comes in tight tonight, he's out,' says Archie.

Supper.

'See that rice there, it's no hauf-cooked. It blows up twice that size in yer guts.'

Archie does the serving. Enter Hughie, the joker of the establishment. Two friends of his mentioned: Flossy Bumfluff and Midnight Mary. It's Hughie does the rounds with the hot water bottles.

I'm to get a call 'wi' the boys' at half past six.

5

Breakfast. Ham and eggs, tea and rolls. I talk with a lorry driver from Lesmahagoe. The black frost again. And with the load he's got. He'll take me up as far as Lochgilphead. He gets his flask of tea made up (six spoonfuls of sugar).

The lorry's hard to start. At last, he goes down to swing the handle while I press the starter. It works.

Down the road to Lochgilphead. Have to watch the camber. The lorry's meant to carry seven tons, and it's carrying nine. Weighs four tons itself. If it starts to coup, it won't stop.

> *It's a lonely road between Lochgair and Lochgilphead*
> *early down the morning*
> *the sky gravid with snow*
> *a light blinking on the loch*
> *a trawler out in the grey smoor*
>
> *twilight is a bad time for lorry drivers*
> *the lamps are not much use*
> *without their complement the darkness*

and the light of day has not yet come
an uncertain time

especially if you're on a seven-ton lorry
with a nine-ton load
and the whole thing swinging like the devil
and the engine so weak
it wouldn't pull a fish out of water.

6

The Argyll Café, Lochgilphead. Hector and his mother. A customer:
 'Four quarters o' big peppermints. Sorry to bother you Hector wi' the four quarters.'
 'I've got a man buys two pounds a week.'
 'You would think that widna be good for him.'
 'Ay, I would think that tae.'
 'I've heard McKellar the ARP man during the war bought seven pounds at a time.'
 'By Christ, it must have been the nerves.'
 Another customer, young woman:
 'Jesus Christ, it's bloody cold,' says Hector.
 'It wid freeze you.'
 'Freeze whit?' says Hector.
 'Oh, you know better than me,' says the girl.
 'You're a comedian of a woman are you not,' says Hector's mother, and continues:
 'See Barbara Stewart the son, he's come back to the Co-operative.'
 'I've just been to buy a leek,' says the woman, and holds it up: '1/4.'
 '1/4!' says Hector's mother.
 'For a wee leek the size o' ma finger,' says the woman.
 'A bloody bit o' grass,' says Hector.
 '1/4!' says Hector's mother.
 'Och, well, it's Christmas,' says Hector.
 When Hector sees the postman coming, he starts singing:

There's no a team
like the Glasgow Rangers
No, no, not one...

'I think that's true,' says the postman with religious conviction, and hands over the mail. Hector's mother opens an envelope:
 'Christmas cards,' she says. 'A've never seen her in thirty years,

never sent her a Christmas card, an' she sends me one every year. It's a shame, hee-hee.'

'That's whit ye call a Christmas card relation,' says the postman.

'It's all Christmas, now,' says the mother. 'It used tae be the New Year.'

7

I hitch a lorry up to Ardrishaig:

> *What a welter of seagulls*
> *and a wind whetted by the Arctic*
> *and the brown-and-green sea*
> *cowping great masses of surf*
> *over the rocks*
> *while the* Cretan *of* Glasgow
> *and the* Halcyon *of* Irvine
> *are unloading coal . . .*

From Ardrishaig to Tarbert. Up there, the nets are lying about in wispy piles, bracken-red and brown, and the mending's being done. The names of boats:

Brighter Morn
Our Lassie
Golden Chance
Caledonia
Dalriada . . .

I hitch a lorry going back to Lochgilphead. The sky's growing heavy and dark.

'That's the east wind blowin' the smoke over from Glasgow,' says the lorry driver.

8

In Lochgilphead, the main street branches off into two roads. The one leads to Oban and the other to the lunatic asylum. I take the one to Oban.

I've been walking for a while when a car stops, unsolicited: 'I wonder if you'd like a lift. You looked so independent striding along there.' I get in. She's a queer mixture, this woman, a cross between the lady-of-the-hall and the land-girl, her speech a mongrel blend of the most effete southern English and the most homespun Scotch. 'Ay,' she says every now and then, 'Ay, Ay.' The real doric touch. And the number of 'wee' things that enter her conversation is astounding. She tells me the old chemist at Lochgilphead was a jolly good fellow. Private concern, you know. Whereas the new thing's a multiple store, only intake considered. She likes the Lochgilphead shops, though, in general – 'they wrap your purchases in a nice bit of paper that doesn't have the name of the shop all over it.' One of the English immigrants to the Highlands. Jolly old Scotland.

Kilmartin. I go down into the neolithic burial cairns. Walk round the stone circles also. Just-over-half moon in the sky. The light, yellow as of fire, and a dark-blue earthy light. This is my territory.

Sleep the night just outside Kilmartin.

'We don't hold Christmas here,' says the host.

'They're gettin too Englified,' says his wife.

9

The next day, before dawn, I'm on the Oban road:

> *Winter, and a wild wind, and I walk a dark road.*
> *Dawn gathers like a pool of blood in the hollows of the mountains.*
> *Then the sky opens the eye of its mouth.*
> *From the black rocks, an icy lustre.*
> *Fish of ice all along the shore.*
> *Two gulls flying catch the first light, and gleam.*

A dusky redness, about eight o'clock. I wash my feet in the loch. The telephone wires are howling.

At Kilmelford, I hitch a lorry collecting milk from the farms.

10

Oban. I go into a restaurant for a breakfast. Coffee and a scone. There's a school-master lives here, supposed to be great on Kierkegaard. I had been thinking of going to see him. Then just as I'm deciding not to bother making the visit, a man passes by outside under the rain, against a background of wheeling seagulls, wearing a black coat and a stiff, black hat, with a bit of beard wispy in the hat's shadow. It pleases me to think that must be the man. Walking about Oban the way Kierkegaard walked about Copenhagen.

But I feel so faraway out on my own – among the neolithic rocks and the arctic seagulls – that I don't want to talk.

11

Late December by the Sound of Jura:

Red bracken on the hills
rain snow hail and rain
the deer are coming down
the lochs are gripped in ice
the stars blue and bright

I have tried to write to friends
but there is no continuing
I gaze out over the Sound
and see hills gleaming in the icy sun.

The Inhabitant of Edinburgh

She's an allagrugous auld city in this allerish licht
Hugh MacDiarmid

I

Grey grey grey white grey grey black
grey white grey grey grey grey white grey
grey grey black grey grey . . .

I was walking down by Cramond, having taken a No. 18 bus out from the city. 'Dull, wet day,' as the weather forecast chalked up on a blackboard outside a petrol-station had it: 'Dull, wet day. But will probably clear up in the afternoon.' It was the back end of the afternoon, and there had been no clearing up. But in my room, after a bout of work and writing, I wanted to be near the sea, so I went to Cramond.

The tide was out. Only in the farness, after the dark yellowgrey sands with the long gleaming streaks of water, the white ruffle of a surfing wave on the grey width of the firth. I decided to walk over to the island.

Silence out there on the sands. Only the sound of rain spitting into the pools, and the occasional cry of a seagull. The big greyness all around. Away to the right, the cranes of Leith; away to the left, the span of the Forth Bridge.

When I got to the island, after all the quiet and the greyness, my attention was held by the ridge of shingle along the tideline, littered with bright blue mussel-shells.

It seemed a miserable little island, waste and derelict, and I did not know its name. But it was good nevertheless to be walking there. And as I walked further along the path, the bushes and shrubs became more compact, and there was even a woodland, whereas at the point of arrival there was only coarse grass and a ruckle of stones.

I walked among the trees and bushes, and every now and then a bird would whirr away in the silence, leaving a trembling twig with rain drops scattered from the leaves.

Then there was a bright-yellow gorse bush. And further on, here and there in the wet tangled greenness, small clumps of bluebells.

I went to the other edge of the island, where the grey sea came surfing in against the rocks, and watched where all around it swirled with thin white surfings shorewards. There was no seeing Fife, the other shore of the firth, only the greyness, and a lighthouse there.

When I got back to Cramond, it was well after five o'clock. There was a strong smell of coal-smoke clinging to the village. The tide was coming in fast.

2

Just along from where I live, lived Velvet Coat, which is the name Robert Louis Stevenson liked to assume when he left respectable Heriot Row and, long-haired and velvet-coated, went damnably bohemian, seeking out crepuscular and crapulous realities among the howffs of the Calton Hill, or the sailors' dens and kitchens down Leith Walk:

> *Oh fine religious decent folk*
> *In virtues flaunting gold and scarlet*
> *I sneer between two puffs of smoke*
> *Give me the publican and harlot!*

It's Saturday night, raining, and I'm out for a walk, passing here in Heriot Row

The Home of
Robert Louis Stevenson
1857–1880

with the lines of tall, goldfish-bowl street lamps strung elegantly along the two pavements, moving on into Abercromby Place, where the *Scots Greys Memorial Club* emits sounds of revelry by night, and further along, past a *Royal Artillery Club*, and a *Masonic Hall*, to Albany Street and the *Hall of the Rechabites* ('Oldest, Largest, Wealthiest') and further on still to the Forth Street Corner with the *Church of the Nazarene* still loud with an old poster depicting a Man and a Whisky Bottle connected by a Chain and the Bible between them, sundering the evil connection. And then, near enough the church to make it humorous (for in Scotland there is a trinity of Whisky, Religion and Sweets) there is a sweet manufacturer advertising:

> *Boilings and Toffees*
> *Pandrops*
> *and*
> *Lozenges*

But now we're in Leith Walk, which is one of the 'Glaswegian' or Hyde parts of this Jekyll and Hyde city.

Full moon in the sky. The smell of chips and beer. A disagreement at a corner – 'A'll fuchin boot yer mouth in.' The further you go down Leith Walk, especially on a Saturday night, the more language diminishes, various intonations of 'fuck' adequately satisfying the needs of communication, until, when you get right down to Leith, it's only the sea you hear slowly and disconsolately murmuring 'fuck ... fuck... fuck' on the shore.

But we're not there yet. We're at the *Halfway House Bar*. And the *Boundary Bar*. And the *Scandinavian Lutheran Church* (*Den norske Sjømannskirken*). And further on the smell of the sea's beginning to mingle with the smell of beer.

East Old Dock. West Old Dock.

Along to Newhaven, along the Granton shore road, the rain still falling, the moon swollen, the sea fucking away there in the darkness, to the crowdedness and hazy light of this pub at the sea's edge, this pub full of bric-à-brac culled from sundry sources: shark skins and shrunken heads, old flags and new flags, exotic curiosities dangling from the roof, in the dull yellow light full of drifting blue smoke, with the gaudy old landlady in a canary-yellow kimono and magazine portraits of breasts and buttocks and cunts pinned to the walls.

Plank it here. Have a jar.

> *O wat ye aught o' Fisher Meg*
> *And how she trow'd the webster, O*
> *She loot me see her carrot cunt*
> *And sell'd it for a labster, O*
>
> *An' heard ye o' the coat o' arms*
> *The Lyon brought our lady O*
> *The crest was couchant sable cunt*
> *The motto 'ready, ready' O ...*

An ordinary evening in Leith.

3

If you saunter down the High Street and the Canongate, and turn right, in a matter of minutes you're up and out on the windy hills. I was up there this evening (it's early November now, the trees are bare but for a few tipsy yellow leaves; the houses show up long, gaunt and black under the grey sky; and these last couple of days a tough wind has been blowing, carrying rain and ice and the occasional white flash of a snowflake.) It was still light when I climbed up the Mound from Princes Street, stopping at a bookshop for a quick reconnaissance, but as I went down the Canongate the sky, from grey, took on a dark purple colour, with the spires and gables of the city outlined black and stark against it.

Very curious are the closes and the courts of the High Street and the Canongate. Anchor Close there, where the howff of the *Merry Muses of Caledonia* was situated (whisky, smoke, pen and paper for baudy creations, and raucous voices, Rab Burns above them all):

Green grow the rashes, O
Green grow the rashes, O
The lasses they hae wimble bores
The widows they hae gashes, O

and where the first *Encyclopedia Brittanica*, under austere auspices and after much laborious compiling, was printed – a strange (antisyzygical, is that how you spell it?) combination and juxtaposition. Another pleasantly grotesque neighbourhood is constituted by *World's End Close*, which occupies a site down from a dancehall called *McGoo's*, which stands directly opposite the house of the most undancing fellow in christendom, Maister John Knox himself.

Well, I went down the Canongate, then the High Street (is it for history-hungry tourists it's called the Royal Mile?), and it was dark as John Knox's vision of the future when I got to Holyrood Park and climbed up into the hills. There was a rough wind blowing with rain. And I walked over the hills there with Edinburgh pin-pointed in yellow lights below me, and beyond it the dark firth and the coast of Fife. Walking up there, I was filled with exaltation at being on those heights, above this once life-teeming Edinburgh, sending out salutations to the living poets of the place – to Hyuk MacTaggart, salutations; to Iain McKeg, salutations; to Robert Garrulous, salutations; to Rid Biddy McKay, salutations – and with bits of old poetry driving gustily through my brain as if blown there by the wind, driving through there vigorously, blackly, pungently:

> *Auld Reikie! thou'rt the canty hole*
> *A bield for mony a caldrife soul,*
> *Who snugly at thine ingle loll,*
>   *Baith warm and couth*
> *While roun they gar the bicker roll*
>   *To weet their mouth*

which of course is Robert Fergusson (*The Daft Days*). Here's Dunbar (*The Dance of the Sevin Deidly Synnis*):

> *Than cryd Mahoun for a Heland padyane;*
> *Syne ran a feynd to feche Makfadyane*
> *Far northwart in a nuke;*
> *But he the correnoch had done schout,*
> *Erschemen so gadderit him abowt,*
> *In Hell grit rowne they tuke.*
> *Thae tarmegantis, wi tag an tatter,*
> *Full lowd in Ersch begowth to clatter,*
> *An rowp lyk revin an ruke:*
> *The devill sa devit wes wi thair yell,*
> *That in the depest pot o hell*
> *He smorit thame wi smuke.*

Fergusson, Dunbar – but not forgetting the Sculemaister from Dunfermeling, Mister Robert Henryson, and that great beginning to his *Testament of Cresseid*:

> *Ane doolie sessoun to ane cairfull dyte*
> *Suld correspond, and be equivalent,*
> *Rich sa it wes quhen I began to wryte*
> *This tragedie, the wedder richt fervent*
> *Quhen Aries in middis of the Lent*
> *Schouris of haill can fra the North discend*
> *That scantlie fra the cauld I micht defend.*

4

A word or two (how to avoid it) on the Glasgow-Edinburgh dialectic.

If, according to the old song, there's something the matter with Glasgow, for it goes round and round, there's damn little the matter with Edinburgh, for, apart from some few pockets of circular cosmo-hilarious activity (as down Leith way, or at times in the shady rooms of Rose Street), Edinburgh stands stock still, and has been so since its last fling in the eighteenth century.

To put it in another way: if Glasgow is an old whore that would like to be loved, and is full of life enough to be lovable, despite some surface characteristics that tend to the repulsive (to put it mildly), Edinburgh is a well-preserved (*preserved*) stuck-up bitch that says: pay me homage, or else.

It must have been a West Coast man, in revolt against this rigidity and snootiness (Glasgow breeds radicals, while Edinburgh breeds bridge-players – I exaggerate, I exaggerate, but there's no fun in talking about the Glasgow-Edinburgh nexus unless you exaggerate) who made up the rhyme we used to say as kids in Ayrshire:

> *Edinburgh Castle stands on a rock*
> *And every time you pass by, you must show your cock*

The only morally safe place, by the way (Edinburgh can be a helluva moral place), to put these verses into practice, is the WC at the corner of Princes Street Gardens, just opposite the National Gallery, a delightful little convenience (as they say), interior-decorated in tasteful mauve paint and tiling, which is the Festival City's answer to Glasgow's huge underworld of an antediluvian lavvy in Central Station. Which, again, points out another distinction between the two cities (for a city can be judged by its water-closets, culture, as Nietzsche says, being manifested in all aspects of civic life): the capital is, or would be, intellectual-artistic, whereas Glasgow is mythical.

If Edinburgh is Athens, Glasgow is China. Edinburgh is formal, Glasgow is grotesque. Edinburgh is apollonian, Glasgow is dionysiac. Edinburgh prides itself on its admirable architecture, Glasgow is rank with what James Joyce called 'monstrous marvellosity'. And so on.

Carlyle, who lived a good part of his young years in Edinburgh, before he became the prophet of Craigenputtock and, with the help of Ralph Waldo Emerson, invented American literature, described the city as: 'this accursed, stinking, reeking mass of stones and lime and dung.' That's not how we tend to see Edinburgh today – though it's how we might well describe Glasgow. Edinburgh is not so much, nowadays, a reeking mass, as: form. And when I say form, I mean, of course, New Town – but the form that attracts me most is not that of Georgian architecture, but the kind of thing you see in Huntly House in the Canongate, or Andrew Lamb's House down at Leith. There is stone-mass strictly (and yet freely) held in shape (a curious, lively shape), and I love it. There's something in that late sixteenth, early seventeenth-century architecture which, for me, is of the essence. Glasgow, I think, has nothing like it. If Edinburgh, at its best, means a conscious ordering of energies, the big gallo-western sprawling chaos of a rain-drenched, grimy and greasy metropolis is a subconscious running riot. A man from the east coast where, in general, things are neater (and narrower) once regretted that the west coast had all the imagination and wished that the eastern seaboard might get an infusion of this volatile stuff. Then he reflected that it was perhaps safer to leave things as they were. What exactly, he thought, had the Gaels, those so imaginative tribes, done with the old Scots city of Glasgow? What indeed? A big waste, a bloody mess, a hideous chaos – right. The 'id' of western civilization. No wonder that, after seeing it and living in it for a while, Gerard Manley Hopkins was convinced that there was something badly wrong with the Western world. As for Blake, it's been said he'd have thrown away his bow of burning gold and agreed to call it a day.

We better leave it at that for the moment.

5

It was a chill afternoon in April when I went to Greyfriars Churchyard to visit the tomb of Duncan MacIntyre, or Donnacha ban nan Orain, that is, White Duncan of the Songs, the gaelic bard who was born in Glenorchy and died at Edinburgh in 1812, of whom MacDiarmid writes:

> ... *only in* your *poetry can we feel we stand*
> *Some snowy November evening under the birch-trees*
> *By a tributary burn that flows*
> *Into the remote and lovely Dundonnell river*
> *And receive the most intimate, most initiating experience.*

The tomb, an obelisk decorated with emblems of hunting (for Duncan of the Songs was a gamekeeper before he enrolled in the Edinburgh City Guard), is inscribed on one panel with the words:

> *A few admirers of his genius*
> *have erected*
> *this monument*
> *to denote the last resting place of*
> *Duncan ban MacIntyre*
> *the celebrated Gaelic Bard*

and on another with the elegy MacIntyre wrote for himself.

> *marbh raun an ugudair dha fein*
> *fhir tha d sheasamh air mo lic*
> *bha misa mar tha thu n drest ...*

On the ledge of the stone, the only stone in the graveyard so adorned, was a bunch of daffodils. Which reminded me of a haiku by Buson, *suisen ya samuki miyako no koko-kashiko:*

> *Daffodils*
> *here and there*
> *in the cold capital*

My next stop was the graveyard of St Cuthbert's, at the tip of Princes Street Gardens, and the gravestone therein of Thomas de Quincey. During his last years, de Quincey would roam the nocturnal streets of Edinburgh, a congenial labyrinth, lost in his dreams that took in misty sphinxes, Manchester fog, Welsh roads, a little Whitechapel prostitute, poppy juice, murderers, seas of faces and, in general, the burden of the Incommunicable. He had rooms rented all over the old town, transcendental ratholes he would use for working in, cramming them with papers, files, books, till they became 'snowed-up' as he put it, at which moment he'd close the door behind him and look for another place. When he died, there were several such rooms still rented in his name:

> *Thomas de Quincey*
> *who was born at Greenhay*
> *near Manchester*
> *August 15th 1781*
> *and died in Edinburgh*
> *December 5th 1859*

After that little necropolitan exercise, I walk down to Rose Street where I nick into a pub for a glass of whisky, because it's very chill weather indeed, with a thin, bitter wind scything up the melancholy streets. It's lugubrious enough in the pub too: a lofty-roofed Victorian place it is, with antiseptic tiles on the walls to make the surroundings as uncouthy as possible, and only a tired gas fire to afford a wheezy and reluctant warmth. I get my whisky and retire into a corner while the bar-lady in sheer boredom heats herself a pie that sends, momentarily, a whiff of hot, greasy air into the general frigidity.

From scenes like these . . .

The Big Rain at Tigh Geal

> *When I first saw him, he was slightly drunk, and said:*
> *'Could you paste this paper on the wall?' Then he rose*
> *and painted two bamboos, a bare tree, and a strange rock.*
> Mi Fu, referring to Su Shih

I

The 'white house' of my title is an old Skye cottage which, abandoned for years, was taken over recently by an Irishman from Glasgow, and it was this Irishman from Glasgow, Michael Mulligatawny by name, who invited me here. In Glasgow, Michael is as civilized a solicitor as you'll find between Scotstoun and Camlachie, but here in Skye he goes native, with a big heathen kilt round his hurdies, a Celtic football strip on his back, and boggy wellingtons on his feet. He is 'chust sublime', as one of his favourite characters in literature would put it. Some wee English woman writer avid for local colour is bound to put him into her book one day ('Miss Effie Dudds has written yet another charming account of life in the Western Highlands'). Anyway, Michael took over this cottage which was falling to rack and ruin, and made a good job of putting it together again, adding a few Irish features on the way. There's the half-door, for instance. When he'd finished it, Michael asked his neighbour, Big Donald the postman, what he thought of it, and Big Donald thought of it and then said thoughtfully: 'Oh, it iss a very fine door, Michael, a very fine door indeed – but where iss the horse?' Another Irish feature is an ingenious bellows which Mulligatawny imported from an antique shop in Dublin. It's fixed into the hearth, and you work it by turning a wheel, which puts a fine rumbustious flame into the sometimes reluctant peat. There's a fine fire glowing at the moment back of me there. I'm seated at a big table beside the window, and outside the rain is coming down, naturally enough, in buckets. There's the smell of peat in my nostrils and even a little taste of it on my tongue-coming from the bottle of island whisky just a few inches nor-nor-west of my left elbow. Everything is chust sublime. Michael has gone back to Glasgow, leaving me the cottage for ten days, though he tells me there may be some sporadic visits from other island-hungry Glaswegians. Back in Scotland after five years and having travelled about a bit, some kind of a reckoning and an accounting I suppose is called for (you can't just come and go without a cheep), but we won't make it circumstantial, no, we won't make a day's work of it, we'll just let it come as it likes, out of the rain ... 'All our troubles,' as Gogol's madman says, 'stem from the mistaken notion that thoughts originate in the brain, whereas, in fact, thoughts are not born in the brain, no, not at all, they are blown in from somewhere around the Caspian Sea.'

2

Talking about the Caspian Sea (now *there's* a nifty transition), that's probably where we all came from anyway. Before we started moving up the blue Danube (*die schöne blaue Donau*) and along the shores of the Mediterranean, and then fanned out further into the secret mists. I mean those stone-working, stone-obsessed tribes, moving out in successive waves from that original area. I like the etymology of the word Keltoi as 'mountain men' – and if they raised stones elsewhere, it might have been, apart from anything else, to remind themselves of their origins. A big question, origins. The primal concern: gods, ancestors, homelands. And a vexed problem, identity – *who am I?* That's been my *koan*, as it were, the insoluble question. But when you've worked at it long enough, there comes a kind of solution. I've worked at it for a long time, if not long enough. Looking for the real space, the real self. From imaginative extravaganzas concerning Indo-Scythians, steppe-wandering and maybe touching the Indus valley; through contemplation of that yogi-type figure you can see on the Gundestrup Bowl, and on the stone in the museum at Reims: yogic posture, antlered cap, holding – on the bowl at least, an earlier piece – a snake in one hand, and a bracelet in the other, surrounded by animals, as though the aim were an integration into nature; from and through all that to the consideration of closer family alchemies:

> *When I think of them all*
>
> *a dancing rascal*
> *a red-bearded fisherman*
> *a red-flag waver*
> *a red-eyed scholar*
> *a drunken motherfucker*

*I take a look in the mirror
and I wonder . . .*

Scot. I like the etymology of that word as 'wanderer'. Yes, that's it. The extravagant (*extra vagans*: wandering outside) Scot. *Scotus vagans*. Wandering, more or less obscurely, in accordance with a fundamental orientation. Which brings us (going hither and thither, but you get there in the end) to the Orient. I no longer remember when that seed of the East got planted in me, but the soil was ready and it took root, naturally, unobtrusively, without straining or excessive flourish. It went along with that urge, always present, not to be embedded in history, but to work a way out of it. Out of MacNies and Camerons and Mackenzies and MacGregors – the white. A kind of transpersonal thing. A breathing space, a cool area. *Kensho jobutsu*. Seeing into your own nature is becoming Buddha. But what is Buddha? Seeing into your own nature . . . Listen to that curlew out there.

3

Not knowing where you are, who you are, in order to get into the nowhere, the no-who-where, and let the essential images come. Sitting here fingering a piece of purple coral from a beach a few miles away. Aloneness, with glimpses of grey seal, heron, bog-cotton in the wind. Outside in the greyness, if you listen, listen, in addition to the curlew's ripple, the yelp-yelp of the redshank and the sempiternal *ka-gaya-ka* of the gull. To know how to sink deep into that aloneness, which becomes an at-one-ness.

4

The smell of dawn goes well with porridge . . . Sitting at the window, looking out at the dripping rowan tree, and beyond it the misty rain and beyond the rain, though invisible, the mountains and the sea:

> *Ninnin kono shōen no tokoro ari. Ika naru ka kore nanji ga shōen no tokoro?*
> *Sōshin no hakushuko o kissu; ima ni itatte mata ue o obou.*
> Everyone has his own native place. Where is your native place?
> Early morning I ate rice gruel; now I feel hungry again.

5

Coming back into Glasgow. The mauve evening thickening into purple above the orange-lighted streets. A drunk bleeding in a close. A woman's voice on Exchange Square: 'She had a bad time wi yon bastard.' Late final, late final. The old room:

> *On the first wall*
> *was a print of Hokusai*
> *on the second*
> *was an X-ray photo of my ribs*
> *on the third*
> *was a long quotation from Nietzsche*
> *on the fourth was nothing at all*
>
> *that's the wall I went through*
> *before I arrived here.*

But the old haunts of the thaumaturgic errancies no longer there. Charing Cross blasted by motorways. Is the White Tower still there down by the Tollcross? I didn't go to see. 'They're destroyin' the image of Glasgow.' The old stinking bog out of which, potentially, the lotus could grow. But nothing can grow in money. Offices and hotels. A place defined only by cash. Let Glasgow flourish, b'jees – the damned place is booming (big deal, big deal), but not blooming (two or three tubfuls of geraniums thrown to the pedestrians don't mean a thing). The future, a flyover. Remember St Enoch's? Remember? Remember? Remember? No use going over to Crown Street, nobody there any more. A sterile, desiccated purgatory (no wonder the seven-day licence has such significance). Witness this delightful gang song I picked up:

> *A went tae a pary wan Friday nite*
> *The Tongs wur there an' wantit tae fite*
> *A drew ma blade oot quick as a flash*
> *An' shoutit' Young Team, Young Team, Ya Bass'*
> *The first wan that came wis five foot four*
> *A liftit ma boot an' he fell tae the floor*
> *The cunt wis in agony, the cunt wis in pain*
> *So a liftit ma boot an' a fuckt him again.*

Even the eyes of the Pakistani girls don't seem so much 'like silver fish' as they did in the city's old murky ocean.

6

Went out, the rain still falling, for a walk along the shore:

> *A grey shore*
> *and a battered herring box*
> *'Scott of Stornoway'*

7

A thin drizzle was drifting over the Black Isle (it seemed a concentration of so much of Scotland) that Sunday when I arrived at Cromarty, making for Hugh Miller's cottage. 'The playing of football on Sunday is strictly forbidden in this park,' by order of Cromarty Town Council. Sounds of hymn singing from a radio somewhere. *Jeannie's But 'n' Ben* was open, selling knick-knacks (Jeannie herself, a grey wiry-haired old crone with a glass eye and a tartan shawl round her shoulders), and further on, a place offering tea and sandwiches: *The Friendly Shop*.

Inside the cottage, a woman goes into a disconnected spiel about Miller: 'He cut stones for the graveyard ... skin disease ... he was consumptive, he had a hard time as a child ... second sight ... he worked in a bank ... people wrote to him from all over the world, he was a famous geologist ... involved in church politics, he said that people should be able to elect their own ministers, ye know ... he killed himself in Edinburgh.'

The upper room has manuscripts and specimens. 'And there it lay, as it had been deposited, far back in the bypast eternity, at the bottom of a muddy sea. But the mud existed now as a dense grey rock.' Ten thousand miles over the fossiliferous deposits of Scotland. Miller's landscape:

> *A grey smir over the Black Isle*
> *the town dismal*
> *chimneys smoking greasily over the Firth*
> *the Friendly Shop offering tea*
> *happy hymn singing on the radio*
>
> *fossiliferous deposits*
>
> *I come away*
> *with the image of a dark figure*
> *hammering reverently at a rock ...*

But I didn't leave Cromarty right away, for there was also Urquhart, who had had great hopes of developing the foresaid town and making it into a hive of commerce and culture before he was attacked by a 'plague of flagitators'. I went up to the Old Kirk, vaguely thinking I might see a gravestone, and I was strolling about in the wilderness of the Old Kirk's graveyard, among the tall weeds and the stones, quiet under the drizzling rain, when I heard a car draw up, and then the gate clanged, and there was this beefy blond-haired Englishman (I heard him) in a kilt (no doubt he had Scottish ancestors), followed by a wee pimpled bespectacled bit of a woman done up in tweed, who barged up to the door of the Kirk as if he owned it, pushed it, banged on it, realised it was closed, and barged off again, with the wee woman scampering behind him. I let the bully boy go, then I left myself.

8

Reading Marpa (another dawn):

> *When the tiger year was ending*
> *weary of the things of the world*
> *I came to the sanctuary wilderness*
>
> *the elements of wind and water seethed*
> *the dark hills were clad in white*
>
> *I don't philosophize but I keep at my task*
> *I sleep little but meditate often*
>
> *when named I am the man apart.*

9

'The islands and promontories along the western seaboard of Scotland are noted for their records of intense and prolonged igneous activity during early Tertiary times. At that period, some 40 million years ago, volcanic plateaux forming part of a continental region must have extended continuously along the western coast. By now, owing to prolonged denudation, vast amounts of the volcanic materials have disappeared and the broad pipes of former volcanoes are revealed, as well as still more deeply situated plutonic rocks.'

Official geological survey.

10

Brief statement (serio-comic) roughly in the style of MacDiarmid:

A rock and river province defying description
(we have of course read all the literature)
but inviting instantaneous perception
à propos red rowan grey heron
lichen grass stone and running water
(see X. Dubrovski on ecological syntax)
with as final metaphysical orgasm
the penetration through to the white

which not only defies description
but cannot even faintly be suggested
(as de Gourmont said: suggérer n'est rien*)*
implying a disgust of metaphor
and even of speech itself
a rarity though a reality
bithidh e goirid do mhuir-làn a nisd
whose concreteness is almost an abstraction

from negation to negation, the mind
arrives at this clear space, beyond
opacity, opinions, history, the all-too-human
(cf Coomaraswamy on Nietzsche in The Dance of Shiva*)*
and it is here the aesthetic of almost nothing
comes into action, the merest sign is enough
(see Kuno Meyer: Einführung in die Altirische Dichtung*)*
if prepared by a spaced-out silence

as a thin blaze of quartz in sandstone
nan tàrladh dhuibh a bhith air leirg
has behind it the whole of geology
and in its purity is beyond perfection.

11

Jimmy McGinty was here for the weekend – turned up with a bottle of whisky in one pocket and a bit of shit in the other. He said Alec Tweedy would have liked to come up as well, but it was his guru's birthday, and he was away to see him in New York. 'It's his guru's birthday,' says Jimmy, going into one of those convulsive laughs of his. It was a long time since I'd seen Jimmy. Last time I saw him was about five years ago in London when Joe Torelli was gathering in the boys for his intergalactic tea party ('cosmonauts of inner space'). 'What have you been doin'?' says Jimmy. 'Oh, this and that,' I said, 'coming and going' – I meant 'travelling in the drifting dawn' – and I asked about him. He told me he'd been getting on and off junk. And he had a guru now, too ('I'm supposed no tae drink'), one Klong Rampa, from the land of snows, who had recently settled in Scotland; the same guru as Babe Ruth MacBlake, the American poet, whom he'd just seen in Edinburgh. He asked me if I didn't have a guru. I said, none or many, depending how you looked on it. He looked at me questioningly. I'm a secretive bugger, I said. He went into one of his laughs. For the moment, it's Sgurr Dubh, I said. Who's he, where's he come from? asked Jimmy. He neither comes nor goes – he's a mountain, I said. We got to talking about Buddhism. I suggested all these guru-seekers were just putting Hindu features on to their Christian Father – we had to get further out than that. He claimed I was making too many distinctions (between Buddhism and Christianity, e.g.), and that I was a scholar. That's right, I said, a *wandering* scholar. I like Jimmy. *Namo guru*! And may he plunge, beyond the guru-pond, into the book of a thousand white lights. It turned out, by the way, that Klong, his guru, had quit his monastery, with all those guru-boys flocking to it (bound to stifle any man), and had run away with a wee Scots girl. I said he'd had the right idea. Jimmy went into one of his convulsive laughs. 'A canny get off the women maself,' he said, and told me how, the last time he was down in the Galloway monastery, there was this wee pippin, mmm, with her breasts just about breakin' the sound barrier washing the dishes beside him and he, er, started to chaff her up, ye know, but she turned round to him, as cool as a Tibetan cucumber, and asked did he not remember the guru had said they were to respect complete silence, and that turned him radically off. I said that was probably the wee girl (*oh, mannie, pad me home*) Klong ran away with. Jimmy went into one of his convulsive laughs.

12

Out of the world and into the Applecross. To get into Applecross, which is a rocky promontory out off from the rest of the mainland, you have to pass through the beetling Pass of the Cattle which, if it is raining and the mist is thick, can be like going through the gates of a nordic hell (you can take it I've been there). But it's worth it on the other side. You hit a kind of Keltic garden of Eden, less well-known than the islands – even its name suggests that Eden touch (in fact it reads like a synopsis of the whole of Christianity). I was looking for an old friend, a Keltic scholar by the name of Coinneach

MacMhaigstir, whom I had known in Glasgow years before. When I finally located the MacMhaigstirs' house, his mother told me he was away, at some celtology congress in Wales, but that I was to come in and have some tea. While she made the tea, I looked out at a couple of fishing smacks at anchor in the rocky little harbour with the thick edge of dark golden weed, and the afternoon sunlight, making a late appearance now with the stopping of the rain, glinting on the sea's dark waters.

Mrs MacMhaigstir knew Glasgow well, she had been there several winters with her son. She remembered particularly McLaren's wee bookshop in Argyll Street, which was the place to buy Gaelic Bibles. As for Applecross, she said, there were 'a lot of English moving in, buying up cottages for their summer holidays – our own boys can't afford them'. She said it would soon be like the Clearances again.

13

MacCrimmon will never come back, never come back, never come back. That '*Cha till, cha till, cha till MacCruimean*' is what Donald ban MacCrimmon, the renowned piper, wrote in the song he composed when he left Skye to take part in the '45. He said MacLeod might come back, but that the MacCrimmon never would. The MacLeod did come back, though he'd have better stayed away, for it's a MacLeod offspring who wrote the verses ('Skye is My Home'), which are presented in the tourist shops as 'the ideal souvenir':

> *Sad songs of the islands, bring memories ever so clear*
> *Of pictures as in childhood days, my Island, oh so dear*

But to leave the kitsch, and come back to the pibroch, it ends:

> *Mo chirl tuilleadh riut*
> *Gun dùil tilleadh riut*
> *Gun dùil tilleadh riut*
> *Gun dùil tilleadh riut*
> *Mo chirl tuilladh riut*
> *Gun dùil filleadh riut*
> *Mo chirl ri d' chirl na deòir à sileadh*

> (*My back to you forever*
> *No hope of your return*
> *No hope of your return*
> *No hope of your return*
> *My back to you forever*

No hope of your return
My back to your back and tears flowing)

It's a little beauty of a pibroch song, and could be seen as a lament not only for MacCrimmon but for the whole of Gaelic culture which his piping represented.

Cha till, cha till, cha till MacCruimean

– sitting here at the window, I'm singing that line over and over to myself, Keltic *mantra*.

But we probably have to go further back than the Keltic. Back to the Thulean, the pelagian. At least for the ground. But who cares about the ground any more? Everything's up in the air. And the air's polluted.

14

At Ullapool, I was fed up going about with wet hair, so I bought myself a cap, a sailor's skip-cap, which I happened to set eyes on in an outfitter's window. Later on, I was standing watching the fishing smacks:

Quiet waters
Harvest
Kittiwake
Dauntless Star
Catriona

(and, oops, there's a seal's head sleekly breaking surface) when this English yachtsman asked me which boat I was off. 'The drunken boat,' I said.

15

That branch among the fern
was a red stag
sheltering from the rain

16

To travel north is to travel into the mind. I suppose the same might be said for the south, the east, and the west (any 'pure direction', as it were), but I'm not sure if the north, with maybe the east, isn't privileged. As you go north, the landscape becomes more naked, points of interest become rarer. The self becomes spaced-out. That blue-grey silence among the reeds of the stream – a heron! Wind scouring the sands, and a grey gull struggling to make headway. Little black lochans full of water lilies. Spaced out, and lost in the high open joyance. When you get to the edge, there's next to nothing. Up there, there was a break in the rain, it was at Kyle of Tongue:

a bird yell
emptied my skull

ricks of hay
lined the fields

a fishing smack
lay at quiet anchor –

it was Kyle of Tongue
on a blue morning.

17

Here endeth the Book of the Big Rain – interrupted by the arrival at Tigh Geal of Dougie Moffat, the author of the All-Scottish-Arts-Committee prize-winning novel, described in the Scottish press as 'authentic', 'down-to-earth', 'pungent', 'real life', 'crying with truth', entitled *Flies in the Porridge.*

PART II

THE GATES

"There are the gates of horn and the gates of ivory"
Homer, The Journeyings of Ulysses

"The great path has no gates
When you go through the gateless gate
You walk freely between heaven and earth."
Mumonkan

The Blue Gates of Brittany

Who's never dreamt of opening the gates of some strange silent region?

Georges Bataille

1

They say it rains four days out of three in Brittany, which doesn't leave a lot of time for anything else. Well, maybe I'm just lucky at the moment, but it's the middle of January, and the sky is gloriously blue. The sky's blue, my coat's blue, my shirt's blue, my franciscan bluejeans are blue, and there's a blue flame glowing brightly in my brain.

Travelling this way, where am I going? – nowhere. I pass through many places of the mind – to get nowhere. Nowhere is difficult, but I'll get there some day . . . Nowhere is anywhere, is mywhere.

Who am I? – just a sign for the infinite; maybe a zero.

And, writing this, this way, what am I? A writer, a poet, a literary person (all tied up in the literary nexus)? Hell, I'm not wrapped up in that gangrenous context. I'm just writing a few strong sheaves for the Book, a few chapters maybe of the coming Bible. I'm part of an answer maybe to a question that hasn't yet been formulated, that can be formulated only by a madman, and maybe that madness hasn't been invented yet.

2

Saturday night at Nantes, on the Quai de la Fosse. Soiled girdle of the goddess. Putanas on the way down and out. '*Le commerce baisse.*'

Next morning, Sunday, on the road to Quimperlé.

La Roche-Bernard.

Vannes.

Auray.

Lorient. All the tramps of the vicinity gathering here at the harbour, earning a coin or two unloading fish.

Then, after six hours holy hitch-hiking – Quimperlé.

3

Baudelaire talks of 'means of multiplying the individuality', of 'augmenting personality', of an 'intellectual paradise', of 'a paradisal state of the mind and senses', of 'angelic excitation', of 'immaterial voluptuousness', of obtaining the 'objectivity peculiar to pantheistic poets . . .'

He speaks too of the Scythians, the Sons of the Wind, gathering hemp seeds and scattering them on red-hot stones for an ecstatic vapour-bath. I'll try that bath some time, a super-sauna with intellectual projections, and all of Baudelaire's phrases go straight to my mind.

But I'll still continue to travel a step at a time, believing that the 'paradise' comes out of the most ordinary reality, and out of 'normal' states. Less spectacular maybe, but more lasting; less intense, but with a greater density.

Gather and control the energy (wakened by movement) of the complete being (the full psychic spectrum), and place it in the midst of naked elements ('nature'), and from there on, I think, you're really on to something substantial.

I'm writing this in Quimperlé, in a little café opposite two buildings: one, the ruins of Clumban's place, two, a cinema called Eden. I want more than the cinema – looking maybe for a stone, a flower, a key, among the ruins.

4

Leaving Quimperlé on this chill blue January morning, white frost on the fields, my breath steaming – 'now I know my nostrils are turned towards the earth!'

Pont-Aven:

Bonjour, monsieur Gauguin:
'D'où venons-nous . . . où allons-nous?'
(Good mornin', Mr Gauguin:
'Where do we come from? Where are we going?')

Down on the Quai Théodore Botrel. An old woman washing clothes in the river, a pile of steaming linen beside her on the stones.

Quraak, quraak of gulls. Gulls fat, white, swift. Never fixed, always in flight. Dancing the pantomine of pure vitality.

Then into the little *Café de la Régie* – smell of dark, polished wood; fire burning – where I slowly drink a bitterblack coffee before moving up out of Pont-Aven on the road to Concarneau.

I arrive there (hitch-hiked with an ex-cabin-boy who had done ten hard years on the Dakar run), at midday, coming along the docks with gulls (small pure-white fellows with red beaks, and big brown-flecked guys with black beaks) clamouring crazily all over the place.

Over to the *ville close* in the midday silence. *Tempus fugit velut umbra* – on a sun-dial at the gate. Old folks' home. Two old men muttering Breton on the ramparts.

Along to the edge of town, to the Quai de la Croix and the lighthouse, then back, and out towards Quimper.

5

From Renan (*The Poetry of the Celtic Races*). 'Their mythology is nothing more than a transparent naturalism'; 'the cult of nature ... of landscape'; 'that impulse of imagination'; 'the principle of the marvel is in nature herself, in her hidden forces, in her inexhaustible fecundity'; 'an unlimited faith in the possible'; 'the Scots ... doing duty, until the twelfth century, as instructors in grammar and literature to all the west'; 'studious philologists and daring philosophers'; 'perhaps the profoundest instinct of the Celtic people is their desire to penetrate the unknown'; 'we are far from believing that this race has said its last word ... who knows what it would produce in the domain of intellect, if it hardened itself to an entrance into the world, and subjected its rich and profound nature to the conditions of modern thought? It appears to me that there would result from this combination productions of high originality, a subtle and discreet manner of taking life ...'

That is pretty much my programme.

6

Rue de Rosmadec:

> *White walls and gulls*
> *extremity*
> *impossible blackness*
> *rapacious solitude*
> *the narrow garden of joyance.*

7

By eleven o'clock the next day, a clear, blustery morning, I'm in Pont l'Abbé, with three old women, two of then, limping, in bigouden costume (black dress and white lace bonnet), going to market on the Place de la Republique.

Then, away out beyond Penmarc'h (after hitch-hiking with a girl who talks with pride of her people, the fisher-folk round Penmarc'h – 'we're different here, we're afraid of nothing' – and dismisses Quimper as '*bourgeois*'), nothing but rocks, the wind, and the clamour-shriek of gulls.

It was out here by Penmarc'h (meaning the Horse's Head) that the crazy Breton poet Tristan Corbière imagined his *Casino des Trépassés*, a 'winter station', where he'd bring together Homer, Dr Faust, Rabelais, Jean Bart, Saint Antoine, Job, and other '*anciens vivants*' (great fellows of the past), there to live a 'high wild life' (*la haute vie sauvage*) between the wilderness and the sea . . .

I go along to the beach of Pors Carn and, sheltering beside a rock, out of the cold wind, eat some bread and cheese, then come back into St Guénolé and a harbour full of multicoloured, fish-smelling. weather-beaten, wave-ridden boats:

> *La Chaumière du Pêcheur*
> *Men-hir*
> *La Petite Jacqueline*
> *Fils de l'Océan*
> *L'Etoile Filante*
> *Mousse-Bihan-Coz*
> *Koroller ar Mor*
> *Flibustier*
> *Cinq Frères Ademo*
> *Ketty et Micau* . . .

On the shore-road between St Guénolé and the Eckmühl lighthouse, two men and a woman loading a cart with dark-red wrack.

8

I spent that night in Audierne (walking in the cold evening on the Quai Thézac, with the moon scudding through cloud and the red harbour light shining at the limit), and next morning, very low down the morning, after drinking coffee to waken me and some milk to keep the whiteness in my teeth, I got on the road, making for the extreme point of the Pointe du Raz. A chill morning, overcast, with streaks of dawn redness raw in the sky. Along the road, gorse, fern, heather, and boulders. When, finally, after one or two short lifts, I arrived out at the Pointe, the rain was beginning to come down with a vengeance. I passed by the huddle of tourist shops and cafés now, at this season, all apparently closed, and walked and clambered out over the boulders, right to the extreme tip, where I sheltered from the torrential rain under an overhanging rock, with the sea turmoiling viciously green and white below me, gulls keeping up a perpetual caterwauling, and cormorants roosting silent, black, solitary.

9

>   *Grack*
>   *rudd*
>   *assilsh*
> *shoo and shaa*
>   *radgrack*
> *shoo*
>   *yaler*
>   *radgrack*
>   *shaaaaaaaa*

10

As I sat out there under my rock, a bedraggled starling came to visit me, and then a butterfly, looked like a red admiral, and I wondered what the hell a butterfly was doing out there at that time of year, especially as it fluttered away *seawards.*

So I sat out there for an hour, maybe more, then came back to the little ghost town of tourist shops, where I found one café open. and went in to drink a cup of hot something, discovering at the same time there was a bus leaving in half an hour's time for Douarnenez. I decided to take it, and sat there in the café, with the rain battering against the big, sea-filled windows, and slithering down them, waiting till it came.

'*Hé, vous avez un client!*' (Hey, you've got a customer!) – and I'm rolling out on the way to Douarnenez.

Down to the harbour:

> *La Belle Garce*
> *Astarté*

piles of blue and green nets on the railings, blue and green dreamy clouds of nets, and the rain still falling. I go into a *crêperie* for a bite to eat (a *crêpe* with egg, and a *crêpe* with cheese, washed down with cider).

It's about five miles from Douarnenez to Locronan, and I saunter along them, passing men in farms bagging spuds, and in fields a family howking dark-rosy-red-beets from the heavy, wet, rain-soaked, darkly-juiced earth.

In Locronan, then (perfect little town of solid granite, with the story of an Irish saint sculpted in coloured detail on its church's pulpit), as evening's coming on, I take the bus for Camaret, arriving there in pitch darkness. There I find myself a room (room zero) overlooking the harbour, where I leave my things, before going back out to stroll around the streets of the town in the thick-hanging mussel-blue night.

11

In Camaret, I'm thinking of the poet Saint-Pol-Roux (a Provençal, but who opted for the Breton milieu), 'Saint-Pol-Roux the Magnificent,' whom André Breton called the 'master of images,' and who lived here in Camaret for years:

> *The Universe is a quiet catastrophe; the poet searches for what is scarcely breathing under the ruins and brings it to the surface of life.*

> *Every being during his life is the centre of Eternity.*

> *Poetry must augment its own Eden.*

> *The poet is a prodigious explorer of the Absolute.*

> *Poetry's becoming bourgeoisified in ordinary gestures.*

> *Widen the circle.*

12

Next morning, early on, after dreaming of myriad red herrings, I'm walking along the harbour to the little chapel of Roc'h-a-ma-dour (The Rock amid the Waters), the air thick with the stench of fish, past lines of black hulks in various stages of skeletonisation when I come across the Saint-Pol-Roux (number CM 3092), one of the many boats reposing in harbour, waiting to leave again for the fishing grounds off Ireland, or Portugal or Morocco, on the hunt for crayfish (green, red and rosy), lobsters, crabs, spider-crabs, scallops, mackerel, or tunny-fish.

I stand out at the end of the breakwater (there's something very fishy about the sky this morning – a pale golden light shining, also silver and blue). Then I come back into town to a café for some breakfast – a jug of coffee and a pile of hot butter-cakes.

13

Gaya gaya gaya ka gaya gaya gaya gaya gaya gaya ka ka ka ka gaya ka – keeya! keeya! keeya! – ka ka ka ka gaya kaa kaa gaya gaya gaya gaya . . .

Two silver gulls with pulsing breasts, beaks raised to the heavens, yelling on the gable of a whitewashed house, as I come along the harbour-front at Camaret and climb up out of the town by the Street of the Four Winds.

14

The hazards of hitch-hiking take me down that morning, along the lovely, misty coast, to Châteaulin, then up to Le Faou, from there into Brest with its little hell of a military port which you look down into from a metal bridge, its once-hot Rue de Siam, and its long, long, long Rue Jean Jaurès. Out of Brest, I wait in its dooly suburbs of Tourbian-Coataudon, whence a car at last takes me in the late and murky afternoon to Landernau, so that finally, with evening coming on fast, I arrive at Huelgoat where, after falling in love at first sight with this small greystone village, I decide to hang around for a while.

15

In the Huelgoat woods, a blue and gold morning. Beech, oak, and pine – a great coloured, trembling ecstasy. Smoky sunlight. Sound of waters. The rich chack-chack of a blackie. Red leaves of the beech thick on the earth.
Wood-silence, big fertility, gloriousness. Massive rounded boulders. Rich water-sound of life flowing deep in the silence. And grotesque, sap-filled roots heaving up out of the pungent earth.
Five hours in the woods.
Then back into them in the evening.
Red ground. Night gathering. Watching the lovely folly of the river, the water coming blackly pulsing and purling in the slits and holes among the rocks.

16

It was in the woods of Huelgoat that the poet Victor Segalen (born in Brest) died, in 1919, after wanderings that took him to China and Tibet, on a solitary quest for what he began by calling 'the last pagan' and which he understood finally as a state of sensuous and intellectual plenitude.

'China,' writes Pierre Jean-Jouve, 'was for him the projection of his psychic life, of his ghosts, his erotic ardour, with the deep, very deep call of a spiritual reality.'

What interests me about Segalen is that he seems to epitomize exactly ambitions and desires which, though I'd have difficulty in defining the term, seem peculiarly 'celtic': the search for 'pagan' living, and the search for a spiritual 'China'.

Segalen, travelling through the yellow lands, along the Blue River, into the empire of himself . . .

17

At Morlaix, on the Saturday morning, I'm in the town museum, strolling around there in the musty silence, when I come across in a dark corner and unlabelled, what I'd vaguely hoped to find: a portrait of Tristan Corbière. There he is in his boat, the grotesque face with the long pipe, a red cap on the head and red jersey on body, against the dark green of sea and the rough whiteness of the sail where the weird profile of the face appears as blue. A crude, but expressive little picture – like Corbière's poems, those acrid, smoky, harsh, poignant, delirious, coarse, tragic, comic, brain-storming, soul-tearing texts that made at least one Parisian critic say he didn't talk French at all.

A very strange character, who gave himself the romantic name of Tristan by derision and, to underline the derision, bestowed the name also on his dog, a beshitten little tike of the most mongrellish origins. A gargoylish figure there in the ports of Brittany, up to crazy doings with his cutter, *Le Négrier*, purposely waiting for the worst weather to go out in it and court there death, maybe his only love. 'Outside the human track,' as he describes himself, 'a wild poet with a lead pellet in his wing.'

Tristan, *salut*.

18

And it's on up to St Pol de Léon and Roscoff, then land's end.

It's there, in the sand, I close this little blue notebook of Brittany, with a coastal signature, so:

```
        W W W W
        W W W W
        W W W W
    K   W W W W
        W W W W
        W W W W
        W W W W
```

Letter from Amsterdam

A kind of eternity

Spinoza

1

The *Gare du Nord* was the first foreign station I knew, and as I was leaving it that morning, years after I'd first set foot in it, I had the feeling of a recapitulation, of having come full circle, of having come to the end of something, and maybe the beginning of something else.

There were a few other people in the compartment with me: three Parisian hippies, *Bill, l'Abbé* and *Etoile Filante* (they had their hip-names painted on the backs of their army-surplus jackets), making for the *Paradiso*; a German girl, studying psychology in Amsterdam, with a little dog she called Woodstock; and an American soldier on leave who, like he was needing a piss, 'just couldn't wait' (as he said to a Belgian boy who came in at Brussels). Later on, a Surinamese came in, and sat staring darkly out the window at the rain.

2

After getting myself a hotel room in the quarter of the Oude Kerk, I found myself, like everybody else whose intentions on going to Amsterdam are vague, walking up the Dam Rak, past the American Express with young Americans offering for sale anything from a Volkswagen to a pair of shoes, till I came to Hippie Square, with its horde of vague-eyed wanderers sitting on the steps of the national monument, waiting for the end, or the beginning, sitting mostly in stolid silence, though the odd guitar strumming – like a tribal group when its shaman dies, showing signs of unrest, distracted, unable to work, sleeping a lot, talking in their dreams, fleeing individually into the tundra. Well, I'd been like that too, and maybe still was like that a bit, but I was no longer of the tribe, and wasn't waiting for another shaman. I'd maybe just gone a bit further out into the tundra than my companions, and was concerned with my own dance there. The 'underground', as they called it, was so full of phoney shamans (and every shaman is at least part-phoney), that it was better to be entirely out on your own – better, and harder.

3

So I walked round the Dam, and up to the Spui, where I went into a smoky little howff for a drink. It was there I met Jaap Kroll, a musician, mawkit-drunk, who told me that earlier that year he'd been in New York and in 42nd Street he'd come across this place where you could put a penny in a slot and see a sexfilm, and he'd gone in there – 'bekoss I am innerested *also* in pornograffy' – but what had delighted him was not the sex-films themselves, but the noises. After taking a peep or two, he'd just stood in a corner listening ecstatically to all the sexy moans and groans coming from the boxes, and that had given him the idea for his new work, *Fuck Symphony No. 42*, on which he was now working. All he had to do, and it was really combining work with pleasure, in a big way, was record in his room the utterances of the women he fucked ('the other night, I haff a new sound produced . . .'), and then work them up kosmically on his electronic equipment. With luck, he would fuck it to a finish by the end of the year, and get it performed in Amsterdam. I said I'd look forward to hearing it. He said to come out to his workshop in Haarlem and hear what he'd already done. I said I might at that.

When I got out on to the street again it was dark, and I went back down towards the Old Kirk, past all the little crimson-lit hole-in-the-wall bordellos.

'*Hé, motje nog een ritje?* (Hey, would you like a little ride?)'

But that night I was happy enough as a pedestrian.

4

I'd sat in my hotel room for a while, glad to be completely alone with my silence, then, feeling hungry, I went out into the streets again, looking for a tavern where I could get a bite to eat.

I found a good place eventually, and sat in the smoky heat listening to a Dutchman half-seas over telling his life story, in Dutch, to two Turkish 'guest workers' who didn't understand a word he was saying but gave an occasional nod and smile to show they were friendly disposed. '*Duitser's zeggen tegen ons,*' said the Dutchman, '*jullie zijn verdomde kaaskoppen*' (the Germans tell us we're damned cheeseheads), but, he went on, they're just '*klootzakken*' (bags of balls), and he looked round the room as though to say 'so there!' 'A man must live', he continued, 'a man must live, drink up!' But the two Turks made signs they had to be going, and made for the door. 'Take care of yourselves!', cried the Dutchman and relapsed into a murmured interior monologue, in which I could just make out the words 'old prick' (*ouwe lul*) and 'the cholera' (*de klere*). Then he beamed at the company, said 'Good night,' and staggered out himself. I ordered another glass of *jenever* ... When I finally made it out myself, a few *jenevers* later, there was a big full-circled moon sailing grandly over Amsterdam and I felt strangely at home.

5

Next morning in the Rijksmuseum, having asked my way to the Asian Art section and followed a whole maze of rooms, past furniture and dolls' houses and crockery and God knows what all else (they seem to have hidden Asia away in the far-away basement, lining the way with futilities), I cross yet another threshold and come up against a big bronze of Shiva Nataraja, the Lord of the Dance, four-armed Shiva in a dance posture, within a circle of flames, signifying the five-fold action of Creation, Conservation, Destruction, Incarnation and Deliverance.

I hadn't expected to come smack up against the most profound religious symbol I know.

That night in my hotel (I'd bought a newspaper with the photo of an Indian woman in it and I'd cut out the photo and pinned it to the wall of my room), I write:

Rain and the Pariah Woman

It's raining,
it's been eight weeks long dark raining
and I've been sitting in this empty room
listening to the rain
it's a Europe of rain
(all the bullshit of Europe
washed away in the rain)
and if I speak of Europe
it's because I'm thinking of India
looking at a photograph
cut from a newspaper
pinned to my wall:
the photo of a woman
an Indian woman

a pariah woman
her dark (very dark) face
lit by a smile
a very naked smile –
the WHITE LAUGHTER *of Shiva!*

I spend a long time with the photo, the poem, and the rain.

6

I'd come across two hippie-boats (barges on which wanderers could lodge) moored in the Amstel, called *Exodus* and *Orpheus*, and the names seemed appropriate to me. *Exodus* for the big secession, and the wandering in the desert; *Orpheus* for the descent into the underworld in search of lost being. But I felt there should he a third boat, and wondered what its name should be. Dionysus? Buddha? Shiva? I'd seen another similar boat, it was true, the boat belonging to *The Lowlands Weed Company*, 'offering you hemp seeds and plants that will grow the purest quality of marijuana', but it seemed to me rather an adjunct of the *Orpheus* boat than another stage. There really should be a third boat after the exodism (allied to exotism), after the orphism (music and wandering and undergrounding), there had to be something else, but I couldn't think of a satisfactory name for that third conjectured boat.

Exodus, Orpheus – then what?

7

I'm sitting quietly in a little coffee-house in the old Jordaan district, then I go out into the Haarlemmer Straat, the rain is still falling, and it's there, as I'm walking along with nothing in my mind (except the vague idea of a rain raga) I smell a faint smell of jasmine and I'm standing in front of an Indian shop, and I go in, and at first there's no one there and I'm standing alone among the many-coloured shirts and saris, with the smell of smoke-perfume stronger in my nostrils, when this young Indian girl appears from the backshop, dressed in a blue sari, long black hair, red circle on forehead, large round ear-rings, beautiful. The same blue sari as I saw at fleeting moments in Glasgow, and even in Edinburgh, and in Paris, a kind of star in my nights, the same Blue Sari. I'd just have liked to sit there and contemplate her, be with her, not even hold her slender brown wrist, not immediately anyway, just look at her moving about, in her quiet young beauty, but I don't say that because other people, noisy characters, have come into the shop, so I ask her for a box of perfume-sticks ('made of indigenous raw materials', as I see later), jasmine perfume-sticks, and I go back out into the street and the rain, with the sensation of jasmine perfume, slenderness, darkness, her body, her smiling, the blue sari, her hidden nakedness and that all as I walk on under the rain gathers into a feeling of joy, sheer joy, pure unadulterated joy.

I go back to my room, rain failing over the window, dark sky, my mind whole and concentrated, and I light the stick of indigenous raw material and watch the blue smoke dancing fragrantly in the emptiness.

8

Kroll's workshop, Haarlem. When I arrive there in the late afternoon, he's got company: a girl friend, a woman painter, a classical scholar, a professor of literature and a poet. Kroll himself with a coloured bandanna round his cranium, stoned out of his mind. He gives me a smoke, so I can get in tune with the others. The poet talks about 'the hemping of Dutch culture.' Kroll puts on his fuck-music, and does a crazy lurching to it in the middle of the floor. He tells me in a rush that the poet is from the Friesian Islands and that his nickname is Iceberg; that the professor of literature is a Structuralist, with a difference, not like the damned Parisians; that the woman painter is working on orgiastic abstracts inspired by his fuck-music; and that the classical scholar had come to speak with him about Spinoza, because Spinoza was the only philosopher he'd ever thought he might be able to read, because Spinoza wrote music. The classical scholar told me that he'd studied in the States and that he'd been to see Pound recently, which got us on to the *Cantos*. As for Spinoza, they hadn't got round to him yet. They had been talking about the Kabbal. The Kabbal! That started me off about the Shekinah, the meeting which communicates the power of opening the gates of the inner world (I was thinking of Blue Sari). The Shekinah, often associated with the sense of smell (Aaron's rod had the perfume of the Shekinah on it) – I was thinking of the jasmine. The Shekinah, I said, was that thing, or notion, or power called the Eternal Feminine. '*Das ewig Weibliche zieht uns hinan*.' quoted the professor of literature. Yes, I said, the Eternal lovely Feminine, and I told him (I was wound up and rarin' to go) of the labyrinthine fogs of Glasgow, and the Blue Sari, and the grim frozenness of Edinburgh, and the Blue Sari, and the fumey confusions of Paris, and the Blue Sari, and how I'd met it again just yesterday, and how I felt I didn't care about anything else any more, just the Blue Sari, that was maybe some innermost essence of myself, and that I was full of it, and that from that moment on I was going to be living in a kind of Blue Sari India. '*Passage to India*,' said the classical scholar (this guy could quote till the cows come home). Yes, I said, and the woman painter started talking (everybody was making crazy connections) about the union with reality of the Sufis, the mystic travellers, advancing towards reality, or Reality, which is maybe just a certain sensation of reality, and I said, yes, and for that the best word I'd ever come across, for that sensation of reality, was the sanskrit term *samarasa*, and that's what it was all about – travelling in the fields of chance, and occasional *samarasa*. And the classical scholar said this was maybe what Spinoza was talking about too, what he called the third kind of knowledge, and his philosophy too was a philosophy of joy –'joy is the passage of a man from a lesser to a greater perfection,' he quoted in Latin, and just as he said it, Kroll's cabin, I swear on this book, blew up into the air, right up into the air, and we were all flying about there on wings of cosmic laughter.

Yes.

'This is too much', said a girl at my side.

She was right.

But Amsterdam was like that, then.

Winter on the Plains

It's a vast field open to the deployment of an energy.
Roger Caillois

1

I take the underground to the Gare de l'Est. At the station, trains are howling on all sides. But I'm in no rush. I like hanging around stations. So I go for a breakfast – to one of those big cafés where the light is yellow and acrid as vinegar. There are lengths of buttered bread piled up on the counter. I'll have one of these and a coffee. I find myself a seat. A child is wa-waaling somewhere. My neighbour is reading the *Parisien* with a surly expression on his face.

2

In the train, the long green train for Châlons-sur-Marne and then away out into the khaki grounds of the east.

Hordes of soldiers, making for Nancy.

Carriage full of the noise of farts, chops moving, and the raking of throats and noses. I'm longing for the open country, longing to get out of Paris, into clear space.

I look up at the high walls of the city as we pull out along the line. 7:40. It's still dark. Waiting for the dawn.

3

Epernay, with its green river and smoke stacks, the river frozen in its narrower reaches.

As we rush along, I see sudden flashes of whiteness in the woods. Patches of snow still lying.

Saw the sun just outside Châlons, already a good way up the sky, apricot-coloured, clear-defined, sailing through cloud. Had it in view for about ten minutes, then it paled, quince-coloured for a last moment, and plunged away.

4

Open country:

> *The cry now is for a wide-open writing*
> *a language plain but curving with power*
> *set bare on reality, a january script*
> *for whiteness and the winter of ecstasy*
> *lonely on fields of sand and salt, birds*
> *wheeling in wild flight, walking through woods*
> *where streams are frozen round birches*
> *the sun sailing through cloud, burnt-yellow*
> *seen and unseen in swift-running cloud*
> *moving on soil virgin and desolate . . .*

5

Writing this in an open field – Paris no longer exists – in the lee of a pile of straw bales. Patches of snow still on this straw. I've made myself a resting-place in out of the keen wind. The sun's a mass of sparkling whiteness, the sky blue with cloud like the first seizure of ice on water. Twittering and chittering of birds, their leaping lunging flight. A bell ringing far away at a levelcrossing. Trees look so complete with their bare branches and twigs you wonder what they ever do with foliage. The zero degree. The straw's rustling all around me in the wind and my writing hand is growing numb with cold. Time to go.

6

Just moving. The sheer sweep of the land, peppery-brown and pungent.
   Walk another while, then sit down at the base of a tree, in a little fir copse at the side of the road.
   But must keep moving. Can't stop for long. That Siberian cold.

7

A circle of peppery fields, some closely harrowed, others with the stubble still on them and round the stubble a thin frost haze. I'm at the centre of these fields now, that radiate away from me over the horizon, with small birds chittering all around me and further off the lazy black flap of a crow. A goods-train passes on the line through the fields, smoke belching from its funnel in thick white curdles then greying and disappearing.

8

Hawthorn tree. Crabbed and spiky. Green-yellow lichen on its branches. At its base, husks of berries left over from a bird feast.

9

Steaming lines of dung on the fields. Mounds of beets encased in earth and straw – at places they've been eaten into and the beets appear red and sore, glistening, chapped by the frost.

10

Birch wood: glistening, slender strength. Saw it suddenly, gleaming there, glistering, with a halo of frost above it.

11

Near a village now, here at the graveyard. Before the yard, a tree with great clumps of mistletoe hanging from its branches, the berries gleaming.

I go down into the village. Hens and duck. The stream frozen. A red tractor there in a farmyard. Four men on a massive pile of dung – hot and steaming, the dung in the frosty air – forking the stuff on to a cart.

12

This cold is killing the seed. The snow is good, brings down the azote from the air, and is a fertiliser. But this cold is deadly.

It is minus 17 degrees here in Champagne. In the Vercors, thirty below. The road to Spain is blocked, and all the canals of eastern France have frozen over.

13

Along the river – icy green, the river, still flowing, the banks ruffed with ice. Where trees bowed branches down to the river and where twigs touched the water, ice had formed, ragged white patches of ice on the green water surface and at the tip of the twigs, arctic blossom.

Today in the plains area of France the temperature is 20 below. But in the wood on the other side of the river, it was quite warm. A sun of distant gold was shining, glinting in the frosty haze around the trees and on the clumps of mistletoe on every hand. It breaks easily, the mistletoe, its twigs being hardly made of wood, but of a kind of fleshiness which fastens on the tree-bark and drinks in the sap.

Saw many other berries, crimson and black, with birds frantic among them. There was a hawthorn in particular weighed down with dark-red clusters, a ferocious nourishment and fertility in this frost. Ate a few berries myself.

14

Went out this night along the road that leads southwards out of the village. The moon a yellow sliver in the sky, clutched in a cloud of frost. About a kilometre out, I come to a level-crossing, its twin oil lamps burning. I pass over it. Darkness and silence – save for a little black and white piebald dog who's been strolling around me for some time and can now be heard rustling in the frosty grass. It unearths a bird that whirrs off into the darkness. A light, and a car comes up behind me, lamps wide, and is forced to slow down for the little dog now trotting in the middle of the road. It comes close to my legs as it has already done once or twice, and I stroke it. Only the two of us in that road, in the darkness. A train rushes through the fields, a murky orange crest whooming above its engine. Then silence again and darkness. The village has disappeared under the curve of the plain. There is only the dark curve of fields before me, and the frost and moonlit road. As I go on and come near other villages (St Etienne, Les Grandes Chapelles, Villette), I hear dogs howling and barking on all sides. When I get to the crossroads, I think it is as good a moment as any to turn back. But before doing so, I stand still, for a long time.

15

Dawn came this morning in a wet mist, visibility about twenty yards. As I looked from my window, the first thing I saw was a row of cabbages, green tousled cabbages, thirty-three of them.

16

The mist lifted during the day, but has come down again now at half-past-five. I went for a walk along the southern road. Quarter moon, yellow in blue. The lamps at the level-crossing reddish, their flame throbbing. Mist and that feeling of distance.

17

In my room, as I was sitting quiet, I heard a fluttering behind me at the window, and looking round saw a butterfly, red, yellow and black, beating its wings at the glass.

Maybe, with this thaw, it thinks that Spring has come already.

It's crawling over the floor now, stops for a few moments with wings spread, then folds them.

I go out for a walk, but when I return, I look for the butterfly, which I find eventually under the bed, with wings closed.

It's not Spring, yet, fella, but I hope you'll see it.

Flemish Weekend

Over there in the hamlet of Saint-Job a big fair was in full swing.

Michel de Ghelderode

1

Paris was plunged in the smoky redness of a June sunset when my train pulled out of the gloomy Gare de l'Est. I had my old torn and battered grey suitcase with me, in which I'd thrown a change of clothes, and was making for Meaux, where my friend Christian Vanderloo was to be waiting for me with his car to take me to his place, an old farmhouse he'd bought just a year before in the village of Foligny, where he lived with his wife and three kids. There was an old man from Charleville in the compartment with me – I knew he was from Charleville, because he kept asking me if the train was going to Charleville – and I felt like asking him if he knew the Rimbauds, but didn't.

Vanderloo was waiting sure enough at the station, and we drove through the now thick blue night to his house. He'd painted some of the rooms, but the room in which we ate dinner was still bare, with a whitewash that had gone grey and yellow over the years. On one of the walls, in a big way, and in red he had calligraphed two Chinese characters: *t'ai ch'i* (First Principle).

First principle, no principle.

2

The idea was that we make a trip to Belgium together to see some people, friends of his, friends of mine (though I'd never met them all, just corresponded with them). So next morning, around nine, in clear sunlight, and with the wind shaking hedges and trees, we were on the road – first stop Louvain, where Vanderloo teaches the history of Buddhism, and where that afternoon we were to listen to a comrade of his presenting his thesis on the *Samantapasadika*. Vanderloo was also working on a thesis, a translation with notes of a sutra called (OK, take a deep breath) the *Pratyutpannasammukhavasthita-samadhisutra* ('the sutra of the samadhi in which you get the Buddha to appear before you'), and he wanted to see how things went.

It was good travelling up to the border – the poplars swaying smoothly in the wind, and the June sun fixed in a bright blue sky. And then we were over the line, into Belgium. The time to have a meal, and it was Louvain, redbrick and Roman Catholic, the thesis-writer, just back from Japan, with a little blue silk bundle of necessaries (*furoshiki*) before him on the table, nervous as hell.

The buddha didn't make an appearance.

3

It had been arranged that we'd meet Isenbrandt, a sculptor, and Susie Coecke his lady-friend, who'd both been fellow-students of Chinese at Louvain with Vanderloo, at the thesis-do, and the four of us left the academy together – Isenbrandt to make a bee line for home where he had a bit of work waiting for him, the other three of us to take it easier and buy in food and drink for the night.

We made for a supermarket, and went through it like the Mongols invading China – weaving up and down the aisles, picking up booty here and there: rice? sure; vegetables, galore; noodles, of course; wine, chocolate, whisky, bread, cake, pork, spices, sauces, bacon, prunes, you name it . . . till we had two prams full, loaded them into the car, and brought it all home.

Through Brussels, getting lost in the suburbs: Vilwoorde, Melsbroek, Grimbergen, Wolvertem . . . the night ripening fast . . . till we get to the village of Rambroeken, and go through it down to the canal to this building beside the lift-bridge with the lights blazing, which is the workshop.

It's a huge barn-like room, with a great fireplace, the walls painted a lurid, house-of-Usher red, an antique sturdy fantastically carved table in the centre with two tall silver candlesticks, and all along the walls, bronze sculptures, all on the one theme: dongs and ballocks. Massive bullroarers in bronze, dark glowing bronze, all over the shop. All those heavy genitals hanging from the shadowy pelvis of the world, filling the air with a deep silence, and in this deep, red silence, Tibetan music (*b'dong . . . b'dong . . . ksh!*) booming and clashing away from the recordplayer . . .

While Isenbrandt puts the finishing touches to a wax dummy,

Vanderloo and Susie go into the kitchen to get the meal started, and I set about lighting the fire, bringing in wood from the big straggly pile outside, twigs, branches, and logs, till flames are leaping, and unctuous smells are wafting from the kitchen, and Isenbrandt (work put by for the day) is calling for wine and beginning to swing lumberously to his Tibetan jazz.

The fire roars and crackles, the music clashes and booms, the smells of food get thicker and thicker, the cocks and balls glow darker and darker, shadows prance wilder and wilder on the walls, the candles are aglow, the bottles are open, the glasses are full and empty and full, the food is on the table, rice and meat and vegetables, in vast quantities; and we all fall to.

4

In the middle of the meal, the door bell (a big bell, like the one Frère Jacques was supposed to ring Matins with) rang, and it was an architect and his wife who were clients of Isenbrandt's.

At this point, I became solipsistic, because everybody, who'd been speaking French before, started speaking Flemish, and my notions of Flemish don't rise to architecture or whatever, so I went off into a little reverie on my own – about the mad Fleming Hieronymus Bosch, his gargoylian visions, his medieval devilry, his hellish horrific humour, and his strange, subtle quietness. Which meditation was interrupted an hour or so later when the clients left taking a couple of hundred quids' worth of bronze genitals with them.

5

It was then, close on midnight, that the two Dutchmen came in: Pieter and Joachim, who help Isenbrandt to cast his bronze. It was Friday night, and they'd been out on a spree – now returned with about ten glasses of strong Belgian beer behind them, in their long trail along the dark canal.

Woops! – they weren't too steady on their pins, at least Joachim wasn't. He had long black hair and the face of a mystic ascetic: something like the Ancient Mariner. Pieter was a sight for sore eyes too, with his blond hair and beard, his copper rimmed glasses, his red shirt, covered in a fine, white dust as though he'd just taken a quiet crawl through a flour mill.

I took to these two right away.

'*Yum, yum, yum, yum,*' said Pieter as he sat down at the table while Susie served him with food and put a fork in his groping hand. While the same was being done for Joachim, pale as death, gleaming-eyed, he kept staring at me and said something in Dutch. Pieter, who knew a little English, translated.

'He says you have a mind, and you know how to touch it.'

While Joachim after that million-dollar remark retreated into silence, I got into talk with Pieter.

He told me he'd been to Scotland once. In Edinburgh. He'd got off the boat at Leith, and couldn't find his way back to it, lost in the Edinburgh streets. He'd stopped two or three people asking them: 'Tell me the way to heaven, please,' but they didn't seem to catch on. Probably thought he was off his nut. He thought they were all off their nut. All he was asking them for was the way to the *haven*, the harbour (they looked like he was asking them something weird, wonderful, and probably wicked). It was only two years later when he knew a bit more English that the mystery cleared.

He also told me he was saving up to go to Japan – to get tattooed.

6

Snooping around the room while everybody was busy talking, Joachim had discovered a bottle of whisky and was swallowing it down lustily as though it were Vichy water. Before he conked out definitively, I went over to have a friendly go at him with the couple of Dutch phrases I retain from a month's intensive study with Assimil. He thrust the bottle of whisky at me. I took a drink, and handed him the bottle back: '*Dank u*,' I said, '*De grote, rode Boot is op de Kanaal!*' My informing him that the big, red boat was on the canal seemed to delight him (maybe it reached him as a remark of esoteric significance), and I was just about to go on to tell him that the baker in this street makes tarts and cookies (and that one would certainly have blown his mind) when somebody suggested we all go out on the canal.

'*Geweldig!*' said Pieter, which I took to mean 'great!' – so we all went out on to the canal, Joachim included, drunker than Li Po, under the moon.

7

There was an old, iron canal boat fastened by a chain to a ring on the canal-side near the bridge. After some ineffectual chugging at the chain by sundry hands, Isenbrandt went back to his workshop and reappeared with a pair of pliers with which he prised open one of the links in the chain, so that the boat was ours to do with what we liked.

The trouble was that on one side our way was cut off by a big, fat barge that took up all the room, and on the other by the lift-bridge, too lowset for the boat to pass under, so that all we could do was go symbolically round and round or to and fro in the small space at our disposal, paddling with shovels (which Isenbrandt had also resourcefully produced from his workshop).

Tiring of the sport this afforded, Vanderloo and Pieter and Isenbrandt started climbing monkey-wise up and along the lift-bridge, while Joachim started to take off his clothes and wanted to jump in the canal, dissuaded only at the last minute by Susie who caught him by the hair, and I knelt up at the prow of the old canal boat till we all decided we'd had enough, fixed up the boat chain again, and went back into the house, where the conversation drifted around for a while, got lost in murky creeks, and sleep began to seem a good idea.

Pieter and Joachim (Pieter on Joachim's back – he'd gone back to the whisky-bottle and dropped into a solid coma) left for the house they lived in on the other side of the canal, and the rest of us went to the sleeping quarters upstairs.

It was close on dawn.

8

At one point there was a ladder, and I climbed up the ladder into an egg, and the egg burst, and I fell into the canal ... At another, there was a red bagpipe in the sky blowing furiously over Brussels ...

9

Next morning, after breakfast with lots of coffee, while Vanderloo took a run into Brussels on business, I walked along the green waters of the canal, its banks thick with wild iris and weeds, and then went over the lift-bridge to the house of Pieter and Joachim, where they were busy, up to the eyes in plaster, making moulds for future casting.

Quiet, the June sun at the window, and the work going on. A girl went by on a bike along the path. Joachim said something. '*Me kloten*,' said Pieter ('balls').

There were bits of bronze sculpture on a table. One, a nude girl, a dancer maybe, about a foot long. I picked it up, admiring it. Pieter came over, telling me how as bronze it was a failure, but fingering the smooth belly, saying: 'It's the most best.'

Then a nun went by on the path, like a two-wheeled bat, and Joachim made some comment to which Pieter answered: '*me kloten*,' which seemed to be a habit with him.

And the work went on, surely, quietly.

10

At dinner, there was talk of art-communes (we'd all get together and live happily ever after), then Vanderloo and I left for Bruges where his parents lived.

Lovely, quiet Bruges.

I promised myself I'd spend a week of winter up there some time, in some clean, simple room.

Yes, I'd spend a cool week up there.

In Bruges of the canals and quiet courtyards.

11

It was already late afternoon when we left Bruges, making for Ghlin, in the Hainaut industrial belt.

Along the road, red sky, scarred fields, here and there the metal and smoke of a factory.

When we got to Ghlin, the town was quiet, the streets empty. We asked at a *bistrot* for the street we were looking for, finally got to it, dark, with small red-stone one-storeyed houses lining it, found the door we wanted, rang.

It was Marc came to the door. I hadn't seen him in years – since he'd made a trip up to Scotland to see me. He'd come off a fishing-smack at Fairlie Pier, asked where I lived, and been directed to my parents' home. He was sitting there having a meal when I got a phone-call (I was living in Edinburgh at the time) from my sister, who'd run out to the phone-booth on the corner, to tell me that this character, a Belgian, had turned up out of nowhere, with a bushy beard, a bulky rucksack, and about ten words of English. She wanted to know if they were to send him on to me. I said yes.

So they put him on the train for Glasgow, and told him to change trains there for Edinburgh, where he arrived about three hours later. He'd been on the road for about ten days.

Long-haired and straggle-bearded, with that rucksack (he had volumes of Fulcanelli and Ouspenski in it), and a tall, thick stave, he made a little sensation in the Calvinistic coffee-house we went to next morning to talk.

He finally stayed in Edinburgh a fortnight, and we spent the time walking and talking, from Princes Street to Leith, from the Calton Hill to Arthur's Seat, and from Thomas the Rhymer to Ruysbroek passing through Whitman and Henry Thoreau . . .

And now here he was again, clean-shaven this time, looking younger though he was five years older, and I was glad to see him. We took each other by the shoulders and embraced. 'We've been waiting for you,' he said.

Behind him was Marthe, the 'mother' of the group, with eyes like anemones and emotion written all over her.

I introduced Vanderloo, and we went into the living-room, where he and I were introduced to Jacques, Marthe's husband, and the three children, and Max, a poet, and his wife, and Marc's girl. That made quite a little crowd in there.

The table was ready set, and we sat down at it right away, to eat, drink, and talk: a feast of union.

Four hours later, we were still at it. Max, who had been going steady at the wine, was now speaking up about death, rosy death. Writing for him wasn't communication, it was already a 'being beyond'. When he came home from the bank where he worked, he'd shut himself up hermetically in his room, drink wine, smoke oriental cigarettes, and write his (morbid nineteenth-century) poetry. His wife, who was eight months pregnant, said he was too much absorbed in himself, he should quit that job in the bank, and he'd be less obsessed by death. Maybe she was right. Anyway, having solemnly made his statement, Max sank back into himself.

Meanwhile, the table cleared, the general conversation (revolution, communities, writers, books, drugs, children, education, Buddhism) went on, and then became more mobile – till at one point Marthe dramatically took the centre of the room and, gesticulating with her cigarette in the air, half-sobbing, her eyes full of tears, her body one quivering flame, made a long, incoherent speech in which she said it was fortunate that I existed, that she had faith in me, that I would pretend not to understand what she was getting at, yes. I would just sit there watching her 'making a fool of herself....'.

To cool the atmosphere, I suggested a walk under the stars.

12

Four in the morning, and I was talking in a corner with Jacques and Marc. Vanderloo was talking in another part of the room with Marthe and Max's wife. Max himself was in a dwam, and Marc's girl was sleeping in animal beauty on the floor.

Then somebody suggested another walk. This time we took the cars – Vanderloo and myself, Marthe, Jacques, and Marc – and made for a wood in the vicinity, a fine substantial beech wood over which dawn was just beginning to break.

We walked through the wood (I was desperate now for a little silence), among the beeches and the holly-bushes, and dawn grew in the sky. and it was chilly there in the wood, especially as we'd had no sleep, but had talked, and talked, and talked.

We all lay sprawled on the grass for a while, half-sleeping, half-watching the rising sun and the dew on the spiders' webs, but it was too cold for comfort, so we went back to the house, and everybody drifted off to bed, closing the curtains to keep out the Sunday daylight.

13

After coffee and rolls in the early afternoon, Marc and his girl and Marthe accompanied Vanderloo and me into Mons, to visit the town before heading back for France. It was meant to be a quiet stroll of about an hour or so, but we ended up in a café with round after round of beer talking our heads off again.

It was late on in the afternoon before we finally got on the homeward road. I spent that night at Vanderloo's Place, delving into his Chinese and Sanskrit bookshelves, and next morning took a train from Meaux back to Paris, with fantastical books in my suitcase and a little Flemish flame flickering in my brain.

Grass on the Streets of Antwerp

Among all seatowns old Antwerp stands supreme.
Max Elskamp

I

I blew into Antwerp on the back of a hurricane, at a cool 120 miles an hour. Don't know where it came from, hell-holes of Iceland maybe, had turned the North Sea upside down, bruised Britain, skimmed Scandinavia, whoomed over Holland. That's where I'd met it, just outside Dordrecht, coming down from Amsterdam – wires down along the line, so the train had to shunt back to Dordrecht, where we had to take a bus to a doll's house village, from there another train to Roosendael, where we finally made the through train for Brussels. All this allowed me to make the acquaintance of Poepke, a bank clerk who does the exchange service on the train between Dordrecht and Roosendael and can say 'Do you want to change money' in thirty languages including Eskimo (you never know) and Welsh. Also Else, who works as a freelance interpreter in Brussels of the intergnashional organisations. But it was the wind that got closest to me. And there it was in Antwerp when I got off the train that night, ripping TV aerials off the cowering roofs, splintering any glass in sight and in general having a randy time. The newspapers (I saw 'em in the morning) were already at their machines pounding out headlines on it. '*Grote Stormschade in onze Gewesten,*' said the *Gazet van Antwerpen.* '*Noordwester geselde ons Land,*' said *Het Volk.* '*Orkaan raast over ons Land,*' said *De Telegraaf.* And so on. *Chaos in Verkeer! Catastrofe in Westland!*

The wind blew me through the dark and shuttered streets. Blew me down to St Jacob's Market, along the Kipdorp, to St Paulusstraat, where I saw this one-eyed place offering lodgings, with special conditions for travellers, so I barged in, bringing a few miles of hurricane with me, and there was a room, way up on the sixth floor, up the long narrow staircase, and I open the door and fall into the bed, and, yes, it'll do. A print of *Rosa centifolia foliacea* on the wall, the hundred-petalled rose.

2

A raw blue morning:

> *The rumbling of lorries*
> *along innumerable quais*
>
> *Bataviastraat, Montevideostraat*
>
> *the sun's an eternally*
> *uncut diamond*
>
> *while the* Nove Anna *from Copenhagen*
> *unloads tomato juice*
>
> *Maria José counts her cash*
> *in the* Caribbean Bar.

3

There was the copper-haired beauty of Brabant, watching Lohengrin's boat coming wagnerianly up the Escaut. And there was the hedonist communist from Old Zeland, Tanchelin. And Eloi the Slater, who had no big ideas – the big dumb ideas that turn the machinery of history – but just wanted to enjoy his life, and encourage others to enjoy theirs. All in the Chronicles of Antwerp, *Semini God!* And weren't the skippers of the river a wild lot of anarchistic kerls who didn't suffer authority gladly? And wasn't the place rank with *klompdragers* and *turlupins* and *homines intelligentiae*? And didn't Thomas the More publish his *Utopia* from here? So if you ask me why the devil I should come to Antwerp, without having raw diamonds in my pocket, there you have your answer, *Semini God* – apart from the mere drifting here and there that does without a reason.

So it's Waalsekaai and Vlaamsekaai, Van Dijckkaai and Jordaenskaai, Brouwersvliet and Ankerrui, Paardenmarkt and Klapdorp, Melkmarkt and Eiermarkt, Vlemindkveld and Schoytestraat . . .

Hour after windy blue hour.

4

A freshly extroverted Englishman with a wee beard and big glasses is waltzing round in gay abandon.

'*Le beau Julien*' is at the counter, starched collar turned up, starched cuffs wide open, a drunken Byron, and flanking him are his two cronies, a thin and long-nosed character who might be a reincarnation of Villon, and a leather-coated, stoutish, middle-aged gent straight from a Simenon novel. There is also Willy, a pixilated old loon with grey flax round his poll who wanders around from beer to beer rubbing his hands and muttering dark secrets. And at the table next to mine sits a boyo with a bloody bandage round his fist and in it a mug of beer, sullen, sullen. The rest is noisy background, conversation, music, tinkling of cash. We're in the café called *De Muze*.

> *Oh to be in England*
> *now that April's there*

sings the liberated Englishman. 'Ah, Spring,' he continues, hyper-lyrically, 'sweet lovely Spring.'

Julien looks up glowering: 'Spring is a crying window!' he shouts.

The Englishman opens his mouth in mock wonder, and nods his head in exaggerated appreciation:

'That's an interesting line,' he says, 'but it's only one line.'

'I am a one-line man,' says Julien magnificently, straightening up and towering over the little Englishman:

'Do you like two-line men?'

'I like women,' titters the Englishman. Then he says to Long-Nose: 'Is he a poet?'

'He is a lion,' says Long-Nose. 'He will eat you.'

'Oh, not now please,' says the Englishman, 'I don't taste good at this time of night.'

Pause all round. Julien is back to his beer. Long-Nose glares crazily at the Englishman.

'You look drunk,' says the Englishman to Long-Nose.

'You look stupid,' says Long-Nose.

'Let's have some music,' says the resourceful Englishman, and he waltzes over to the juke-box, takes a coin out of his pocket with a flourish, and sets the thing going:

'I wanna be elected . . .' sings a voice. Julien looks up from his beer:

'I *am* elected!' he roars.

5

Cold outside, the gale still hugely enjoying itself, no one in the streets to ask the way, and I want to get to another place called *De Engel*. I hoof it for a while in the blustery dark, getting nowhere, then I see someone coming towards me on the pavement, young fellow, all muffled up. I stop him, ask him how to get to the *Engel*. He's silent for a moment, then he says:

'I'll show you. Can't explain. I'm stoned. Nearly always stoned.'

'What on?' I ask, as we go down a sidestreet.

'Shitraal,' he says.

'What's that,' I say.

'A mixture of Nepal and Afghanistan,' he says.

'Good?' I say.

'Not bad,' he says.

'Try this,' I say, and offer him some of my noola grass.

'Where are you from?' he says.

'Paris,' I say.

'*Alors, tu es Parisien*,' he says.

'More or less,' I say.

'Me, I'm an Antwerpenaar,' he says.

'What's it like in Antwerp?' I say.

'Stoned,' he says, and laughs.

'That's *De Engel*,' he says.

'How about a drink?' I say.

'Okay,' he says.

6

It's the time of the great quiet drifting, and the age of the *aurora borealis*. Lodged in a decomposing city, Master Unckebunck plays a blue-toned clarinet. Soul to soul. Jefferson climbs into his aeroplane, Credence looks for clear water. This is real shit, paint a masterpiece with it. High-high Joe gone to Mexico, composing mescaline poetry. That crystal skull. The solution. Earth diamond. It's not what it means, it's what it does – but it's also what it means. In a country devoid of negativist dialectic, there's always the madman. Quick movers in clod-hopping England. Kit, Will and Dylan. The French dawn-men: Breton, Artaud, Bataille, Char and Valéry. Cosmic signs. Not so long ago, that Spring sky, the wisp-drift of the white cloud, and a rainbow circling the incandescent sun. Perfect. Cool euphoria. White world. Quiet. Naked girl quiet. The red dakini danced out. The golden Egyptian girl swimming. Yellow body adored. Brown, red, yellow, white, brown, yellow, red. Cosmos. To make cosmos. Earth diamond. The solution out of the dissolution. Art, a hazardous dance. Break your neck. Wandering. Dark streets, blue mountains. Rooms and islands. Clouds of poetry, he thought, clouds of poetry, but where's the lightning? Aesthetics of light. Erigena. The Arabs. A medieval ghost in the Rue St Victor, saw it, shining, while cops gathered like bats around the Mutualité. Solidarity of the peoples of Indochina. Yellow body adored. Under the red flag, the purifying wind. *Don't politicize art, artify politics.* Synthesis, dancing synthesis. The purifying wind. The cold wind of dawn. Beginnings, beginnings. Once I lived among pigs, now I live among gulls. The gull academy. Taoist scholars and poets. Cool, clear, dancing, laughing spirits. The minister of war glowers, and brings up his values in armoured tanks. They executed Hi K'ang. They chased Brecht. They – the undrifting, the undancing. Who do not know the dialectic. The mono-men. Reducing the space of living. So the Romantics went into the Gobi desert of the mind. If you tie subtle movements to less subtle movements (even if you approve of 'em), which themselves are ... the very subtle is going to get lost in the crush, so it all has to go on at different levels. The hundred-petalled lotus grows in its own space. Master Unckebunck understands. Master Unckebunck smokes the noola grass and understands. Who are *you*? asked the caterpillar. The modem poet – a fisherman in winter. The Eskimo smelled out the lie of the land. Do you know the story of the Eskimo who went to India? That's me. In a kayak. In a kayak with no name. Here's to Eloi, Eloi of Antwerp.

7

Next morning I'm on the train to Paris. Two Moroccans in the compartment, on leave from Dutch factories, going home; an American girl with a rucksack reading *The Scientific Analysis of Personality* (now what would that have to say about Master Unckebunck?); and a man (he turns out to be a South African from Jo'burg) reading an English newspaper. This gives me a chance to catch up on the news. The Soviets have made a move against the Buryat Buddhists and against women wearing trousers; and Mohammed Ali has been nominated for the Chair of Poetry at Oxford ... So everything's fine. I go to sleep.

A few kilometres from the French border, the Customs come on the train. I'm asked to open my case. The man rummages in it:

'What's that?' He holds up a package.

'A book.'

'Unwrap it.'

He takes it, looks at it, sniffs it, flips through its pages. Then he says to the plain-clothes police-fellow who's come up behind and is quizzing the two Moroccans: 'Where's your casbah?'

'I've got a book here.'

'Okay, I'll take a look at it.'

He finishes grilling the Moroccans, then comes for the book, asking for my papers. I give him my *carte de séjour*. He looks through my card, then examines the book, flipping through its pages like the other, coming back to the title, which was:

Psycho-cosmical Evolution
by Prof. Konrad Unckebunck
with the research assistance of
I. M. Shitraal

'What's it about?' he says.

'The expanding universe,' I say, 'from a psychic and a physical point of view.'

'Where did you buy it?'

'In Antwerp.'

'Why did you buy it in Antwerp?'

'Because that's where I came across it. I buy books all over the place.'

He considers my statements, then looks again at the book, putting two and two together and getting Suspicion.

'I want you off the train at the next station,' he says.

'Why?' I say.

'Explanations later,' he says, and disappears with the book and my card. Meanwhile the Customs man has been rummaging on faithfully inside my case, uncapping a toothpaste tube. Now he's trying to twist the heels off my shoes, pawing everything in sight. He's looking for marijuana, heroin and all hell's pharmacopeia, and he damned well isn't finding it. If you're wondering where my noola grass is, it's invisible. At last the Customs man leaves me alone and heads for the South African. He's tapping dutifully at the man's tape-recorder when the police-fellow comes back.

'All clear,' he says to the Customs-man, and gives him my book and card, saying nothing to me. He must have gone to consult his secret list of badman books, and Professor Unckebunck wasn't on it. Which was very cunning of Professor Unckebunk, and very lucky for me.

In the familiar Paris underground again, making for my lodgings, I find myself singing:

*Now Sinbad was in bad
in London and in Rome
in bad in Trinidad
and twice as bad at home . . .*

Where in hell did *that* come from???

As a Breaking Wave

> *She will plunge into the house and there will be light in the body.*
>
> Kanha

1

That Spring, I was wandering about in the South, around Arles, on the Plaine de la Crau, in Les Saintes Maries-de-la-Mer, and in the Camargue. Of all the places I'd been through, it was the Camargue that had attracted me most and left me tense with expectation.

A land of pools and marshes. Of wind, solitude, and silence. A land of light, where water becomes light, where the flow becomes an essence. A nakedness, an austerity, a monotony, an abstraction. A clump of reeds shaken in the wind; an angry blue squall of rain rushing across the sun; white sand rivuletted by wind and water; a snake slithering over the mud; the carcass of a bird half eaten away by the salt, for the salt is everywhere, the earth is impregnated with it. The Camargue is the hieroglyph of a stump of branch projecting above the surface of a marsh, or the ideogram of a shell encrusted in sand. It is the quick excitement of seeing lithe forms in rippling water and the feeling that at any moment you may meet that girl, that woman, 'her smooth legs still bearing the salt of the primal sea' . . .

2

When I saw her that morning, she was wearing a dark red poncho. Long, very long black hair. My whole being gave a jolt when she appeared there on the road, so perfectly southern she looked Indian.

She lived in Lyons, but was spending a few days on her own in a little *calanque* on the coast near Marseilles, where she was born. She had just driven out to the Camargue for the day, and was going back that evening.

We spent the day together, and a good part of the night. It was about five in the morning when we made back for Marseilles, passing through the still slumbering suburbs. Then it was up the chalky crest covered with scrub-oak, grey and darkgreen, dawn breaking, the smell of the sea – and down to the *calanque*. A gull's cry out there in the dawn, all of life gathered in it.

3

We were up about ten. While she made some breakfast, I climbed up the slope to get a bird's eye view of the place. A creek between chalk cliffs, a cluster of cabins, smoke rising blue in the cool morning air, boats in the harbour, two or three fishing smacks. The kind of place I like to live in . . . I saw her come to the door of the cabin, waved, and went down to her.

While we were eating our bread and coffee, three Swiss members of a Geneva diving club, passed on their way to breakfast in the café. It appeared they had achieved a monumental *cuite* the night before, with pastis, wine and cognac, and were pleased with themselves. The captain of the team was a little brown-bearded man with a red tartan cap on his head, always telling the others: '*Ne soyez pas si Suisses en quelque sorte!*' ('Don't be so damn Swiss!'). The big milky-faced one was a travelling salesman in chocolate. Then there was the gendarme, amateur geologist, always picking up stones and enquiring after their identity. They invited us to a *raclette* in their cabin that evening.

4

We walked out to the cape, along a narrow path among rocks and shrubs, climbing till we were well above the *calanque* and walking along the skyline, in the openness. Desertic flowers among the rocks, intense concentrations of colour all the more remarkable for their rarity. That deep attraction to the desertic landscape, with thought concentrated on only one or two signs, concentrated to the point of a kind of madness, 'normality' being a state of soft incoherence. Blue-flowered romarin. Thyme strong in the nostrils.

Walking there together, on that narrow path, in the openness. With these signs of intense life around us.

We went right to the extremity of the cape, watching the sea come pounding in against the rock, and the dance of gulls there. Out on the edge, together:

like sea-birds on a cliff

always alive to desire
always at the knife-edge of life.

5

At the knife edge. Let there be no talk of love. Let nothing dull the sharpness of the reality. Nothing of the sentimental, nothing of the social. Sudden and absolute, and though tempted to make a halt, keep it that way, pure and unencumbered, pure as a breaking wave ('the hollow curve of a wave about to break,' she'd said), yes, realise the wave.

Thinking all this disjointedly as we came down the narrow path from the headland, then back into the clear country of ten words, seeing the sun reflected on the sea:

sun reflected on running waters
a jewel for her nakedness.

6

There was a big crowd in the cabin of the Swiss that evening. A great plate of baked potatoes on the table, and a shining array of bottles of white wine, and Henri the gendarme sweating away at the big fire where he had a massive slab of Swiss cheese resting on a plank with its bared edge to the flame. He holds it to the fire till it is soft and scrapable, then cradles it in his arm and scrapes the softness with a big knife on to a plate, then starts all over again, red-faced and serviceable, dousing the plank with water when it catches fire, making heavy ('don't be so Swiss!') jokes with the Captain who is expounding his Swiss chauvinism (and it's all so noisy and unreal), saying he'd go through the country to the north (i.e. Germany) with a flame thrower, and how much he loathes even to hear the language he calls '*schnock*'.

The cabin's full of heat and smoke, the wine going down and the Swiss have already moved from wine to schnaps, intending to get '*carbonisés*' (boozed up) again. Getting '*carbonisés*' seems to be their favourite sport, at least on land.

Only time they aren't '*carbonisés*' must be when they're underwater.

We leave about eleven – intending to sleep under the pines. Go to the cabin to collect sleeping-bags and walk out then along the left branch of the *calanque* till we find a convenient place.

7

Pine, moon, the sound of the sea. We take each other there, under the big wild drifting of the moon and with the curvings and swirlings of the sea out there in the darkness. And when we're quiet again, I'm grateful, to all of creation, to have her there with me, all the beauty of her: hair, jaw-bone, breasts, belly, buttocks, cunt, all the lovely substance of her being, and we lie there together, watching the pine-tops swaying in the little breeze that has sprung up, and the moon veering down the sky in its cloud-drift, till we move again into our own delirium.

8

The cave in the great mountain is deep. There the whole world breaks.
He who knows the jewel of the spirit that flourishes in the Innate, knows the way. Who else knows it, among all the talkers?
He who has stilled his mind by joyance in the Innate, achieves sovereign presence in that very moment.
He who has understood this has understood everything.
It is the best of mountains, the place of the greatest joy.
When the whole earth is gathered into the body, word and spirit go far.

9

If I say that what I'm trying to write here, however clumsily, is a metaphysical text, though not as the philosophers, if I even go so far as to say that my meeting with that girl was metaphysical, the pigs, and I don't blame them, will snigger and titter. Trampling under their feet the subtle physics of life, they can hardly have the slightest inkling of meta-physics. Ruysbroeck talks about 'the essential meeting with God in the nakedness of one's being.' That's what I'm trying to get at. The purely physical rising into the metaphysical, beyond the personal nexus. Though I'd never speak of 'God'. My world isn't a God-world. Before, the world was full of God, now it's full of Man, and I'm at home in neither. Both of them are noisy, heavy, and burdensome.

For me, the free play of emptiness-plenitude, and the truth, that is the pure wave – a precarious form, an illuminated nothingness, a power that knows no domination – rising from it.

Truth, as Hegel says somewhere (I used to read so much philosophy) being a delirium in which each of the participants is dissolved, but which, once this dissolution is complete. is itself simple and transparent. Simple and transparent. Almost nothing.

10

On the afternoon of that day, we went to visit the widow of a German who had lived in the *calanque*, making his living as a fisherman, and had been drowned off the Cape five years before.

I noted the books on the shelves: Hesse, Rilke, Nietzsche (one line in the Nietzsche strongly underlined: '*I am alone, and I want to be alone, with the clear sky and the sea*'.)

But what struck me most was a musical instrument, now lodged in the upstairs room, which he had been working at when he died: a stringed instrument, its base a drifted treetrunk. I had never played a musical instrument myself, but for years I had had the idea of a musical instrument, *sui generis*, which would play an absolute music.

I would like to have known this man. Also trying to express, by some *unedited* sound, what was deepest in himself.

11

Two days later, I left from the station of St Charles in Marseilles, making for Paris and the north ('You come and go, you come and go, where will all this end?'). It was a beautiful, clear Spring morning, and it was all in her eyes. A line from the Greek anthology came into my head: 'No girl so lovely as you, no girl who ever looked into sunlight,' and I spoke it aloud. On that station platform, beside the train, and a few miles away the sea was dancing, with a thousand sun-crested waves.

Night in Barcelona

The effluvium of beauty one receives through the eyes
Plato

I

Spain (and in this of course it's only representative, part of a world with the mangies) has got a gigantic advertising itch, at least on that coast road down to Barcelona. Not only is every farm surrounded by four or five 400 square-footers, huge multicoloured hoardings advertising anything from whisky to underpants, but they've even got adverts floating in the briny sea. If you go swimming on that part of the Spanish coast, especially, if you're one of those professional-style people that forge ahead with face in the water not looking much where you're going, be careful you don't collide with a yoghurt – yes, there they float, and there they bob, the yoghurt adverts, huge whale-like tubs, exact replicas of the real small thing, and the jocund bathers frolicking and dallying all around them. There's something almost mythological about it. I mean, does this setting of yoghurt right in the middle of nature make people accept it as *part* of nature, the way they accept trees and mountains? When, their holiday over, they rememorise the natural scenes of their joy and freedom, when they see the blue elemental sea coursing in against the ever-virgin shores, do they also see those big tubs bobbing into the picture, and when they say over to themselves the mystic words such as Costa Brava–Sun–Sea–Beach, do they also say Danone, the trade name of this particular product? Are there maybe even poets in the making who will compose odes to Danone the way Tennyson did to Oenone? Will Danone be the new god of the sea? Has Poseidon, that mythical old salt, had it? Is the child now being born who will grow up to think that those tubs have *always* been there, that they are part integral of the sea-landscape and will it wonder maybe (like that kid in Sandburg's poem) what the sun advertises? – in the poem it's the moon, I know.

I came down that road two days ago. I'd been wandering about in the Corbières district (an interesting area, with vicious little ranges of white hills in a Colorado landscape) and I'd decided to come down further and have a look at Spain, by way of the coast. So I went to Perpignan, where you could hardly move for traffic, great circus hordes of it in every square, honking and fuming and apparently getting nowhere, and got a car to take me over the frontier as far as Ampurias. There, after a couple of hours on the beach and strolling around the graeco-roman ruins, the grey walls and the olive trees, the sea-patterned tessellated floors, I slept the night on the sands, and next morning, after a leisurely swim and another walk round the ruins, struck out again on the main road, heading for Barcelona.

I made it finally with two sun-burnt boys from Birmingham in a rattling Ford (they told me it was a Ford, my own technical know-how stops somewhere around the neolithic) that rattled up to a camping-ground just a couple of miles from the city, where we parted company, and I hoofed my way into Barcelona on my own.

2

The hotel I was in that night was some ancient palace with pillars everywhere, and tarnished mirrors, and brown lighting scarcely penetrating the dusty gloom. I think it was called *El Paraiso*. For sheer worn-out elegance and decrepitude, I'd never seen anything like it.

But there was something better to come. The next morning, I was walking quietly through the streets of Barcelona, minding my own business, when this hideous monstrosity howled up in front of me like a nightmare. 'What is it?' I asked a passer-by. 'It is a church,' he said, 'it is the church of Gaudi.' For a moment I thought 'Gaudi' must be a Barcelona nickname for God, so completely had this apparition shattered my nerves, then I remembered about that architect who'd taken it into his head to out-grotesque the grotesque, out-baroque the baroque and build his visceral vision in stone to the glory of the Holy Family who, however much at one time they may have been preoccupied with lodgings, could never in their wildest dreams have imagined this. It out-Danted Dante, it out-Swedenborged Swedenborg, it positively out-Popocatapetled Popocatapetl.

I walked on – 'live and go', that's the motto. And ended up around midday at a café near the metro station of Triunfo Norte, where I ordered a beer with tapas (first a plate of anchovies, with bread, then, still being hungry, a plate of olives, with more bread) and gazed out upon the world. And what did I see? I saw a van go by bearing an advertisement for a film: *El Hijo de Jesse James*; then I saw a second van go by bearing an advertisement for *Panico en Bangkok*; and pretty soon I saw a third van go by bearing an advertisement for *El Regreso de Fu Manchu*. At this, I began to feel melancholy. The day before it was yoghurt, and now it was Fu Manchu. I felt abysmally melancholy. The beer also was having its effect. Beer always makes me feel melancholy. I began to wonder what I was doing there in Barcelona, why the hell I had come there in the first place, I should have stayed in the Corbières, away from yoghurts and Fu Manchu, and I said to myself, aloud: 'You bloody idiot'. But no sooner had I done so than a shoe-shine man who'd settled down a few seats away with his box for a breather, thinking I was addressing him, came up to do business. Now I've never had my shoes shoe-shined in my life, and hadn't intended it this time, but I liked the look of this little Charlie Chaplin man so much I didn't have the heart to say him nay. The only difficulty was, I was wearing those Japanese rubber no-shoes called tongs which, apart from the sole, consist of two thin straps connected at and held by the big toe and the second toe. They are quite unshoe-shinable. But that was a minor difficulty. Before there could be any misunderstanding between us, I delved into my rucksack and pulled out a pair of good shoes which I presented to the shiner, and on which he got immediately to work. He made a marvellous job of it. My shoes were beaming. I thanked him and paid him, he thanked me and pocketed the money, and went off on his business. I left soon after, having put on a pair of socks, wearing the shoes. I felt better for it. There's something in having a good pair of kicks on your feet.

3

By early evening, after having spent most of the afternoon in the area of the harbour, where there was a naval exhibition going on, with modern ships and shiplets moored beside a resplendent Santa Maria and where I saw behind a counter in a shop a beautiful young dark lovely girl with whom – God, she was lovely – I tried to talk in Spanish, I found myself in what I now know was the Barrio Gotico, the gothic district, which wholly deserves its name. It's grim. It's religion and history, two depressing subjects (give me metaphysics and geography any day). Long, gaunt, imposing architecture full of gloom, and streets that lead you to an overwhelming question – 'Oh, do not ask what is it, let us go and make our visit', as the man said (he always turns up in the most miserable precincts).

Well, I'm wandering round that murky gothic district in the rainy afternoon, and I come into this weird building that is a huge church with chapels built in dark niches all round its walls, and which is at the same time a public square with people crossing it from one street to another, a great dark covered square with a murky yellow light around the altar where a service is going on. It's a real horror of a place this, rank with the smell of piety, and with the signs of piety hanging everywhere on the iron gratings closing off the chapels: waxen arms, waxen legs and hearts tied with string to the bars in grateful remembrance of, or anticipation of, miracles. In one chapel a wedding's going on, in another a baptism – and all the time there's the dark crowd moving through the darkness from one greyness to another. I go outside again where there is a little kind of cloister with colonnades, and a couple of swans floating in a pool of water, a couple of degenerate swans floating about in the dubious water, pale in the darkness of evening coming down among the gruesome gothic stones.

I make my way over to the *ramblas* and ramble there for a while, with the strolling crowd, past the flower stalls and the café tables, till the night really gets thick. Then I go down into the Barrio Chino, the Chinese quarter. Symbolic journey – out of the nightmare of history into a China of the mind!

4

So I'm down there in the hot, seething little *calles*, with a roasting chicken spurting grease in blue flames in a sooty corner, and light dripping on the painted lips and eyes of queens, fairies and other creatures of the night, and the crowd packed in those narrow ways jostling past bodegas and bars (*San Francisco–Texas–Moby Dick*) and where food lies fishy and colourful and smelling on trays, in barrels, in pails, clawing at the air.

'*Yoop-yoop! yoop-yoop!*' – that's an American sailor-boy coming out of a hotel with a catalan whore: '*yoop-yoop! yoop-yoop!*' he cries to the bunch of old wineys in the café. '*Yoop-yoop,*' what is it: an infantile cry of triumph from the great grandson of big chief Brooding Buffalo? – something like that. '*Yoop-yoop!*' America calling. Texas Tim on the rampage.

Three others coming up the *calle*, their arms interlocked, a big one, a medium one, and a little one, in that order, three yankee sailors, totally sozzled, singing:

> *I got a girl her eyes are green*
> *She goes down like a submarine*
> *Yoo! Yah! Yee!*

(the last three sounds proferred by the big one, the medium one, and the little one respectively). America calling again. America calling. '*Me cago en la puta*' (I shit on the bitch), says a Spanishman darkly, chewing on a vicious peppercorn.

And then it gets quieter and darker and miserabler, I'm away at the bottom of this street I think is called the Calle San Pablo, away at the dead end of the Calle San Pablo, where there are no longer any women visible, only men humped in sordid drinkshops with pale blue TV screens flickering in the darkness, yes this is the end, with a pale-green-painted little hospital-looking shop there advertising *lavajes-siphilis*, the syphilitic end of the overhumanized bloody world.

5

So I retrace my steps, back into the noise and the spurting of an aliver at least reality. And it's passing in front of a bodega with big windows that I see this woman of dark stunning beauty that stops me deadstill there on the sidewalk, fascinated, staring at her, till she turns round, and a whole table of faces turn round with her, and she gives me a smile that melts the marrow in my bones, and she says, her divine eyes flashing, '*le gusto*,' do you like me, do you want me, and I say '*si*,' and the crowd of faces with eyes like coins drag her away into the noise, drag her away into the hectic noise, while I lurch away into the darkness towards the dark-swirling animalistic waters of eternal eros.

Insular Delirium

We all follow an eccentric path and there is no other way possible from childhood to completion.

Hölderlin

1

The ferry made back to the mainland. Hitching my pack on my back, I made out on the road up the island. It was raining. The equinox. Big tides. You could hear the calm force of the green waves exploding lazily on the beach. The world a grey wet greenness. I met no one on the road.

Having found myself a hotel room in the island's main town, I went out again to buy some food. I was being served with cheese in a grocery when my eye fell on a shelf bearing bottles of golden whisky, like a symbol of the past. So with the cheese, and a loaf, I purchased also a bottle of whisky, and thus provisioned came back up to my room. It was already dark. From my room I could still hear the sea, pounding away in the darkness. I ate some bread and cheese, and then uncapped the whisky-bottle and (riding on the whisky) went back home for a while (I do this kind of thing now and then) to the *Skotlandsfirdir*.

2

>   *goddess*
>   *dark wind blowing in from the sea*
>   *this dawn*
>   *the deepblue mussel-beds*
>   *writhe and crackle*
>   *the salt sand*
>   *reflects in its pools*
>   *the awakened gulls*

  and the first
    redness
      as you open your belly
        over the island
  and the day comes cold and howling.

3

Next morning, another grey, drizzling day, the horizon silvery, I went down to the shore early on – there were two men with a cart gathering in seaweed – and walked along the edge of the tide for a mile or so, and then came back slowly along the shingle-line picking up shells:

Venus ovata
Venus sasina
Venus mercenaria . . .

I went back to the hotel then, made up my pack, and was on the road again further up the island. I was making for the lighthouse: the Lighthouse of the Whales, at the extreme point.

4

It was a long walk up to the Lighthouse, past the small fields fertilised with wrack, the dunes and the pine trees, the oyster parks and the salt-marshes, and when I got up there, I was the only visitor – the tourist season was over – so the guardian, to save himself the climb, let me go up the tower on my own.

At the top of the stone steps was the guardian's cabin, which I passed through and went up the few remaining steps to the bridge directly under the light. The wind was blowing strong, with grey-white cloud breaking in the sky, a green sea scudding against the shore, a green sea with blue reflections here, pale sandy reflections there, and the whole coastline of the island hazed with spray.

I stood up there for a while, then went back down to the little round, wood-panelled, brass-fitted cabin, whose sole furniture was a bunk fitted into the wall. It had apparently not been used for some time.

The cabin had two windows. it was very silent in there, though you could hear the wind, subdued, outside . . .

I was thinking of other such tower-rooms I'd visited: the tower study at Culross, Yeats' tower at Galway, and Montaigne's tower library: 'It's on the third floor of a tower . . . In shape it is round, the floor being just flat enough for my table and chair . . . It has three wide, unobstructed views, and is sixteen paces in diameter ... very windy ... that it be difficult of access pleases me ... I try for pure self-possession there ...'

5

They call this island (probably because its base is limestone): the white island. Maybe also because it is a place of salt, a place where salt concentrates, the salt of the earth.

The search for a place of concentration, that's what my travelling is all about, the travelling-writing as one indivisible process.

The centre is where I space myself out.

6

Yes, what I am aware of in my depths is an energy (which does not very well know what to *make* of itself, and perhaps prefers to remain pure, undefined, energy), pursuing wildly conjectural figures in open space.

7

During another evening with the bottle of golden whisky, this chant for childhood:

Birch rites
empty moors
raw skies
incredible snow

mussel beds
gull screams
lost islands
moonglow

wet woods
heron shells
crimson leaves
dark rain

hare pads
lightning flash
written rocks
begin again.

8

Sitting on the shingle-line, facing the sea, remembering Baudelaire's: 'In certain, almost supernatural states of mind, the entire depth of life is revealed in the spectacle, however ordinary it may be, which one has under one's eyes,' and Boethius' definition of eternity: 'the presence, with measureless intensity, of unending life.'

Plenitude of life. It exists under an apparent stillness, lack of 'interest'. All the occupations and interests with which we concern ourselves, and which are called 'living', are, to someone who knows, or who desires (and to desire is at least to know in part) the plenitude of life, quite beside the point, mere diversions, nuisances. They have nothing to do with the deepest desire, the life-desire. In so much of our living, truth, life-truth, gets in only by chance, and is quickly stifled, or translated into insignificance (even poetry can be just a kind of wordy deflection).

To maintain desire *in its whole form* – that is my ethos. What do I mean by the 'whole form' of desire?

Desire can be fragmented. It can he reduced to a hundred little satisfactions. *Ad nauseam.*

Desire in its whole form is indivisible. It is the *intention* of the whole body, the whole being.

9

Thinking now of Archilochus, first of European lyricists, born on Paros (a few fig trees, goats on the rocks) in the Aegean, who wrote of himself: 'I am plunged in desire . . . So violent was the desire that swelled in me like a sea and covered my eyes with mist,' and of a girl: 'like the halcyon on the promontory rock, she would beat her wings and take her flight.'

The always original situation.

10

Last image as darkness begins to come (I've been sitting all afternoon on the shore):

On the point of an anfractuous rock, a sturdy, crazy and determined-looking gannet, swiping the air with its wings, ready to make off somewhere, I wondered where.

The Tunisian Journal

> *How can people know what we have been journeying towards?*
>
> Al Hirrâli

1

Let it begin with the young American, member of the Peace Corps, reading Rimbaud there in the harbour at Marseilles, and the talk we had about 'wild mystics'. Or better, with the young girl, lovely to look at, standing at the ship's rail, her blue dress blowing in the wind.

That evening there'd been a storm, the sky let loose thunderously over Marseilles, and now the sun had gone down in a great smothered glow, and that girl there had appeared it might seem out of the storm itself.

> *What remains in the mind*
> *in the storm-washed emptiness:*
> *a blue dress*
> *blowing in the wind*
> *and the sheer live beauty*
> *of her sixteen year old body.*

2

Roundabout reflections in a ten-foot square cabin:

In the beginning Lieh Tzu was fond of travelling. The adept Hu-ch'iu Tzu said to him:

'I hear you're fond of travelling. What is it in travelling that pleases you?'

'For me,' said Lieh Tzu, 'the pleasure of travelling consists in the

appreciation of variety. When most people travel, they merely contemplate what is before their eyes. When I travel, I contemplate the processes of mutability.'

'I wonder,' said Hu-ch'iu Tzu, 'whether your travels are not very much the same as other people's, despite the fact that you think them so different. Whenever people look at anything, they are necessarily looking at processes of change, and one may well appreciate the mutability of outside things, while wholly unaware of one's own mutability. Those who take infinite trouble about external travels, have no idea how to set about the sight-seeing that can be done within. The traveller abroad is dependent upon outside things. He whose sight-seeing is inward, can find all he needs in himself. Such is the highest form of travelling, while it is a poor sort of journey that is dependent upon outside things.'

After this, Lieh Tzu never went anywhere at all, aware that till now he had not really known what travelling means.

I suppose I'm still at the stage of 'going places' – yet this going from place to place always leads me, sooner or later, to a no-place. It's the no-place that fundamentally attracts me. Whether or not it is possible to settle there, that remains to be seen.

But even then, even if I really get to the no-place, that won't mean the end of drifting. As the Ch'an master O Hu says: 'Do not say that only those who have not realised the Self are forced to drift about. Even those who have clearly realised it continue to drift.'

They continue to drift, just as they continue to eat rice. Otherwise they would be imprisoning or corpsifying the living truth.

You've got to remain in the current.

3

Tunis. The Arabs used to call it 'Tunis the White', and the whiteness is still there, if a bit soiled, especially in the old quarters that are still Arab. They used to call it too 'the sweet-smelling, flower-bedecked,' and the jasmine-sellers do their best by hawking their little posies of white flowers to keep it that way, though car fumes make it a losing battle. Once unequalled in the Muslim world, maybe Tunis too is destined to become just another city of illusion.

Anyway, I haven't come here for Tunis. I'll only be in Tunis a few days, lodging with a friend, a Frenchman, scholar of Arabic (glasses, goatee, and a ruined stomach), before moving southwards.

4

There are eight of us, sitting around a big basinful of couscous in the house of Harouk, who is a Customs man at the port of La Goulette, and there's a good half-dozen bottles of red Mornag on the table. In the couscous, along with chicken and mutton, there are partridges, though the shooting season doesn't open for another three weeks... 'the ways of Allah'. Harouk talks through the wine of flush times at La Goulette, and of high jinks when he was a randy youngster among the Italian girls, and about later flush times at Marseilles. Then he gets on to his favourite author, Alexandre Dumas, all of whose novels are ranged behind him on the bookshelves. Then back to the Thousand and One Nights of La Goulette. If I told you it all, you could write a book about it, he says: '*Tu pourrais écrire un bouquin.*' And it strikes me that I might at that. A picaresque and picturesque recital of adventures, – yes, The Thousand and One Nights of La Goulette. I'd turn Harouk the *hâbleur* and *bon vivant*, in reality a bit of a bore, into a culture-hero, a Gargantua, a Don Juan and a Haroun al Raschid all in one. What he's saying now, '*tu pourrais écrire un bouquin*', is exactly what an old acquaintance of mine, up in the Gorbals of Glasgow, told me one night he'd invited me over to *The Rising Sun* for a 'refreshment': 'All y'need's a tape-recorder, boy, and it'll put y'right on top'. Up there in Glasgow I did actually start in on a book of this kind, or at least started noting down incidents and anecdotes around a character called Mungo Reilly, a kind of incarnation of the spirit of Glasgow. But it got lost along the way. Now, however, the idea's fleetingly back, with Harouk here and the port of Tunis, and the red Mornag. Maybe some day. Some day in the evening. But no. The time for such books is past, I tell myself. It's now a new drifting dawn, and there are other, more radical, things to be done. No drama, no romance, just the truth of the drifting – the free mind's arabesque.

5

There's a little library, belonging to the Pères Blancs, in the old quarter of Tunis, impasse Kradechji, and I spend a good part of my afternoons in there, with Tunisian students around me working on Middle Eastern politics, the economic situation of the Maghreb and other themes of the kind – university students preparing theses, working at national problems, self-consciously modernist, while this drifter is sitting in there among them, nation-less, and not only not moving with the times, not even moving against them: working in sheer idiosyncrasy (but beyond that, the cool universal stream). He's not reading Bourguiba, but the tenth century Abu Bakr al-Kalâbâdhi: 'If the ecstasy of a man is weak, he will be all out to make a show of it. But if it is real and strong, he will be silent.' And Hâfim al-Asamur: 'Every morning, Satan says to me: What will you eat, and what will you wear, and where will you dwell?' Or again: 'On the hat of poverty are inscribed three renunciations – quit this world, quit the next world, quit quitting.'

Wandering with the Arabic scholar through the streets; learning a few phrases of the language; reading in the library – then, after five days or so, out on the road.

6

I'm back in biblical country. I'm moving with my feet through the pages of a book, and it's the illustrated Bible I possessed as a child, and large chunks of which I knew by heart.

That old shepherd, and his flock of sheep and goats spreading slowly over the sunburned landscape . . . That young veiled girl passing:

'Thine eyes are like the fish pools of Heshbon, by the gate of Bath-Rabbim.'

The feeling that I'm starting from the beginning again.

7

There's a race of French schoolteachers, called *'co-opérants'*, lent by the French government to Tunisia for varying periods, bearers too often of a semi-colonialist mentality, earning fat salaries (about twice what they would earn in France, and at least three times what the normal Tunisian teacher can make), that infest the country north, south, east and west. It was my misfortune to hitch-hike with a couple of them on the road from Tunis to Nabeul.

One was a teacher of philosophy, who'd already spent a couple of years in the country and, as he never tired of saying, 'knew the ropes', and 'everybody worth knowing'. He was acting as guide and chaperone to the other twerp, a teacher of French and Latin, who'd just arrived, and was full of illuminating questions such as:

'Is that a lycée, Hervé?' to which Hervé would reply authoritatively: 'Yes,'

or

'How much can you get me a meergoum for, Hervé?', to which, after due reflection, Hervé would reply, equally authoritatively and categorically:

'Fifty dinars.'

In fact, the conversation between these two shits was all about hotels, their lay-out, the food in them (*'Excellent'*), the price of the rooms (*'C'est correct'*), and about their salaries, exactly how much they'd have at their disposal, and how much they would be able to bank in France. As the philosophy teacher put it:

'*Avec du fric, tu peux tout faire*' (with cash, you can do what you want).

Tunisia being 'culturally under-developed' too (the people here having 'no notion of rationality': 'simple intuitives', 'subjective'), they wouldn't even have to work hard at all, just put in a few easy hours, draw their salary, and enjoy the luxury of their villa at Sidi Bou.

I was glad to see the last of these two when they dropped me in Nabeul, making for their rooms in a 'palace' at Hammamet.

8

That night, I saw a yellow flame dancing. But it was nothing so insubstantial as a flame, it was the solid body of an Arab girl doing a belly dance, prophesying fleshly delights with breasts, hips, belly and thighs, *ghoonjing* (arab: *ghoonj wa taghneej* – the art of moving in coition) for all she was worth. And next day the sun did a belly dance all day in the sky.

9

> '*The wine-seller
> pouring the golden wine
> and me drinking
> beside us a girl
> with perfect breasts
> dancing*'.

10

'*M'sieu, M'sieu, donne-moi l'argent*' (Mister, Mister, give me money).

It's Youssef puts forward the request, but he is not alone, around me with him are Ahmed, Habib, Abd-el-Karim, Moncef and Brahim, kids who have seen me walking here through the medina of Monastir, and have latched on to me. They all know too, or at least the sharp-eyed Youssef knows, that I have a packet of biscuits in my rucksack, for he saw me buying them at the little grocery. But he hasn't got round to the biscuits yet, he starts off with the usual: '*donne-moi l'argent*'. Just to set the ball rolling, I say I don't have any money to give away, for if I gave him a coin right away there'd be no game, and no fun. We walk together through the streets of Monastir, and I learn their names, and they ask me where I come from and where I'm going ... At length, with a smile and a nod at the rucksack, Youssef says: *'M'sieu, donne-moi l'argent, et j'achèterai biscuits comme toi'* (Mister, give me the money so I can buy some biscuits like you). We all squat down at a corner and I share out the biscuits among us.

11

In Kairouan, the wool merchant (multi-coloured hanks of wool piled all around) offers a glass of tea from his little blue enamel pot set on the charcoal-burner. His son then suggests a tour of the carpet-weaving families in the street. In one, working at a loom with her mother – hanging at the top of the loom are a hand of Fatma in metal, a shell, and a smaller Fatma hand cut out of cloth – there is a lovely young girl about fifteen years old. She's sitting like a tailor before the loom, her skirt up over her thighs, and while I'm leaning over supposedly to admire the pattern of the carpet, it's those lovely thighs I'm also looking at, and I'm not sure she doesn't know it, for when I get on my way again, she gives me a smile that outsmiles the angel of Reims, and leaves me, out in the sunlit street, full of a longing more than desire that the Grand Mosque can't satisfy, can't satisfy at all.

12

'I will take her to the desert and speak to her heart.'

13

I'd picked some Barbary figs, for a midday meal, and my hands were covered with the prickles. Just outside Msaken, I'd got a lift with a French couple, and now at El Djem, where they'd come to admire the colosseum, the woman had taken a pair of tweezers from her toilet bag, and was extracting the prickles as we stood beside their car. Pretty soon, there were a dozen men of El Djem around us, all wanting to have a go at me with the tweezers, and one hurried back into his shop and comes out – with a pair of pliers, intending to have a go with then. When my hands had won the attentions of five El Djemians, all expert prickle-extracters (the man with the squint wielded the tweezers with great confidence and delight, closing them all the time, except maybe for the odd chance, on sheer vacuity), I was advised to finish off the process by rubbing my hands in sand – there was a pile close by, where two or three men showed me the best way of going about it, each according to his idea. Then the woman recovered her tweezers and, with numerous farewells, we got on the road again.

14

'I have extracted by means of the pincers of self-knowledge the thorns of divers opinions from the deep recesses of my mind.'

15

At night, in the old quarter of Sfax, after wandering among the little workshops of the tailors, the cobblers, the smiths, the jewellers, etc. (and when I say little workshops, I mean *little* workshops – the Arab can live and work on the space of a mat; though it may be this same Arab, or his brother, you see out in the vastness of the countryside, miles of desertic landscape all around him, on foot, a single point in the emptiness), I go into the mosque, evening prayers are on, and, sandals in hand, find myself a spot away in a corner, in semi-obscurity, a spot which is visited later only by a wandering cat. And I sit there, with the murmur of prayer from the large hall, doing a little concentration on my own – religionless, prayerless, but concentrated:

'The truth flashes by like lightning in between the gaps left by thought.'

16

Near Gabès:

> *The old black man*
> *in tattered shirt and faded blue shorts*
> *walks up and down the beach*
> *up and down the beach*
> *slowly*
> *all morning*
> *on the lookout –*
> *then suddenly he crouches*
> *eyes fixed*
> *and stalks into the sea*
> *his net at the ready*
> *casts it*
> *and carefully*
> *hauls it in:*

ten silver fish
flapping in its meshes.

17

Out of Gabès, moving west. Wind blowing. Little sand columns whirling and whisking out in the scrubland. A herd of black goats. Long line of telegraph poles leading into nothingness. My dusty feet. A woman goes by, water jar on her back, dark red robes, heavy silver jewelry. Sidi Mannsour. Then the scrubland again. Tents stretched over walls of earth and brushwood. El Guetar. Soon after, the palm trees begin, and it's the oasis of Gafsa.

In the Oued Gabès I touched the breasts of the wind.

18

I'd wanted to move on further down to Tozeur and Nefta and the Chott El Djerid, but heavy rains had fallen in Algeria, and the oueds were flooded, and the car I'd travelled with decided it was dangerous to go further and was making back to Gabès, so I went with it. Back to Gabès, and then from Gabès to Medenine. And from Medenine all the way down to Foum Tataouine, and the berber country around it.

19

When Morienus the Alchemist was asked by the Prince Kallid (seventh century) why he preferred to wander in mountains and deserts rather than live in a monastery, he answered: 'I do not doubt that in monasteries and brotherhoods I would find greater repose, whereas it is tiring work in the mountains and deserts, but ... the gateway to peace is narrow, and no one can enter it without some suffering.'

20

Guermessa is built on three hills, the houses inserted in them, distinguished by a flash of whitewash round the doors. Halfway up the middle hill, a dark red *malhafa*, spread to dry on a wall, attracts and holds the eye.

The three hills are named Margab Essallah, Matmana, and Aigri. I climb up the central hill, Matmana, with two young boys who've offered themselves as guides. On rocks on the hill top, footprints marked in paint or carved, with names and dates, sometimes the outline of a fish as good-luck sign. The boys tell me that the men of the village climb up here on the seventh day of their marriage and make these marks.

An *instituteur* from Tataouine – '*Moi, j'enseigne le langage arabe aux Français* (I teach the Arabic to French people) – met up there on Matmana says that 'the people are hard here, but they have white souls' ('*Les gens sont durs ici, mais ils ont l'âme blanche*').

Rocky, desertic landscape. Down in the village, a gathering of red-robed women – it's a marriage, the boys say. And then a chanting rises in the clear air, a chanting interspersed with calls: red cries in the clear air.

Down off Matmana, we go to the village café, a hole in the rock, with a couple of shelves bearing packets of biscuits, coffee, and tins of sardines. The little pot is set on the *kanoun*. A 33 *tours* is set on the record-player. And the six of us huddled there in the hole in the rock have a little festival.

21

'*I would have you strip away every impediment of your body, scour your your heart till it is free of passion, and travel through the desolate wilds. For to the south there is a place called the Land of Power. Its people are ignorant and unspoiled, negligent of their interests, and of few desires. They know how to make, but do not know how to hoard. They give, but seek no return. They live and move thoughtlessly and at random, yet every step they take tallies with the Great Plan. They know how to enjoy life while it lasts, and are ready to be put away when death comes.*'

22

Lines for a Berber brooch:

> *Crude silver*
> *crescent-shaped*
> *berber moon*
>
> *figure of the fish*
> *and the bird*
> *and the flower*
>
> *heavy in the hand*
> *gleam of last light.*

23

A circle of sphinx-like hills, and in the centre a rocky pile. On this rocky pile, Chenini, the dwellings worked into it: cut into the rock, or made with its stone. Many ruins, but livable places still among the ruins, and one or two houses even have the firm appearance of little forts.

Middle of the afternoon. Hard white sunlight. The men are gathered in the shade of the mosque. Asses and camels in the courtyards. Figs and dates drying on the roofs. Women in dark red going about their tasks.

I follow the track up to the top of the hill.

Up there, suddenly, the crying of a hundred cocks, all the cocks of Chenini crowing in the mid-afternoon. There's knowledge and ignorance, desperation and joy in it.

24

> *'Ah, marvellous obscurity*
> *seed of my whiteness.'*

25

There were three of them round that table in the café at Medenine, drinking beer and eating beans – a pile of brown bean-shells growing steadily under the table. I'd come in for a cool, quiet drink myself, and was making for the door when one of them got up and came over to me, asking if I was French. To keep it simple, I said yes. He told me he was taking a correspondence course in French, and had a problem in grammar which I would be able to solve for him. When we'd got the grammar straightened out, he invited me to their table. They were teachers of Arab literature.

They asked me what I was doing in Tunisia, and I said I was just travelling around. And they asked me what I'd liked best of all I'd seen, and I talked about the girl dancing, and the smile of the girl in Kairouan, and the man moving across the scrubland and the wind blowing, and the crying of the cocks on Chenini. Then one asked me out of the blue what were the finest lines about love in modern poetry, and I said the first lines that came into my head, and they weren't modern, and were they even about love:

> *There is nothing here but this cave in the field's midst*
> *A wild place, unlit and unfilled.*

26

On the market at Mount Souk, I meet the Professor of Sheep, alias Semi-colon. That requires perhaps a little explanation.

Semi-colon, who sells everything from sheepskins to dried scorpions ('If these damned creatures don't find anything to kill, on Fridays they kill themselves,') introduced himself as a Professor of Sheep ('*professeur de brebis*') to a French tourist who'd said he was a '*professeur*'. And he elaborated: 'I am Professor Ali Habib, professor of sheep, famous in the entire universe. I am the big chief. When I say to my sheep, go, they go, and when I say, come, they come. I have four houses, and four wives – one German, one French, one American, and one Tunisian. I am looking for a fifth. She must weigh two hundred kilos. But the women never stay long. Only five or six days at a stretch. They are happy and contented till they see me take my *neffa*, then they skedaddle.' At this, he gives a demonstration of how he takes his *neffa* (snuff), producing a little tin box from his pocket, pinching in his forefinger and thumb, then sticking his thumb into the right hand corner of his mouth, between gum and lip, then running it along to the left. 'You see,' he says, reperforming the gesture, 'that is why I bear the name of Semi-colon.'

27

'With a little earth, one makes many forms,' says the potter at Guellala.

28

'*L'essence pure, sans alcool* (pure essence, no alcohol),' explains the perfume-merchant, dressed in a spotless jebba, bringing out his 'secret of the desert', which he says is made from a blue flower growing in the wastes.

29

'Since we took leave of you, we have gone down to a sea and the shore of that sea is our abode.
And above this abode of ours there is a sun. The setting of this sun is within us and its rising is also within us.
What is this sun? What is its meaning and its secret?
We have gone down to a sea whose name is emptiness.'

EU Authorised Representative:
Easy Access System Europe Mustamäe tee 50, 10621 Tallinn, Estonia
gpsr.requests@easproject.com

Printed and bound by CPI Group (UK) Ltd, Croydon, CR0 4YY
19/08/2025
01939360-0012